FRACTURED REPUBLIC

ERIC BOHL

DUAL COLUMBIA PRESS

info@ericbohlbooks.com
www.ericbohlbooks.com

Book cover design by ebooklaunch.com

Back cover photo by David Strom Photography

DEDICATION

To my father, who sparked my interest in politics,
and my mother, who inspired me to love writing.

PROLOGUE

At 3:35 a.m. on a warm, muggy Monday in July, the middle-aged man's dark Chevy Tahoe moved briskly northward on Interstate 395. The highway was nearly empty; a rare occurrence at any time, day or night. He was deep in thought as his car began a long, slow curve to the right.

Out the driver's side window, the faintly glowing lights of an enormous, five-sided building came into view. This storied, low-slung structure was the first recognizable landmark indicating his arrival into the greatest political city in the world - the pinnacle of the intersection between strategy and power.

As the Tahoe lumbered past the Pentagon, it began a long, slow curve back to the left as it approached a long bridge. Directly in front of him, across the Potomac River, the monuments and memorials of Washington, D.C., shone brightly under artificial light. The driver scratched his left cheek as he hunched down to get a better look at the skyline.

"Always so beautiful," he said to himself. "It's a shame what these dirtbag politicians have done to it."

He had been driving all night to make it to Washington by daybreak. After an unexpected Sunday morning phone call from an old friend, he had cancelled all of his appointments for the week. A quick visit to the secure room in his home's basement produced the supplies he kept on hand in case he ever faced a situation such as this: a military-grade knife, a list of trusted names and phone numbers, and a large amount of untraceable cash.

From the sounds of it, this could be a long and complicated trip. He would not delay a second more. He grabbed some granola bars from the pantry, threw a few clothes in a bag, and headed east. There were only a handful of people in the world he would have done this for on such short notice, but this particular old friend just happened to be on the list.

He steered the car into the center lane, gently gliding past the Jefferson Memorial on his way into the heart of the city.

He had been a patriot since his earliest memory. His father made sure of that. As an adult, he followed politics as if the outcome meant life or death, watching cable news and checking political Twitter like it was his religion.

In the day and a half since his beloved nation had fallen into complete political chaos, his anger and frustration had only grown. The United States of America had withstood two World Wars, numerous terrorist attacks, and countless outside threats. Now these spineless idiots were destroying it from within for no reason other than ego.

His old friend had played on every emotion within him during that early morning call. A sentimental commemoration of the good old days. A passionate denouncement of the coming effects of the political parties' implosion. An urgent, personal plea for help. An insistence that only he had the perfect combination of skills, experience, and resources needed to set things right again.

It was true, he *did* have a unique toolkit. Combining his recent decade in the FBI with his previous, more dangerous line of work, he had many trusted friends in valuable places. More importantly, he had a track record of getting things done while keeping his mouth shut.

Now, hours before daybreak, he was nearing the meeting place where his old friend would be waiting. He had no idea what, exactly, he would be asked to do. At this point, he really didn't care. The United States was on the verge of collapse and he might be able to help stop it. The driver was resolved to do whatever his friend might suggest. The stakes were too high to say no.

PART I

FALLOUT

1

Anna Rothwell didn't know who to trust. In her 31 years on Earth, she had never faced this much uncertainty.

Anna knew that it was pointless to rely on people in Washington, D.C., but she always felt like she could at least count on the institutions of government to provide security and structure to her life. Now even they had suddenly disappeared, and Anna found herself lost in an alien landscape.

Two days earlier, the complete and seemingly final collapse of the Republican and Democratic Parties had stunned the world. Everything happened so quickly, Anna felt like it had been a dream. She wished she could wake up from this new reality before it turned into a nightmare.

Things had been rocky for a long time. There was no arguing that. Congressman Willis Montgomery, Anna's boss, had been in Congress for 23 years. Since he arrived, the parties had grown further and further apart with each passing year. Each side used cable news and social media to push their supporters to the extremes, with constant purity tests and purges of ideological heretics.

As the chasm grew wider, the threads tying the nation's political class together finally became so frayed, only a few strands remained. Once the last bits unraveled, the entire system crashed down overnight, taking with it any sense of stability Anna had enjoyed. For once in her life, she wished she had a friend to help her navigate this new world.

But truly close, trusting, vulnerable relationships had never been easy for Anna. While most of her colleagues were put off by President Truman's old quip, "If you want a friend in Washington, get a dog," she was oddly comforted by it. She'd always felt a certain kinship with Truman, as he was the only President to hail from her home state of Missouri, and she thought he was on to something. Anna knew other people couldn't be trusted. She misused Truman's line as a justification for avoiding intimate relationships, both platonic and romantic. In a city where everyone would stab you in the back at their first opportunity, what's the sense in showing your weak spots?

Paradoxically, even though she trusted almost no one, Anna knew almost everyone responsible for pulling the levers of power in Congress. As Montgomery's Chief of Staff, Anna had used a methodical approach to create a wide network of powerful ties on Capitol Hill. Well, ties that seemed powerful at the time. Her carefully built spiderweb of connections was now crumbling along with the foundations upon which it had been built. Now no one could tell who was on what side. Really, Anna didn't even know what the sides were anymore.

For an ambitious young civil servant who loved politics and thrived on order and routine, the situation was terrifying. Anna feared the country and political system that she loved might be torn apart forever - and she would never achieve the recognition and success she deserved.

2

MONDAY, JULY 17

On this Monday morning, when it seemed like her whole world was collapsing, Anna drew comfort from sticking to her normal routines. For her, this meant immersing herself in work as soon as possible. Other staffers joked about setting their watches by Anna's rituals, and they weren't wrong. She typically arrived at the office at 6:00 a.m. every day, long before anyone else. This was usually her favorite part of the day, since no one was there to ask her questions, make her decide anything, or try to chitchat.

However, today she found herself hoping that Montgomery would be in early. As a lifelong family friend, he was a father figure to Anna and the one person in town she felt like she could rely on in an emergency. Although he had seemed withdrawn and preoccupied the past few days, Anna secretly hoped that today he would provide some guidance and comfort to her in the midst of all this upheaval. But when she got to the office, she found herself alone as usual.

After arriving promptly at her normal time and situating herself in her office, Anna logged in to her computer at 6:10 a.m. and opened her email. At least there was one person in Washington, D.C., who could help her make sense of this new world - even though that person was someone she had never met.

Four years ago, on her first-ever day on the Hill, an experienced staffer gave Anna a piece of advice that stuck. He said that 20 minutes of reading about people was worth more than an entire day of reading about policy. Knowing all about the latest gossip, rumors, infighting, friendships, alliances, and political positioning is what separates the amateurs from the professionals.

Since that day, Anna had never missed reading DC's preeminent daily House of Representatives rumor mill, *Quincy's Whispers*. Nearly every staffer on the Hill read Quincy's morning email newsletter because it was always entertaining, sometimes salacious - and usually surprisingly accurate. The website, quincyswhispers.com, was named for a likely-apocryphal story that interns loved to tell during Capitol tours.

The old House chamber, now known as National Statuary Hall, is a marble room with a domed ceiling. As with any such room, two people on opposite sides of the room can hear one another clearly even if speaking only in a whisper. The acoustics of the dome and marble create an unmistakable amplifying effect.

After leaving the Presidency in 1829, John Quincy Adams went on to spend the last 17 years of his life as a Member of the House of Representatives serving in the old House chamber. As the story goes, Adams' health declined as he reached his upper 70s and early 80s. He often would lay his head down on his desk and appear to have fallen asleep. Unbeknownst to his political opponents, he was actually wide awake, intently listening to the strategy discussions of his opponents on the other side of the chamber. The sly old fox continued to use this trick to his political advantage for many years.

The story is almost certainly not true. The room was carpeted and much less acoustically resonant in the 1830s and 1840s than today. Even if the whispers were as easy to hear back then, many other

Members could have heard the strategy discussions too. It would have become obvious to everyone very quickly that there was a problem, and Members would have moved sensitive conversations elsewhere. But interns serving as tour guides never let little things like facts get in the way of a good story, so the tale has survived and grown.

Quincy's Whispers was now about 10 years old and wildly popular among House staff. "Quincy's" true identity remained a tightly held secret, although rumors and speculation abounded. Since John Quincy Adams had served as the sixth President of the United States, each daily edition contained the Hill's top six rumors of the day.

Despite the fact that "Quincy" trafficked in rumors, his track record was very reliable. Today Anna was especially grateful to have a reliable source of information to help her understand everything that had happened over the weekend.

From: Quincy <quincy@quincyswhispers.com>
Subject: Quincy's Whispers - Monday, July 17
Date: July 17 at 4:31 AM
To: Anna Rothwell

Quincy's Whispers
251 days since the Midterm Election
477 days until the Presidential Election
What the House is whispering about...
but doesn't want you to hear.

Good (insane) Monday morning! Since I last came to you on Friday, a magnitude 10 earthquake destroyed what was left of DC's two-party system. The Republican Party - the Grand Old Party, the party of Lincoln, formed in 1854, home to 20 Presidents - formally dissolved on Saturday. This, only a week after the previously unthinkable implosion of the Democratic Party. The nation's political leadership is now left with zero major parties and nothing but chaos in the halls of Congress.

Selecting the top six Whispers is never an easy task, but for yours truly, this day is unlikely to ever be topped. The old electric mailbox has been stuffed to the brim with e-parchment all weekend long. Ever true to my word, I have read every tip and pulled out the best and most-plausible rumors.

What I'm hearing today:

Whisper 1 - Speaker of the House Julie Mathes (AZ) is privately telling confidants she does not see a path forward for her continued Speakership. Sounds like she's leaning toward jumping ship before she gets thrown overboard. Close aides expect her to make an announcement today.

Whisper 2 - President McCullough has ordered the Pentagon to increase its alert level to DEFCON 2. Whisperers say there is no specific credible threat to the country, but the heightened alert was warranted because of the unprecedented political instability.

Whisper 3 - The power struggle has already begun. At least six House Members are confirmed to have already been making calls to test the waters for their own runs at Speaker. Expect rumors to explode today as the House will be in session for the first time since the World's Greatest Power Vacuum opened beneath Capitol Hill. I expect it to be difficult to downright impossible to separate signal from noise - the incentives to backstab and start false rumors about opponents are just too tempting for bad actors to refrain.

Whisper 4 - Everyone is still trying to wrap their heads around Saturday's dissolution of the GOP and what the new reality means for them. Thousands of former party staffers are now unemployed... all staffers at the RNC, DNC, NRCC, DCCC, NRSC, and DSCC are now on the street, since their salaries were paid by the Republican or

Democratic Parties... which no longer exist. And these are just the tip of the iceberg. All Leadership office staff aside from the Speaker's Office are also out of a job, since their positions were actually party positions rather than employees of the whole House or Senate. The former big shots who were working for Majority and Minority Leaders, Whips, Party Chairs, and Secretaries yesterday just might be delivering your pizza tonight. Many of these highly connected and influential staffers are already loudly whispering vows to return to relevance, power, ...and gainful employment. Lots of folks swearing to "get even."

Whisper 5 - It's only been two days, but judging by the nonstop talking heads on TV and course of discussion in D.C., it sounds like the end of the two-party system is starting to be widely referred to as "The Collapse."

Whisper 6 - Great timing... Hearing lots of terrified Whispers from staffers and Members who have an eye on the calendar. Treasury estimates we will bump up against the Debt Ceiling by mid-September unless it's raised, and the Fiscal Year ends September 30. The House has passed ZERO appropriations bills this year. Accomplishing all of this in the next two months would be a heavy lift under normal circumstances... and our circumstances are a galaxy away from normal. I'll keep my ear to the desk.

Until tomorrow, I have the honor to be,

Your obedient servant,

~Quincy

Sign up at www.QuincysWhispers.com to get
every edition delivered to your inbox!
Watch for breaking Whispers on Twitter @quincyswhispers.

Hear something good?
Whisper it to me at tips@quincyswhispers.com.
All Whispers are reviewed and kept
strictly anonymous and confidential.

3

As she skimmed and re-read the email, Anna did her best to focus on the words and think through their implications.

Not surprised to see the rumor mills are already on fire. The one about Mathes is a bit surprising... I really thought she'd try to hold on to power. I'll believe it when I see it. I wonder what will happen to Heather! Is she going to just be out on the street like everyone else?

Heather Townsend, Speaker Mathes' Chief of Staff, had been Anna's role model since the day she started in Montgomery's office. Strong, confident, and beautiful, Heather embodied everything Anna hoped to someday become. She knew everyone in D.C. and was a constant surrogate for Speaker Mathes on the cable news channels. Anna would kill for her job.

Like all Hill staffers, Anna knew that Speaker of the U.S. House of Representatives was one of the most powerful positions in all of world politics. Unlike in the Senate, where archaic rules and traditions allow for more of a balance of power between parties, in the House the majority party holds almost unlimited command of the chamber. With few exceptions, the Speaker can set the body's agenda and move it forward so long as he or she maintains the support of a bare majority of Members.

On top of the Speaker's day-to-day powers, he or she is second in line to the Presidency, behind only the Vice President. While no Speaker has ever been elevated to the Presidency through the chain of succession, James K. Polk did serve as Speaker before being elected as the 11th President.

Anna dreamed of being the top staffer for the Speaker. It was an incredibly difficult job, but its holder was in the driver's seat for much of the political agenda of the U.S. Congress. When Anna started working for Montgomery, her personal resume was far too thin to take her into the type of high-powered job she really wanted. She was a Congressional Chief of Staff only because her boss had known her since she was a child and trusted her implicitly; not due to a long record of political accomplishments. If she ever wanted to move up the ladder, she would have to make her own way. No one else was going to build a career for her.

Fortunately, the job she had was an extraordinary perch from which to meet people and build a name for herself. The network of connections she'd developed in her first four years had just begun to feel strong enough to use for a leap to a higher rung.

Right now, though, Anna was glad to not be in Heather's shoes. She couldn't get past how completely The Collapse had toppled the whole power structure. Before the parties collapsed, she could use her knowledge of the Hill to navigate and exploit the arcane hierarchy and power players of the Republican and Democratic Parties. Now she just felt weak and vulnerable.

For the next two and a half hours, Anna read through the headlines of the *New York Times*, the *Washington Post*, and the local Capitol Hill newspapers. She saved the articles that sounded the most interesting, then finished her survey of headlines before beginning to read the stories in full. Given the scope of the weekend's events, today's stack was voluminous.

The noise and prattle accompanying the rest of the team's arrival at the start of the workday was a good signal it was time for Anna's mid-morning break. Without fail, she rose from her desk in the Chief of Staff's office at 9:00 sharp each morning. Today was no different - despite the rest of her world being turned upside down.

With headphones firmly placed in her ears, Anna exited the office and entered the hallway, eyes to the floor. She made the short four-minute walk to the coffee shop in the basement of the Rayburn House Office Building, filled her mug, and paid. Anna allowed herself 15 minutes to enjoy her coffee - no creamer, but two pink artificial sweeteners - while she absentmindedly scanned her phone to catch up on the latest headlines. After her early arrival at the office, this was a great way to refuel for the second half of her morning. This week's situation made the short coffee break feel absolutely necessary.

Although she kept up her routines, today Anna's brain felt like mush. She rubbed her temples with both hands as she read the news, hoping to massage some of the stress away. Anna was moving on autopilot. Despite this being the four-year anniversary of her employment in the U.S. House of Representatives, the milestone never even crossed her mind. Her thoughts were so consumed with the events of the weekend, she'd had no time to think of herself. Like practically every other person on Capitol Hill, Anna had hardly slept for the past few days. The chaos and uncertainty had been emotionally draining, and they were beginning to take their toll on even her young and physically fit body.

The hallways were unusually full this morning. No real surprise, given the weekend developments. The slow, rhythmic pounding of her high-heeled shoes echoed through the corridor as they hit the marble floor. Anna grasped her disposable coffee cup with two hands and stared at the lid as she walked. Her headphone wires dangled from her ears, the end disappearing into her jacket pocket.

Anna's headphones were never actually playing music, but they did a great job of keeping other people from talking to her. Before she learned this trick, Anna could hardly make it a minute without yet another entry-level male staffer trying to chat her up.

Contrary to some pop-culture depictions, Washington is a city full of tall, beautiful women and handsome, clean-cut men. The center of power and money has a tendency to draw the best and the brightest. Even in this environment, Anna stood out from the crowd. Her 5'9" height was not exactly unusual, but her striking shoulder-length red hair and piercing light blue eyes turned heads wherever she went. She was youthful and athletic, and men of all ages took notice. But to her, these self-obsessed fraternity boys were nothing but an irritation. She didn't have time for pointless flirtation.

Anna opened the door to Congressman Montgomery's office suite at precisely 9:25. She passed through the foyer while walking briskly toward her desk. The office setup was pretty standard for Rayburn. Visitors entering the front door were welcomed in a small reception area with three rooms splitting off from it: Congressman Montgomery's large personal office to the right, Anna's Chief of Staff office directly ahead, and the rest of the staff in a large open room to the left.

Lily Villareal, the Congressman's Staff Assistant, occupied the left side of the foyer. Joshua Harper, the Scheduler, was on the right side, nearest Montgomery's personal office. He was the Congressman's gatekeeper, and he was fiercely protective of his post. A small back-door passageway between Montgomery's office and Anna's office let them work together outside of the public eye.

This morning, every telephone line in Congressman Montgomery's office was lit solid. It seemed like all 750,000-plus constituents from the district were calling at once, demanding that Montgomery and his Congressional colleagues do *something* to stop this catastrophe.

Staffers and interns fielded calls nonstop, listening to constituents yell, scream, and cry as they helplessly took the callers' names and contact information. The best answer they could give was a promise to pass along the concerns to the Congressman. Anna felt so sorry for them - the thought of facing the furious constituents on the other end of the incessantly ringing phones made her want to crawl under her desk.

As usual, Anna avoided making eye contact with Lily as she breezed by. Lily was incredibly friendly - making her the perfect receptionist - but small talk made Anna too uncomfortable to engage in it with every trip through the foyer.

Within seconds of walking into her office, the boss's deep baritone called for her through his open personal office door.

4

"Anna, could you come in here?" Montgomery asked loudly.

She stopped mid-stride and switched directions toward his office.

"Close the door, please," Montgomery requested. He leaned against the front edge of his large oak desk; hands clasped in front of him. His eyes had dark circles under them, and he looked like he hadn't slept in days - probably because he hadn't. Despite his haggard appearance, his thumbs tapped his hands with nervous energy.

At only 51 years old with a photogenic smile and a movie star head of dark hair, Willis Montgomery's 6'3" frame cut an imposing figure in the marble hallways of Congress. He was still younger than the average Congressman but had nearly two dozen years of careful study and experience under his belt. When Willis Montgomery entered a room, people felt his presence. He was neither a loud man nor charismatic; he simply commanded attention through gravitas. Serious and knowledgeable with a dry sense of humor, other Members loved spending time with him.

Anna waited a few moments, but Montgomery did not acknowledge her presence. His eyes were glued to the television perched in the corner of his office opposite his desk.

"Yes sir, what can I do for you?" Anna asked crisply.

As one of the youngest female Chiefs of Staff on Capitol Hill, Anna was eager to show her willingness to help her boss with anything he could possibly need. Montgomery was a lifelong bachelor who never seemed much interested in dating. His work was his life, and he expected his staff to treat their work similarly. He had known Anna since the day she was born, and she would do anything to avoid letting him down. Given the political situation, she knew he would need plenty of help today.

"Have a seat, Anna." Montgomery looked like he had been mulling over an idea. "I've hardly slept a second the past two nights, you know?"

"I'm not surprised," Anna said. She was already thinking it looked like the stress of the past two weeks was starting to get to him. "You're not alone. I'd be shocked if anyone has gotten more than an hour since everything fell apart. I certainly haven't slept much myself." This was not the kind of thing Anna would admit to many people, but Montgomery was apparently so deep in thought that he didn't even acknowledge she had spoken.

"I've seen some crazy things happen up here over the past two decades," Montgomery mused. "I can honestly say I never thought the actual collapse of the parties would be one of them."

Willis Montgomery had been through many difficult situations in his 23 years on Capitol Hill. None came close to this. He had been only 28 years old when first elected - at the time making him the youngest Member of the House. Now in his 12th term representing a predominantly blue-collar district in Missouri, he had a sterling reputation as a sharp, pragmatic statesman, albeit one who didn't seem too ambitious or concerned with his own political standing.

Montgomery stepped away from his desk. He walked past Anna toward the television, never moving his eyes from it. Anna noticed it was tuned to CNBC - an unusual choice for Montgomery. Most days he was continuously flipping his TV through the cycle of 24-hour news channels, not watching the financial networks.

Although the TV was muted, the anchors' facial expressions told Anna everything she needed to know. They weren't just reporting the news today - they were visibly distraught. They were obviously bracing themselves for an unprecedented day in the markets.

"No one knows what to do, Anna. The Members are in full-fledged panic. With the collapse of the parties, there's literally no elected leadership in place anymore other than Speaker Mathes. President McCullough seems clueless. The stock markets are opening in a couple of minutes, and they're going to immediately go into freefall. Once the markets bomb, it'll almost certainly dump us into recession. We've already been close enough to it anyway - it wouldn't take much of a shove. Every lobbyist within 500 miles will try to buttonhole me for information or to plead for government money to prop up his industry. The entire world is going to look at the U.S. government for answers. Right now, the House doesn't have any."

Montgomery's tone of voice sounded odd to Anna. She tried to figure out why as he continued. "For God's sake, it's basically anarchy out there. Everyone's acting like it's *Lord of the Flies*."

Anna studied her boss's face intently. Although it sounded like he was describing a doomsday scenario, he seemed to be trying to contain some bubbling pleasure.

Surely he's not actually happy. No one's happy today, least of all a senior Member of Congress.

Still staring at the television, Montgomery stopped talking as he watched the seconds tick down to 9:30 a.m. and the start of the week for the New York Stock Exchange. 4-3-2-1... At the sound of the opening bell, the entire electronic board lit up red as investors rushed to cash out stocks as fast as possible.

Anna and Montgomery stared in silent amazement as the S&P 500 Index plummeted more than five percent within seconds. A mere 18 seconds after the bell, the Exchange halted trading, as the S&P had hit its seven percent "circuit breaker" that required a mandatory 15-minute cooling-off period. The word "unprecedented" didn't even begin to describe what they were experiencing right now.

As Montgomery turned to Anna, she thought she saw a slight twitch in the corners of his mouth. "This is only the beginning," he said. "This place is going to be complete chaos for the foreseeable future. I hope you're ready for this."

"So do I," Anna said quietly. She tried to maintain a concerned but strong exterior, but her insides were doing somersaults as anxiety took hold.

What do either of us know about economic collapses and fiscal policy? Absolutely nothing... so why's he smiling? Maybe he just doesn't know what to do. Gallows humor or something.

"You and I are going to accomplish great things together in the next few weeks," said Montgomery as he turned back to the TV.

Anna's cool blue eyes stared at the back of Montgomery's head with a quizzical look.

What on Earth is he talking about? Why is he acting so happy while the world is burning down in front of us? Out of everyone here, why would Willis Montgomery be on the verge of doing great things? He's a good man, but he usually goes out of his way to avoid controversy and leadership roles.

Despite her impressive title and important responsibilities, Anna's job had never been nearly as high-stress as others assumed. With Montgomery playing a back-bench role, she had never seen the need to grind herself down like so many of her colleagues who worked for more ambitious bosses. On the other hand, it hadn't provided the same opportunities to gain valuable backroom experience as some Chiefs of Staff. The staffers closest to power were the ones with the highest street value.

Three and a half years ago, after just six months on the job, she had recognized that Montgomery's distance from true power meant she would never really be where the action happened. Being on the Hill was exciting, but Anna wanted to be *in the room*.

Anna puzzled over Montgomery's cryptic comments while his silent gawking at CNBC dragged on.

It's always felt like he doesn't want to have any leadership role, even though he probably could have had just about whatever he wanted. There's no way he'd suddenly want to poke his head up now that all the guns are going to be pointed at Congress.

As the silence grew increasingly uncomfortable, Anna spoke to fill the void. "I've been flipping around through the news channels all weekend. All of the 'experts' seem to think Congress has some master plan behind the scenes that we're hiding from the public. As far as I can tell, *no one* knows what's going to happen."

Montgomery snapped out of his daze and responded with a hint of excitement in his voice. "You're absolutely right. No one knows what's going on. There literally is no Congressional Leadership left. There's not a Star Chamber or the Illuminati or the Masons running this show. The show is running *itself* right now. It's complete and utter anarchy. That's why you and I need to move." He turned away from Anna so quickly that he missed the look of shock that flashed across her face at his sudden, uninhibited ambition.

Montgomery began to pace back and forth behind his desk while looking out his window. He was struggling to contain his nervous energy. The second-floor room looked into the Rayburn House Office Building's courtyard; a square park fully enclosed by four stories of Member offices. Its center fountain and many flower beds were designed as a respite from the grinding work of Congress.

After a few moments of thought, Montgomery stopped pacing and turned to Anna. His entire demeanor was intense. "What are we desperate for right now? Congress is in anarchy. What does it need more than anything?"

Anna swallowed hard.

Great. He's playing professor again.

She hated these lectures full of seemingly rhetorical questions. Anna could never tell when he wanted her to actually answer and when he was just pausing for dramatic effect. As she pondered the question, she realized this time he was waiting for her to speak. She focused her thoughts.

Everything is spiraling. Mission number one needs to be stopping the spin.

"Congress needs stability," she answered.

"Exactly. But given our current situation, where could we find it?"

Again, she took her time to consider the question. She bit her lip and looked down as she thought.

If stability was easy to find, surely someone with enough knowledge and experience would already be stepping up and providing it...

Anna realized she had answered her own question.

"Knowledge and experience," she said. "You can't stabilize an institution as large and complex as Congress unless you know what all the pieces are and have the experience to know what to do with them." Anna felt proud of her answer.

Montgomery looked impressed. "You got it. Congress has functioned for two and a half centuries. It has grown in complexity and tradition. The intricate procedures aren't just an annoyance - they're the glue that holds the body together. Or *held* the body together until recently, I should say. Knowledge and experience will be what restore it."

Montgomery again turned to look at the courtyard. After a few moments' reflection, he again addressed Anna. "That's not enough, though, is it?"

The lecture isn't over yet? How much more is there?

Trying not to show her annoyance and frustration, Anna said, "I'm not sure, sir. What do you mean?"

"Lots of people here have knowledge and experience. Twenty-three years may sound like a lot of time, but 45 other Members of Congress have been here longer than me. That's one-tenth of the House. They all have more experience than I do, and many know the processes as well or better."

"Yeah, I guess that's true," she said.

He turned again to Anna. "Are those 45 Members interchangeable? Do they all have what's necessary to put Congress back together?"

Anna gazed at the ceiling as she mentally ran through some of the names who were likely on the list of 45 more-senior Members.

Stephenson... clown. Neville... well, he's senile. Jackson... totally incompetent.

Some of the long-timers had almost become caricatures of themselves over the years. Remembering some of their more boneheaded moments made her begin to smile. Montgomery picked up on her thoughts and smiled himself.

"Yeah, I didn't think so. Some of my more-senior colleagues are wonderful people, but I wouldn't trust them to manage a baseball team full of eight-year-olds, much less the entire United States Congress. So, what is it? What else does a leader need?"

Montgomery's hints clarified Anna's mind. "Competence," she said. "Knowing something and having seen similar patterns before doesn't help at all if you can't do anything with it."

"That's right," said Montgomery, forcefully pointing his index finger at Anna. "Saving this body will take knowledge, experience, and competence." He turned to the window and began to pace once more. "Anything else come to mind?"

Oh, come on... Can't he just say what he's thinking like a normal person?

Knowledge, experience, and competence seemed pretty thorough to Anna. Knowing how things work, having been through challenges before, and being good at executing a plan felt like fairly strong leadership qualifications.

Montgomery could tell she was stumped. He again gave a wry smile. He was enjoying this way too much. "Think pragmatically, Anna. If someone put three candidates in front of you who were equal in knowledge, experience, and competence, which one would win?"

He let his words hang between them while Anna's mind raced. She thought of three Members she respected and imagined them standing next to one another on a grand theater stage, as if in a three-way Presidential debate. She mentally zoomed in on each Member's face and tried to think of their characteristics.

What makes any one better than the others? So many of these politicians just sound the same... same canned answers, same plastic smiles. The only ones that are any different are the ones who seem like real people.

This gave her an idea. "Authenticity," she said. "If they're equal on everything else, the ones who stand out are the ones who feel like they are real people."

"Precisely," said Montgomery, again swinging an index finger Anna's direction.

Hopefully that's Test Over.

"The elite are not set apart by who has the best ideas, the strongest policy proposals, or the most spotless resume," Montgomery continued, waving his hands for dramatic effect. "Knowledge, experience, and competence are necessary elements. In reality, though, no one cares about that stuff if they don't like and trust the person. The only way they like and trust a candidate is if they believe the candidate isn't just in it for himself. It has to feel like the candidate cares about people like them."

Anna knew this made sense.

Sure, plenty of people have made the same observation. Reagan, Clinton, Obama, Trump... in some ways they couldn't be more different, but they all had the ability to make their voters feel like they weren't just spouting canned lines for their own gain. It was like they were actually just talking straight and saying what they really thought.

"There's no doubt that's right," she said. "But Congress is a bunch of politicians. Don't they all know this? Don't they all follow that advice anyway?"

Montgomery laughed a bit too loudly. "Do you really think that?" he asked. His laughter continued as he spoke. "You think everyone in Congress is authentic and comes off as altruistic?"

Anna tried to keep her face neutral so Montgomery wouldn't see how much his laughter stung.

Alright... yeah. That was pretty dumb. Congress is basically the Inauthenticity Hall of Fame.

"Yeah, yeah," she said quickly. "True. They are all successful politicians, but there aren't many of them who ever learned how to be authentic. So why do some have it while most don't?"

"That's a good question, Anna. I don't think anyone knows for sure. My theory is that most people can just smell it when someone is constantly angling for their own gain, and once they get a whiff of it, they're forever on guard against that person. They want someone smart, competent, and experienced, but they really want someone who seems more likely to fight for them than for himself."

"Of course," Anna said. "Everybody wants to be inspired. Does that really apply to internal elections too? The voters in Congressional

Leadership elections are just other Members of Congress, not the general public."

Montgomery stretched his arms wide, palms to the ceiling. "100 percent," he said. "Contrary to popular opinion, Members of Congress are just as human as anyone else. We're slaves to our emotions every bit as much as an average voter. And with Congress in complete anarchy and chaos, they're going to flock to someone who has a big vision for fixing it."

"Good points," said Anna. "A crisis election is definitely a completely different animal than any normal election."

5

Montgomery nodded, then turned his attention back to the television. The first circuit breaker had just been lifted, and the market continued its tumble. The second circuit breaker, requiring another 15-minute cooling-off period after the market shows a 13-percent drop, took only another 41 seconds to trip. Combined with the morning's initial 18-second trading session after the bell, the market had now tripped its first two breakers in only 59 total seconds of trading.

As Anna watched the screen in silent shock, Montgomery resumed pacing the office and returned to professor mode. His left arm was folded across his chest while his right hand grasped his chin. "Who do you think are the most likely candidates to be the next Speaker?"

Anna tore her attention away from the TV and considered this for a moment. *Pretty obvious he's got himself in mind... every Member has an ego.*

She decided to give in and do a little brown nosing. "Well, I think the country could really use a statesman like you right now."

Montgomery sat down in his chair and sighed. He again clasped his hands in front of him.

"Well, that's very nice of you. I appreciate it. But you know, I've been thinking this through for several days. I've gone over the membership list and challenged myself to question my assumptions. At the end of the day, I think there are four possible Members who have what it takes."

"Only four? Out of 435?" Anna asked. Her surprise at the small number was feigned - in reality, she had assumed he was only thinking of himself. "Who do you think it'll be?"

"Well, first off, I'm immediately tossing out anyone who was in Leadership before. After this debacle, they are as toxic as rat poison. Zero of them stand a chance. So, when I look at who's left, the ones I see as plausible candidates are Jonathan Garcia, Ted Alber, and Christine Franklin. And, yes, myself," he said with a smile.

There it is.

Despite the mental confirmation that this was indeed about Montgomery, Anna was actually quite impressed with her boss's assessment of the field. These were three formidable opponents who could each plausibly cobble together a coalition that would bring them to power. Still, she struggled to wrap her mind around why Montgomery would even consider getting in the race for Speaker himself.

In his high-flying wunderkind youth, Montgomery had a few misfires. He had tried to rise too high too fast, reaching for positions in Congressional Leadership before he was ready, and suffered some embarrassing defeats in the process. For more than two decades since, Montgomery had been lying low, toiling in relative obscurity. Even to his friends, he appeared to be an aloof idealist - respected for his intellect but relatively unambitious.

Unbeknownst to his colleagues, Montgomery was actually building the foundation that he hoped would someday enable him to seize the right moment. He became friends with Congressmen and Congresswomen of all political stripes. He memorized their birthdays, their kids' names, and most especially, their grandkids' names.

Montgomery collected phone numbers as methodically and dependably as a Swiss watch ticks. Ever since the advent of cell phones, he had religiously sought out and saved every new Member's number and given them his own. Every tidbit of information he learned about another Member, he made his staff input into a special computer database they had nicknamed Alfred, after Batman's famed butler who always seemed to have the perfect tool close at hand.

Montgomery made sure Anna backed up Alfred regularly and kept the information under tight control. He kept it fresh by texting each Member first thing in the morning on his or her birthday and anniversary. If there was no response or the line had been disconnected, he made updating the number his top priority.

When Montgomery had started this conversation, Anna had assumed it was just his turn for the self-indulgent "why not me" moment every Member on the Hill had been having for the past week or two. He was serious, though, and she could tell he had thought it through. She started to consider his prospects for becoming the next Speaker as well.

Maybe he has a point. It's not as crazy as it sounds... and it would definitely be a career lifeline for me. What if he could pull it off? We'd be in the catbird seat... the center of the political universe. I could be Chief of Staff to the Speaker of the House! I can't even imagine that kind of visibility - the important decisions to be made, the national network interviews... but that's a long way from becoming reality.

Anna thought about the three other Members Montgomery had named.

Garcia, Alber, and Franklin. At least two of the three would most likely beat Montgomery. Garcia's an asshole, but he's been here for ages. Everyone on the Hill knows Garcia isn't trustworthy, but that's not exactly unusual, and his constituents love him. Franklin and Alber are polished and have national followings, and they're well-respected among their colleagues. Plus, they're smart and have kept their noses clean.

Anna could feel Montgomery watching her intently, so she collected her thoughts. "I can't say I'm surprised that you'd mention Christine Franklin. She's obviously substantively qualified and tough as nails. Garcia is a little unexpected, but I can see why you'd think so. And Alber? I bet most people will see him as the early favorite."

Montgomery again rose from his chair and walked across the room, trying to tame his nervous excitement. He agreed with Anna's assessment of Alber. "Yes, he has quite a following and is very charismatic. He's going to play the 'centrist' card pretty far in this environment. I know he's younger, but I think in today's day and age, experience is the least important of the qualities we talked about. People want someone who is able to get things done."

"Fair enough," said Anna. "He's certainly formidable." She thought through their conversation as Montgomery pulled an index from his suit coat pocket and scribbled some notes. He was barely listening to a word she said.

"And yourself…" she began timidly.

What's the diplomatic way to say this?

"Do you really think that's something you'd want to put yourself through? This is bound to be the ugliest fight this body has ever seen, and you're usually not one to enjoy those kinds of battles."

Montgomery stopped his pacing and looked toward Anna. He nodded thoughtfully and rubbed his mouth with his hand. "I know that's how it looks, Anna. You were probably irritated last December when I didn't make a play for Chairman of the Appropriations Committee, weren't you?"

Anna was caught by surprise.

He had just seemed so oblivious to the opportunity... seemed like he was too aloof to even notice he could have waltzed into it if he wanted it.

"Honestly yes, it was a little frustrating," she said, at the risk of going too far. "You could've beaten Duncan for the Chairmanship if you wanted to. You have more seniority, know the process better, and have stronger relationships in Leadership."

Montgomery nodded again. "What about right after you started working for me? I had the chance to lead the budget reform bill but passed it off to Morgan. Did that get under your skin?"

Passing up this opportunity had been the first major disappointment for Anna in her job. Every staffer wants their boss to be in the middle of things and do important work, and Anna wanted it more than most. Montgomery was presented with a golden opportunity just weeks after she started with him, and he didn't seem remotely interested. After only a day of consideration, and almost wholly without comment, he had suggested that Congressman Morgan lead the bill. Anna was beside herself but did not make a scene. As the saying went, her name wasn't on the door, so she dutifully did as she was told.

"Actually yes," she said. "From my perspective, I couldn't see why you wouldn't want to take on such a high-profile piece of legislation. It could've launched you into the national conversation."

"What were the rumors about why I didn't?" he asked. "I'm sure people talked about it."

Does he really want to know that? Just about everyone thought he was too lazy or afraid to do it - that's the honest truth.

"Hmm, it's hard to say. There were a lot of different things," she hedged.

"Oh, come on, Anna, just say it."

"Well... most people thought you were afraid of the backlash you'd

take for it," Anna said with a slight cringe. "A few said th
think you wanted to put in the work."

Montgomery looked at his shoes as he processed her words. He took a deep breath and turned to the side as he began to respond. "The truth is, I've bitten my tongue for years. I've deliberately avoided middling leadership positions and taking on controversial projects. I've pretended to be distant, acted disinterested in flashy accomplishments and positions of power. I'm just like everyone else in DC, though - when I see an opportunity, every fiber in my being wants to jump on it. I would love the attention, the praise, the victory.

"But I promised myself long ago to not let myself get bogged down with illusory accomplishments. At worst they could damage my reputation and hand me a defeat over something that barely mattered anyway. At best they would distract me from the bigger picture and consume my time while not getting me any closer to what I want."

"And what is it that you want?" Anna asked cautiously.

Montgomery waved his hands, correcting himself. "It's not about what I want, necessarily. That was the wrong phrase. It's about being ready to act when my country really, truly needs me. Everyone was born for a purpose, and I have always felt that my calling was for something larger than a petty Chairmanship or a minor party office. I believe I owed it to myself and to my Maker to fully prepare myself for my destined purpose."

Wow... he's really gone off the deep end. I've never thought of him as super religious... I guess either I've been missing some serious piety or he's having a sudden attack of ego fever.

This conversation was so out of character from her first four years' experience working for Montgomery, she wasn't sure how to take it.

But what if it was real? If he pulled this off... no, best to not get my hopes up about it yet.

Montgomery sat down on the edge of a chair directly across from

Anna. He looked at her intently as he rested his elbows on his knees and touched his fingertips together in front of his chin. "I'm sure this sounds incredibly megalomaniacal. That's why I have never breathed a word of it to anyone. However, as my Chief and the daughter of my lifelong best friend, I feel like I can trust you. Your dad and I used to dream about an opportunity like this, and I think my moment has arrived. It's finally time to step out of the shadows and get into the arena."

The intensity of Montgomery's words made Anna a little uncomfortable, but she knew his heart was in the right place. Plus, she was ecstatic to finally get to be part of something real. She appreciated the nod to her father, as well.

"So, you plan to run for Speaker?" she asked.

"No. My plan is to *win* the Speakership," Montgomery replied seriously.

Anna suppressed an eye-roll. "Yes, of course," she said. "Well, what's the plan? Where do we even start?"

Montgomery smiled at Anna. "You know what they say - a leader without followers is just a man on a walk. Step one is to get a few people to quit running around like their hair is on fire and form a group."

Anna smiled back and agreed. "Sounds like a great idea. Let's get after it."

Montgomery laid out a few preliminary ideas and gave Anna some tasks to knock out. She returned to her office feeling energized and excited for the first time in days.

~

As soon as she sat down at her desk, Anna turned the flat screen TV mounted high in the corner above her doorway to CNBC. The second

15-minute circuit breaker was about to expire. The financial commentators were in what could only be described as a panic.

Unfortunately, the stock market's circuit breakers did almost nothing to slow the economic collapse. The third and final circuit breaker of the day, designed to trigger after a 20-percent drop in the S&P 500, tripped after just another 53 seconds of trading. This previously unthinkable milestone caused the exchange to close for the remainder of the day - after being open a total of only one minute and 52 seconds.

Anna again stared in disbelief as the CNBC anchors tried to make sense of it all. The Collapse was inflicting pain on the economy at a scale she could not have imagined. What's worse, this time it was directly caused by the tiny group of people for whom she worked - the United States Congress.

Anna's stomach dropped for about the tenth time that morning as the reality of her situation set in. It was all falling apart. Her dreams, her future, her country... The Collapse was shaking the world's belief in the entire American political system to its core, and all fingers were pointing directly at Congress in blame. And now her boss was planning to step directly into the maelstrom and make a play for Speaker of the House. It was somehow terrifying and exhilarating all at the same time.

6

At 10:00 a.m., the former Republican and Democratic Leadership teams from both the House and Senate held a joint press conference to formally resign their positions. Although the Democratic Party had technically collapsed a week earlier, most Members had continued to recognize the former party's elected officers as de facto leaders. Now that the GOP had fallen as well, everyone knew they really had no other choice but to step down.

Anna called in the rest of Montgomery's staff and told them to send the office phones directly to voicemail so they could all watch on her office's television. She considered asking Montgomery to join them but decided against interrupting him. He had seemed pretty focused when she had left his office a few minutes earlier.

On the screen, the entire Leadership teams of both chambers neatly filed into a small studio space inside the Capitol Visitors Center. Their faces were somber as they stood shoulder-to-shoulder behind a podium emblazoned with the seal of the United States Congress. Until just days ago, this collection of lawmakers had been some of the most powerful individuals on the planet. Almost 30 people, representing hundreds of years of ambition and experience, were about to say goodbye to their positions of power.

Although they were now planning to formally resign, technically The Collapse had already eliminated all of their jobs instantly. All of their roles were Republican or Democratic Party Leadership positions. Now that those parties were gone, so were their positions.

There was only one exception to this general rule. Procedurally, Speaker of the House is not a position that is elected as an officer of his or her party; they are elected to the position by the entirety of the chamber and serve all Members as their leader. Therefore, Speaker Julie Mathes of Arizona was technically the only remaining Representative or Senator holding any position of actual power.

Despite this quirk of history saving her job for the moment, Speaker Mathes joined her colleagues in solidarity at the press conference. The Leadership teams' four highest-profile members approached the podium together. Senate Majority Leader James Heaton from Oklahoma, Senate Minority Leader Jessica Beck of Oregon, Speaker Mathes, and House Minority Leader Clarence Goforth of Illinois stood stone-faced as cameras snapped thousands of photographs.

Majority Leader Heaton stepped to the microphone first. For years he had been seen as one of the few Senators who really didn't sling mud. He had appeared to be in it for the right reasons - he cared about Oklahomans and the issues that mattered back home. Unfortunately, he had been caught up in the wave and swept away along with all of the worst actors.

"Thank you all for joining us today. The statement I am about to read is issued on behalf of the entire Leadership teams of the House and Senate, with the exception of Speaker Mathes, who will speak following me."

Heaton put on his reading glasses and slowly began to read. His words were filled with emotion and his voice trembled as he spoke.

"The past two weeks have been incredibly difficult for all Americans to watch. We, as their elected representatives, have failed to act in accordance with the high ideals and expectations of the American people. For years, politicians in Washington have grown further and further apart, even to the point of losing sight of each other's humanity. Civility has been eroding for decades among Members of Congress. In the actions of the past two weeks, we have finally seen the end-result of these trends: a complete dissolution of both major American political parties.

"As you all know, with the exception of Speaker Mathes, the positions each of us here today have held were elected roles within our respective political parties. Now that the Democratic and Republican Parties no longer exist, our former roles correspondingly are no more. Our former powers and duties are now void, and we will immediately end any efforts to exercise them.

"Each of us has agreed to vacate our Capitol Leadership offices and dismiss our Leadership office staffs by the end of this week. Decisions about future Leadership positions will be determined by the will of each chamber over the coming weeks."

Heaton removed his reading glasses and placed his speech back into his suit coat pocket as the cameras continued to snap. Flashes lit the room like a lightning storm, reflecting off his glistening eyes as he continued to speak.

"As a personal point, let me say that serving as Majority Leader in the United States Senate has been the greatest honor of my life. Each of us is responsible for the failure to heal the wounds of our parties. I am no exception. For my part, I deeply regret the damage I did to my party through my careless or passionate words. I regret even more deeply my failure to do my part to bring others together and unify our brothers and sisters under a common purpose. I, for one, pledge from this point forward to be a unifier rather than a divider. I pledge to learn from this situation and help build a brighter future for America.

Thank you for your time. May God bless the United States of America."

As Heaton spoke, Anna kept an eye on the large crowd of Members behind the podium. While Senator Heaton was eminently respectable, she could not say the same for many of the others.

Especially in the past couple of decades, rhetorical bomb-throwing had become one of the fastest paths to Congressional Leadership. Several Members from both former parties on that stage were among the worst of the worst - seeking out TV cameras to deliver ad hominem attacks against their colleagues. She could honestly say many of them had developed true hatred for one another, and their disdain showed through on their faces. It was clear they could hardly even stand to be in the same room anymore.

As the cameras endlessly snapped and flashed, Speaker Mathes took her turn at the microphone. Her eyes were also teary as she began to speak.

"Thank you, Leader Heaton. I appreciate the partnership you and I have had in these roles and your honest determination to get work done for the American people. I can personally attest that the acrimony and division that we've seen recently happened in spite of your example, not because of it."

The two exchanged a painful smile and nodded in acknowledgment of one another.

"I would like to echo the words of Leader Heaton. I also accept responsibility for any of my actions that have contributed to the climate of discord in our politics. I have often behaved in a ruthless manner and spoken harshly about my opponents and their motivations. We should all be better than that.

"Under the rules of this body, my position is not tied to either party. However, after consultation with my family and colleagues, I have decided it is in the best interests of the House of Representatives that I resign my position and allow for a completely clean slate of new Leadership to guide our chamber into the future."

As Speaker Mathes spoke the word "resign," an audible gasp and murmur filled both the press conference studio and Montgomery's office, quickly followed by a loud "shhhhh" as people strained to hear the next words. The cacophony of camera shutters rose to a previously unreached volume.

"In order to retain some continuity and stability while the House chooses its new Leadership, I will remain in my role in a caretaker capacity. As soon as my successor is chosen, I will step down. In order to move the process forward quickly, the latest I intend to remain as Speaker is August 14, four weeks from today.

"It is impossible to adequately convey what an honor it has been to serve as Speaker of the House. I look forward to working with our next generation of Leadership as it begins to take shape. Thank you. We will now take a few questions."

The small studio erupted into shouts as reporters, crammed into the room in numbers far beyond the fire code, each tried to get their questions answered first. Speaker Mathes eventually pointed toward a respected long-time Capitol Hill reporter from CNN.

"Madame Speaker, what will be the process for electing your replacement?" the reporter asked.

Speaker Mathes responded. "We have not yet determined that. I expect the Members of the House to agree to an appropriate timeline and procedure in the coming days."

The yelling began again, and Speaker Mathes picked out a young reporter from NBC News.

The reporter spoke loudly from the back of the room. "Who will you be supporting in the Speaker election?"

Mathes replied quickly. "I do not intend to influence the election in any way. I believe the mandate of our Leadership team has expired, and clearly the Members and the public desire a new slate. I plan to stay out of the politics of this election."

The reporters again roared their questions, and Speaker Mathes selected a tall man from Fox News Channel in the front row.

"Senator Heaton," the reporter said, "do you expect the Democratic and Republican Parties to largely form again under different banners?"

Senator Heaton slowly returned to the podium. He grabbed the wood on both sides and exhaled loudly while looking down.

After a few seconds, he turned his gaze upward, seeming to stare off into the distance just above the heads of the room full of reporters. The room was silent, except for the shutters clicking every time Senator Heaton's expression changed. Finally, he broke out of his deep thought and began to answer slowly and deliberately.

"I think we have seen the last of these former parties," he said. More murmuring and shhhh-ing echoed through the room. "Think about it. The Democratic Party and Republican Party each had abysmal approval ratings way before all of this. I mean almost single digits. The only thing worse than the parties' ratings was Congress's rating overall. Both parties have seen increasing infighting for decades. To be honest, they've probably both been on the verge of collapse for a long time - we just didn't realize how fragile they were. It's not like anyone's clamoring to get them back… except the people who worked for them.

"Everything about our culture has been moving towards a more individually-tailored experience for a long time. Until now, the two monolithic parties have stood in the way of that trend. They strained against it for years. I think it's more likely that we see a more fractured political landscape for the foreseeable future."

Senator Heaton's candid comments sent the reporters into an eruption. They also set off some of the other former Leadership Members, who began launching invectives at Heaton, Mathes, and each other.

With fire now incoming from all sides, Speaker Mathes stepped to the microphone and cut off questioning. The Members of Congress raucously left the room amidst a roar of reporters and shutters.

Despite the fact that everyone already knew these leaders' power had evaporated along with their parties, the formal announcement sent a new shock wave through the Hill and the media. Hearing these Members speak the words of resignation somehow made it finally seem real. Most staffers would later agree that this was the moment it hit home. The parties were gone. They were all now adrift in the unknown.

BACK IN ANNA'S OFFICE, Montgomery's team sat in silent shock as the press conference wrapped up. After a few moments, Josh spoke. "So, what now? Who's in charge? How are they going to do anything without any Leadership?" He was visibly upset, voice shaking. A circle of eyes stared at Anna, looking for reassurance and answers.

Anna was rattled. Her mind was filled with the competing noises of about six different lines of thought. Anna knew she had to maintain her typical stoic demeanor and hopefully reduce the staff's anxiety, but deep inside she felt sick. Finally, she found some words to share with her team.

"I know how you're feeling, Josh. I'm feeling it too. We all need to remember that this institution has been around for hundreds of years and will be for hundreds more," she said with more confidence than she actually felt. "I don't know exactly what the path forward will be, but we *will* find one and we *will* move forward."

Behind her impassive face, Anna's insecurities were raging.

They're not buying a word of this. Obviously they all know I don't have any clue what I'm talking about. They're scared out of their minds, and I have nothing to offer.

She knew the team needed her to be their leader. If this crisis was going to be her opportunity to achieve greatness, she'd better figure out how to fake some confidence.

"Other offices are going to be in full-fledged panic mode. Everyone's afraid for not only their jobs, but the future of their country. It's hard to blame them - this is probably the biggest political crisis this body has ever faced, aside from the Civil War. Here in Willis Montgomery's office, we are not going to panic. We are going to press forward with confidence. With a crisis comes great opportunity for leadership, and we will be taking that bull by the horns and leading.

"I actually talked with the boss just a bit ago. That's how he sees it too. He has been here a long time, knows a lot of people, and has some legitimate wisdom and good judgment. Even more importantly, he's stayed out of the fray and has not been tainted by the party collapse. I think he can offer a lot to the conversation, and we are the ones who can help him succeed.

"So I know things are looking bleak, but we're going to make the best of it. We have one of the best teams on the Hill, and we've got each other's backs. Sound good?"

Anna tried to flash a hopeful smile towards her colleagues, who returned varying degrees of optimism in their faces. Josh still looked pretty bothered, but Kyle Helms, the Communications Director, and Des Parker, the Legislative Director, seemed fully on board. Everyone else looked somewhere in between.

"Alright, I hate to say this, but... let's get those phones back on," said Anna. "Thanks everyone."

The team filed out of her office and Anna shut the door behind them. She sank into her chair and dropped her facade. She began to flip through the cable news channels as a feeling of despair overcame her.

7

Without exception, Montgomery's staff believed Anna did not possess any emotions. She was kind and pleasant to work for, but she never seemed to get either excited or upset. Day after day, month after month, Anna led their office with steadiness, logic, and reason. Behind her back, robot and Vulcan jokes were common.

This outward patina of stability masked a tumultuous inner world. In reality, Anna was a jumble of emotions beneath the surface. Her youth and her personal connection to Montgomery fed insecurities that everyone else thought she was an unqualified fraud. Privately, she questioned almost every decision she made and, perhaps more than anything, worried about whether she was making her father proud. As someone who depended on routine and constancy to soothe these self-doubts, the instability The Collapse introduced to her world was tying her stomach into knots.

Since her father David's sudden and surprising death 17 years earlier, Anna had tenaciously attempted to eliminate any trace of weakness from her persona. Anna had been his spitting image in looks as well as temperament, and they shared almost all of the same interests. As his precocious only child, David had given Anna constant attention and care, teaching her the subjects he was most passionate about. In many ways she was mature beyond her years, but at the same time never seemed to fit in with other kids.

Her dad's favorite hobby was following politics. After David Rothwell and Willis Montgomery had met and served together as 24-year-old kids in the Navy, they had mutually reinforced each other's interest in the topic. Immediately after his discharge, Montgomery dove right in to his first Congressional race. Anna's dad supported him every step of the way. After she was born a few years later, she began to hear the stories of their early years together. She listened with eyes wide, imagining someday being on the world stage herself, maybe as a Member of Congress like Montgomery.

After his own discharge from the Navy, David worked tirelessly as a civil engineer at a local architectural firm. He always seemed to volunteer for longer hours than anyone else, yet he never complained once. Work was a privilege to him, not a burden. He took care to instill this point of view in Anna whenever he could, and she admired him deeply for his dedication.

On the weekends, her dad would take her camping and fishing in the Ozark Mountains of southern Missouri. Anna's mother had zero interest in sleeping in the woods, so these trips became their own special getaways. David taught Anna outdoors skills to rival most amateur survivalists and tested her to build her mental and emotional strength. He believed a strong mind was every bit as important to success as a strong body.

Her dad had been her rock, her constant protector and supporter. He was physically and mentally unmatched by anyone Anna knew. And then suddenly, he was gone.

To Anna, then a brilliant but awkward 14-year-old girl, losing her main source of stability was crippling. The grief was unbearable. For months thereafter, she was silent throughout the school day, then retreated to her locked room the moment she returned home. All too often, her mother could hear sobs late into the night as Anna cried herself to sleep in anguish for her departed father.

Time did not make the loss hurt any less, but it allowed Anna to gain some perspective. She had relied too much on her father. She never should have become so attached to any other human being, even one as strong and intelligent as her dad.

By the time she turned 15, Anna emerged from her locked room a new person. She was focused and determined. She was going to honor her father's legacy by immersing herself in the world of politics and becoming the best of the best. But if she was going to make it in this world, she would need to reinvent herself in the image of her father: strong, tough, self-sacrificing, and determined. And to do this, she believed, she could not ever be reliant upon anyone but herself.

Willis Montgomery had been at her side at David's funeral, comforting and guiding Anna and her mother. Willis had no wife or children of his own, so the Rothwells became his surrogate family. He remained close to them, both literally and figuratively, over the succeeding years. The two men's friendship had been the closest of either of their lives. Once David was gone, Willis did all he could to ensure Anna and her mother were taken care of.

Throughout high school and college, Willis called to check in on Anna every few weeks. He would ask probing questions about her schoolwork, her after-school activities, and the sports she put so much time and effort into playing. It was not unusual for Anna to see him in the stands at an evening soccer game during a Congressional recess.

Anna would never forget the things Willis Montgomery did for her during these crucial years. He gave her his most important possessions: his time and attention. She knew that anyone who would truly give of himself in this way was someone she could trust and confide in.

When Montgomery had called her four years ago to see if she was interested in becoming his Chief of Staff, Anna did not hesitate for an instant. This would be her opportunity to repay his kindness with loyalty and service. She had put her heart and soul into her work over the past four years. He had done so much for her in her time of need - she was determined to fight for and protect him wherever he might lead. And if that meant standing in front of a room full of staffers and faking confidence and vision, then that's what she would do, no matter how much her stomach churned.

THE PANIC and anxiety that seemed to be spreading across every news channel only worsened Anna's frazzled nerves. The inner stress caused by the morning's events had begun to feel crippling. Anna knew she needed to get out of the office and calm down.

She composed herself, inserted her decoy headphones, and left her office, telling Lily she would be back in about 30 minutes. Many staffers liked to take "nature walks" around and around the Rayburn courtyard, but Anna had always consciously avoided the ritual. There were far too many office windows peering down upon its walkways and benches.

Anna preferred a nearby, but far more secluded, retreat named Bartholdi Park. Lying just to the west of the Rayburn building, this tiny, triangular, two-acre green space was part of the U.S. Botanical Garden. Its central fountain was created by Frederic Auguste Bartholdi, designer of the Statue of Liberty. The numerous trees, bushes, and flower beds made it all but impossible for any colleagues to watch her from their windows.

Anna walked to the park in under three minutes. Her growing anxiety made her feel an urgency to get out of Rayburn. She circled to the far side of the fountain and found an empty bench facing away from the office. After thoroughly surveying the park for familiar faces and seeing none, she sat on the left end of a park bench and exhaled deeply.

She relaxed her usual perfect posture and sank against the back of the bench. The hot, muggy summer air was already oppressive even though the bench was shaded from the morning sun. Anna didn't really mind, though - it was a nice reprieve from Rayburn's freezing A/C.

The white noise from Bartholdi Fountain's crashing water soothed and cleared her mind. She closed her eyes and listened to the water as the cars rushed by on Washington Avenue. A group of schoolchildren noisily passed, but she was not fazed by their chatter. She felt her anxiety ease away as she began to imagine lying in an Alpine meadow, a mountain stream trickling by.

"Anna?" a loud voice called.

She jolted upright and looked for the source of the unwelcome noise.

Just perfect. It's Kit.

She tensed up again.

Kit Lambert was the 33-year-old Chief of Staff for Congressman Ted Alber of Kentucky. While Anna's path to her position was as far from normal as possible, Christopher "Kit" W. Lambert IV, followed the standard route like a roadmap. He was the fourth generation in his family to attend Phillips Academy in Andover, Massachusetts, one of the most prestigious boarding schools in New England. He then followed the footsteps of both his father and grandfather to Dartmouth, graduating with highest honors and two majors. He had also managed to win All American honors swimming the breaststroke and had been selected as a Rhodes Scholar. A more pristine resume was hardly possible.

Kit's father had been a Congressman before being named Secretary of Labor, and his grandfather served in the Senate for five terms. Most of his friends assumed it was only a matter of time before he attained a similar position.

Kit started on Capitol Hill with Congressman Harlan Davis two weeks after graduation, beginning as an intern and working his way up through the ranks. His father had gotten him the internship, as he and Davis were very close friends while serving together in the House. After being elected to succeed Davis, Congressman Alber asked Kit to stay on, offering him the Chief of Staff position.

Kit's hair was a world-class example of what Anna called the "politician's cut" - never out of place and always ready for a photo. His rugged good looks and impeccable pedigree intimidated most younger staffers. However, Anna was not the type to be afraid of anyone. Her outward Midwestern confidence included a deep-seated distaste for East Coast entitlement. Anna hated everything about him.

"Kit," Anna said in a low, cold, formal tone as he stopped in front of her.

"What're you doing out here?" he asked. He looked around the small park and glanced at the nearby Capitol dome. Kit seemed preoccupied with other thoughts, only giving Anna about half of his attention. "Isn't your office crazy this morning? Ours is a madhouse."

"How would you know?" Anna responded curtly. "Isn't this about the time you show up to work?" Anna wasn't even trying to hide her distaste for Kit.

"I just had to run over to HHS to deliver some paperwork to one of my dad's old buddies," he said. The Department of Health and Human Services was indeed just across the street from Bartholdi Park.

Anna rolled her eyes at the mention of Kit's father. He was still a very influential man in Washington, and she was sure Kit milked his connections for all the advantage they were worth.

"I just wanted to get some fresh air; clear my thoughts a bit," Anna said curtly. "The past few days have been pretty heavy."

Without asking permission, Kit put down his messenger bag and sat on the bench next to Anna. She instinctively straightened up and scooted a few inches away from him. She adjusted her skirt to adequately cover her thigh, which had been more on display than she wished. Kit folded his hands across his stomach and leaned back on the bench.

What is he up to?

She stared at the side of his face.

If this overgrown frat boy is trying to hook up with me, he's got another thing coming. How can guys still be thinking about that stuff this week? Don't they have bigger things to be worrying about?

He continued to absently gaze straight ahead. They sat in silence as Anna imagined the horrible pick-up lines Kit might be preparing to try out.

"I talked to my grandfather last night," Kit finally said in a quiet voice. He leaned forward and put his elbows on his knees, hands supporting his chin.

Anna was taken aback. This was not what she expected. "And… How is he?" Anna asked guardedly.

"My entire life, I've never heard him like that." Kit was solemn. "He told me this was the first time he has honestly feared for our country's future."

Anna's face relaxed a bit more as she studied Kit's serious demeanor. She couldn't tell if his tone was truly sincere. "That must have been hard to hear. Your grandfather is a true statesman. I've always respected what he stood for."

"Thanks. He's the wisest man I know. What he said scared me."

Why is he really telling me this? Did he know I was here, or did he really just happen by? Does he have some angle? Everyone says Alber will run for Speaker… I bet he is just trying to manipulate me for something. But how on Earth would him tracking me down to tell me some sob story about his grandpa benefit him and Alber?

The questions rolled through her mind all at once as she tried to evaluate his motives.

She and Kit knew each other through work events and the occasional group lunch, but they had never been anything close to friends. She had generally been cold to him in the past - if his name alone didn't get on her nerves, his pretentious background was plenty enough reason to keep her distance.

For some reason Kit seemed to occasionally enjoy talking to Anna when he found himself near her. It was a habit that made her uncomfortable. People didn't tend to seek Anna out to spill their guts, so it raised her suspicions for it to randomly happen with someone who was more or less a stranger. It did so even more when it was a near-stranger whose boss was likely to challenge hers for Speaker of the House in the coming days. Anna decided this was unlikely to have been a chance encounter.

"I think everyone is rightfully concerned," Anna finally responded, stiffening again and resuming her formal tone. "It's unprecedented. No one truly knows what will happen, and the speculation is so wild I don't think any of it is believable."

"I guess it'll all play out before long," Kit said. He picked up his bag and rose from the bench. "Take care of yourself. It'll be a bumpy ride."

"Thank you. Same to you," she said as he walked away toward the Rayburn building.

What a bizarre thing. Better keep an eye on him.

Anna stayed a few more minutes while she tried to clear her mind, but Kit had invaded her solitude, and she could not find the sense of calm she had been desperately seeking. Instead, she now had even more questions bouncing around inside her head. Frustrated, she headed back to her office.

8

As Anna was trying to compose herself in the park, chaos was breaking out in the halls of Congress. With the former Leadership stepping down, Capitol Hill was now one big free-for-all. Nothing governed the chambers but the centuries of parliamentary rules and precedents. Speaker Mathes was doing her best to keep some semblance of normalcy in the House, calling on popular and well-liked Members and asking for them to help talk to colleagues and keep them from losing their composure. Unfortunately, her power was so limited by her lame-duck status that she could only bring the barest order to the chamber.

Throughout the morning, lobbyists for every industry imaginable rushed around from office to office trying to get a handle on what was happening. Many of the industries and companies they represented were heavily dependent upon government money. The economy's freefall, combined with the complete evaporation of Congressional Leadership structure, took away all certainty that these contracts would be continued.

Even more acute were the personal fears and anxieties of the lobbyist corps. Most of them had built their entire career on their inside knowledge of either the Republican or Democratic party. The relationships and influence they had carefully built over decades were directly tied to the continued success of the old two-party system. The Collapse suddenly tossed these relationships and influence in the air - no one had any idea if they would be worth a nickel when they landed.

Reporters from every national outlet swarmed the halls of Congress. Any person spotted walking in public while wearing a Congressional Member pin on his or her lapel was bound to be accosted by at least a half-dozen cameras. No one had any new information to offer, but many Members were happy to stop and talk in exchange for a splash of face time.

Few had eaten, no one had really slept, and everyone was consumed by stress. Tempers flared all around as the lack of information continued and the economic pressures mounted.

Amid the growing chaos, Montgomery stayed in his closed office, working out his plans to build a foundation of support. Meanwhile, the rest of the staff was growing increasingly uncomfortable and anxious fielding angry phone calls from constituents. Despite some frustrations, most of them had generally enjoyed working for a relatively unambitious Member, since it usually meant less incoming fire. But now it seemed to them like he was hiding in his office, buckling under the pressure. As far as they could tell, it looked like Montgomery wanted to crawl into a hole and disappear.

ANNA RETURNED from the park just before 10:30 a.m. As usual, she breezed through the foyer without a word and quickly entered her personal office. Seconds later, Montgomery exited his office and silently shot by on his way out the door to meet a colleague. Josh and Lily, each on the phone getting an earful from angry constituents, glanced at each other across the foyer and shrugged.

As Montgomery strode purposefully through the hallways on his way to his first target, he checked his watch - 10:28 a.m., just in time for his first meeting. He could not hide his smile as he neared the office of target number one: Benjamin Petrowski. Once he opened the door to the suite located at 2004 Rayburn House Office Building and crossed Congressman Petrowski's threshold, there would be no turning back.

This would not be a shoot-from-the-hip effort. Montgomery had quietly been planning for a campaign like this for decades. While he didn't know when his opportunity would arise, he knew all he needed was a catalyst to launch his plan into action. The Collapse was clearly that moment.

In his early days in Congress, Willis Montgomery had made three unsuccessful attempts to gain positions of influence. Each time, he picked out a low-level party Leadership position for which he felt qualified, then set his sights. As a young, tall, handsome, well-spoken Member, he believed his colleagues would quickly see him as Leadership material. He would make a list of the Members whose votes he needed, then run around to each of their offices and make his case for why he was the best fit. After rattling off his resume and qualifications, he would ask for their vote.

Being professional politicians, his colleagues were adept at making you *feel* like you had their support without ever actually *saying* so. And in the end, each time the votes were counted, Montgomery came up short.

Montgomery was an analytical type, so he did not just sweep these defeats into a mental dustbin of failures. Since he had arrived in Congress at the incredibly young age of 28 and quickly became beloved in his safe district, he knew he had time to get this right. He dissected each defeat like a scientist, cataloguing each error to ensure he never repeated it.

One of his favorite post-mortem strategies was seeking the advice of senior Members of both parties. They were always happy to offer their thoughts, and it was often substantively valuable.

After suffering his third consecutive defeat for a minor Leadership post, then-32-year-old Montgomery had decided to talk with Herbert Steffens, one of the Members who had been a strong supporter of his opponent. At that time, Steffens was one of the most senior Congressmen in the House. Montgomery felt it couldn't hurt to ask for some advice to improve his future runs.

He set up an appointment through Steffens' Scheduler and waited patiently in the foyer. When Steffens came out to greet him, Montgomery was extremely humble and well-mannered. He told Steffens his purpose in meeting and asked for any guidance on how he could do better.

Congressman Steffens had the air of a wise grandfather who was teaching a young pupil. Nothing flattered him more than having a fledgling Congressman ask his advice. He sat in a comfortable chair in his office and motioned for Montgomery to sit on the sofa, a small coffee table between them.

"As I recall," Steffens began, "you were very thorough in your Leadership race. You came around to every voter and explained to them why you believed you should get their vote. You displayed an excellent resume and clearly have a first-rate intelligence."

Montgomery thanked Steffens for his kind words.

"But," Steffens continued, "your entire presentation was focused on what *I* could do for *you*. You never mentioned what *you* could do for *me*. You see, it's human nature to want to do things that are beneficial to yourself. In the world of politics, you can multiply this basic truth tenfold. As long as you're talking about why *you* should get something, you'll rarely get it. Talk about how you can deliver to others what *they* want, and they'll be apt to let you."

Montgomery profusely thanked Steffens for sharing his wisdom, then walked back to his office deep in thought. He decided Steffens was right. If he ever wanted to get anywhere, he had better learn how to make people think it's all about them. Most people will not voluntarily sacrifice their own interests to help someone else - they will only do something if they think they will personally benefit.

In addition to being too self-focused, Montgomery determined that the root cause of each loss mainly came back to two other big-picture errors: he had failed to think strategically, and he had not been thoroughly prepared. Whereas Montgomery had rushed into battle as soon as he spied an opportunity, the victors had taken a more strategic approach in picking which battles to fight in the first place. And, they only fought if they were already well-positioned for victory. He needed to learn how to say no to mediocre opportunities while preparing for the incredible one that would someday come.

This epiphany years ago had been game-changing for Montgomery: If he was patient and methodical, he could achieve whatever he wanted. No more chasing shiny prizes; he would take his time and build his foundation and ladder. The right opportunity would eventually arrive.

He now sensed the preparation and waiting were about to pay off. Finally, he would undo the shackles he had placed on his own ambitions so long ago and step forward toward his destiny. This time, he would not fail.

CONGRESSMAN BENJAMIN PETROWSKI had represented a district on the outskirts of Pittsburgh, Pennsylvania, for nearly 30 years. Like Montgomery, Petrowski was well-respected among his peers as a pragmatic statesman who truly cared for his hometown. He had been one of Montgomery's closest friends for many years. The similarities in their districts and temperaments had brought them together early on, and they remained close through the ups and downs of the past two decades.

Back in the glory days of the steel industry, the district had produced more steel per capita than any other in the nation. The last few decades had not been kind to its residents. Still a working-class area, the citizens had felt left behind by the global economy.

Petrowski welcomed Montgomery into his office and offered something to drink. Montgomery accepted a bottle of water from Petrowski's Staff Assistant, who quickly scurried out the door and back into the foyer.

"Good to see you, Willis," Petrowski said. He looked tired as well - just like everyone else on the Hill that Monday morning. "What's on your mind?"

"Oh, just a thing or two lately," Montgomery replied. The two men laughed.

"What an understatement," said Petrowski. "Anything in particular this morning?"

"Well, Ben, I was actually wanting to pick your brain on something. You've been here a long time - longer than me - and I think you have a good feel for how things work."

"How things *worked*," Petrowski corrected.

"Fair enough. How things worked. I have been trying to figure out what the best path forward is for this body and wanted to hear your thoughts. It's uncharted water and I don't know how to navigate it. Where do you think we go from here?"

Petrowski let out a long sigh and looked at the coffee table between them. "I wish I knew," he said. "This place is such a mess right now, I'm not even sure where to start."

"What are your constituents telling you?" Montgomery asked. "Our districts are not that different. Both very blue collar. Salt-of-the-Earth people."

"The best people in this nation," Petrowski agreed. "In between people yelling at me and telling me what a lousy S.O.B. I am, I occasionally hear some real suggestions. Mostly, people want us to quit fighting and get along. They're tired of the bickering and partisanship. They're sick of the swings from ideological extreme to ideological extreme. First the Tea Party, then the Democratic Socialists... none of it seemed to make their lives any better. They want people who can get things done. Pragmatists."

Montgomery smiled. "Sounds like you do indeed have wise people in your district, Ben. I hear almost all the same things back home. You know, I would bet you most of the people up here are hearing that every time they set foot in their districts - the ones who still have the guts to actually do so, that is."

"I think that's absolutely right, Willis." Petrowski's eyes were starting to show life. "It's not just Pittsburgh or Kansas City, it's all across America. The people want pragmatic leadership."

"I couldn't agree more. But I'm afraid without any cohesive group up here who stands on that message, it just gets drowned out by the shouting from the ideological extremes," Montgomery said with a tone of resignation. He let a few moments of silence hang in the air.

"It doesn't have to be that way anymore, Willis," Petrowski said. "I know it's hard to think this way, we're so used to the Republican and Democrat system... but we can put together any group we want now."

"It's like the wild west, isn't it?" Montgomery said, as if just beholding the political blank canvas for the first time. "Except there's not even a sheriff to tell us we can't get our people together and have our own posse!"

"A group of Members who puts pragmatism first and sets aside old ideological fights...who fight for the economic security and success of hardworking everyday Americans… I think we could get some traction with that," said Petrowski. "Who else might be interested?"

Montgomery took a blank notecard from his shirt pocket and the two began to make a list. After several minutes of brainstorming together, the two men rose and shook hands heartily. "I am so glad I sought your advice today, Ben," Montgomery said. "I think we're really onto something!"

Petrowski nodded in agreement. "You let me know how I can help. I think this is the first glimmer of hope I've seen for our country in weeks!"

Willis Montgomery replicated this scene a dozen times over the next several hours. Here is where Montgomery used Alfred as his secret weapon. He knew other colleagues were likely testing the waters for their own Speaker bids, but Montgomery could focus with precision on exactly who he needed to talk to, knew how he could finesse them to get on board with his ideas, and meet with the maximum number of people possible to grow his team.

He picked out Members from mostly blue-collar districts who he knew would not be seeking the limelight themselves, but who were likely to support a respected elder statesman promising to stop their world from spinning out of control. Each time his colleague would offer a slight twist on the same advice, and each time Montgomery would respond with the surprise and thankfulness he had shown Congressman Petrowski. He always let his colleagues believe that they were the ones who had come up with the idea in the first place.

Just as Montgomery had predicted, the Members he spoke to were so worried about Congress's precarious situation and craving leadership and stability so badly, they were excited to follow this respected leader offering a solid plan.

9

Just before 10:45 a.m., as Montgomery was beginning the first phase of his strategy, Anna shut the door to her office and started to sketch out her own plan of attack. She completed each of the tasks Montgomery had specifically asked her to do, then filled a sticky note with some feedback and follow-up questions and stuck it on Montgomery's desk.

For the next several hours, Anna sat at her desk working through spreadsheets, calendars, and lists, trying to war-game the Speaker race. Since her first day on the job she had been acquiring cell numbers and personal information of all the other Chiefs of Staff and feeding them to Alfred. Although at first she didn't want to do this tedious and annoying work, Montgomery absolutely demanded it. She now realized it was beginning to pay off in spades.

Since Anna decided three and a half years earlier to focus on building connections, she had placed relationships with other Chiefs as her top priority. She attended every meeting for Chiefs she could get to, regularly asked her counterparts to join her for lunch, and sent each one a handwritten birthday card every year.

Lily was extremely helpful in making this happen, keeping close track of the birthdays and cards. Her cheerful demeanor extended beyond greeting visitors and answering phones. She loved to brighten someone's day with a personalized card. She created printed instructions for Anna with personal details from Alfred, then placed the blank cards on Anna's desk a week ahead of time.

Montgomery encouraged Anna to use his campaign bank account liberally in developing her professional relationships. As a senior member of the House, he had no trouble raising money. Without a legitimate campaign challenge in almost 20 years, he believed the best use of his war chest was for relationship-building. Montgomery gave Anna nearly carte blanche to pay for meals with her colleagues.

She used Montgomery's generous spending authority to support a standing lunch reservation each Wednesday. Just before noon, she and nine colleagues could be found in a back room at Live Oak, an upscale Southern cuisine restaurant a few blocks northwest of the Capitol. This steak and seafood restaurant had a well-deserved reputation as one of the best in town. Anna's table for 10 was seldom short of its full capacity, as the regular events became a popular invitation among House Chiefs of Staff. Since the crackdown on lobbyist gifts in the early 2000s, Hill staffers rarely were offered a meal on someone else's dime anymore. They were also always happy to get away from the Capitol's gravitational field for an hour or two.

To Anna, the meals served a dual purpose: they were an excellent opportunity to glean information about her colleagues that she and Montgomery could later use, and they raised her own stature among people in the know. Like the Parisian salons of old, Anna made her Wednesday table at Live Oak a status symbol at which many other Chiefs sought to be seen.

Despite all her efforts to build social standing and relationships, Anna's generally introverted personality and hesitancy to trust others sometimes made her struggle to make true personal connections. Her defensive walls were typically raised so high in conversation that she had a hard time lowering them enough to let others in, even for benign friendship. Anna was fully aware of how this came across, but it was a hard habit to change. She consciously tried to save up her reserves of extroversion for these weekly lunches.

Anna's uncommonly good looks helped mask these struggles. Rather than seeing her as cold and unlikeable, her male colleagues generally fell prey to wishful thinking. They interpreted her high emotional walls and lack of flirtation as a deliberate effort to create a feeling of mystery and intrigue. Though this worked to her advantage, Anna did little to actually lead them on. Despite all the attention Anna garnered, she had no use for dating. She poured her heart and soul into her work and left no time for personal trifles.

Besides, all men had ever been good at in the past was disappointing her. Anna had long ago learned there was only one person in the world upon whom she could truly rely - herself. She was all business, regardless of the fairy tales her hopeful colleagues spun in their own minds.

Anna's weekly lunches were, in fact, modeled off of the weekly dinners Montgomery had been holding with his colleagues for nearly 15 years. Each week that the House was in session, Montgomery invited nine fellow Members to a Wednesday dinner in the same back room at Live Oak.

Lily and Josh spent several hours a week organizing these dinners around the infinitely complex schedules of other Members. Whenever possible, they tried to coordinate Chiefs and their bosses to attend Anna's lunch and Montgomery's dinner on the same day. This way, Anna could probe the Chief for information that she could use to prep Montgomery on the Member's latest priorities before dinner.

Montgomery had always insisted that Anna devote equal attention to Chiefs of both parties - an act that bordered on heresy in the hyper-partisan environment of the Hill. At first Anna had chafed at this directive. But she and Montgomery also insisted on civility at these meals, so everyone knew they would not be ambushed or ganged up on, making everyone more relaxed and willing to talk to one another. Because of this, she grew to enjoy meeting her counterparts on the other side of the aisle even more than her own. She realized that she learned more by listening to a variety of viewpoints (even when she didn't agree with them) than she would have learned from staying inside of her echo chamber.

Montgomery and Anna strived for partisan parity at these weekly lunches and dinners, never allowing more than a 6-4 tilt either direction. Over time, their consistent bipartisanship at mealtime helped develop reputations for statesmanship and sincerity among their peers.

Now that the parties had dissolved, the wisdom of Montgomery's nonpartisan approach was looking prescient. It was unlikely anyone else had as thorough of a contact list of former partisan opponents as he and Anna had created.

To prepare for Anna's Wednesday lunches, Lily created table place cards containing each person's name, office, and state. An hour before leaving for lunch, Montgomery's Legislative Director, Des, and Communications Director, Kyle, helped Anna set up a dry run around the conference table in Montgomery's office.

Des was one of the most interesting people Anna had ever known. Baby-faced and barely five feet tall on a good day, many people thought she looked a full decade younger than she was. Anna learned quickly not to allow Des's diminutive size and youthful looks to deceive her. She was incredibly smart and knew the Hill's legislative procedures like the back of her hand.

Physically, Kyle was nearly the mirror opposite of Des. Standing over six feet, three inches tall and thin as a rail, the two made quite the odd couple when standing next to one another. On the Hill, the most successful Communications Directors were those who could speak the reporters' language, and Kyle was an expert at it. He had served over a decade as a linguistics officer in the Air Force prior to joining Montgomery's office, learning to pick up foreign lingo and assimilate like a native. These skills had come in handy with the tight clique of Hill reporters. His trendy glasses and fashionable clothes helped him fit in with them as well.

At dress rehearsals for Anna's lunches, Des played the part of female Chiefs while Kyle stood in for the men. They went around the table, switching chairs rapidly, taking on the persona of each of the nine guests. Anna was focused and engaged, scribbling notes about each person's kids, alma mater, and favorite policy issues.

Lily always left 10 minutes early in order to claim the room and set up the place cards in proper order. Josh gave Anna and three of her colleagues a lift to the restaurant, while Kyle usually helped chauffeur the others. This kind of coordinated service was doubly impressive to their guests, who were accustomed to driving themselves to events downtown or securing their own ride - a nightmare for parking and logistics.

At lunch, Anna invariably sat at the head of the table. After welcoming her guests and thanking them for taking time out of their busy days to have lunch at her favorite restaurant, she asked each of them to go around the table and introduce themselves. As an icebreaker, she also asked each one to share a fact about themselves that others might not know. Anna used every memory device in the book to squirrel away these tidbits for later.

After each meal, Anna pulled out a cell phone and quickly recorded a short audio memo cataloguing everything they wanted to remember from the event. Anna usually did this with her eyes closed, mentally scanning the table from left to right and making note of anything memorable that each lunch guest said. Lily uploaded these files to an automatic transcription service, cleaned up the output, and inserted the relevant facts into Alfred.

In her four years with Montgomery, Anna had used a combination of these lunches and other efforts to become one of the best-known Chiefs of Staff in Congress. In the end, her struggles to open up to colleagues did not push anyone away - they just made her friendships shallow. Anna knew just about everyone and almost everyone knew her... but she had very few people she could truly call "friend." Nevertheless, from a career perspective, she was still many steps ahead of most people - even the most charismatic of her peers.

After these years of effort, her substantial knowledge about other Chiefs was now helping her instinctively navigate the relationships and personalities of her colleagues to Montgomery's maximum benefit. She pored over the information she had gathered and created a ranked list of Chiefs to contact herself and Members for Montgomery to speak with.

Anna might not have become best friends with any other Chiefs through her lunches and other outreach, but she had definitely stored up a massive amount of goodwill and positive reputation. She would need every ounce of both for the task she now faced.

10

Toward the end of the workday, Anna could tell the staff was running on fumes. Each time she overheard a staffer take a constituent phone call, the staff responses got shorter and more terse. They needed some encouragement.

At 5:30 p.m., she knocked on the passageway door to Montgomery's office. She had heard him return a few minutes earlier from making his Member visits. Montgomery told her to come in.

"Hey boss, did you have good meetings this afternoon?" Anna asked.

"Yeah, they went great, actually," he said. "I really think we're onto something here. How have things been in the office?"

Anna considered the grim tone she had witnessed getting progressively worse throughout the afternoon.

"Eh, not good, really," she said. "What do you think about letting everyone in on your idea and sending them home early? They really don't need to sit here and keep getting yelled at on the phones all night."

"I think that's fine," Montgomery said. "It's really not a secret that we're trying to get some like-minded folks together. If it helps them feel like they're doing something more worthwhile, all the better."

Montgomery called his team into his office. He sat on the front edge of his oak desk as everyone gathered around.

"Come on in, guys," he said. "Close the door. Don't worry about bringing in chairs, I won't keep you long."

The last few stragglers squeezed in the office and shut the door as Montgomery began to speak.

"I just wanted to thank you all for the effort you've put in today. I have heard your end of some of the phone calls, and I can tell it's rough. No one should ever get talked to like that, much less all day long. I do appreciate your efforts on behalf of our district."

The mood eased slightly as the staff felt some appreciation for the first time all day.

Montgomery continued. "I also wanted to let you know what I've been working on. Now more than ever, our nation and our Congress needs strong, competent leadership. People who are of like minds need to come together and work for the common good. In this spirit, I have begun reaching out to colleagues to gauge interest in forming a new coalition. If we are successful in gaining a critical mass, I will offer myself to my colleagues as a potential leader of this new party."

Excitement filled the staff's eyes as they glanced back and forth toward each other. Montgomery had never been in the mix as long as any of them had worked there, and the young team was hungry to get involved.

He continued to explain his plan. "We are laying the groundwork for what will be the future of this institution, and I am thrilled to have each and every one of you with me at the beginning. No one is better-positioned and better-equipped to take the mantle of leadership in this new reality than us. We have strong relationships and outstanding organization.

"Success will depend on how well we execute our plans right now. I think the next seven to 10 days are crucial for us to either succeed or fail. I don't know about you all, but I plan to succeed. I need you to give us everything you've got in that time. It'll be a lot of early mornings and late nights - grunt work that no one enjoys - but if we bear down together, we can do this.

"I apologize that I will have to be out of the office quite a bit as I meet with other Members, but that's where I can be most useful. I trust Anna fully and ask that you help her in any way she needs over these next few days.

"Now I know everyone's worn out from today. All of you go ahead and get out of here. Go home and get some rest. I'll see you back here at 9 a.m."

The team was energized by Montgomery's words. They were thrilled to be in on the ground level of what could be something big. Excited chattering filled the office as the staff gathered their belongings and headed home. Everyone except Anna. She had much more work to do.

AFTER EVERYONE ELSE LEFT, Anna stayed behind to debrief with Montgomery.

"Why don't you go ahead and give me the rundown of your meetings from today?" she asked.

"There were some great meetings," Montgomery said. "Talked with Ben Petrowski this morning. He's dying for some leadership he can trust. I think he's going to be a cheerleader for us."

Anna made notes as Montgomery talked. She did this religiously every time they spoke, collecting anything relevant to feed to Alfred.

"That's great," she said. "He's really well-respected. I think that'll really help. Who else?"

Montgomery unloaded his thoughts on several more conversations, excitedly telling Anna about all of the support he was accumulating.

Once he finished his debriefing, he asked Anna if she had any new information.

"You know, I've been here in the office planning things out most of the afternoon. Sent out a bunch of emails and texts but haven't had the chance to look through the replies yet."

"Not a problem," Montgomery said. "That's just what we need right now."

"Oh, hold on," Anna said. "I just remembered I did run into someone today when I took a break, and it was a little bit weird."

"Alright, who was it?"

"Kit Lambert. I took a walk in Bartholdi Park mid-morning and he came up to talk to me."

"Kit Lambert? Which one? The kid?"

Of course. He's the least-famous of three people in this town by that name. Anna had forgotten that Montgomery had known the Lambert family for decades.

"Christopher Lambert the fourth," she said. "Ted Alber's Chief of Staff."

Montgomery's face was sullen. "Ah. And what did he have to say?"

"Like I said, it was kind of weird. He really didn't talk about much of anything. Just sort of stared off into space and talked about his grandfather."

"Did he ask about the Speaker's race?"

"Nope."

"Say anything about what Alber plans to do?"

"No. Not a thing about work, actually."

"Alright. Well, be careful around that kid. From what I know of him, he's a snake. I served with his dad and have heard stories about his grandpa. All three of them are playboys of the first order. Being born into money and power doesn't usually make people upstanding citizens, and Kit is a prime example."

"Duly noted," said Anna. "Don't worry, I'd prefer to keep my distance from him anyway. I don't trust him. I always sort of feel like he's trying to get with me."

"You aren't the first to feel that way about him and his family. Just watch him with a skeptical eye and don't get too close. His dad also had a bit of a conspiratorial streak in him when he was in the House. Not sure if he passed that on to his son, but he was always cooking up some nutty theory about people or groups being out to get him." Montgomery clearly had a deep-seated distaste for the entire Lambert clan.

"Will do," said Anna.

"Good," said Montgomery. "Okay, I'm heading out to dinner with some Members. You good here?"

"Yep. I have a ton to do - will probably be here late."

"Alright. Well, be sure to take care of yourself - you need sleep too."

"I know... I'll get to bed at a reasonable hour."

Depending on your definition of "reasonable," that is.

Late into Monday evening, Anna pored over the information in Alfred, picking out details and using them to compose personal text messages and emails to dozens of her colleagues. She knew that most people enjoy having a colleague reach out and ask their thoughts on something. It makes them feel as if the other person truly values their opinion and sees them as important. Anna exploited this tendency to the fullest in her messages, asking for opinions and advice from as many people as possible. However, she was careful to not ask for any favors or seek their support in these messages; the point was to soften them up for a future ask. She took copious notes, marking each person for follow-up in a few days.

As the night dragged on, Anna found herself daydreaming about being Chief of Staff to the Speaker of the House. This brought her mind back to Heather Townsend, Speaker Mathes' Chief of Staff.

She has to just be overwhelmed. What's she going to do? Start a lobbying shop? But all of her best connections are out of power now. If I ever get to be where she was, I sure hope this isn't how I go out. She has to be feeling absolutely hopeless. Maybe I should let her know I'm thinking about her.

Anna shot Heather a quick text.

> **Anna Rothwell**: Heather, this is Anna Rothwell in Willis Montgomery's office. Just wanted to let you know I'm thinking about you tonight. If I can do anything for you, please let me know.

She rarely texted Heather, preferring to save those contacts for when she really needed them. The Speaker's Chief of Staff is one of the busiest jobs in Washington, and the last thing she wanted to do was irritate her idol. Besides, Anna figured that to Heather, she was hardly more than a face in the crowd. They'd spoken many times, but with Montgomery being a fairly low-key Member, Anna wasn't high on Heather's list of priorities.

A few minutes after Anna's short text, Heather responded.

> **Heather Townsend**: Thanks Anna. Rough day. Appreciate the kind words.

Anna's heart sank for Heather. She leaned forward with her elbows on her desk, chin resting on her hands, trying to imagine how Heather felt. This was every staffer's deepest fear: getting caught up in the gears of politics and spit out onto the street. The excitement of working on the Hill was worth the risk, but it really was rough to see good people lose their jobs.

Around 9:30 p.m., Anna decided she could use some friendly commiseration, so she sent a text to Florida Congressman Martin Wilson's Chief of Staff, Peter Garibaldi. She had known Peter since soon after coming to the Hill. Peter was not nearly as high-strung as most other Chiefs, and he usually was straightforward about what he knew and wanted. She had never known him to be conniving or to stab a colleague in the back. Anna would still hesitate to call him a friend, but she felt more comfortable with him than most other Chiefs.

> **Anna Rothwell**: Hey Peter, hope you're holding up ok. I feel like I'll never feel rested again. Been thinking about all this stuff and wondered what your take is on Mathes stepping down. How soon do you think they'll schedule a vote?
>
> **Peter Garibaldi**: Hi Anna - I'm feeling worn out too - not sure on the vote. My guess is it'll be at least 2-3 weeks. People need time to campaign and whip votes - but who knows anymore.
>
> **AR**: I think that's right. Can't just spring it on people. It'll take a while to sort out who's running.
>
> **PG**: Yep. Probably half the House.
>
> **AR**: I bet you're not far off. Hope your nephews are doing alright and enjoying summer. Let me know if you need anything.
>
> **PG**: Appreciate it. Hope to see them again someday. :) Take it easy.

Anna stopped sending texts and emails at 10:00 - she thought anything later seemed unprofessional - but stayed at her desk until late into the night, long after her self-imposed texting curfew. The sheer volume of logistics involved in keeping track of this many people was overwhelming. Each conversation had to be tracked in

Alfred. She took note of any public statements she came across and even made note of nonverbal cues from personal interactions.

She continued to work until sometime around 2:30 a.m., when the adrenaline wore off and fatigue hit her like a sledgehammer. She decided to lie down on her office couch for a quick 20-minute nap and then get back to it.

PART II

FACTIONS

11

TUESDAY, JULY 18

After what felt like five minutes, Anna was awakened by a gleam of sunlight coming in her office window. She had completely crashed.

She groggily sat up and rubbed her eyes, then checked her watch and exhaled a massive yawn. 5:30 a.m.

I feel like I got hit by a bus. I've got to get up. Come on... this is my chance to be somebody - I can't waste it asleep.

She lay flat on her back, head on the couch's small armrest, and closed her eyes.

After six additional minutes of rest, Anna decided she had better get off the couch and prepare for the day. Fortunately, she always kept a change of clothes in her office for situations just like this. Once she had put on a fresh outfit, washed her face, and applied some minimal makeup, she felt awake enough to start thinking again.

Anna decided she had already thrown her routine off enough, she might as well go ahead and read the overnight rumors. Maybe the early treat would help her feel a tiny bit better. She logged back into her computer and checked her email.

From: Quincy <quincy@quincyswhispers.com>
Subject: Quincy's Whispers - Tuesday, July 18
Date: July 18 at 4:27 AM
To: Anna Rothwell

Quincy's Whispers
252 days since the Midterm Election
476 days until the Presidential Election
What the House is whispering about...
but doesn't want you to hear.

Good Tuesday morning! As predicted right here yesterday, as soon as the House returned to session, everything went crazy on the Hill. Leadership formally resigned. Everyone who's anyone is jockeying for position right now... and quite a few who are no one. The markets' panic sent the Hill's anxiety meter through the roof... and don't expect it to go back down any time soon. We're just getting started on this wild ride.

What I'm hearing today:

Whisper 1 - After Congressional Leadership resigned yesterday, the House now has only one formal leader - Speaker Julie Mathes. Aaaaand she also announced she plans to resign in about six weeks. No one person can single-handedly hold 435 Members together and do anything productive, and Whisperers say this is even more true of Speaker Mathes than most others. Via tips from Members and staffers alike, sounds like almost everyone on the Hill is completely at a loss for how the chamber will run now. Many Whisperers are asking for procedural guidance... My advice is to crack open Jefferson's Manual and get to know the House Parliamentarian - he just became the most important man in Washington. We're going to be traveling back in time to the era before modern parties... the name of the game will now be *precedent*. In the absence of a controlling party to set the daily rules of debate, the House will simply revert to the centuries-old traditions and precedents that were its original foundational rules. Rather than the majority ramming through its agenda and overriding rules, the body will now effectively defer to the Parliamentarian's rulings on proper procedure.

Whisper 2 - It's hard to find someone in D.C. who is NOT mad about the current situation - and most are mad at almost everyone. However, my Whisperers are clear - the hottest fires are burning within the ashes of each of the old parties. Former Dems have formed cliques and factions that are at each other's throats casting blame for their party's implosion. Former GOP'ers are doing the same, with many swearing permanent oaths against their former brethren. The damage won't be repaired quickly. The blame game over last weekend's events might be fought for 100 years. We're talking Hatfields and McCoys here.

Whisper 3 - The big question... Now what? Will two new parties form? One major party and a slew of minor ones? A bunch of splintered factions? It's anyone's guess at this point. Smart Whisperers seem confident that whatever happens, we will see a lot of formerly-strange bedfellows ending up in the same coalitions. The hurt feelings among former party colleagues are just too raw to see either old party re-form in anything like its old image.

Whisper 4 - Circling back on what only a few days ago actually seemed like big news (my how quickly perspective can change)... The latest on the situation we codenamed "Bunker Hill" is that prosecutors of Congressman Steve Weher's alleged campaign finance law violations will receive a boost today, as Whisperers tell me two more eyewitnesses to the alleged crimes plan to go public. Maybe worse for

Steve, it's hard to see anyone responding to a Member's screams for help over pre-Collapse troubles. Truth is, this story is old news, and Weher is toast.

Whisper 5 - A big question on Whisperers' minds: What happens to all of the legislation that was in process when The Collapse occurred? The short answer is: We have no idea. We're entering uncharted waters here. Will Committees dissolve? Will their bills just live in limbo until new parties and Leadership form? And what about the Approps bills and Debt Ceiling I mentioned here yesterday? Tons of unanswered questions; even more wild speculation and rumors floating around. As of now, no one really has the answers.

Whisper 6 - While you were busy with The Collapse... rumor has it that at least one, and possibly up to three, high-profile Members are involved in a new FBI investigation. In keeping with our recent Revolutionary War-themed naming convention, we'll give this alleged scandal codename "Yorktown." Potential for financial crimes, FEC violations, and/or bribery charges. I'll be listening closely as the situation develops.

UNTIL TOMORROW, I have the honor to be,

Your obedient servant,

~QUINCY

Sign up at www.QuincysWhispers.com to get
every edition delivered to your inbox!
Watch for breaking Whispers on Twitter @quincyswhispers.

Hear something good?
Whisper it to me at tips@quincyswhispers.com.
All Whispers are reviewed and kept
strictly anonymous and confidential.

~

After skimming the Whispers, then reading back through them more carefully a second time, Anna felt a little better about the growing anxiety she had been feeling. She was strangely happy to know that she was not the only one who had no idea what was going on.

Everyone within 100 miles is probably freaking out about all of the same things. For a town full of type-A control freaks, nothing could be worse than being cut loose of all moorings. Funny how much more interesting that last Whisper about the FBI would have been a couple of weeks ago. Now most people will hardly notice.

Anna's email inbox contained 632 unread emails from the past week. Usually she kept her inbox completely clean - efficiently triaging, processing, and categorizing her work. Falling this far behind was completely out of character. The unbearably large "632" stared at her in bold.

She processed a few dozen more emails.

So much junk. None of this seems half as important as it did last week. Nothing like an existential crisis to bring perspective to your job.

Her eyes blurred and her gaze began to drift, but she made herself snap to attention.

What's my problem? I've got to get my stuff together. I think if I knock out my emails right now, I'll be able to stay on top of it going forward. Time for a fresh start.

Anna clicked on the "Select All" command. She marked the emails as read, then dragged them into an archive folder.

Tada, inbox zero.

Cleaning her digital slate eased Anna's mind less than expected. No level of organization and tidying up was going to calm her today. Deep inside, she just wasn't quite herself.

12

By 8:30 the first few staffers started to drag themselves in. When the clock reached 9:00, the whole staff had arrived. Anna put everyone to work as soon as they walked through the door. The team was making good progress with their whip operation, but there was a long way to go.

Anna had been keeping track of every conversation, every commitment, and every offer to help as quickly as Montgomery could relay the information. Organization would be key to success, and she was one of the best at it. She mindlessly tucked her red hair behind her ear as she opened Alfred and began sorting out potential Members for Montgomery to target.

Skimming through the mounds of personal information, she contemplated the categories that could even possibly be helpful. She quickly highlighted tidbits to call to Montgomery's attention before he reached out so he could be fully prepared. These personal details could help him connect with each Member on a more intimate level.

She also tried to figure out who the most likely supporters would be for the three opponents who worried Montgomery the most. Christine Franklin was staunchly religious and had a reputation as a sweet, grandmotherly woman who was smart as a whip. Montgomery had gone to church with her for years and occasionally attended a Members' Bible study that she led each week in the Capitol. He knew that Franklin's faith was serious to her. She would pull in many socially conservative supporters, but Anna wasn't sure where else her reach would extend.

Jonathan Garcia would probably have a ton of support from minority Members and others representing more urban districts, but his gruff demeanor and bad reputation would limit his appeal. Ted Alber had a lot of star power and could probably pull from all different corners of the ideological map.

As she scanned Alfred for grandchildren's names, favorite foods, anniversaries, and notable friendships, Anna ruminated on the situation.

I wonder how many other Chiefs are doing the same thing right now. This complete power vacuum probably has everyone thinking they have a legit shot at Speaker. A blank slate makes everyone imagine filling it in with their own name. No doubt there's a ton of people who are going to try for it. Maybe we're just one of that delusional pack? No... I really do feel like we're ahead of the curve.

But aren't there other offices that keep track of this kind of information too? Nah... I'm sure there are a few that have cell phones and birthday lists, but there's no way anyone else has anything close to what we have. They could spend a week working round-the-clock and not end up with one-tenth of our info. They're all still shell-shocked and scrambling to make a plan while we're going to be blasting forward. By the time they get up to speed, it'll be too late. We're going to knock them out.

Anna smiled to herself. She was excited - but cautiously so.

~

Montgomery arrived just after 9:00 and burst into the office with even more enthusiasm than normal. He greeted everyone on his staff except Anna and asked them how they were, giving each person a minute's worth of his full attention.

After hanging up his suit jacket, Montgomery knocked on the passageway door linking his personal office to Anna's, then entered. "Good morning, Anna," he said cheerfully. "You doing ok?"

"Yeah, absolutely. Making good progress on things. I think we ought to go ahead and book a room to pull all these people together for a meeting tomorrow morning. At the pace we're getting commitments, we should have a good crowd by then."

"Perfect. Tell Josh to book a room for 10:00 tomorrow morning. Something in Rayburn - make sure it's big enough for about 30 people. I think we'll get close to that."

"Will do. Shouldn't be hard - most committees have called off all of their hearings for the week."

"And that helps our cause," said Montgomery. "Fewer competing events on the schedule. They'll be looking for excuses to get away from reporters and constituents anyway."

Anna laughed and agreed.

"I'm going to head out and make some more visits," Montgomery said. "I'll give you my iPad. While I'm out, I want you to use it to individually text each Member on this list."

He handed her a handwritten list of about three dozen Members he had already met with in person.

"You can just copy and paste the same message to everyone. When I get back, let me know who you've heard from."

They created the draft script together:

> *Hi __________, great to talk with you yesterday. I took your advice and*

> *talked with some of the others on the list we came up with. LOTS of interest. I've reserved ________ Rayburn tomorrow at 10 am to get everyone together. Can you make it?*

"Let me know if you need anything," he said as he headed for the door. "You're doing an awesome job."

Montgomery closed the door behind him as he exited Anna's office. She felt a warm rush of positive energy in response to his quick compliment. It was good to hear that he thought she was on the right track.

Anna got to work sending texts to each Member and keeping track of their responses. She enjoyed the banter she got to engage in after receiving a reply. It was fun to occasionally play Member.

Throughout the morning, Anna kept an eye on her office TV to see how the markets were faring. The day started out massively better than Monday had, with some investors buying up stocks at a discount after their historic fall. After a couple of hours, though, the mood swung back south. It would turn out to be another abysmal day for stocks.

After finishing the Member texts, Anna contacted the Chief of Staff for each Member on the list. Anna invited each Chief to attend with his or her boss. She knew one of the best ways to get a Member to a meeting was to make their gatekeeper feel important by inviting them as well.

Anna stopped to take a quick break in the middle of the day. Out of curiosity, she turned on C-SPAN to see what was happening on the House Floor. Each of the past two mornings the chamber would gavel into session, attempt to approve the prior day's journal, and open the Floor for motions. Some of the ornerier Members saw this as a prime opportunity to both try to sneak through some of their priorities and irritate their colleagues. They had taken to spending most of the day on the Floor debating ideologies and generally blowing smoke.

Monday this group of lawmakers had numbered about 80. Tuesday it grew closer to 100. The count ebbed and flowed throughout each day, but a few almost never left. It wasn't that they were overwhelmingly interested in the subjects under debate; most of them just went to the Floor to avoid the angry constituent calls, drop-ins by frantic lobbyists, and constant pestering by reporters. So long as they were in the chamber, they had some peace and quiet. Others' main motivation was making rousing speeches for the C-SPAN cameras. It was great for name ID and fundraising.

Members who stayed away from the nonstop blathering on the Floor started derisively referring to this crew as the Debate Team. They thought hanging out on the Floor all day was either cowardly or shameless camera-chasing, and perhaps both.

Anna had no respect for such showboating and meaningless prattle. After watching for a few minutes, she turned off the TV in disgust. As she returned to her work, she felt even more proud that she was working for a Congressman who was taking real action to heal political rifts and improve things for his constituents.

For a solid 10 hours, Montgomery personally visited Members and Anna texted Members and Chiefs. They both stuck to their strategy of using personal details and open conversations, trying to do more listening than talking.

When Montgomery and Anna circled back at the end of the day, they had received commitments from 21 Members for the meeting. Together with Montgomery, this would make 22; a psychologically important number, as it constituted 10 percent of the 218 votes necessary to reach a majority in the House of Representatives.

Montgomery and Anna worked in his office until 12:30 Wednesday morning creating and rehearsing the plan for the 10 a.m. meeting. They decided Anna would arrive an hour early to get the room arranged. Montgomery would get there by 9:30 for a last-minute run-through and to begin greeting guests.

As the Members and Chiefs arrived, Montgomery would personally thank each one for coming and for sharing their advice. Anna would pull each Chief aside and thank them for bringing their boss, then tell them how happy she was to also have the Chief there for the meeting.

The excitement of being in the middle of something that really mattered was intoxicating. Anna had never imagined that she could play a potentially critical role in a turning point in American history. After everything the country had been through over the past two weeks, she was ready to help bring peace and stability back to the nation… and at the same time become a power player herself.

AT 12:45, as she made the short walk home to the townhouse in which she rented a third-floor apartment, Anna did her best to stop imagining the press conferences where she would be taking questions from the national media as the Speaker's Chief of Staff. The prospect seemed too good to be true, plus it was incredibly scary to think about actually having the responsibilities that came with such a job. She climbed the stairs as quietly as possible. The building was over 80 years old and its wooden steps betrayed every movement with loud creaks and groans.

She opened her door and flicked on the light. After spending almost two entire days in her office, she was happy to finally have a chance to relax in her own space - even if there was not much "space" to speak of. Her studio apartment was hardly any larger than the bedroom she'd grown up in. The townhouse was actually not three stories, but rather two and a half. This meant the ceiling on both sides of the converted attic space that was her apartment slanted at a 45-degree angle. The stale fluorescent glow of the 40-year-old light fixture in the center of the ceiling made the tiny room feel even smaller.

Summertime heat made the room even more uncomfortable. The intense sunlight beating on the asphalt-shingle roof throughout the afternoon heated up the former attic, which trapped heat like an oven. Her tiny window air-conditioning unit just couldn't keep up.

Anna dropped her keys and bag next to the door and immediately kicked off her heels. In the middle of this nightly ritual, her best friend slowly tiptoed across the room towards her on soft paws. Delta was excited to see her finally home again. Half Siamese, half Persian, Delta had the exotic look befitting the companion of a Ming-dynasty emperor. Anna felt blessed to have such a gorgeous roommate.

"Good evening, beautiful!" she said as she picked up Delta.

Delta rubbed her fluffy white cheek against Anna's face, purring gently. Anna had been gone far too much the last few days.

"I'm sorry I was out late again," she said, but Delta was not interested in hearing her excuses. The cat jumped out of her arms and pointedly stalked over to a pillow on the other side of the apartment, where she quickly resumed her beauty sleep.

Despite being mentally drained from the long work day, Anna was so pumped full of adrenaline that she still felt wide awake. Her mind was so consumed with speculation and ideas that she could not shut it off. The feeling reminded her of when she bought her first lottery ticket. The jackpot was over $800 million. The next two nights she laid in bed fantasizing about all of the ways she would spend her new fortune. But this time the dream actually had a chance of coming true: she could actually be the new Heather Townsend, Chief of Staff to the Speaker of the House.

Every five minutes or so she would pick up her phone from her nightstand to quickly jot down an idea or reminder, lest she forget it by morning. After a couple hours of this, she forced herself to stop and call it a night.

13

As Anna was restlessly tossing and turning upstairs, a dark Chevy Tahoe cruised slowly past her townhouse. The driver nonchalantly peered at the building's front stairs as he made a mental record of its appearance. He mindlessly rubbed his left cheek as he thought about the ingress and egress routes from the property. As he drove on to the next property on his list, he wrote some coded notes on a small pad of paper balanced on the car's center console.

His old friend had requested some heavy lifts in their early Monday meeting. He had accomplished harder objectives in the past, but usually with many more resources and men at his disposal. Frankly, given the incredibly tight and inflexible timeline, he wasn't sure he could do it. Nonetheless, he had sworn he would develop and execute a plan, and he wasn't about to fail on such a crucial mission.

One thing was for sure: he would have to call in every favor from every trusted source he knew if he was going to be successful. For now he needed to gather intelligence as quickly as possible. There was no time to waste. He was already setting plans in motion… even if he wasn't sure exactly where they were going to end up.

14

WEDNESDAY, JULY 19

When Anna's alarm blared at 5:00 a.m. after a second sleepless night, she still felt bone-tired and unrefreshed. Her routine was shot to hell.

Maybe it was time to re-evaluate her schedule. These days she needed to be on her toes and perhaps she should be catching up on the day's gossip before grabbing that seemingly important first cup of coffee. Anna picked up her phone from the nightstand and scanned through her email.

~

From: Quincy <quincy@quincyswhispers.com>
Subject: Quincy's Whispers - Wednesday, July 19
Date: July 19 at 4:33 AM
To: Anna Rothwell

Quincy's Whispers
253 days since the Midterm Election
475 days until the Presidential Election

What the House is whispering about...
but doesn't want you to hear.

Good Wednesday morning! The craziness doesn't seem to be settling down on the Hill. The financial panic just seems to be adding fuel to the fire. Every CEO in America (rightly) blames Congress for what's happening to their companies right now. And that's not to mention how the general public feels about their retirement accounts and investments. The consensus seems to be that current Members had better figure something out - and fast - if ANY of them want to keep their jobs come next November.

What I'm hearing today:

Whisper 1 - My inbox was flooded yesterday afternoon with tips from Whisperers about a new caucus/party/faction/something that may be forming as soon as today. Rumor has it Willis Montgomery is leading the movement to bring together some of his colleagues from more blue-collar districts. It's yet to be seen how this group may style itself, but I hear a large group of Members will gather this morning in Rayburn.

Whisper 2 - Wild guesses about who will become Speaker continue to pour in. At this point, there are no leading candidates. Whisperers have suggested no fewer than 36 - yes, that's right, THIRTY SIX - Members may be testing the waters. Until that number becomes manageable or a frontrunner or two emerges, everything is just rank speculation.

Whisper 3 - But so long as we're in the business of rank speculation... the name I'm hearing loudest from the great hallowed halls is Ted Alber (KY). This young star will be a force to be reckoned with as this fight plays out. All signs point to a squeaky-clean background, and he is clearly one of the sharpest young minds in the chamber. Doesn't hurt that he's very photogenic and well-spoken, too.

Whisper 4 - The power vacuum has shaken loose some dust from the rumor mill. With so much opportunity for power, clearly some operatives are using the opportunity to dirty the reputations of their rivals as things get heated. Starting to get plenty of tips from intrepid Whisperers about a particular Member who has developed quite the reputation for drinking too much and carousing with staff after hours. We'll give this rumor codename "Brandywine." And yes, it just so happens this Member is one of the names being tossed around for Leadership positions. So, take that with a grain of salt.

Whisper 5 - Yesterday's Whisper about the FBI investigation of rumor Yorktown pushed a few people's buttons... quite a few new tips and guesses about who it might be pouring in throughout the day. Will be looking into the tips... which cover the actions of not one, not even yesterday's rumored three, but up to FIVE Members.

Whisper 6 - As for that power vacuum rumor mill, I'm hearing some pretty loud Whispers about yet ANOTHER Member. We'll give this alleged situation codename "Ticonderoga." This one is quite the doozy... SHE is actually rumored to have an ongoing romantic relationship with her young male Chief of Staff. Will keep this one close to the vest for now - but if it gains corroboration... we'll be in for quite the juicy scandal.

UNTIL TOMORROW, I have the honor to be,

Your obedient servant,

~QUINCY

Sign up at www.QuincysWhispers.com to get
every edition delivered to your inbox!
Watch for breaking Whispers on Twitter @quincyswhispers.

Hear something good?
Whisper it to me at tips@quincyswhispers.com.

All Whispers are reviewed and kept
strictly anonymous and confidential.

READING Montgomery's name in the morning Whispers was a thrilling new sensation to Anna. She had gotten so used to reading rumors about other people, she'd never considered what it would feel like to read one about her own boss. Now that it was happening, she felt a sense of pride and importance. It made it much more pleasurable that this Whisper was completely accurate, and it was a positive rumor at that.

Anna also took a few moments to appreciate the fact that she had never had to worry about her boss getting wrapped up in a sex scandal. Like all Members of Congress, Montgomery had his ego and his quirks, but physical relationships had never been a distraction. He deliberately steered clear of potentially compromising situations. He was never anything but professional to even the most attractive staffers and interns. She was confident it would be a cold day in hell before Willis Montgomery ever did anything along those unsavory lines.

After a few more minutes of rest, she pulled back her covers and got out of bed. She got dressed and ready, fed Delta, and grabbed a cup of coffee and a handful of pink sweetener packets on the way out the door at 5:45 a.m.

15

With the big meeting happening at 10:00 a.m., Anna and Montgomery had called off their longstanding Wednesday lunch and dinner meetings, and instead had the entire office focus on preparing for what might be the most important hour of their political lives. Anna had asked everyone to be at the office by 7:00 to help get ready. She pulled the team together at 7:15 to take stock of where everything stood. Each person reported the status of their area of responsibility. It looked like everyone was pitching in wherever needed and getting along perfectly, just like she had hoped.

Des made contact with all of the other Legislative Directors in the offices scheduled to attend and promised to fill them in on any details after the meeting. She and Lily dubbed themselves the "party planning committee" and took care of refreshments and decor in the meeting room. Combining Des's huge network of connections on the Hill with Lily's irrepressible cheerfulness and love of decorations and details, the two were a great pair. Kyle was a huge help as well - his years in the Air Force had made him as dependable as a Swiss watch. Each time he finished a task, he asked Anna what more he could do to help. The team was ready to roll.

Montgomery and Anna finished their 9:30 a.m. walk-through without a hitch. They positioned themselves near the door to greet their guests as they arrived.

By 9:45 Lily, Josh, and Des had set out cookies, crudités, iced tea, and lemonade for their guests. They arranged 30 seats with care and turned the air conditioning on high.

Kyle stationed himself outside the room to fend off any reporters who may have caught wind of the meeting. The place was still crawling with members of the media who had nothing better to do with their time than sniff out secret Member gatherings and try to weasel their way inside. Not to mention, the blurb in *Quincy's Whispers* was sure to have them on the prowl. The event was private, however, which helped Kyle shoo away nearly 10 reporters who eventually noticed something was going on.

Kyle was shocked when the first Members showed up at 9:50. Washington is not an "early-arriver" town - most Members' schedules are at least triple-booked every moment of the day, leaving them to jet from meeting to meeting with rarely a moment to spare. Things were different now that the parties were gone.

The attendees seemed to share a hopefulness and spark that had been absent from D.C. since The Collapse. Everyone was excited to be talking about a possible new path forward. They wanted to put this craziness behind them and find a new normal.

Once all of the guests arrived, Montgomery stood at the front of the room and raised his voice to get their attention.

"Thank you, everyone, for taking time out of your busy schedules to come together today," he said. The 22 Members in the room quieted down as the last conversations trailed off.

Anna made sure to position herself at the back of the room in direct view of Montgomery. She wanted to be able to signal him if anything started to go astray. Anna was intensely focused on the task at hand -

she did not want to miss a single tell, sign of discomfort, or building disagreement from the audience.

Travis James, the 27-year-old Chief of Staff for Congressman Michael Bianchi of Massachusetts, approached Anna from her left and took up a post next to her. "Quite a turnout you got here on short notice," he said.

Not now...

Travis's invariably cocky demeanor was hard to stomach. He obviously thought Anna ought to be interested in a catch as great as him. Since Travis was rarely paying attention to the discussion in any meeting, he had long had a habit of focusing his efforts on finding any thin excuse to talk to her. He never seemed to accept that Anna had zero interest in him - he decided she was just playing hard to get.

She ignored him and wrote a few words in her open notebook to try to give him the hint that she was focused on her job at the moment. Travis continued trying to make small talk.

"I bet you made all of this happen yourself," he said.

If that's a line, it's the most pathetic one in history. Clearly, he must be yet another of those guys who has a thing for redheads. Can't he take a hint? I am not into you. I have never been into you. I WILL NEVER BE INTO YOU.

Anna wanted to summon every bone-chillingly cold emotion in her body and send them Travis's direction, but she knew she had to be on her best behavior. Montgomery needed her help now, and that meant playing nice with people she didn't like. She gave Travis a nod and a tight smile, then turned her attention back to her notebook, hoping that this would head off any more conversation.

Unfortunately, Travis seemed to interpret her cold smile as a thaw in her usually icy demeanor. He decided to test the waters further. He leaned too close to her ear for comfort and whispered loudly, "So, is Montgomery going to run for Speaker?"

It took every ounce of Anna's self-control to not cringe and recoil at the feeling of his breath on her ear.

Be nice... His boss has a lot of friends. I won't have to put up with his crap for long... as soon as Montgomery either wins or loses, I can go back to normal and tell him exactly what I think.

She turned her head toward Travis. With a much friendlier tone than she could usually summon for him, she whispered in return, "Sorry Travis - the boss has asked me to take detailed notes. Let's catch up later. Is that ok?" She ended with a smile and a charming glance from her crystal blue eyes.

Travis shot back a smug grin and winked at Anna. "You got it," he whispered.

Anna turned her attention back to the front of the room and took a step forward to distance herself from Travis. She closed her eyes and tried not to physically shudder at what had just happened.

I can't believe I basically just flirted with Travis James. This election had better get over quick.

Montgomery was just getting into the heart of his speech.

"I don't have to tell you all how difficult the past few days have been for me," said Montgomery. "I know from speaking to each of you individually that it has been every bit as hard on you. We love this great nation and hate to see our citizens at each other's throats.

"Our constituents are begging us to put our differences aside and work together for the good of the country. They don't like political bickering one bit. But much more important to them, they don't like their 401(k)s losing two-thirds of their value in a week. They don't like their brother, their sister, their neighbor, or - heaven forbid - themselves being laid off. They don't understand why our petty bickering is more important than their jobs or their children's future.

"And from my conversations with each of you, it's clear none of us in this room understand it either. I don't have any answers. The path forward is complicated, and I know I don't have the map. That's why on Monday I started the week by going to some of the wisest, most practical people I knew and asking their advice. This room is now filled with those men and women.

"The thing that struck me the most from our conversations was how similar they were. Most of us in this room represent districts that are not wealthy. Our constituents are hard-working, blue-collar people who just want us to get along and get things done. They want us to stop the pain, stabilize our country and our economy, and just get back to business.

"You all know me and what I have always stood for. I don't care about honors, glory, power, or positions. I care about relationships with my colleagues and solutions for this country. Those are not hollow words - my track record proves it. When I look for the solutions the United States Congress needs right now more than ever, I honestly believe the people in this room can be the catalysts for change. If we unite together under the principles our constituents are begging for, we can make government work again for the people. We can return to a politics of civility and progress. And we can make our constituents stop hating our guts."

The room erupted in laughter.

"I'll open it up for comments," Montgomery said as he sat down.

A tingle ran down Anna's spine.

Perfectly executed.

~

As the elder statesman in the room, Benjamin Petrowski was first to speak.

"Thank you, Willis, for taking the initiative to come talk with me on

Monday. I have been here far too many years, and it is unfortunately very rare that a Member has the humility to acknowledge he doesn't have all the answers. Reaching out to your colleagues and asking their insight speaks volumes about your character.

"We've worked together a long time. I can vouch for the veracity of your track record of honest and wise leadership. You have passed on chance after chance at seeking powerful Leadership positions. Each time, you have humbly deferred to a younger or more junior Member who you thought could use it more than you. When someone with such unimpeachable integrity speaks, we should all listen.

"I agree that our country needs and wants a return to normalcy. The majority of the public is not clamoring for the entire American political system to be destroyed. They don't want anarchy; they want pragmatism and real solutions. They want us to put down our swords and get along. They want us to fix things that will improve their everyday lives.

"I've been thinking about this a lot since we spoke, Willis. I think it's time for those of us who agree on these points to join together and formally create a group."

The room filled with agreeable sounds from the other attendees.

Pamela Bartholomew, a young Member from West Virginia's coal country, rose to speak after Petrowski. "The folks in West Virginia are tired of going to work every day and watching jobs disappear because of the circus going on here in D.C. I agree with Ben. We should join together in a group that just wants to get things done. I'm no marketing expert, but I suggest we call ourselves something like the 'Blue Collar Party.' That name would instantly tell people that we're for the working men and women of our country, and we're not going to take any BS from the snobby intellectual class that got us into this mess!"

Again, the room filled with murmurs of agreement.

Petrowski called out, "Second!"

Montgomery laughed. "I don't think Congresswoman Bartholomew made a formal motion. More importantly, I don't think this meeting has a chairman!"

The rest of the Members broke out in laughter again.

Bartholomew jumped back in. "Alright, then, I move that we form a group and name it the Blue Collar Party. And I further move that Congressman Montgomery be named its Chairman."

Again, Petrowski called out, "Second! Twice!"

Anna was in disbelief over how well this entire event was unfolding.

Good Lord, he's barely had to say a word... They're about ready to anoint him their leader, and all he did was call a meeting.

Montgomery shook his head with a self-deprecating grin. "Alright, all those in favor?"

The Members unanimously yelled "Aye!"

"All those opposed?"

The room remained silent.

"Well... I guess that's it. Welcome, everyone, to the Blue Collar Party," said Montgomery.

"And congratulations, Mr. Chairman!" someone yelled from the back of the room.

Couldn't have scripted it better myself.

Montgomery flashed his trademark smile. The group broke out in cheers and applause. Anna could feel her optimism rising. That lottery ticket just might pay off.

Some of the guests hung around to talk strategy for their new party while others headed off to other meetings. Anna and Montgomery stood near the door to personally thank each Member for coming as they left. The mood was electric - everyone was excited to be moving toward something positive.

Travis and his boss were some of the first to leave. Congressman Bianchi stopped at the door to talk with Montgomery and congratulate him on his new role. Travis seized the opportunity to have another chat with Anna.

"That was pretty great, right?" he said. "You're about to be one of the most powerful staffers up here. You know I like it when a lady's in charge." Travis was anything but subtle.

Anna suppressed the urge to roll her eyes and responded politely, "Far from it. I think this bunch can really help bring Congress together, though. I'm looking forward to making a real difference."

Travis was convinced that Anna was flattered by his compliment. "Well, when you're ready to bring you and me together, just shoot me a text," he said with another wink.

Anna smiled weakly in response as Bianchi and Travis exited to the hallway.

Not on your life.

16

Montgomery and Anna walked back to the office together while the rest of his staff cleaned up from the meeting.

“Well that was much easier than I expected,” Montgomery said.

“I could hardly believe it,” she replied. “I feel like that couldn’t have gone better if we had planted people in the crowd!”

“It was a good first step. We have a long way to go, though. Remember, our goal isn’t to form a little clique; it’s to win the Speakership so we can make real change in Congress. We need to rebuild it into what it originally was - first among equals in the three branches of government.”

Montgomery’s focus on the big picture filled Anna with pride. Everyone wants to make a difference in their job. Not many would ever get the chance to restore to glory what Anna believed was the greatest force for good the world has ever seen.

Montgomery was filled with excitement and ideas for what to do next. He was animated as he talked.

"I want you to take good care of the Chiefs. We have to build up a loyal foundation if we are going to build this movement beyond the size of that room. I have a few more people I need to talk to myself. Keep pushing. This is going to be worth it for both of us."

Anna made mental plans to check in with each of their supporters again that day and tried not to gloat over her boss's major success. All of her colleagues were still grasping for something stable. After the founding of the Blue Collar Party, she was the top staffer at the only place in town that was starting to establish any sense of stability. Four years ago, she had to beg other Chiefs to talk to her. Now they would rush to leave meetings to take her calls.

She loved the warm rush she felt when other people wanted to be in her good graces.

WORD of the morning's events spread like wildfire through the early afternoon. National and international media quickly started clamoring to interview Montgomery for their evening newscasts. The Blues, as reporters started to call them, were the first formal faction to coalesce after the dissolution of the two major parties. Every station wanted to speak with their leader, Willis Montgomery.

Anna and Kyle, Montgomery's Communications Director, worked feverishly all afternoon to keep track of all of the requests. They lined up 16 interviews back-to-back in the course of two hours in the early evening, a gauntlet that would have exhausted even the most seasoned veteran. Kyle did a masterful job of arranging the hits and keeping the boss moving from camera to camera near the Old House Chamber in the Capitol.

Anna and the rest of the team stayed back in the office, frantically flipping channels to keep up with the schedule and catch every interview. Through each one, Anna thought Montgomery remained cool and composed. If he was getting tired, he certainly wasn't showing it. If anything, he got stronger as the evening went on. He was so energized that he looked almost ten years younger.

Montgomery spoke movingly of the sadness he had for the state of American politics today and his constituents' loud and clear directive to fix it. When reporters pressed him on his motivations for forming the group, Montgomery was deferential to his colleagues and portrayed it as an altruistic team effort. His humility was almost palpable, even through the camera.

When the final interview wrapped and the lights powered down, Montgomery and Kyle raced back to Rayburn to recap his performance with Anna and the team. Everyone knew his face and message would dominate every nightly news program and political show for at least one full news cycle, giving him a major leg up in the campaign for Speaker.

As Kyle opened the office door for Montgomery, the team inside burst into cheers and applause. For the first time in forever, they felt like they had something worthy of celebrating. Even better, they all knew it was for a good and noble cause. Montgomery instructed Anna to buy pizza and beer for everyone and handed her two $100 bills to cover the cost. Kyle cranked up a dance mix playlist, kicking the mood up another notch. Montgomery went home to his Capitol Hill apartment at 10:30, but the party lasted well past 11:00 as the team basked in the glow of victory.

At 11:45, Anna turned down the music and addressed the team.

"Today has been a great day, guys. This was just the first step toward bringing America back to normalcy. Now everyone get home and get some rest - we have a lot more work in front of us."

The team let out a collective cheer, then began to gather their things and head out. A few of the team members were talking about heading to one of the nearby bars to grab a few drinks before calling it a night.

Their voices trailed off as they neared the end of the hallway. Anna shut down her computer and was the last one out of the office as she headed out the door behind them.

BY THE TIME Anna reached her townhouse, it was five minutes after midnight.

Anna dropped her work bag next to the door and took off her heels. She stretched her feet to relieve the pain, then reached her arms as high as possible in an effort to work out the tension built up in her shoulders. These long days were starting to wreak havoc on her muscles.

Delta immediately came over to greet her, and Anna scooped her up into her arms.

"Hi beautiful. I'm so glad to be home. Did you have a good day?"

Delta purred and rubbed herself against Anna.

"Yeah, mine was fine too."

She set Delta on the floor and continued changing out of her work clothes to get ready for bed.

"I guess I'm a little run down," she finally said, acknowledging the fatigue that permeated her from head to toe.

Delta sat on her favorite perch - a 15-year-old IKEA chair Anna had inherited from a previous tenant - and stared at Anna while she undressed.

"I know I haven't been getting enough sleep. I just have too much to do at work."

She tried to avoid Delta's knowing gaze.

"It's different this time. Willis is trying to be Speaker of the House and everything's just crazy with that. I have hardly had a moment to even think, much less relax."

Delta gave Anna a disbelieving look.

"I'm serious, you wouldn't believe it. Our phones never stop ringing, and every caller wants to bite your head off. I feel bad for Lily and Josh - they're taking the brunt of the calls. Constituent email volume was more than eight times normal yesterday. *Everybody* back home hates us."

Delta raised her head and voiced a loud, drawn-out "meowwww."

"Alright... not *everybody*," said Anna. She resented the look Delta was giving her from the chair. "Yeah, yeah. I know it's just the loudmouths who call every day. It just feels like the whole world is against us right now. It's hard to stay positive."

Now in her pajamas, Anna stepped over to Delta's chair and ran her hand down her silky back, eliciting a low rumbling purr. Anna felt like Delta was still not satisfied with her explanations, though.

"What are you still unsure about?" Anna asked. "Is it Montgomery? He's actually doing really well. Surprisingly well." Her voice was filled with uncertainty. She knew Delta could see straight through her.

"I don't know what it is... it just seems weird. It's just so out of character for him to be this way. He's never seemed interested in any kind of leadership roles before, and now he's jumping in headfirst. I really am not sure what to make of it."

It felt good to have the warm contact of another living being to comfort her. Delta's love was unconditional. Anna could trust her to keep any secret.

"You know, the weirdest part to me is that I'm starting to really love it. Everyone I call sounds like they're stumbling over themselves to be nice to me. When I text people, they text back instantly. A couple of years ago, Lily and I had to call 40 people to get our little Wednesday lunch booked. Now I think I could fill the whole restaurant - I probably wouldn't even have to call them, they'd just ask me! It's pretty great."

They sat in silence for several minutes while Anna stroked Delta's back.

"The other odd thing is that I still feel this tension in my chest. It's probably just too much caffeine. I don't know."

Delta laid her head back down and closed her eyes. Anna kept thinking, trying to probe the depths of her mind and figure out what was still giving her hesitation.

"One thing I'm not sure about is what Montgomery is doing all day, but he's out of the office constantly. I only hear from him in the morning and at the end of the day."

Delta kept purring under Anna's hand, but she tilted her head to the side and opened one eye quizzically.

"Yeah... I guess that's why lots of people think he is aloof," said Anna. "He's acting like this is the best thing that's happened to him in years while everyone else is losing their minds. In some ways it makes me worry we're doing something wrong."

Delta was beginning to doze off under Anna's strokes.

"I know I can trust him," Anna said quietly. "He's always been there for our family. He saved Dad's life before I was born. I literally wouldn't even exist without him."

She moved back to her bed, as Delta looked to have fallen completely asleep.

Anna tried to wrap up her thoughts so she could get some rest.

Maybe he's quirky, but I know he'll always be there for me and would never do anything to hurt me. That's worth a lot. I'm sure it's fine. I'm just not sure how to process everything. He obviously has been making these plans for a long time. I guess I'm just a little hurt that he never thought to tell me about them.

Delta snored with a gentle purr as Anna did her best to get comfortable in bed. She drifted off to sleep as the clock ticked to 1:00 a.m.

17

THURSDAY, JULY 20

If there was one thing Anna had learned in her time on the Hill, it was that Congress is a jealous workplace. Once Montgomery's colleagues saw his face on every TV channel known to mankind, several of them wanted a piece of the action. It didn't take long for the chatter to begin.

By the time Anna woke up at 5:00 a.m., she had already received four emails from other Chiefs of Staff about Montgomery's media tour the night before. One was a genuine congratulatory note; the other three masqueraded as such but were really thinly veiled sniping.

She briefly scanned the other subject lines in her inbox, then opened Thursday's Whispers.

~

From: Quincy <quincy@quincyswhispers.com>
Subject: Quincy's Whispers - Thursday, July 20
Date: July 20 at 4:39 AM
To: Anna Rothwell

Quincy's Whispers

254 days since the Midterm Election

474 days until the Presidential Election

What the House is whispering about...

but doesn't want you to hear.

Good Thursday morning! Post-Collapse DC has moved into a new phase: rebuilding. Willis Montgomery's meeting that we first reported on in this newsletter yesterday morning gave birth to the first formal post-Collapse political party. While Montgomery has been coy about the precise number of Blue Collars, saying it's a quickly growing faction, several Whisperers tell me yesterday's meeting had 22 founding Members. Rumors are swirling about additional groups forming soon - they don't want to miss their chance to pick up Members while the slate is clean. Look for much more action on this front before the weekend.

What I'm hearing today:

Whisper 1 - With his actions yesterday, Willis Montgomery (BC-MO) (Like that? First time this newsletter has ever used anything other than a D, R, or I in a tag) established himself as a leader in post-Collapse DC. Members were VERY impressed with his interview appearances last night, with several of them referring to him as "Washington's last true statesman." Several Whispers are floating around speculating that he may have the skills and connections to make a run at Leadership. The biggest caveat to that is... no one has any idea how that will work or when it will happen.

Whisper 2 - One Whisperer astutely compared our current situation to an old-school college fraternity Rush Week. Similarities: lots of booze, empty promises, and preening overachievers. Differences: no established houses, fewer attractive people, and many more people who should be using walkers. And... many corners of this particular Rush Week will look more like Revenge of the Nerds than Animal House.

Whisper 3 - So much is unknown right now, but it's never too early to speculate on the top prize - Speaker of the House. As I relayed in Whisper 1, Willis Montgomery has earned a slot on many people's short lists. He will have an uphill battle should Ted Alber (I-KY) jump in the race. Don Stephenson (I-CT) is likely to jump in today, but few take him seriously. Yesterday's reported three dozen interested Members has continued to grow, but it's hardly worth even mentioning most of them. Bottom line: no one knows what's happening.

Whisper 4 - With everything going on in DC, I haven't even mentioned the financial meltdown going on all around us. The stock markets' plunge this week has enraged citizens and businesses alike, and their target is Congress. Ordinary people's life savings have evaporated, and this time they have one clear group of 535 people to blame - the Members of Congress who bickered so much they exploded, causing the financial panic. Capitol Police tell us death threats against Members have multiplied to over 30 times their normal level this week. Angry protestors seem to be around every turn. Whisperers expect Congress to move today to allocate resources to triple Capitol Police presence until things calm down. This might be the ONLY thing they can agree on this week.

Whisper 5 - Now that the initial shock of The Collapse has passed, President McCullough ordered the Pentagon overnight to reduce its alert level to DEFCON 4. No specific credible threats were identified since the level was elevated to DEFCON 2 on Monday, but the President said he wants to maintain heightened readiness until the country has gained more stability. For those unfamiliar with Defense Readiness Conditions, DEFCON 5 is for normal peacetime, and DEFCON 1 means that nuclear war is imminent. Let's hope none of us never see that.

Whisper 6 - To answer our question from Tuesday's Whisper 5, the House agreed by unanimous consent yesterday to suspend all committee activity for the remainder of this week. The sole exception was for the House Intelligence Committee, as it was deemed necessary for national security to continue their work. I don't expect the other committees to return to work next week either - it may be a long time before we get back to regular order.

UNTIL TOMORROW, I have the honor to be,

Your obedient servant,

~QUINCY

Sign up at www.QuincysWhispers.com to get
every edition delivered to your inbox!
Watch for breaking Whispers on Twitter @quincyswhispers.

Hear something good?
Whisper it to me at tips@quincyswhispers.com.
All Whispers are reviewed and kept
strictly anonymous and confidential.

~

ANNA MADE a cup of coffee and thoughtfully reviewed the morning rumors.

Nothing too shocking today... for once. That "BC-MO" tag actually looks pretty good. Hadn't thought about how they'd handle that. I wonder if Montgomery will be excited or annoyed that they're talking about him on the shortlist for Speaker... he usually likes to stay under the radar and out of the rumor mill, but he's not acting normal these days. It'll be interesting to see what other groups start to form now that the race is on. Didn't really expect us to have zero competition for long... The longer people are in limbo without a party, the more anxious they'll be to grab onto something that feels stable.

Congress's lack of substantive business was also frustrating to Anna.

In reality, though, they were light years away from working on any real legislation. It was doing its best just to not completely fall apart.

She finished getting ready for work and headed out the door at 5:45 after giving Delta a quick goodbye hug.

~

AFTER SETTLING in at the office, Anna leaned back in her chair and tried to game out what factions might be next to form. There were so many moving parts, it was hard to sort out a pattern.

The most active Members might be the last ones to group up. The movers and shakers, the politically engaged Members, the ones who had the most at stake - they're the ones whose disagreements really blew up the parties in the first place. Most of them are so mad at each other, it'll take a while for them to cool off enough to move forward. A few individuals may rise to the top, but I can't see a formal party coming together out of those ashes very quickly. Doubt the rank and file are going to become the new early adopters - they'll wait to see which way the wind is blowing and then follow it. Other than that, you just have the Members who were already on the political outskirts before this all started. The radicals, the troublemakers, all the ones who barely had a home beforehand. A lot of them were basically operating like their own parties pre-Collapse anyway.

The other topic consuming her mind was what Ted Alber, Christine Franklin, and Jonathan Garcia were planning. All three seemed to be laying low so far, keeping their names out of the headlines.

Alber and Franklin seem like they'd stay away from the hard-core ideological groups. They're both pretty centrist in their politics, except that Franklin is so conservative on the social issues. Maybe she'll try to pull together some of those folks into their own group. And Garcia... not sure about him. I'd guess either some type of Latino Members' group or perhaps a big-city or urban party. New Mexico isn't exactly New York City, but he has much more in common politically with the large-city Members than anyone else.

Anna knew she had another packed day ahead of her. Although her Wednesday lunch had been cancelled outright, Montgomery had rescheduled his dinner for tonight. This week's edition might be the most consequential Member dinner any Montgomery had ever had, and Anna knew she had to ensure that the guest list and Montgomery's prep work was top notch. She also needed to follow up with every Chief and Member who had been at the Blue Collars meeting yesterday. With a deep breath, she pulled out her to-do list and got to work.

18

Anna's analysis of how other factions might form was quickly proven prescient. Since before she could remember, strongly ideological groups had held outsized sway within the House of Representatives. The Republicans or Democrats often had held the House by relatively narrow margins of control in recent years. These narrow margins made the governing party susceptible to a small, cohesive group holding their own party hostage for its pet issues.

Unsurprisingly, then, the next new parties to form were vestiges of the interest groups that had controlled the former parties in recent years. Over the course of the previous days, the ideologically-minded Members of the Debate Team, the blowhards who had been holding court on the House Floor, had started coalescing into more cohesive groups. These Members were already bonded from their dogged pursuit of niche platforms in previous years, and were used to steering much larger bodies into giving them concessions. They understood the power of small but tightly-bound factions far better than anyone else, having already lived it for the past few decades. Even if they did not gain a majority of members, their factions' organization and experience would likely give them an outsized influence on all the workings of Congress for the foreseeable future.

These power players for the Debate Team had generally divided into two camps on opposite extremes of the ideological spectrum. On the far right was a group that became known as the Gadsden Guard; on the far left were the Americans for Social Justice.

The GGs, as many called them, were composed of the remnants of the Tea Party of the early 2010s. By the last years of the decade, the few remaining Tea Partiers had formed newer factions and evolved their positions beyond those of the original wave. The GGs now constituted an extremely vocal, and notoriously headstrong, minority of 27 Members. Unlike some previous iterations of their caucus, the remaining GGs were all male.

Ever since they appeared on the scene following the 2010 midterm elections, these Members had identified themselves by attaching yellow "Don't Tread on Me" Gadsden flag pins on their lapels. Uncompromising on principles of limited government and staunchly conservative on social issues, this group had been a constant headache for their colleagues since their formation.

Around 11:00 Thursday morning, the GGs huddled in their corner of the House Floor and decided to formalize themselves as a party. Their principles made them loathe to name a leader, but they eventually decided they would be more effective with one spokesman than five. After six rounds of hastily created paper ballots, the GGs chose Congressman Steven Reed of Wyoming as their founding Chairman.

Never ones to miss an opportunity for press attention, they poured out into the Capitol hallways in search of reporters willing to hear their story. Unfortunately for them, neither the media nor their colleagues were any more interested in talking to them after the formalization of their party than before.

~

On the other side of the chamber sat a group every bit as passionate as the Gadsden Guard but polar opposite in every conceivable philosophical way. These stalwarts of the ideological left traced their lineage back to the Democratic Socialists who came to prominence in the Democratic Party by way of the 2018 elections.

Like the Tea Party, the Democratic Socialists had seen their day in the sun come and go. Shortly after their rise to prominence, internal squabbling led to the group's demise as a political force. They were now barely larger than the GGs, numbering somewhere between 25 and 40, depending on who was counting.

The only thing this group hated more than free-market capitalism was seeing their archenemies gaining media attention. Literally moments after they heard that the GGs were forming an official faction, 30 of the Democratic Socialist remnants gathered in the opposite corner of the chamber to formalize their own group.

The resulting Americans for Social Justice Party elected Congresswoman Nadia Lewis of New York as their Chairman. The obligatory round of camera-chasing and interviews ensued.

Most other Members felt like "Americans for Social Justice" was too cumbersome and didn't roll off the tongue. Plus, pretty much everyone thought of them as the "Social Justice Warriors" anyway. Media and colleagues quickly adopted the shorthand nickname "the Warriors."

The ASJ did its best to force its formal name into the public lexicon, but it was no use. For those on the left, they used the nickname as a positive, as they were proud to fight for social justice. Their right-leaning opponents used it as a pejorative, viewing the ASJ as modern-day Don Quixotes.

The next vote series on Thursday afternoon was the first time the

House had been back in the same room since the formation of the Gadsden Guard and Americans for Social Justice. As the chair of the only other party currently in existence, Montgomery felt he needed to stand toe-to-toe with these new faction heads to assert his leadership, yet he knew he had to tread carefully in his interactions with them. The GGs and the Warriors had the ability to be very powerful in this new environment. They were each large voting blocs who understood their ability to make or break an issue. If Montgomery was going to become Speaker, he would need to be able to work with both extremes and help them get what they wanted in return.

Montgomery entered the chamber from the center-rear door. He immediately looked for Congressman Reed to congratulate him on the formal creation of the Gadsden Guard. Montgomery spied Reed in the far back corner of the chamber, talking and joking with some of his close GG buddies.

The GG crew was riding high after their formal announcement that morning. Montgomery approached the ring of Congressmen and patted one on the back as he stepped in.

"It is so good to see other people in this chamber who can work together," Montgomery said. "It sure has been a wild ride the past few days, but I think we're starting to see that people can put their differences aside and get along."

The GGs were in a celebratory mood. "Why thank you, Willis!" Congressman Reed said. "I think it's fair to say your little group inspired us. We realized we are stronger together than we are apart, and I think our constituents are going to agree."

For as long as most of the GGs had been in Congress, they had known Montgomery as a kind, friendly colleague who was quick to praise their successes. His words today did not seem out of character.

"I know I certainly do," Montgomery said. "Whatever the name - Tea Party, Freedom Caucus, Gadsden Guard - I have always respected you all and your predecessors for having a strong sense of right and wrong. You know what you believe, and you stick to it through thick and thin. Congress needs people who will stand by their principles."

Congressman Reuben Pruitt, a freshman legislator who had joined up with the Gadsden Guard, thanked Montgomery. "We appreciate that, Willis. I've only been here a few months, but so far, the only thing I've gotten for standing up for my beliefs has been mockery and scorn from other Members. My colleagues here have been in the fight much longer than me, but I doubt they'll say any different."

"That is inexcusable," Montgomery said sternly. "Every Member of this body deserves to have their opinions treated with respect. Personally, I think Members who stand by their positions even while taking heat should be *more* respected, not *less*. You and I may not see eye to eye on every vote, but I'll always respect your integrity."

The ring of Guardsmen nodded in agreement and thanked him. Despite him heading up a rival party, they knew from experience that he would treat them fairly.

Montgomery wrapped up the conversation. "If there is ever anything the Blue Collars and the Gadsden Guard can work on together to restore respect to the United States House of Representatives, my door is always open. Congratulations again, gentlemen."

He waved to the circle as he turned and made his way across the chamber.

AFTER STOPPING to chat with a handful of other Members in the center of the chamber, Montgomery made his way to the far opposite corner to find Nadia Lewis, newly elected Chairman of the Americans for Social Justice.

Lewis was a middle-aged African American woman who had represented a portion of Queens, New York, for just under two decades. She and Montgomery had served together since her first day. While they had never been close, they always had a cordial relationship. Lewis and her colleagues were just as bombastic as their GG counterparts, although they would have rather died than admit any similarities.

The Warriors were also riding high after announcing their formation and were in a similar celebratory mood. Montgomery approached their circle and raised his hand to wave to Lewis and give her a thumbs-up. Lewis smiled and waved Montgomery over to the group.

"Willis, so good to see you. You were all over the TV last night," said Lewis.

"Oh Nadia, the press must be running out of stories to cover," Montgomery replied with a laugh. Lewis waved off his humility with a smirk. He continued, "I didn't come over to talk about me, though, I came to talk about you. Congratulations on forming your group! I think it is wonderful that people are finally starting to come together after all of this craziness."

"That's very kind of you, Willis," said Lewis. "If we can't make groups of Members with whom we agree, how will we ever bring together Americans who disagree?"

Montgomery laughed. "Well count me as one who agrees with that!" he said. "Americans deserve a Congress that actually works for their best interests, not one that just fights with itself nonstop. You and I have not always seen eye-to-eye on matters of policy, but I have always respected your strong sense of right and wrong. Sticking by your beliefs when you're under heat from all sides is incredibly difficult. Congress is better with people of principle like you all here."

Congresswoman Vanessa Abrams reached out to shake Montgomery's hand. "Thank you, Willis," she said. "Far too many people just can't see their political opponents as human beings. I know you and I don't agree on all that much politically, but I've always appreciated that you see me as a person. I feel like most of our colleagues just look at us as caricatures."

"That is absolutely unacceptable," Montgomery said with disgust. "Every Member of this body deserves to have his or her opinions respected. Personally, I think Members who know what they believe in and won't back down should be *more* respected, not *less*. I know we won't always vote on the same side of issues, but I'll always respect your humanity and your integrity."

Montgomery's response was met with warm smiles and several "thank yous."

"If there is ever anything the Blue Collars and the Americans for Social Justice can work together on, my door is always open. Our constituents deserve a Congress that can get along. Congratulations again."

Montgomery waved goodbye as he returned to the center of the chamber. He felt confident that his wooing of these two large, important blocs had been a great success. As the final votes were cast for the afternoon, Montgomery exited through the same door he had entered with a pleased smile stretching across his face.

19

Around 5:30 p.m., Montgomery asked Anna to come into his office to recap the day. They reviewed the dinner prep sheets together and went over final details.

Two minutes before he had to be out the door to head to Live Oak, Montgomery pitched one more idea to Anna. "I've been trying to come up with an idea for something that could really set the Blues apart," he said. "All of the other Members who are trying to get parties off the ground are doing small, exclusive dinners at the swanky joints downtown to try and get uncommitted Members to join them. What do you think about having a 'Blue Collar' get-together that's open to everyone - staff, Members, friends - some real fun for normal people, not just snooty elitists in back rooms with $100 steaks? More like a block party than a smoke-filled room."

Anna contemplated this for a few seconds.

The idea's intriguing... it'd be hard to pull off, but probably could really make hay with it. Our party's selling point is that we're in touch with ordinary people. If there was ever a good time to not look like Washington elitists, this is it.

"I actually think that's genius," she responded. "We need to claim the mantle of representing ordinary Americans... send a message that we have open arms to anyone who wants to work together for the country."

Montgomery agreed as he headed out the door to catch his ride to dinner. "Perfect. Can you get to work on that? I want to do one of them tomorrow night, Saturday night, and Sunday night. Thanks Anna!"

The door shut behind Montgomery as his last words trailed off. Anna stared at the door as she tried to wrap her head around what he had just asked.

THREE? He's got to be kidding. Planning ONE block party on 24 hours' notice would be a big enough pain in the rear, and he just drops this bomb and runs out the door?

Anna leaned back in her office chair and looked at the ceiling, exasperated. A few seconds later, she heard a light knock at the door.

"Hey Anna - need some help?" Anna quickly sat up and composed herself. It was Lily, her ever-present smile beaming across her office's threshold. Her desk was just outside Anna's office door. Sometimes Anna forgot Lily could hear almost every word spoken inside - Capitol Hill offices were not the most soundproof on the planet. She and Des walked in timidly.

"Sounded to us like we need to get the Party Planning Committee back together!" Des said gleefully. She loved nothing more than planning events with Lily.

Anna tensed up at their move to take over the event.

"Thanks, you're both very thoughtful," Anna said. "I'm sure I can handle it though."

Des and Lily exchanged glances, then advanced on Anna. "We're going to take this off your plate," said Des. "We need you focused on what only you can do - working the Chiefs and Members."

Lily chimed in next. "Let's make a plan together and divvy up the tasks. That way you'll be able to give input on every piece, but we can take care of the grunt work."

Anna knew they were right. She did need to focus on other things right now, not plan a party. Make that *three* parties. She locked eyes with Des for a moment, stared at her to make sure she was serious, then gave in.

"Alright, you make some good points," she said. "Let's get on it. There's a lot to do and not much time to do it. I'm going to order some sandwiches for delivery - on me."

Des and Lily thanked her, then turned to each other and let out squeals of excitement usually reserved for middle schoolers.

TWENTY MINUTES LATER, Anna found herself standing just outside the entrance to the Rayburn House Office Building known as the Horseshoe. This circular drive, shaped like a horseshoe as its name implied, was the best-known meeting place for delivery drivers. At mealtimes it often had a crowd of staffers awaiting their bicycle-riding couriers.

Anna mindlessly checked the latest news stories on her phone while she waited for her delivery to arrive. Combined with her decoy headphones, keeping her eyes buried in her phone served the dual purpose of helping her catch up on the latest developments and deterring other staffers from talking to her.

She had scrolled through several screens of headlines when she heard a familiar voice just over her left shoulder.

"Hey Anna, having a good afternoon?"

Without looking up, she knew it was Kit.

Why does he always have to talk to me? Can he not take a hint?

"Doing fine, Kit," she said coldly. "And yourself?" She did not glance up from her phone.

He didn't even seem to notice that she was trying to blow him off.

"I'm good - just waiting for some pizza. Thought the team needed a little pick-me-up. They've been working their tails off this week."

She rolled her eyes and continued staring at her phone.

Let me guess - you put it on your dad's credit card while pretending like it came out of your own pocket.

He was silent for a few seconds as if waiting for a response. When none materialized, he said quietly, "Well then, never mind."

Anna spun around and looked directly at Kit. She pulled out her headphones and held them in one hand.

"I'm sorry, Christopher, did you need something?" Anna said pointedly.

He was stone-faced, not the least bit shocked by her sudden confrontation. No one used his given name, not even his mother when he was in trouble.

"Nope. I'm doing fine. Just trying to make conversation."

Kit's smug, annoyed demeanor confirmed Anna's long-standing feelings about him. Even in the middle of a potentially existential crisis for the nation, he was a smart aleck who was more interested in hitting on her and spending his family's money than minding his own business.

"I'm very busy right now and need to respond to my boss," Anna said unconvincingly as she spun back around and took a handful of steps to her right. She re-inserted her headphones and stared down at her phone again. She began playing a matching game to keep her thumbs looking occupied.

She heard Kit sigh loudly, then watched him out of the corner of her eye as he began talking to another pretty female staffer.

“Shocking,” Anna muttered under her breath.

20

FRIDAY, JULY 21

After a long night of event planning with Des and Lily, Anna grabbed about four hours of sleep. When her 5:00 a.m. alarm went off, everything ached so badly she could barely move a muscle. She reached for her phone and began to look through her email.

From: Quincy <quincy@quincyswhispers.com>
Subject: Quincy's Whispers - Friday, July 21
Date: July 21 at 4:23 AM
To: Anna Rothwell

Quincy's Whispers
255 days since the Midterm Election
473 days until the Presidential Election
What the House is whispering about...
but doesn't want you to hear.

Good Friday morning! As I first dubbed it in these electronic pages yesterday, Rush Week is rolling along here on the Hill. The two most predictable factions to form did so yesterday, with the Gadsden Guard and Americans for Social Justice making it official. The stock market is still unhinged, gaining back 4% yesterday... but overnight trading is predicting more losses to close out the week. Progress has been slow in this first week post-Collapse. Everyone is ready for a weekend, but don't expect many members to head home - they don't want to get tarred and feathered.

What I'm hearing today:

Whisper 1 - By my count, 79 Members have formally joined new factions: 22 Blue Collar Party, 27 Gadsden Guard, and 30 Americans for Social Justice. Of those three groups, don't expect the Gadsden Guard or ASJs to grow much - their appeal is pretty limited outside of their own borders. The Blues definitely have potential to grow dramatically, though - Willis Montgomery (BC-MO) is a respected leader, and their message will have broad appeal to constituents hungry for compromise.

Whisper 2 - The Gadsden Guard was not pleased to share its spotlight with the ASJs (or the Warriors, as everyone is calling them) yesterday. Nothing new to see these two squabbling, but their sniping was taken up to another level on last night's cable news shows.

Whisper 3 - More news on Wednesday's Whisper about Ticonderoga... which, as you'll recall, involves a female Member allegedly in an ongoing romantic relationship with her Chief of Staff. Sounds like the lovebirds' secret wasn't as secret as they thought. I've heard from four different Whisperers who offered details about the relationship. The Member is indeed married, as is the COS. Much more to come on this one.

Whisper 4 - Update on Yorktown's FBI investigation: Lots of agent sightings on the Hill the past few days. Of course, when rumors are largely based on staffers spotting tall, handsome men wearing black suits entering a Congressional office, I'm taking these Whispers with a grain of salt. This is the preferred uniform of plenty of constituents and lobbyists as well. As a reminder, I do not publish names of alleged wrongdoers until I have absolutely confirmed that charges or an indictment are imminent. Does not sound like that is the case on this one.

Whisper 5 - A late-night tip from a Whisperer tells me there will be a big party tonight at Union Market. The interesting twist here is that it's connected to Rush Week! The similarities keep growing.

Whisper 6 - I heard my first credible Whisper of another new sex scandal yesterday. We'll call this alleged scandal "Saratoga." Very scant details, but it involves yet another credible Speaker candidate, and the allegations would be immediately disqualifying. Likely much more to come on this one.

UNTIL MONDAY, I have the honor to be,

Your obedient servant,

~QUINCY

Sign up at www.QuincysWhispers.com to get
every edition delivered to your inbox!
Watch for breaking Whispers on Twitter @quincyswhispers.

Hear something good?
Whisper it to me at tips@quincyswhispers.com.
All Whispers are reviewed and kept
strictly anonymous and confidential.

QUINCY'S WHIP count compared exactly to Anna's. She did some quick mental math.

That leaves about 80% of the chamber uncommitted. Tons of opportunity.

She re-skimmed the rumors.

I don't really care about the Member-Chief love affair... salacious, but not unique. The FBI thing is much more interesting long-term... Hmm... I wonder who tipped him off to our party tonight. Would Montgomery have done that? Maybe Des or Lily? No, they wouldn't do that. Probably was one of the vendors we've been contacting. Could have been any number of people.

Anna put down her phone and dragged herself out of bed. No matter how bad she felt, she needed to get moving. She had a lot to do to get ready for the party tonight.

~

Anna stepped inside the office at 6:00 Friday morning and was shocked to see Josh and Kyle already inside. She usually had a bare minimum of an hour to herself before other early arrivers started coming in, and often an hour and a half.

"Happy Friday!" Josh said cheerfully as Anna entered the office. Kyle smiled as well.

"What are you two doing here so early?" Anna asked in surprise.

"What, you don't think we work hard too?" Kyle responded sarcastically.

"We were jealous of all the fun you've been having," Josh said with a smile. "No, really, Kyle and I were talking last night after work. Both of us have noticed you've been putting in a lot of extra hours. You seem like you're maybe overwhelmed with everything going on. We'd like to do more to help out."

This comment hit Anna the wrong way. She gave them a questioning look but kept her mouth shut.

Do they really think I look overwhelmed? These guys have no idea all the things I'm trying to juggle. I think I've kept it all inside pretty well. I'm fine.

Josh and Kyle did not seem to notice her slightly offended reaction.

"Yeah, Des said last night we're having a party," Kyle said. "We want in!"

Anna's face didn't flinch as she stared at them in disbelief. She was still fixated on the word.

Overwhelmed. Overwhelmed... Overwhelmed? Really? Why do they think I can't handle this stuff? When have I ever let a ball drop? When have I needed someone else to take something off my plate or do something for me?

Still she said nothing.

"Is... that ok...?" Josh asked.

Anna snapped out of her daze and smiled broadly. "Of course - absolutely. I'm sorry, I'm still waking up. Lily and Des could use all the help they can get. Just make sure you're completely on top of your normal duties first."

"Will do, boss," Kyle said. "We're all in this together. You don't need to do it all yourself."

"I'm doing just fine," Anna said without emotion. "Thank you for your concern, but I have a pretty firm handle on everything I need to be doing. Now give me a few minutes to get settled and we'll get to work."

21

Montgomery continued to meet individually with Members throughout the day Friday. In each office he entered, he engaged the Staff Assistant and Scheduler in conversation and invited their entire office staff to the Blues' party that evening. Many were a bit starstruck to have the currently most newsworthy Member of Congress paying individual attention to them instead of rushing past them to talk to their boss. To say Montgomery was building goodwill among Hill staff would be an enormous understatement.

But Montgomery wasn't the only one working his colleagues. Throughout the week, a dozen or more Members had floated trial balloons to see if their own new proposed factions had legs. By Friday morning, a few had found enough support to move forward. Before the end of the day four more parties had announced their formation and begun to make the media rounds. As former Senate Majority Leader Heaton had predicted when he resigned just a few days before, it looked as if Congress was likely to be a highly fractured political body for a long time to come.

Some of the most die-hard former Trump loyalists joined together in the Nation United Party, which they styled the "NU Party." They had originally planned to call themselves the United Nationalists, until an intrepid staffer pointed out that the party's initials would be "UN" - perhaps the most hated and antithetical organization possible for this collection of Members. The Members decided they liked the sound of "new" made by the initials, so they decided to move forward with it.

Though America's hard-core Nationalist moment had fizzled after the 45th President exited the stage, the NU Party was still able to cobble together more than 20 members. This group took the former Trump "America First" campaign slogan and adopted it as its ideological platform. Believing in a strong government with slightly left-of-center nationalist economic policies, the NU Party was generally in favor of any policy that would place the government's thumb on the scales in favor of America over other nations. They even commissioned a rush order of bright red "Make America United Again" hats and began wearing them any time they were out in public.

Standing firm on right-wing social issue politics, the Christian Conservatives brought together exactly 60 Members to form their own large bloc. Although its Members leaned somewhat right-of-center on economic issues, they were typically open to negotiation on spending. Where they refused to compromise, however, was on the importance of the federal government setting social policy. On issues such as abortion, gun rights, and religious matters, they could not be outflanked to the right. The most recognizable face in this new Christian Conservative Party was Congresswoman Christine Franklin of Idaho. She was selected as the group's Chairwoman and primary spokesperson.

A collection of Members who were focused on strong foreign policy and defense issues gathered and formed another faction. Most of their colleagues referred to this group as the "War Hawks," but they adopted "The Watchdogs" as their formal name; they thought it sounded more edgy and modern. Plus, they liked the defensive posture it evoked rather than the aggressive "hawk" imagery. Economic issues were of secondary importance, so long as the

Pentagon was taken care of. Most of their 31 Members were similarly ambivalent about social matters.

A final group coalesced around a platform of fiscal responsibility. Since its inception, Congress has always had a contingent that was opposed to almost any additional federal government spending. This group has varied widely in size, growing much larger through the Obama years and shrinking dramatically thereafter. Several true believers in fiscal discipline were still committed to the cause. Seventeen of them came together to create the "Fiscal Front."

While they shared many economic views with the Gadsden Guard, the Fiscal Fronters had much less interest in social issues. They were effectively a single-issue party. In contrast to some of the more loosely tied factions, the Fiscal Fronters made a formal pledge to one another to never break ranks on any issue of federal government spending. The consequences for defection were expulsion. While this rather draconian rule certainly made them a formidable bloc to be reckoned with, it was even more effective at scaring away any potential new recruits who feared being handcuffed by such strict rules.

ABOUT HALF of the Members were now tentatively committed to one of the seven new parties, but the rest were in varying stages of limbo. Not everyone fit neatly into one of the new groups, and much of the bad blood that had run so hot this week had yet to cool off. Congress had a long way to go before its Members were settled down.

Members and staff have joked for decades about Congress being like an elite college - a group of unfathomably petty, wealthy people who are consumed by gossip… and nothing but former student council presidents. Never had this been more true than at the end of this first post-Collapse week. Everyone was running on adrenaline and energy drinks. By Friday afternoon, staff was almost universally at each other's throats, even within their own offices. Endless furious constituent phone calls, long work days, and late nights in the office had already worn out most people's patience.

Very few Members decided to return home to their districts over the weekend. There was too much uncertainty to leave town. The nascent factions were doing battle with one another for the 200 or so Members who had not yet committed to a group. Rumors were flying that maybe 10 to 15 more potential factions were still trying to find the strength to emerge from the post-Collapse primordial ooze. It was clear that the weekend was going to be full of extracurricular activities trying to recruit Members to join many different teams.

As Quincy had predicted, Washington had truly begun to resemble the world's highest-stakes Fraternity Rush. Each faction headed to its own favorite restaurant and invited undecided Members to stop by for dinner or drinks. Every faction except the Christian Conservatives, that is. They limited the festivities to dinner and dessert. Each group had its own list of likely targets and assigned the most charismatic and persuasive Members to latch on and close the deal.

MONTGOMERY WAS DETERMINED to blow away every other group with the Blues' block party. Lily and Des had nailed down the outdoor space at Union Market in Northeast D.C. for Friday, Saturday, and Sunday nights. This area that had once been a farmer's market now served as one of the trendiest revitalized areas in town.

Team Montgomery worked like crazy to prepare. Des secured five of the hottest food trucks in D.C. As the office Staff Assistant, Lily was used to knocking out any miscellaneous job that didn't fall into anyone else's wheelhouse. In no time flat she had booked a different band for each of the three nights. Montgomery's Scheduler, Josh, used his skills at juggling invitations and commitments to reach out and invite the entire office staff of every uncommitted Member. Theoretically, if everyone showed up, they could have nearly 1,600 people attend. More realistically, they planned for about 250 attendees Friday night.

Kyle lent his graphic design skills to create fliers, tickets, posters, and a logo billing the three-night extravaganza as the "Blue Collar Congressional Tour." He printed a sheet of 10 tickets on special paper for each of the 238 offices of every uncommitted Member and all of the declared Blue Collars. The office interns fanned out throughout the Capitol complex to hand-deliver the invitations.

After cranking out the paper goods, Kyle rush-ordered 500 trucker-style hats with "Blue Collar Congressional Tour" screen-printed on the front. Next he found a local supplier sitting on a huge stockpile of white t-shirts with dark blue neckbands and armbands. Kyle mocked up shirts reading "Blue Collar Congressional Tour" and ordered 500 in varying sizes. Lastly, he slapped the logo on a blue plastic cup and ordered 1,000 for the party. He was determined that even if the party was a flop, it would be a well-branded one.

Anna asked Kyle to get a special batch of blue-collared polo shirts for the staff with "Team Montgomery Event Staff" emblazoned on the back. Half an hour before the gates opened at Union Market, Anna tracked down each team member and personally delivered the shirts. She thanked each of them for their dedication and hard work.

Friday night the Tour saw over 500 attendees - double what was expected. The swag was so popular, only about a hundred hats and t-shirts remained at the end of the night.

From the moment the gates opened until the bartenders issued last call, Anna determinedly hunted down Chief after Chief and engaged with each one. In between conversations, she tried to keep an eye on Montgomery, who was doing the same thing with his own colleagues. Each time she found a target in the crowd, she tried to ensure they were enjoying their time and had gotten all the swag they wanted.

As she and Montgomery had planned the night before, when wrapping up each conversation, Anna would say, "Willis really appreciates your boss getting together with us! Let me know what I can do for you." Montgomery did the same thing with Members, ending their chats with "Thanks again for coming tonight! The Blues are going to be a much stronger party with you a part of it. We'll be in touch about our next meeting!"

Anna knew how effective the subtle peer pressure of presuming support could be. It put the other person in a situation where the only other option was to overtly reject the statement. After being treated like a VIP at a great party, it would feel rude to do so, and therefore most people would just smile and agree.

This kind of subtle mind trick also contributed to the aura of confidence surrounding Montgomery and the Blues. As human beings, many Members of Congress are liable to follow the path of least resistance. When their friends are headed one direction and it seems like a strong option, they will often follow along.

Whenever she got a chance, Anna took notes on her phone's notepad app to ensure she remembered who she had talked to. She planned to send each one a personal email first thing in the morning thanking them for coming and welcoming them to the Blues.

At 11:30 p.m., Anna was rushing past Kyle on her way to talk with another Chief when he grabbed her by the arm.

"Hey boss," he said. "I just wanted to tell you what a great job you're doing with this party. You are killing it!"

"Thanks Kyle," she said. "Do you really think it's going well?"

"Anna. Look around. Do you see anyone having a bad time?"

Anna took a few seconds to scan the crowd and gauge the mood. She somehow hadn't noticed how happy everyone seemed - this party was *rocking*. Blue Collar Congressional Tour hats adorned about half of the heads in the swarm of people. Just about everyone was dancing and singing along to the band. From the pace at which Anna had seen

Josh change kegs, she knew many of them had gotten plenty of help with their mood.

"Wow... I guess it really is going well," she said. "I haven't seen people in D.C. this happy in quite a while."

"I know, right?" said Kyle. "Let's keep it up. You need anything from me?"

"Nope, I think I've got it under control. Just keep an eye out for anyone who needs help."

"You got it, boss!" Kyle yelled to her as she jogged away to resume firefighting.

The party went past 1 a.m. and was only shut down after the third time the police investigated a noise complaint. Anna could not have asked for a better result.

22

SATURDAY, JULY 22

Saturday morning the team met back at the office at 9 a.m. sporting casual clothes and splitting headaches. They talked through the successes and failures of Friday night and started resetting for Saturday. Lily was still on cloud nine - this weekend she was living a party planner's best life. Not that she was ever much lower than cloud eight. Lily was a true ray of sunshine. Des was wearing sunglasses and a hat. She had obviously had the most fun on Friday night.

Congressman Montgomery arrived around 9:30 wearing sweat-logged workout clothes. He had just wrapped up a run and was stopping by the office to grab a towel before hitting the Members' Gym for a shower. As he entered, he caught a glimpse of the huddle of staffers in Anna's office out of the corner of his eye and jumped.

"Hey guys, already back at it?" he asked peppily.

"Hey boss," Anna replied. "Just recapping last night and planning for the sequel. Anything you want us to change?"

Montgomery grabbed his towel and wiped his face. "Sorry for my… uh… casual attire," he said. "Just ran 6, and that humidity is killer." He leaned against the doorframe and stared at the far corner of the room as he thought. "I feel like it was a HUGE success. You all were fantastic with the logistics. I didn't see a problem with any of that. Today, let's shoot an email to anyone we know was there and thank them for coming. Tell each of them I hope they'll come back again tonight - it'll be even bigger and better. If they do come back, they'll bring their friends, and this will be the hottest place in D.C."

"We'll get on it," said Anna. "Just text me if you need anything else."

"Will do," Montgomery said as he slipped back out the door to head to the shower. "And thanks again to all of you for your hard work."

Kyle bought another 2,500 hats and t-shirts, plus an extra 4,000 cups. He was determined to avoid running out of any special items, and Montgomery had told him late Friday night to make a high estimate for restocking and then buy double. Anna sent all of her follow-up emails to the Chiefs she'd talked to Friday night. She also followed up with any Chiefs who hadn't been at the party but whose bosses Montgomery had spoken with. The team finished preparations in time to grab lunch together and celebrate their initial success.

Anna ran home for a half hour around 4:00 to change clothes and feed Delta. She hated keeping her best friend cooped up inside all day with no one to talk to, but there really wasn't a good alternative right now.

That evening, the crowd quickly swelled to more than triple Friday's count. Clearly word had gotten out around town that this was *the* place to be. For the first hour and a half, Anna personally supervised the admission gateway to ensure no one entered without an official ticket. The last thing she needed was for this party to be crashed by press, lobbyists, or other hangers-on. This also gave her that chance to greet everyone and make mental notes of which staffers from which offices were attending so she could enter the information into Alfred later.

She and Montgomery followed the same game plan as Friday night to great effect. There were many new faces to target tonight, and a lot of repeat customers to shore up as well.

As the party wound down at 2:15 a.m., Kyle and Anna leaned against the bar analyzing the night. As the primary staffer in charge, Anna had not consumed a drop of alcohol. Kyle, on the other hand, had consumed enough for both of them.

"This is really great, Anna," Kyle slurred with half-open eyes. "You've just done such a great job making this happen. You're so awesome to work for." Kyle was obviously a loving drunk.

"Thanks Kyle," she said. "I think we've all had fun with it. And your designs and swag have been a huge hit. I really appreciate you going the extra mile to make it happen."

"Aww Anna." He shook his head and smiled as he playfully pushed her shoulder. "I'm always happy to help you."

"Thanks, Kyle. You guys are the best. We make a great team."

"Naaawwwww," Kyle said. "YOU'RE the best." He stood, wobbled, and prepared to re-enter the crowd. "Two parties down - one more to go!"

23

SUNDAY, JULY 23

By Sunday morning, just about everyone on the Hill was wiped out by Friday and Saturday's festivities, but Montgomery was more energized than ever. He had thought of an opportunity to not only boost the ranks of the Blues, but to purchase some goodwill with the other factions.

The team met with Montgomery again at 9:00 to follow up on Saturday night's party and plan for round three. This time Des wasn't the only one wearing sunglasses and a hat. For the first time in Anna's memory, Lily was in sad shape too. Kyle looked to be asleep, his head lying on a desk. Montgomery joined the circle, bubbling with excitement for his new idea.

Montgomery explained that he had decided to ditch the band they had scheduled for Sunday night. He said he'd called in a few favors, dipped even further into his campaign war chest, and planned to fly in an A-list musician from Los Angeles. They had worked together on a charity event a couple of years earlier and hit it off. Once again, it paid to have Alfred keep all those cell phone numbers.

Also, rather than limit invitations to uncommitted Members, Montgomery told the team to open up the invitation list to the entire House of Representatives, whether they were committed to another faction or not.

If anyone's head wasn't hurting yet, this massive dump of new plans made them begin to rub their heads. It was going to take a ton of work to get it all done in time.

With Des and Lily busy working on party logistics, Josh and Kyle divvied up the invites and started making calls. Even though invitations were much more in the Scheduler's wheelhouse than the Communications Director's, Kyle was a great utility player. He could pick up almost any task in the office and do it well.

After a morning spent emailing, texting, and calling everyone they could think of, he and Josh treated themselves to a couple of the famous "half-smoke" sausages at Ben's Chili Bowl on U Street. The greasy goodness hit the spot and put them back in working order in time for the grand finale.

Sunday night, the crowd overwhelmed Union Market five times over. Everyone who was anyone on the Hill came out to the party to blow off steam, have a good time, and - most importantly - see and be seen.

Even though the crowd was far larger than Friday and Saturday had been, Anna felt much more calm Sunday evening. She had grown comfortable with her routine and easily glided in and out of the masses of people, stopping to say hi to any Chief she saw. She thanked them for coming and reminded them to take home some extra hats, shirts, and cups for their staff members who couldn't come. In all, Anna estimated she bumped into at least 45 House Chiefs of Staff.

Sometime shortly after midnight, Anna literally bumped into the only Chief she absolutely did not want to see there. She was in the middle of helping Kyle make a beer run, struggling to move a keg from a rented refrigerator truck to the main bar. Kyle operated a large red dolly while Anna leaned down, bent halfway to the ground, holding one of the keg's handles to keep it from rolling off.

As they rounded the final corner before the bar, Anna's rear end forcefully crashed into the backside of one Christopher W. Lambert IV. The blindside impact knocked him sideways and sent his full cup of beer flying, landing across the back of Anna's shirt.

Anna let go of the keg and jumped straight up in shock from the ice-cold beer running down her back. She simultaneously let out a shriek two octaves above her normal voice. She turned to see who she had just run into… and locked eyes with Kit. Her face immediately turned bright crimson. She froze in place, speechless.

The keg, bereft of its human stabilizer, began to teeter off the other side of the dolly. It crashed to the floor and began to roll through the crowd, Indiana Jones-style. Kyle dropped the empty dolly and sprinted to halt the keg's progress before someone got crushed by 160 pounds of low-end beer. His military training had not prepared him for this. Anna saw what had happened and dashed to help him.

Kit had been dancing with a stunning young woman with blonde hair and a gorgeous smile. She covered her mouth and laughed hysterically as she watched Anna scrambling for a runaway keg while wearing her beer-soaked Team Montgomery Event Staff shirt.

Anna and Kyle stopped the keg from its rampage and began to tip it upright. Kit quickly joined them to lend a hand. Anna was mortified with embarrassment. The second he arrived on the scene, she snapped at him, "We are just fine, Kit. We don't need your help."

Her harsh words stung. He recoiled and put both hands up. "Fine, do it yourself," he said.

"Yeah, well, we've got it under control," she said, avoiding further eye contact as she struggled with the keg.

"Got it. That shirt looks good on you," he said with the cocky grin she had hated since the day they met. He returned to his date and picked up where they had left off.

"Thanks, jerk" she said under her breath with more than a hint of disgust. She could already feel him and his knockout date laughing at her expense.

No doubt he's wasted too... that bimbo on his arm looks like a perfect fit for him.

As the staffer in charge, Anna only drank water all three nights of the Blue Collar Congressional Tour. Normally she enjoyed exercising this kind of self-control as proof of her dedication to her job, and because she could pick up valuable tidbits of information for Alfred when everyone else loosened up after a few drinks. But tonight, having thousands of drunks surrounding her had suddenly gotten on her nerves.

Aside from Anna, perhaps the only sober person within three blocks that night was Montgomery, who worked to close the deal with his prospective recruits. He methodically zeroed in on his broad list of targets and sewed up their support. By the end of Sunday night, he had brought another 62 Blue Collars on board.

CONGRESSIONAL RUSH WEEKEND WAS OVER, and it had reshaped the layout of the House. The Blues were by far the most successful at drawing new pledges, but several other factions gained members too.

Two Members joined the GGs, but not before riding the fence between the GGs and the Fiscal Front for several days. After plenty of wining and dining, they decided the GGs would lead to better opportunities for face time on cable news. The Fiscal Fronters had a reputation for being closer to stodgy accountants than rabble rousers, and the nerds never win in Rush. They scored a big, fat zero in this popularity contest.

The Warriors had been courting several recruits who were passionate environmental advocates but had some uneasiness about the radical social policies the Warriors espoused. The Warriors basically just ground down two of their targets until they agreed to join. No other group that represented their views seemed to be coalescing, and the Warriors definitely liked to fight for what they believed in.

Despite their best efforts at showering their targets with steak dinners and American-made beer, the nationalist NU Party came up with only two new Members.

The Christian Conservatives' dessert bar actually pulled in five Members who had been waffling between other factions, which led to many prayers of thanksgiving.

The Watchdogs held their gatherings at the office space of one of the local defense contractors. The office's atrium held a public technology showcase where prospective recruits could try out some of the latest and greatest military technology gadgets. This proved very popular with the Members, leading another 22 to enlist in their group.

Several of the smaller groups were pleased with their results, but the time the dust cleared and everyone was ready to get back to work Monday morning, the Blues were indisputably the most dominant faction in the House of Representatives.

24

MONDAY, JULY 24

Although she liked to think of herself as invincible, the unusually long nights and overly stressful days of the past week finally caught up to Anna. On Monday morning, she slept straight through her 5:00 a.m. alarm and only woke up when Delta began licking her face at 7:30.

After scrambling to get ready, she arrived at the office late. To her surprise, when she stepped inside the office at 8:15, Montgomery was already there, dressed in a navy-blue suit and fully engaged in a policy discussion with Des, his Legislative Director.

She rushed past them and quickly unloaded her things at her desk.

He never sleeps, does he?

Anna was 20 years younger than Montgomery, yet she was exhausted while he looked invigorated.

"Hey Anna," Montgomery said cheerfully as he stepped into her doorway. "Great job getting Union Square together this weekend. People are going to be talking about last night for years."

"I think every person on the Hill under 30 was there," said Des. "It was perfect."

"Thanks," Anna said drowsily. She was so worn out she could barely stand. "I'm ready to go. What's on tap for today?"

"Let's get together in a few minutes and recap where we are. Just let me finish up with Des."

Thank God... enough time for coffee.

"I'm going to grab some breakfast downstairs," said Anna. "Be back in a second."

Des nodded in acknowledgment and continued to talk with Montgomery.

Once Anna had stepped back out the door, she exhaled loudly and rolled her head to get the kinks out of her neck. As she walked slowly down the marble corridor, her mind wandered over the events of the past few days.

This whole thing is such a blur... It hasn't even been a week since Montgomery suggested all of this, but it feels more like a month. We only founded the Blue Collars like five days ago, but here we are with 80-plus Members... my boss is Chairman of the biggest group in the House... where does that put us? In control? A target? Presumptive Speaker? Uncharted waters, that's where. I wonder how he sees it all. Seems like he has some plan but isn't fully telling me. I'll ask when we talk. Maybe he's —

"Hey Anna, you holding up okay?" Peter Garibaldi, her friend from Congressman Wilson's office, interrupted Anna's thoughts. She had mindlessly joined the rear of the omelet station's eight-person line and Peter tagged on behind her.

In the time they'd known each other, Anna and Peter generally got along well. She did occasionally get the impression he was feeling her out to see if she was interested in him. Of course, this was a familiar situation for Anna. Her strategy was generally to just ignore it and be extra careful to not give off any reciprocal vibes.

"Yeah, doing great Peter," Anna replied lethargically. "How are you?"

"You sure? No offense, but looks like you're dragging a bit."

Anna laughed and reluctantly agreed. "Alright. A little tired. I've been running nonstop. I actually fell asleep in my office a couple days ago."

"You guys have been killing it. Everyone in my office who was at Union Market last night says it's the best party they've ever been to in D.C. How many new Blues did you sign up?"

"Last I talked to the boss, it was somewhere north of 60."

"Holy crap... well I guess the effort was worth it, huh?"

"I guess," Anna said ruefully. "Sure hope he doesn't tell me in five minutes that he wants another one tonight."

"No kidding," said Peter. "Nothing like a last-minute order. Takes them 10 seconds to demand something, but it takes us 10 hours to do it."

"That's for sure... been there way too many times myself," Anna replied. A moment later, she changed the subject. "Has your boss committed to anyone yet? I don't have him marked down with a group, but most of the newspapers' scoreboards are about three days behind reality and only about two-thirds accurate." Wilson was a three-term Member from Florida who was mostly harmless and never very outspoken.

"If that's not the truth... Two papers have us down as a confirmed Warrior, one as a confirmed Watchdog, and the rest have no idea, which is actually the right answer."

"This town is so messed up," said Anna. She took her turn to order her omelet.

"We've talked to every faction a hundred times, been to every party in town the past few nights… it's wearing me out," Peter said. "The boss is so wishy-washy, he can't decide what to do. Seems like the last person he talks to is always who he is leaning toward at any given time. It's super annoying."

"I can see how that'd be true." Anna's omelet was just finishing up. "If you all are still interested, we would love to have you. We're over 80 Members total now. I think Wilson would fit in well. Could be nice to be part of something big."

"Thanks Anna," said Peter. "I'll keep it in mind. I just hope he figures out *something* soon. I'm tired of dealing with it."

"I understand. Good to see you."

"You too - have a good day," Peter said as he turned to place his order.

Anna picked up her omelet, grabbed some coffee and sweeteners, and got in line for the cash register.

It sucks to be run ragged with no sleep, but it's a million times better than working for someone who doesn't even know what he wants. Montgomery can be a challenge but at least he knows who he is.

As she headed back upstairs to the office, her mind began drifting back to numbers and logistics.

If we have 84 Members and a majority of the House is 218, we're only about a third of the way there... and there's only maybe 120 to 130 uncommitteds left after this weekend. Even if we got every single one to join the Blues, we probably wouldn't get to a majority... so what's his plan now?

Anna stepped back into the office, settled in to her chair, and started to eat her omelet as she pulled up the morning's Whispers.

~

From: Quincy <quincy@quincyswhispers.com>
Subject: Quincy's Whispers - Monday, July 24

Date: July 24 at 4:31 AM
To: Anna Rothwell

Quincy's Whispers
258 days since the Midterm Election
470 days until the Presidential Election
What the House is whispering about...
but doesn't want you to hear.

Good Monday morning! This weekend was quite a bit less somber than last - not that it could possibly have been any worse. Willis Montgomery and the Blue Collar Party put on the events of the year at Union Market. If you missed the Blue Collar Congressional Tour, too bad - it's probably never coming back. They weren't the only ones partying, though. Rush Weekend was packed with high-end Member dinners and special events. These back-room soirees put a whole new meaning to "wining and dining." Don't expect it to slow down this week - there are plenty of eligible rushees still out there who will be fought over like this town has rarely seen.

What I'm hearing today:

Whisper 1 - WOW were those parties rocking! Especially Sunday night. I had to stop reading all the Whispers I received from partygoers - they were overwhelming. The 50 or so I did read, though, were EXTREMELY positive and complimentary of the Blue Collar Party. This group has turned into THE force to be reckoned with in the new post-Collapse Congress... at least so far.

Whisper 2 - Accurate whip counts will probably be delayed a day or two as weekend commitments become public. Whisperers have significant, solid evidence of at least 40 more Members making solid pledges over the weekend, but many Members are trying to keep their heads down for fear they might be chopped off... be it by constituents, former friends, or new enemies.

Whisper 3 - Hearing a little more about Brandywine, which I first reported last Wednesday. Obviously, the Member involved in Brandywine has not been the only one getting a little too friendly with staffers after hours. After my initial report, I received literally scores of Whispers on this topic naming dozens of different Members. Maybe I should've been more specific - this *particular* overly friendly drinking Member has apparently been much more than friendly with one of his fellow Members' staffers. Whisperers in the know on this one say the staffer is convinced their relationship is for real and they will end up together. Poor thing. I've heard that one before.

Whisper 4 - A few new details are emerging about what is probably our most salacious outstanding Whisper - Ticonderoga. Not only have the Member and her Chief allegedly been engaged in an affair for at least three years, an extremely credible Whisperer has provided me evidence that the Member sought to terminate a surprise pregnancy last spring... and her COS was the daddy. Enough said.

Whisper 5 - Unfortunately, Saratoga is starting to sound less steamy and more... well, just troubling. Lots of allegations too intense for even the tabloids. Some rumors make you want to break out the popcorn... this one is making me want to shut my eyes and call the police.

Whisper 6 - Congress may be back in session, but don't expect it to do any actual work. I'm hearing the House will continue to suspend the work of all committees through at least the end of this week, and probably still more. No serious bills will be considered on the Floor either. Keep in mind, we still have a Debt Ceiling looming mid-September and government funding runs out September 30... if they don't get things straightened out soon, we could be in for even more problems ahead.

UNTIL TOMORROW, I have the honor to be,

Your obedient servant,

. . .

~QUINCY

Sign up at www.QuincysWhispers.com to get
every edition delivered to your inbox!
Watch for breaking Whispers on Twitter @quincyswhispers.

Hear something good?
Whisper it to me at tips@quincyswhispers.com.
All Whispers are reviewed and kept
strictly anonymous and confidential.

~

ANNA SMILED TO HERSELF, enjoying the glow of success.

The nice words about the Union Market party really do feel good... especially after so much work and stress. Hmm, these new scandals sound even crazier than the typical garden-variety rumors. Saratoga wouldn't be so interesting if it didn't allegedly involve a Speaker candidate. That could be anything though. Misinformation, disinformation... who knows.

25

Invigorated by the positive Whispers, Anna took an uncharacteristic walk by everyone's desks to say good morning to the team. The office was buzzing with excitement from all corners. Although Anna had been the point person for the last three nights' events at Union Market, the entire team had pitched in to make it happen. They were all physically exhausted, especially Lily and Des. They didn't want to plan another party for at least... well, at least a week. At the same time, the team was full of emotional energy from the thrill that comes from being the talk of the town.

The deluge of phone calls that had been pouring in since the earliest signs of The Collapse still had not relented, but today the tone was different. In contrast to the profanity-laced tirades that had become so common, today's incoming calls from constituents were mostly congratulatory.

The message of the Blues was resonating with everyday people. Montgomery's media blitz had done the trick - anyone who had their TV on over the weekend to watch something remotely news-related had seen him discussing the need for Congress to put its petty bickering aside and come together.

This also made for a much more pleasant workplace. Fielding a never-ending flood of hateful phone calls will wear down the patience of even the most patient staffer. Hearing at least the occasional word of encouragement and positivity can make a huge difference.

Once Anna returned to her office, she settled back into her chair and checked her Google alerts for "Willis Montgomery." She scanned the headlines of the results. The stories were shockingly positive:

> **Former Dem and GOP reps join forces under Montgomery** - *The Washington Examiner*
>
> **Montgomery leads coalition of uniters** - *The Hill*
>
> **Blue-Collar Congressmen first to unite post-Collapse** - *The Washington Post*
>
> **Statesman Montgomery leads the way in Congressional reorg** - *Roll Call*
>
> **"Blue Collar Party" rises from ashes of Collapse** - *The Wall Street Journal*
>
> **Montgomery urges unity as Congressional infighting grows** - *The New York Times*

Throughout each story, one main theme popped out to Anna.

They all talk about Montgomery's 'sterling reputation' as a statesman. Maybe people really do see him as a uniter... that's going to be a good message in this environment.

Even the major editorial boards had glowing reviews. Six of Anna's acquaintances had separately emailed her a piece from the morning's New York Times. In it they wrote,

> Congressman Willis Montgomery (BC-MO) is one of the few Members of the House who, across the spectrum, has the respect of former Republicans and former Democrats. The admiration his

> colleagues hold for him appears near-universal and genuinely deserved. We expect this will continue into whatever new party arrangements Congress forms.
>
> ...
>
> Congressman Montgomery's ability to quickly organize the new Blue Collar faction and grow it overnight to the largest bloc in the post-Collapse free-for-all is strong evidence of his organization, discipline, and the respect he commands.
>
> Combined with his years of experience and the gravitas he brings to any discussion, Congressman Montgomery deserves to be strongly considered as a potential leader who could guide Congress out of this troubled time. His is a name with which we should all become acquainted - it will likely soon become known in every house across America.

Anna struggled to accept their good fortune. The coverage was so positive, it seemed more likely to be an elaborate prank than reality.

I guess keeping his nose clean and staying out of the limelight all those years wasn't such a bad strategy... he has the most experience of almost anyone, and no one has a good reason to hate him.

Anna printed the editorial, highlighted the headline, and with a quick knock slipped through the passageway into Montgomery's personal office. Montgomery was at his desk, engrossed in his study of eight piles of paper randomly arranged across its expanse. "Have you seen this?" Anna asked as she circled to the front of his desk, displaying the editorial at arm's length with pride.

Montgomery finished annotating an article and glanced up. He removed his reading glasses and squinted to focus on the middle-distance paper. He read the headline out loud. "'Congressman Willis Montgomery an emerging star in D.C.' Well that doesn't sound half bad coming from the *New York Times*, does it?"

"This is fantastic!" Anna said. "They say you 'deserve to be strongly considered as a potential leader who could guide Congress out of this troubled time.' Sounds like you've made a real impression!"

"Good. That's good." Montgomery said as he sank into thought. "We still have a lot of work to do, though. You know we only have 84 Blues right now. Yes, it's the biggest in the House... but it's a long way from 218. Unless I can get that many votes, I can't be elected Speaker."

"About that," Anna replied. "I'm interested in your thoughts on how to close that gap. It's 134 more votes, give or take a few. By most estimations, there's only maybe 130 uncommitteds left. Plus, plenty of those would quit Congress before becoming Blues. I'm not sure there's a path to victory."

Montgomery nodded as he rocked in his office chair. "In the old system, you'd be exactly right, Anna. We have to start thinking differently, though. Not just outside of the box - you can go ahead and throw away the box. The parties are dead and gone, so those rules no longer apply.

"Let's be honest. The parties had been fracturing way before The Collapse. Years before. Ever since the advent of 24-hour cable news and social media, groups have been splintering off in ever-smaller and more homogenous segments.

"The two-party system was a dinosaur from a different era. A time when liberal Republicans and conservative Democrats were a thing. A time when sticking together with your group was more important than ideological purity. That system could only last so long in the new media environment.

"So, as we look at the future, what does a more modern political party framework look like? To survive, it will have to be less of a broad, big-party conglomeration and more of a federation of narrower interest groups. A coalition, in other words."

Anna tried to process what Montgomery was getting at. "What's the difference? Isn't that pretty much what the Republican and Democratic Parties were? Coalitions of narrower interest groups?"

"In a sense, yes. But the actual structure really matters. There's a big difference between an interest group within a party - like a caucus - and an actual separate party. The former still has a strong expectation to eventually reach agreement with others in the party. The latter has no such pull. Aside from that, parties are actual legal entities; technically they are private companies formed for the purpose of winning elections."

"Wouldn't lots of little parties make it tough to govern, though?" Anna asked. "The entire system is set up for two parties. It's been calcifying that way for almost 150 years."

"Again, Anna, that *was* true until a week ago. Forget it all. I mean it - get rid of the old box. Burn it. It's gone. Anyone still working in that paradigm is destined for failure in the new reality. It's actually very simple. Rather than a big party with hierarchical control, the new era will be one of coalition governments. You'd be wiser to look to the UK for our future than the old American two-party system. We have to learn to forge parliamentary-style coalitions. It's the only choice we have."

That's not a paradigm shift... that's a completely different universe from the two-party system.

She tried to readjust her mindset to fit the world Montgomery was describing.

"Okay," said Anna. "I'm not sure I can really envision what that will look like."

"I'm not sure if anyone really knows yet," Montgomery said. "But you and I aren't going to sit around and wait for someone else to figure it out. Right now, we are in position to shape things however we want. But to capitalize on this opportunity, we need to think three steps ahead."

26

Montgomery clapped his hands and abruptly rose from his desk. "Alright, let's get to work!" he said. "Anna, do you still have that big whiteboard in your office?"

"Sure do. Want to go in there or want me to bring it in here?"

"Let's just go in there. Get something to clean it off with - we need to war-game a little."

"You got it," she said as she sprang to action. She sensed he was getting into professor mode.

Anna cleared the scribbling off her massive whiteboard and set her dry-erase markers on her desktop.

"Where do we start?" she asked.

"Let's start with what we know," said Montgomery. "We'll list out the parties and their membership, then see what's left. The Blue Collars have 84 Members. The Gadsden Guard has 29 announced Members. The Fiscal Front seems stuck at 17. The Christian Conservatives have 63, including Christine Franklin. I think the War Hawks, or Watch-dogs, or whatever dumb name they're using, have an even 50. The

Nationalists have 26. And the Social Justice Warriors are at 32. What's that add up to?"

Anna neatly listed out the factions, then rearranged them in order of size and totaled the column:

84 Blue Collars
63 Christian Conservatives
50 Watchdogs
32 ASJ/Warriors
29 Gadsden Guard
26 Nation United (NU) Party
17 Fiscal Front
301 Total Committed

"Three hundred and one," Anna said.

"Okay, now how many Members have we not accounted for?" Montgomery asked.

Anna did the math out loud as she wrote on the board. "435 total Members minus 301 committed leaves about 134 uncommitted Members." She added this information to the bottom of the board.

435 Total Members
-301 Committed
134 Uncommitted votes

Montgomery continued his train of thought. "A majority of the House takes 218 votes and we have 84 in the Blues. So how many short are we?"

Anna again subtracted while narrating. "218 minus 84 equals 134." She added this to the list:

218 Majority of House
-84 Blue Collars

134 Additional votes needed

"It's exactly how many uncommitteds are left!" Anna said.

"Yeah, but don't get too excited," said Montgomery. "Not all of them will join the same group. Not a prayer. Let's ignore that idea."

Anna deflated slightly but continued to listen to Montgomery.

"I see two big questions on this board right now, and we need to solve them both. First, who are the 134 uncommitteds? How many can we get into the Blues? And second, how do we siphon off enough of these other factions' numbers, or convince enough of these other factions to join us, to get to 218?"

They both puzzled over this for a few moments. Suddenly, Montgomery snapped his fingers and pointed to Anna. "I want you to pull up the voting history of every uncommitted Member we know of. There are resources that place every Member onto a political compass - you know, economic issues on the X axis, government control on the Y axis. Plot all of them out for me by this afternoon and we'll talk it over then. I have to run to some meetings but should be back by 1:00."

"You got it," Anna said as Montgomery dashed off. She immediately called the team together and started splitting up the work.

By 12:45, the staff had completed a poster-sized chart on foam board with dots identifying the political ideology of each uncommitted Member. Given the time crunch, Anna was pretty proud of the end product.

After plotting all of the Members, the team debated how to separate the dots into groups. They finally agreed to separate them into three main groups plus some outliers. Anna carefully took a picture of the unadulterated chart, then made three large ovals with a red permanent marker, pulling together the three loose clumps of Members. She labeled these "Group 1," "Group 2," and "Group 3." About 15 dots were scattered around the chart outside of the red ovals.

Group 1 contained about 50 dots clustered around the intersection of the X and Y axes. A few marks strayed farther away from the middle than others, but by and large these were clearly the moderates or centrists. Anna erased the label and replaced it with "Centrists."

The second group was firmly to the left of the economic spectrum, but not as strongly pro-government as members of the Warriors would have been. The group was much more tightly clustered than Group 1 or Group 3. Anna asked Des to read off the most prominent names from the grouping.

Des pulled up a spreadsheet the team had been keeping while making the chart. She scanned through quickly and began listing names. "Let's see... Porter of California, McClanahan, Neville, Foote, Tuma, Robinette... seems like mostly the hard-core enviros."

"Looks that way to me too," Anna agreed. She pulled out a green marker and renamed the oval containing about three dozen Members "Greens."

The third and final group was much more loosely spread. It was generally to the left of the economic center but had significant variation among its Members. Anna could not immediately see much of a common thread. Again, she asked Des to read some of the names.

"Alright... Villarosa, Rodriguez, Williams of Alabama, Williams of Texas, Brown, Jones, Hernandez, Johnson of Arizona, Johnson of California, Lopez..." Des trailed off. "Almost all of these Members are people of color," she observed.

No one noticed that before? Of course... almost none of the minority Members joined the existing factions... maybe they're planning to create their own faction, or maybe they're just looking for someone to stand up for minority interests.

"I think you're right," said Anna. "I think they've all been sitting it out to see if anyone would form a faction that would give minority Members a voice."

Anna took a marker and named the roughly 40-Member set of dots "Minority Members." She then took a blue marker and made a fourth oval in the lower-right quadrant, slightly on the economically conservative side of center and towards less government intervention. Next to this oval she wrote "Blues."

"I know this is a broad generalization, but this is more or less where our membership lies," Anna said. "There could be some bleed-over from the Centrists, but most of the uncommitteds aren't within spitting distance of our home turf."

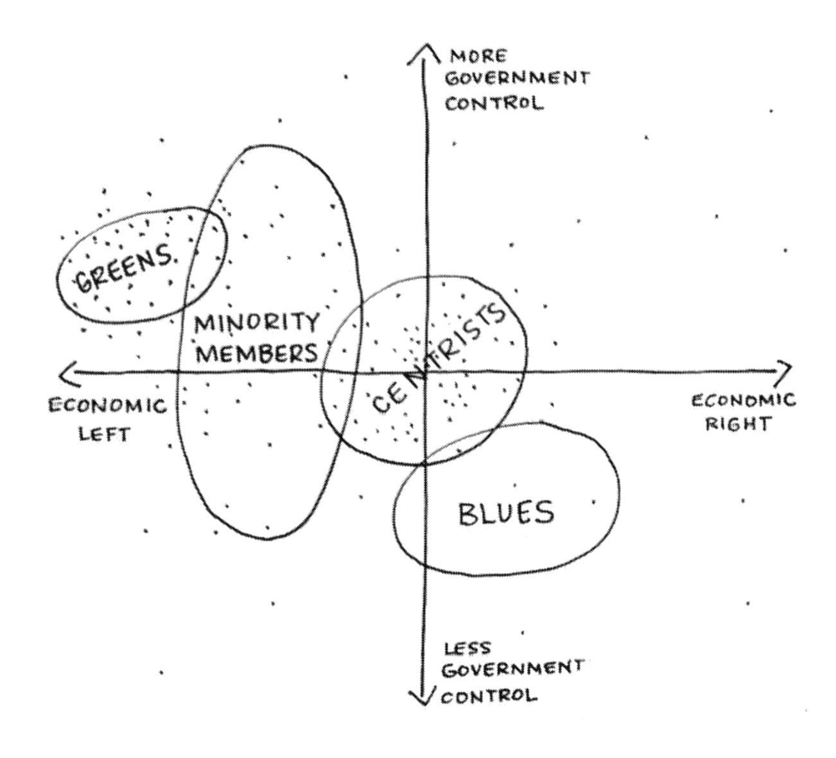

"What about the rest of them - the outliers?" Lily asked. The Members outside of the three main ovals were scattered around the board with no clear pattern.

"I think they're mostly likely to join up with other factions," Anna said. "They're too different from each other to actually join together into a coherent group themselves." She paused and considered the board for a moment. "Alright, anything else?"

A few head shakes around the room showed the team was satisfied with their analysis.

"Sounds good," Anna said. "I'll run it by the boss when he gets back. Thanks for all of your work on short notice."

27

Just after 1:00, Montgomery returned to the office. As usual this week, he was all smiles and full of energy. He had been making the rounds to undecided Members, pitching some on joining his own party, gently nudging others toward a different group. Each push was carefully calculated - some Members could be more helpful in another faction than they could be from within.

After passing off his notes to Lily to be input into Alfred, he tapped on Anna's door and entered. She had turned the foam board around to allow for a dramatic unveiling. She was excited to show it to the boss.

"We looked up every uncommitted Member's ideological voting scores like you asked, then plotted them on an x-y axis," she said, ready to burst with anticipation for the reveal. "It turned up some really interesting patterns. Here, take a look."

She turned around the foam board to display the team's work. Montgomery leaned over the chart and silently reviewed his team's analysis. After a few minutes, he began to pepper Anna with questions about the Members' placement on the chart and the team's thought processes on groupings. In short order, he came to agree with their conclusions.

"Get me a list of all of these Members in the Centrist group with their cell numbers and office numbers," he said. "These centrists are probably our last good bunch of potential new Blues. Since they haven't joined yet I've got to imagine most of them have already thought it through carefully and decided not to. I want to take one more pass at each of them. After that, it's on to phase two."

"And what would phase two entail?" Anna asked.

"Well, if these guys aren't going to form factions on their own, maybe it's time they got a little push."

"I like it," said Anna. She thought through her mental list of things that still needed to be worked out. "What about our announcement for Speaker? I'd like to get going on our plans."

"Sure. I've been thinking about that. I think Speaker Mathes will be setting an election date tomorrow, so we need to be ready to announce."

This took Anna by surprise. "Do you know when it will be?"

"No, not yet. Probably won't be too drawn-out, though. She wants to get out of here."

"I don't blame her," said Anna. "What are your thoughts on an announcement?

"First thing, I need you to get all of the Blues together early tomorrow afternoon. I want all of them completely locked up before I announce."

"I'll get Josh on it ASAP."

"We can't give them an option of not being on board," Montgomery said. "We're going to put the hard sell on them. I need every single one of them in that room."

"Got it," said Anna. "We'll knock their socks off."

"Get with Kyle to prep a statement and start working people off the record. We need to be first to the cameras and get big coverage tomorrow night."

"Will do," she replied.

They split up and began work on their own tasks. Anna started by getting Josh going on the Blues meeting, then strategized media plans with Kyle. Montgomery withdrew to his personal office to give some personal attention to the last few uncommitted Members.

MONTGOMERY SORTED the list of 50 potential centrists into three tiers: the top five he labeled as "leaders," the middle group of 12 "lieutenants," and the remaining 33 "back-benchers." After consulting Alfred for intel, he fired off quick texts to each of the back-benchers:

> *Hey ____________, it's Willis Montgomery. Hope you're holding up ok through all of this. I know it is especially hard on ____________. We're getting close to 100 Blues and would love for you to be part of something special. If you'd like to talk through the pros and cons, no commitment, just let me know. Happy to swing by and chat. Thanks!*

Montgomery filled in the second blank with information from Alfred that he had gathered about the Member's spouse, children, or other loved ones. He knew how emotionally impactful it could be for a colleague to remember your spouse or kids' names, and it was a nice personalizing touch. He knew this was a risky game - if done poorly or awkwardly, it could look insincere and turn off the recipient. It also created a possibility of the recipient believing that Montgomery actually remembered the name of an obscure relative. If they casually mentioned that 4-year-old grandson in a future conversation and expected Montgomery to contribute, he might end up looking like a fool.

Montgomery had enough experience artfully dodging tough questions and uncomfortable situations from his decades in Congress that he felt these were risks worth taking. From the responses his texts garnered, it seemed he had made a good calculation. The personal tidbits and attention to detail made each recipient feel like they mattered and were important to Montgomery.

The 12 Members who Montgomery classified as lieutenants were Members who sometimes led, sometimes followed, and often sat on the fence. They were not A players, but definitely solid Bs who he would love to have on his team. Each of these received a phone call, weaving in a healthy dose of the personal information and emotional appeals he had used in the back-benchers' texts.

28

The back-bencher texts garnered some positive feedback but no commitments. Montgomery made notes to follow up with about 10 of them but marked it as low priority. His phone calls to the 12 lieutenants were more encouraging. Five of them agreed to sit down and talk with him in person about potentially joining up with the Blues.

After completing these contacts, Montgomery hit the marble hallways to personally visit the five potential leaders. Montgomery knew in-person conversations were far and away the most effective way to close deals, and he had always executed them masterfully.

Each of the first four meetings was smooth and friendly. Montgomery had a way of making others feel at ease even when they knew he was trying to persuade them. His sales pitch was never aggressive or overt. He tended to ask questions and have a personal conversation about what was important to the other Member. At the end, he would suggest that the Blue Collars could use a principled man or woman like them and extend an invitation. Even though only one accepted, all were impressed.

The final Member Montgomery personally visited was Ted Alber. Alber had been seen as a rising star before The Collapse. A young, good-looking, well-spoken man with a squeaky-clean reputation, it was no secret why Alber was a five-star recruit for any new party.

After a week of chaos, Alber was exhausted from the sales pitches from colleagues and lobbyists. Everyone wanted a young, charismatic leader to take up their banner as the new era arrived. The deafening rumor mill about his own run for the Speakership was wearing him out. All he wanted was to be left alone for a few moments.

Montgomery entered the foyer of Alber's office in the Cannon House Office Building and introduced himself to the Scheduler. The nice young woman thanked him for coming and slipped into Alber's personal office to let him know another Member was there to see him. It was standard Congressional courtesy for Members to always take a meeting with another Member.

The Scheduler emerged from Alber's personal office and asked Montgomery to follow her. She politely introduced the Congressman, then excused herself from the room.

Alber knew exactly what to expect when Montgomery showed up at the door - yet another plea to join his new Blue Collars group. He'd seen Montgomery's interviews and read probably ten stories about the burgeoning powerhouse of the Blues, but something about the group just didn't quite seem to fit his style.

Alber summoned the energy to fake a warm welcome. "Willis! So good to see you. I've been reading about you everywhere the past few days. Quite an impressive operation you and your team have put together."

"Thank you, Ted. They are a great group of kids and have worked their tails off. The numbers speak for themselves, I'd say."

"Absolutely," Alber agreed. "I am glad to see reasonable people coming together. We're going to need that in the days to come."

"Yes, we are," said Montgomery. "We can't let the fringes run this place anymore. That same thing is what I've always respected about you, Ted. You understand how to work together with others to get things done. Have you decided anything about your own future? Know where your home is going to be?"

Alber flashed a self-deprecating smile. "I haven't settled on anything yet. I'm sure you'd like to tell me more about the Blues?"

Montgomery perked up. "We've got such a *great* group of Members that have joined us, Ted. I haven't felt this good about my colleagues in years. Once we wiped the slate clean, I feel like people finally snapped out of their old partisan ruts. They've realized the best thing for everyone is to find things we can actually agree on and join together on those common principles."

"What a novel idea!" Alber said jokingly. "Seriously, though, it's so very disappointing that it took a collapse of our system to wake people up."

"It saddens me too, Ted. Back when I was getting started here, Members from both sides of the aisle were friends. They went out to dinner together. Their kids went to school together. Heck, a few of them were even in a band together!"

"Times have sure changed, Willis. And I don't think that's a good thing. Those old everyday interactions helped Members see one another's common humanity. We came to see each other as enemies to destroy, not colleagues with disagreements."

"That's right," said Montgomery. "But perhaps this situation will ultimately provide the reset we have so desperately needed for decades. I have seen more friendliness and agreement in the past five days than I had in my past five terms. We're under a very dark cloud, but maybe it has a silver lining."

"I hope you're right," Alber said. "If this doesn't do it, I think we may be out of chances."

“I fear that may be true,” Montgomery said with a sad tone. He waited a few beats to let the import of the realization sink in before switching topics. “So about you, Ted. I don't think there's a soul in Washington who doesn't believe you would make an outstanding leader of this institution. Count me among them.”

Alber’s eyebrows rose in surprise. He was expecting either a sales pitch or a confrontation from Montgomery, not praise. “That's very kind of you, Willis. I respect your opinion immensely.” The quizzical look on his face showed that he was still trying to figure out what Montgomery's angle was.

“Don’t look so worried, Ted!” Montgomery said with a laugh. “I’m not here to co-opt you or try to talk you out of running. I’m not even here to try and convince you to join the Blues. You’re a smart, principled young man, and I know you will make the best decision for your future in that realm.

“I know it may seem bizarre, but I come from a very old school of civic duty. It is my honest belief that the country gets the best leadership when all of the best candidates compete on the basis of ideas, and when they do so on an even playing field. Sounds crazy, right?”

Alber looked as though a thousand pounds of worry, expectations, and anxiety had been lifted off of his shoulders. He looked Montgomery in the eye, trying to decide if his words were as sincere as they seemed or just another cynical line from a double-dealing colleague. Heaven knows he had seen far too much of that in his first few years in Washington.

After a long silence, Alber finally smiled and leaned forward. “Willis, I can't tell you how much I appreciate that. This town has a way of beating all of the hopefulness and idealism out of a person. I’ve been struggling to keep my own optimism, especially with all of the backstabbing and deal making going on since the Collapse. If that's how this chamber is going to continue to operate, I have no interest in leading it. But if we can restore the integrity and honor that used to be more prevalent here, I want to be a part of that."

"It starts with honest leadership - people of integrity," Montgomery said. "Look, Ted. I've made no secret that I intend to run for Speaker. I plan to run hard and I plan to win. But I wanted to let you know that if you get in this race, I will treat you with the dignity and respect you deserve. I will not besmirch your reputation - which is outstanding - and I will not take your words out of context. I will run on my own vision and my own record. I hope you will do the same, and may the best man win."

Alber stood and extended his hand to Montgomery. "You have my word, Willis. I should make my decision very soon. If I do decide to run, I will run honorably and on my own record."

The two men shook hands heartily. Montgomery put his left arm around the younger man's shoulder and gave him a half-embrace.

"I also want you to know that if you come out on top at the end of this race, you will have my full support," Montgomery added.

"And if you prevail, I'll absolutely do the same," said Alber.

Montgomery thanked him and made his way out of the office. He stepped into the corridor and confidently began the walk back to the Rayburn building.

IN ALL, the texts, cell phone calls, and personal office visits to uncommitted Members netted an additional five Blues, bringing their total membership to 89. All of the low-hanging fruit was now gone. While many of the still-nascent factions would continue to gain one or two members here and there, Montgomery was ready to turn his attention to the next phase. If he was going to become Speaker, he would need more than just the Blues.

29

Just after 11:00 p.m., a dark Chevy Tahoe crawled through the 24-hour drive-through lane at a McDonald's on King Street in Alexandria, Virginia, just across the Potomac River from Washington. Willis Montgomery wasn't the only person in the nation's capital who had been working on plans. The past few days had been brutal on the driver. His usual healthy diet had been thrown out the window along with every other routine to which he was accustomed. Living out of his car and "showering" with wet wipes was not his idea of the good life, but it was what the current mission required.

He had only slept in short three-hour spurts and used every waking moment to plan and execute a grand strategy to assist his old friend. He had enlisted three other long-term confidantes to help carry out the plan. The job was too large for one person to handle but too sensitive to entrust even a piece of it to anyone who was not battle-tested.

Over the past week, he had developed plans, contingency plans, and double-contingency plans. He knew the potential targets, their individual strengths and weaknesses, and how to most effectively neutralize them. The only thing he did not yet know was which ones would need action - if any. He would have to wait for his old friend's guidance on this.

As the drive-through line crept along, he scratched his left cheek with his index finger as he thought.

"Six hours of sleep tonight," he said to himself.

He felt he had earned one solid night of rest. Now that his plans were in place and ready to move forward, he needed to be mentally sharp.

The team had a list of targets who would need 24-hour surveillance until the mission completed. The tails would begin first thing in the morning and continue until his old friend called them off.

PART III

RACE FOR THE GAVEL

30

TUESDAY, JULY 25

Tuesday morning, Anna was feeling better than she had in days. She had gone home early at 9:00 p.m. and cooked her favorite comfort food meal: fettuccini alfredo-flavored Tuna Helper. This was one of Delta's favorites as well, since Anna invariably bought a second can of tuna to share with her while cooking. Seven hours of sleep never felt so good.

At 5:45 a.m., she lifted her Pop Tarts from the toaster, said goodbye to Delta, and began her walk to the office. The muggy morning air was the worst part about summer in the former literal swamp that was Washington, D.C.

Today marked the beginning of the next phase of the Speakership battle. Montgomery's plan for a winning coalition still seemed like such a mystery. Anna couldn't figure out exactly what he was doing.

I wonder if he's been lining people up without telling me. Just feels like he's being a little cagey. Hopefully he'll say more today.

Anna made her way down C Street Southeast, passing by the other House Office Buildings on her way to Rayburn. As she slipped between Cannon and Longworth, she took a few moments to peek at the Capitol dome. Three blocks up New Jersey Avenue, it rose out of the surrounding plaza and caught the morning sun. The image was spectacular. This worldwide symbol of democracy and freedom was only a couple hundred yards from her very own office. She reminded herself of her own good fortune.

When Anna had first arrived in Washington, she promised herself that if she ever wasn't awed by the sight of this symbol of power, it was time for her to leave. Four-plus years later, she was nowhere close to tiring of it.

She entered Rayburn and made her way to Montgomery's office on the second floor. These early mornings were so peaceful and quiet - a brief respite before the throngs descended on the halls of power.

Anna settled into her chair and logged in to her computer. She triaged the morning emails, then began to read the overnight news reports.

From: Quincy <quincy@quincyswhispers.com>
Subject: Quincy's Whispers - Tuesday, July 25
Date: July 25 at 4:30 AM
To: Anna Rothwell

Quincy's Whispers
259 days since the Midterm Election
469 days until the Presidential Election
What the House is whispering about...
but doesn't want you to hear.

Good Tuesday morning! After struggling to figure out which way was up last week, everything is starting to move at warp speed now. Yesterday two more groups of Members met to propose the creation of new parties. Nothing concrete to report, but expect news soon. My biggest question: how will all of these groups work together? Clearly no current faction will be getting anywhere near a majority in its own right... so how do they get to 218? Plenty of horse trading will be happening over the next few days.

What I'm hearing today:

Whisper 1 - Discussions initiated by Speaker Mathes with representatives of existing parties proved fruitful yesterday. I'm hearing Speaker Mathes is likely to announce today that a Floor vote to elect her successor will occur next Friday, August 4. Details beyond that are fuzzy.

Whisper 2 - The Whisper lines have been humming with speculation about what coalitions might be built out of the new fractured power structure. Nadia Lewis (ASJ-NY) and Steven Reed (GG-WY) have been actively soliciting partners, but no coalition that forms will contain them both. The bad blood between the Warriors and the Gadsden Guard has always been intense, but it seems to be getting even worse, if that's even possible.

Whisper 3 - Some developments to report on Yorktown. While initial Whispers suggested that the FBI probe involved up to three Members and later reports suggested as many as five, the most reliable Whisperers seem to be retreating from those reports. If I'm hearing right, it sounds like this investigation is focusing in on only one Member. I really am not hearing any clear Whispers about the Member's identity, though... lots of speculation but no certainty.

Whisper 4 - Many Whisperers have noticed that whip lists of the developing coalitions are largely devoid of Members of color. I'm hearing the leaders among said Members have not been pleased with the current options and may even be looking into forming their own party. I expect if they do, they will be highly courted by other groups in efforts to form a coalition. Minority Members historically are very loyal to their colleagues, and they bring a large bloc of votes to the table.

Whisper 5 - Three separate Whisperers from three separate House offices have confirmed that Congressman Willis Montgomery (BC-MO) met with Congressman Ted Alber (I-KY) in Alber's office Friday afternoon. The one-on-one meeting has raised all kinds of speculation, as both men have been on nearly everyone's short list for Speaker. Could a back-room deal be in the works?

Whisper 6 - Brandywine continues to be an intriguing rumor. The young lady who believes she and her Member boyfriend are in love apparently is not much for keeping secrets. I've heard Whispers from seven people who have heard her talk about the relationship firsthand. Most of these Whispers involve incidents that occurred over the past three days in front of multiple groups of people. She wants to shout their love from the rooftops… which is probably making her "lover" awfully nervous.

UNTIL TOMORROW, I have the honor to be,

Your obedient servant,

~QUINCY

Sign up at www.QuincysWhispers.com to get
every edition delivered to your inbox!
Watch for breaking Whispers on Twitter @quincyswhispers.

Hear something good?
Whisper it to me at tips@quincyswhispers.com.
All Whispers are reviewed and kept
strictly anonymous and confidential.

ANNA TRIED to make sense of how these rumors might affect her own plans.

Next Friday sure doesn't seem like a lot of time for campaigning... that's basically 10 days away. Probably won't be much sleep happening between now and then. Good thing I got a full night's rest - it'll need to last for a while. That Yorktown situation could be getting some real legs. Usually best to not put too much stock in these kind of rumors until there's more evidence than this, though.

Whisper Five, the rumor about Montgomery and Alber's meeting, bothered her so much that she tried not to think about it. She skipped down to the final Whisper.

A Member who's a little too frisky with staffers after hours? I could name you six current Members who have explicitly hit on staffers I know personally. That one's not really even news.

Her eyes wandered back to Whisper Five and focused on it intently.

Did Montgomery meet with Alber to cut a deal with him? Would he really have done that behind my back or kept it a secret from me? Surely not. He is so consistent about downloading his conversations as soon as possible, surely he wouldn't have done that without saying anything.

She tried not to let the questions bother her but couldn't completely shake the disconcerting feeling that she had been cut out of the loop.

31

Montgomery arrived in the office at 8:30 that morning. He bounded into the foyer with enthusiasm and chatted with Lily and Josh for several minutes. Anna could hear them talking and laughing through her closed office door.

Soon she heard a quick knock on her door before Montgomery poked his head inside.

"Hey boss, how are you this morning," she said.

"Great, Anna! How about you?" He let himself in and closed the door behind him. He pulled up a chair in front of her desk and sat casually.

"I'm doing well. Got some actual sleep last night, so that felt nice."

"Same here. I'm feeling energized and ready to roll. Are you excited to see some *real* action?"

Hasn't this already been real action? The past week was the busiest of my life by far...

"Sure. What do you expect?" she asked.

"I met with Mathes and a few others last night. We talked

through the Speaker situation and decided we have to have a vote sooner rather than later. As long as we're messing around here, the markets are going to stay in freefall. The best thing we can do to bring stability to the financial sector is to inject some stability."

Anna tried to quell the feeling of hurt rising in her chest.

Would've been nice to know about that meeting before now... but there's quite a bit going on these days. Can't exactly blame him when he mentioned it at 8:30 the next morning.

"The early rumor mill emails are saying it'll be next Friday, the fourth," Anna said. "Are they right?"

"That's the plan. Gives us a solid 10 days to make and execute a plan. Not too little, not too much."

"And how will the election work?" Anna asked. "Any details?"

"Yeah, the plan is to use an 'exhaustive ballot' method. If no one has a majority of all votes cast after the first ballot, we drop the lowest vote-getter off the ballot and vote again. We keep doing this until someone earns a majority."

"Interesting. Sounds fair enough to me."

"Right," said Montgomery. "So, what's key in this kind of race is not necessarily locking down a majority of voters to make you their first choice. Most of the candidates will waste their energy doing that. The smart move is actually getting them to commit to making you their second or third choice. That's where the real action lies. The voters are usually so fixated on getting their first preference across the finish line that they aren't nearly as protective of their second- or third-place commitments."

"That makes total sense," said Anna. "Oh, also, *Quincy's Whispers* had an item today specifically about you, potentially along these lines. Did you see it?"

"It did? Really?" Montgomery asked. "No, I haven't. Can you show me?"

Anna pulled up the email again and pointed out Whisper 5.

"Good Lord," Montgomery exclaimed. "Two people can't even have a friendly talk with each other anymore without making the gossip rags. That's absolutely ridiculous."

"So, there's no 'back-room deal'?" Anna asked, trying to sound casual to mask her insecurity. If Montgomery was cutting her out of the loop on something this important, it could be a bad sign for her future with him.

"Of course not. I was just there to tell him I plan to run a clean race and hope he will do the same if and when he decides to get in. It was 100 percent above-board. We didn't even mention voting or election strategy."

"I figured." Anna said. "Makes you wonder how many of these other Whispers you can really trust."

Anna was kicking herself for even questioning Montgomery's loyalties. He was the one person who had never let her down, yet she still struggled to let him through her shields.

Montgomery was still frustrated. "I'm sure 95 percent of them are exaggerated at the very least, and probably half are made up out of thin air," he said. "How that guy doesn't get sued for libel is beyond me."

"Well, nobody knows who he is, for one thing. Or maybe she. Really no one knows a thing about Quincy."

"And I'm sure he's determined to keep it that way," said Montgomery.

Anna nodded in agreement before switching topics.

"Have you been hearing much about Christine Franklin or Jonathan Garcia?" she asked.

"Not really," said Montgomery. "Well, nothing about Garcia, at least. Franklin and her Christian Conservatives seem to have some real momentum though. I'm just not sure if she'll have enough appeal to other people outside of the CCs to cobble together a coalition. That social stuff is polarizing."

"I agree about Franklin," said Anna. "I definitely want to keep watching Garcia, too. I always feel like he's a little shady, so I want to make sure he isn't kneecapping us."

"He's definitely worth some attention, and more than a little shady," Montgomery agreed.

"Ok, so what are you thinking on next steps for today?" Anna asked.

"Right. Okay. I've been spending a lot of time running the numbers, and I think there are multiple paths to 218 for us. Right now, we're sitting at 89 Members. Let's just assume, for the sake of argument, all of them will support me for Speaker. That leaves us 129 votes short."

Anna walked to her whiteboard, erased yesterday's marks, and took down Montgomery's thoughts.

218 Majority of House
-89 Blue Collars
129 Additional votes needed

Montgomery continued. "Most of the other parties are going to put up one candidate as their standard-bearer. But not *all* of them. A few of these groups are more loaded with loose cannons than a pirate ship in a hurricane.

"The Gadsden Guard will definitely vote in lockstep - they've all sworn it to each other. So, they'll be supporting Steven Reed on the first ballot. He's their Chairman and the one they're going to put forward for Speaker. We know he doesn't have a prayer... but *they* don't. They're so blinded by their ideological purity that they always imagine others will come around and see the light before they have to face reality. I'm pretty confident we can nail down their second-choice votes. Let's make a second column and add them in with 29 people."

Anna did just that:

129 Votes Needed
-29 Gadsden Guard
100 Additional votes needed

An even 100. That sounds doable.

"Next up, I think the Fiscal Fronters will be open to our message," said Montgomery. "As far as I know, they haven't put up a candidate yet. If they do, I'm sure it'll be as a token, just to have someone. That's a pretty good group to angle for.

"Lots of the Blue Collars are fiscally pretty conservative and willing to work with them to keep spending at a reasonable level. That bunch of nerd accountants will just go with whatever group promises to blow the budget less than the others. They'll add another 17."

Anna revised her tallies:

129 Votes Needed
-29 Gadsden Guard
-17 Fiscal Front
83 Additional votes needed

"Looking alright so far," Anna said. "Think we can scrounge up 83 more?"

"Yeah, this is where it gets interesting," said Montgomery. "There are several different pathways, but each has its challenges."

"I'm sure that's right. Like what?"

"Why don't you list out all the other factions over on the side and add their latest whip counts. That'll make it easier to see. Put in the three uncommitted groups from your graph yesterday."

Anna pulled out her foamboard chart and some notes from the previous day's meeting and studied them for a few minutes, counting up dots. She then added the four formal parties and three uncommitted groups to the whiteboard:

65 Christian Conservatives
53 Watchdogs
45 Centrists
43 Minority Members
36 Greens
32 ASJ/Warriors
26 Nationalists

"Alright," Montgomery said. "That's what we've got to work with. We need to find at least 83 votes out of these groups."

Anna studied the board carefully. The two silently contemplated the various possible arrangements of numbers for several minutes.

"If we get the Christian Conservatives to join us, then any one of the others would put us over 83," Anna observed.

"True, but I think it is exceedingly unlikely that they will want to do that," said Montgomery. "Right now, they're sitting in second position in overall membership. It's much more likely they will want to make a hard run at leading their own coalition with Christine Franklin at the head of it."

Anna agreed. "So, unless we can knock out Franklin and become the Christian Conservatives' second choice, we need to cobble together two or three of the others, depending on size. Well, I guess we can scratch off the Warriors if you think the Gadsden Guard is pretty solid. They'd rather eat garbage than be on the same team."

"Yeah," said Montgomery, "same probably goes for the Nationalists.

They can't get along with either one of those groups. Let's take both of them off the list."

Anna revised her whiteboard accordingly:

65 Christian Conservatives
53 Watchdogs
45 Centrists
43 Minority Members
36 Greens

"That does narrow down the options pretty well," she said.

Montgomery studied the list carefully.

"On your chart there, where did you have Alber and Garcia?" Montgomery asked. "Neither one has joined a party yet."

Anna referred to her notes, then pulled out a red marker and circled the dots representing Alber and Garcia. Alber fell squarely in the middle of the group she'd labeled the "Centrists." Garcia was ID'd as part of the "Minority Members."

Montgomery snapped his fingers and pointed at the chart.

"Just what I thought. I bet you Alber is going to pull together some kind of centrist coalition and make a run from there. Garcia is the most senior of the minority Members, so he'll probably bludgeon them until they let him run as their standard-bearer. So that leaves the Greens without any obvious strong candidate... but they're not enough to get us anywhere on their own."

Anna had been doing some mental math to see what different ways they could possibly find 83 more votes. "Let me work out the options," she said.

She erased the rest of the whiteboard, then made a list of potential coalition partnerships, ordered from largest to smallest, then drew a line at the 83-Member mark:

118 CCs +Watchdogs
110 CCs + Centrists
108 CCs + Minorities
101 CCs + Greens
98 Watchdogs + Centrists
96 Watchdogs + Minorities
89 Watchdogs + Greens
88 Centrists + Minorities

----

81 Centrists + Greens
79 Greens + Minorities

"There's our answer," she said. "First we need to nail down the Gadsden Guard and Fiscal Fronters. Then if we get either the Christian Conservatives or the Watchdogs on our side, then any other group would put us over the top of 218. If we don't get either of them, there are only two paths to victory: the Centrists plus the Minorities; or the Centrists, Minorities, *and* Greens. Geez, this is getting complicated."

"Let me simplify it for you," said Montgomery. "No matter what, we're probably going to need to knock out one of the three big dogs - Franklin, Alber, or Garcia - and pick up their voters. Otherwise, the pathway to victory is extremely narrow.

"Really the only option on your board that doesn't go through one of those three is convincing the Watchdogs and the Greens both to join us. Let me ask, how many times have you seen war hawks and greenies holding hands?"

Anna laughed. "Nowhere outside of a tornado shelter," she said.

He smiled as he responded. "Yeah, extremely unlikely. Plus, we'd only have a six-vote margin to play with even if it did happen, which would be cutting it close."

Anna grimaced in acknowledgement of the predicament. She stared at the board, hoping another option would pop out, but none did. The math was undeniable.

Montgomery continued, “Bottom line, I think we have almost no choice but to outlast one of the big three and scoop up their votes.”

“Okay, and what’s the plan to make that happen?” Anna asked.

“Let me worry about that,” Montgomery replied solemnly, and dismissed her.

32

Later that Tuesday morning, Speaker Mathes announced that she was scheduling the vote for her successor on Friday, August 4. Several reporters questioned who she would be supporting in the race, but she remained adamant that she was staying out of it.

Mathes additionally announced she would be resigning her Congressional seat as soon as she stepped down from the Speakership. This was no huge surprise - in recent decades it was almost unheard-of for a resigned ex-Speaker to remain in the House.

Although she still retained the title of Speaker, Mathes was no longer even trying to exercise any of the powers of the office. Each day, she spent several hours at the dais of the House, presiding over meaningless debate. While presiding over the House Floor was technically the Speaker's job, in ordinary times the task is delegated to junior members of the Speaker's party. It was no secret that Speaker Mathes was spending her day in the Chair to avoid the media.

~

EACH TIME the Members came to the Floor for a vote series - still invariably casting votes on trivial matters - Montgomery took full advantage of the chance to make his case seeking Members' support.

This particular day, a vote series was called at 11:21 a.m. The Members all headed to the Floor, many grumbling that they were likely to miss their lunch appointments if the series went too long.

Montgomery grabbed a folder off his desk labeled "Floor" and hustled to the chamber. This vote series was anticipated to last about 35 minutes. Plenty of time for him to work the room.

As soon as he reached the chamber, Montgomery scanned the room for his key targets. Close to the center aisle, about halfway back, he spotted a group of Members chatting. It was just who he was looking for.

Karen Johnson, a 58-year-old African American Congresswoman from California, was engaged in light conversation with Alejandra Hernandez from Texas and Marquez Williams from Alabama. This trio was the epicenter of political power among the ethnic minority Members in the House.

Montgomery approached but was careful not to interrupt their conversation. As he came near, he caught Congresswoman Johnson's eye. She cut off her sentence and turned to Montgomery with a smile.

"Hey Willis, how's my old buddy?" she said with enthusiasm. "You've been all over the papers the last few days. You staying out of trouble?"

"Oh, Karen, you know that's not possible," he teased. "How about yourself? You all doing alright?"

Congresswoman Hernandez spoke up. "Yeah, things are starting to look a little better. I hope I never have another week like last week as long as I live."

Everyone expressed agreement with her sentiment.

"I'm glad you three are together," Montgomery said. "I wanted to bend your ears a little bit."

"Bend away," said Congressman Williams. He and Montgomery had played pick-up basketball in the Members' gym many times and had grown comfortable with one another.

"Alright. You all know about the Blue Collar Party. It's been going really well - I feel like people are starting to come together over things that matter again, not just political squabbling."

"Willis, you're doing a fine job with your group," said Johnson. "I really mean that. I've got to say, though, we're not joining. It's nothing personal - it's just that our constituents would toss us out if we signed up with a mostly-white working-class party. They're looking for something that hits a little closer to home."

"As you absolutely should," said Montgomery. "That's actually why I wanted to talk to you. I think you're right to avoid the Blues. I obviously love my people, but I think you all could be much more effective in a different faction."

Johnson, Hernandez, and Williams appeared shocked. They looked at each other with confusion, then looked back at Montgomery.

"I don't mean to offend - I have thought about it quite a bit and just wanted to walk through my ideas with you. Have you all talked much with the other groups?"

Johnson spoke up for the three. "We're still talking with a couple of the other factions, but joining any of them would mean we'd have to sacrifice an awful lot of what we care about. Right now, we're just feeling it out."

Montgomery nodded. "Sounds like you're doing it right, seeing what all your options are. I'm sure you've already been giving this quite a bit of thought as well, but I wanted to run it by you. I think there may be a lot of merit to forming your *own* party." He seemed completely earnest.

"We've talked about it," Hernandez said cautiously. "Why do you say that?"

"I think there are a lot of advantages to being on your own," said Montgomery. "What are some of the reasons you might be leaning against it?"

"I think I'm most concerned about being pigeonholed," Williams said. "On the issues that really matter, we want to be listened to, not just be tokens."

"That is a pretty universal desire," said Montgomery. "I would argue that you have some strengths that could make you a powerful faction in your own right. You have Members who historically are outstanding at sticking together for what's in their common interests. You have at least 40 Members who would probably band together - about 10 percent of the House... and about 20 percent of what it takes to win any majority vote. That's a significant chunk.

"Keep in mind that *no* faction will have an outright majority. Nowhere near it. If you're holding 1/5 of the chips another faction needs to win a vote, you can be kingmakers."

The trio looked at each other and shared a look that seemed to say, "he has a good point."

Congresswoman Johnson responded. "I think what you're saying makes a lot of sense, Willis. If we do form our own group, what's in it for you?"

Montgomery laughed. "Absolutely nothing. I'm certain we'll be with each other on some issues and opposed on others. I just would love to work with people who are actually reasonable and honest in their dealings."

Hernandez had a skeptical eye toward Montgomery but decided to let it go for now. "We'll give it some thought. But if there's anything you are hoping to get from us, I would suggest you be upfront about it."

Montgomery adopted a somber tone. "I genuinely want the future of this great, historic body to be in the hands of competent leadership. If we let the crazies stay in charge, America as we know it is toast. You can help make it a better place by banding together.

"Yes, I will be throwing my name in the hat for Speaker. But I could take it or leave it. If your preferred candidate does not seem to have the votes to win, I would be honored if you would consider me as your second choice. I can commit to you that I will always work with you and be honest in my dealings.

"What is most important, though, is that we elect *someone* who will provide honest, stable leadership. I will gladly support any candidate that provides that for this body and for our country."

Johnson, Hernandez, and Williams looked satisfied with Montgomery's elevator speech. They were impressed with the case he made, and it did seem like a win-win proposal. They all shook hands, thanking Montgomery for reaching out to them.

Montgomery wandered to the rear of the chamber. After saying hello to a few more colleagues, the last vote of the series was called by the chair. Montgomery inserted his voting card into the electronic reader and pushed the "YEA" button, then quickly exited the Floor and returned to his office.

33

Anna and Josh had again reserved a room in the Rayburn House Office Building for a second formal all-hands gathering of the Blues at 3:00 p.m. By 2:45, Montgomery was milling about the room, full of energy. In addition to inviting all of the Members, Anna had also sent personal texts to each of the 83 other Chiefs to invite them to the meeting as well. These touches both made the Members more likely to come and kept Anna's name in the front of her colleagues' minds.

In what felt like a miracle, every single one of the 83 Blues showed up for the meeting. Anna counted 74 of their Chiefs as well and made a point to speak personally to each and every one of them. She invited them to actually partake in the refreshments provided for the meeting, an act that nearly elevated her to instant sainthood among her colleagues. Staffers were typically forbidden to touch the food or drink provided in meetings on the Hill, no matter how mouth-watering the offerings and how little of it the Members had eaten.

This unspoken rule, born from decades of tradition, was just one of the ways in which Members were still treated like princes by staff. A corollary effect of these traditions was that they often made staffers feel unworthy and undervalued by their bosses. Anna had learned early on that making staffers feel valuable and important went a long way, and the quickest way to their hearts was through their stomachs.

Spirits were high throughout the Blues. Their group was sitting in a strong position so far - the biggest faction in a very fractured House. They were excited to take the next steps as a team. It finally seemed like the future was not all doom and gloom.

When the clock ticked to 3:00 p.m., Montgomery raised his voice to call the meeting to order.

"Thank you all for making it this afternoon! I'm sure you'd all much rather be back home instead of here again this week, but if I have to be in Washington, I can't think of a finer group of people to spend it with."

The Members throughout the room chuckled.

Montgomery continued. "The people in this room have already done something amazing. In perhaps the darkest hour for this nation's political leadership aside from the Civil War, we came together to rise above the partisan bickering. We showed the nation that Members of Congress are not all like the stereotypes - many of us care deeply for our country and our constituents. We want to do what's right, not what's going to make us personally rich or powerful.

"This is the type of leadership each of the people in this room has shown. Two weeks ago, many of us called ourselves Republicans. Many of us called ourselves Democrats. We saw ourselves as members of two completely separate teams playing a zero-sum game.

"Now we've stopped even playing the game and are in the middle of a benches-clearing brawl. Plenty of Members who started out on the same team are now throwing haymakers at each other. It's gotten so ugly that the American people are about ready to toss us all out of the stadium.

"The men and women in this room have decided to step away from the brawl. We're not playing for the Republican team or the Democrat team anymore. We've chosen to play for the American team.

"We're playing for the hard-working, salt-of-the-Earth people who built this country. We have shown our fellow citizens that it's people like *them* that matter, not the donors and the lobbyists and the consultants.

"We are going to go to bat for the American people. With our nation in crisis, we cannot allow its elected representatives in the people's house to be led by special interests or cynical political animals.

"Over the past few days, many of you have encouraged me to consider a run for the Speakership. I have thought long and hard about your words. I have prayed over them. I wanted you to be the first to know that I have decided to put my name forward as a candidate for Speaker of the House."

As Montgomery said these words, the room erupted in applause and cheers as the Members stood to congratulate their Chairman. From the back of the room, a rhythmic clapping began, along with cheers of "Will-is! Will-is! Will-is!"

For about a minute and a half, Montgomery tried in vain to quiet the crowd. Eventually everyone settled down and retook their seats.

"We can do this together - as a team," he continued. "The good people of this country need us to. They want us to put bickering aside and govern as pragmatic realists. That's why the Blue Collars are the right people to make this happen.

"All of us believe in the blue-collar work ethic, right?"

The room murmured its agreement.

"Well this race is going to take an extra dose of it. We are 84 Members strong. That's a big number, but it's still 134 short of a majority. We'll have to talk with our friends. We'll have to talk with our neighbors. We'll have to talk to our former enemies. With our team going to bat for the American people every day between now and next Friday, we *will* get it done."

Growing cheers came from the crowd with each successive line. Watching this rousing, emotional speech from the side of the room, Anna wondered if Montgomery had some Baptist preachers in his family tree. The stirring words, combined with the altar call, seemed straight out of a tent revival.

Benjamin Petrowski had been sitting in the front row during Montgomery's speech. As soon as the final word slipped out of Montgomery's mouth, he leapt out of his chair to stand next to his longtime friend.

Petrowski put his left arm around Montgomery's shoulder and gestured emphatically with his right hand as he spoke to the room. "Only one week ago, I spoke to many of you in this very room. At that time, I told you I believe our nation's people are craving a return to normalcy. I testified to the wisdom and humility of my good friend, Willis Montgomery, with whom I have had the honor of knowing and working for many, many years."

His hand squeezed Montgomery's shoulder and the two shared a warm smile.

"Today, I again am honored to stand with my friend and offer my full support and endorsement for his candidacy for Speaker of the House. Willis is the kind of leader we need at a time like this. We need experience, wisdom, and humility. Willis has all of these traits."

Petrowski turned to Montgomery and offered his right hand, which Montgomery accepted. "Willis, let me be the first to congratulate you on beginning your journey to be the next Speaker of the United States House of Representatives."

The room again erupted in applause and cheers. The chants of "Will-is! Will-is! Will-is!" returned as Montgomery again waved them down.

"Thank you, Ben," Montgomery said. "Thank you. It means so much to have someone as respected as you offer your support."

Montgomery reached beneath a table at the front of the room and pulled out a large poster-sized sheet of thick paper. At the top the words "Team Montgomery" were printed in a big, bold font. The design resembled a baseball manager's lineup card. Below were 84 numbered lines filled in with the handwritten names of every Member of the Blue Collar Party.

Willis Montgomery was listed in the #1 position with Benjamin Petrowski in the #2 slot. Petrowski held the left side of the lineup card and Montgomery held the right. They proudly displayed it to the rest of the room with smiles stretching from ear to ear. The room was full of applause and laughter.

Montgomery again reached under the table and pulled out two crisp new baseball caps. The blue and white hats were emblazoned with a stylized red M logo that Kyle had designed. Montgomery handed one to Petrowski and kept one for himself. Stitched on the back of each hat were the words "Monty's Whip Team."

Next, Montgomery handed Petrowski an authentic baseball jersey with "Montgomery" scrawled across the chest in dark blue, the team logo over the heart, and the number 1 on the back beneath the name "Petrowski." The rest of the group cheered as Petrowski put on the hat and jersey.

Last of all, Montgomery took a pristine wooden Louisville Slugger baseball bat from a box beneath the table. He held it up to show the room that the words "Monty's Whip Team" were burned into its barrel. The room cheered once again as he handed it to Petrowski.

Montgomery was all smiles as he turned back to the assembled crowd. "Our team is unstoppable when we all work together. We have divided up the rest of our 352 colleagues into 83 groups of four and five. My Chief of Staff Anna has a personalized whip card for each of you. Anna, wave to everyone."

Anna stepped forward and waved to the room to let them know who to look for. She held up a poster-sized example of one of the whip cards with text large enough for everyone in the room to read from their seats. The card had the same design as the lineup card Montgomery and Petrowski had been holding moments earlier. Everything was on-brand. Kyle had really knocked it out of the park.

"Each card has just a handful of names on it. Most of the people on your card will be colleagues you already know well - from your state, your region, or people you are already friends with. The other side of the card has three bullet points we'd like you to cover with your targets. They are:

> **1. Servant Leadership** - Willis has demonstrated his selfless devotion to this chamber for 23 years. His record of sharing credit speaks for itself.
>
> **2. Fair Treatment** - No Member should be punished for his or her beliefs. Willis will treat Members equally based on their merits.
>
> **3. Regular Order** - The Speaker should not rule as a dictator. Willis will let committees vet legislation and open up the amendment process on the Floor so *every* Member has a voice - not just an elite few.

"I ask each of you to talk with your targets by tomorrow evening at 7:00. Please write any notes about your conversations on the card and return it to me or Anna as soon as possible. Now let's get everyone dressed out and get a team picture!"

A unanimous cheer arose from the Members as they rose to claim their own hat, personalized jersey, and bat. The room was abuzz with excitement as Members gushed over their new swag.

As Montgomery shook each Member's hand, Anna sought out the Member's Chief of Staff. She delivered each Chief a matching team hat and a "manager's clipboard" with the team logo across the back and campaign materials clipped to the front. Each clipboard also held a note with Anna's personal cell number and email address handwritten on it.

The frenzy continued until every Member in the room had received their gear. Anna marveled at how well peer pressure worked on even Members of Congress. Not a single Member questioned the fact that Montgomery had presumed their support and presumed they would whip colleagues on his behalf.

At their core, even these highly accomplished individuals just wanted to be a part of something. Kyle had done another awesome job sweet-talking his source to get this gear ready in such short order, and it all looked great with the team name and logo.

After all 84 Members had donned hats and jerseys and picked up a bat, Kyle gathered them together for a group photograph.

As soon as Kyle finished, Montgomery stepped forward and turned to address the crowd.

"I could not possibly be more grateful to all of you for your support," he said. "I am humbled and honored to be part of this wonderful group of people. The spirit in this room is precisely what our nation needs in this moment. Together we will heal the wounds of our nation.

"We have nine days to make this vision a reality. Thank you all again for your support. Let's go out there and win this!"

The room erupted in cheers one final time as the Members headed for the exit, picking up their whip cards on the way out the door.

Before the meeting broke up, Kyle clicked "send" on the press release formally announcing Montgomery's candidacy, highly touting the unanimous support of the 83-Member Blue Collar Party. Within

30 seconds, his cell phone began to blow up with texts, calls, and emails from reporters wanting to interview Montgomery. He began to arrange another gauntlet of interviews for his boss that evening, plus booked him on three of the Sunday morning shows that were the rite of passage for any big name in Washington.

After Montgomery's announcement broke the ice, seven more Members announced their candidacies for Speaker by the end of the day... including a few serious contenders. The group of three dozen Members Anna had identified as hard-core environmentalists also announced - to little fanfare - that they were forming a new Green Party. The news about Montgomery's endorsements sucked up all of the oxygen on the nightly newscasts, leaving the Greens feeling forgotten by the media.

~

YET ANOTHER LATE night of data entry and texting fellow Chiefs kept Anna at the office past 1:00 a.m. Much more of this and Delta was liable to run off. Nonetheless, her fluffy best friend was there at the door waiting for her the moment she returned home.

Anna reached into the cabinet and pulled out a can of wet cat food. This special treat was better than catnip to Delta. Anytime Anna gave it to her, she was on top of the world for the next two days.

She dressed for bed and talked with Delta for a few minutes before settling in for the night. "Nine more days," she whispered as she drifted off to sleep.

34

WEDNESDAY, JULY 26

Wednesday morning came far too soon for Anna. When her 5:00 a.m. alarm sounded, she felt like she had only slept for 20 minutes. Delta hopped over to the bed and began snuggling next to her head on the pillow. Anna fought the urge to fall back to sleep, but she drifted off again. At 5:23 she bolted upright, panicked that she was already behind schedule for the day. It felt like the pace of events was chipping away at her sanity.

She hopped out of bed and stepped into the bathroom to get ready. She decided to read the morning news on her phone while brushing her teeth.

~

From: Quincy <quincy@quincyswhispers.com>
Subject: Quincy's Whispers - Wednesday, July 26
Date: July 26 at 4:32 AM
To: Anna Rothwell

Quincy's Whispers

260 days since the Midterm Election
468 days until the Presidential Election
9 days until the Speaker Election
What the House is whispering about...
but doesn't want you to hear.

Good Wednesday morning! As of today, it is formally *game on* in Washington, D.C. The Speaker's race will be decided nine days from today, and we already have eight formally announced candidates for the position. This is going to be an all-out sprint - the stakes could hardly be higher, and the outcome could hardly be less certain. The drama is only beginning.

What I'm hearing today:

Whisper 1 - Whispers have taken a decided turn in the past two days. Most people have turned their attention to the race for Speaker. A highly placed Whisperer tells me one or two more factions may still come together, but beyond that, it sounds like the parties are pretty much set. For now, at least.

Whisper 2 - Here's a sampling of the most interesting questions I'm hearing now: How will these new factions ultimately work together? Will they stake out positions and play hardball? Will they work to build broad, formal coalitions? Will they make shifting alliances based on each issue? Will they operate as blocs at all or loose groups of individuals? So many outstanding questions, and there will probably be dozens of different answers depending on the group and issue.

Whisper 3 - The biggest news coming out of yesterday's Speaker race announcements was the huge number of endorsements Willis Montgomery has already locked down. According to his office, 100% of the Blue Collar Party endorsed his candidacy, giving him 84 votes. I'm hearing Whispers that he may also be in talks to join forces with another faction in the next two days that could take him well north of 100 votes. He will need 218 to win, so there's a long way to go... but this is a very strong start for Montgomery.

Whisper 4 - Tips on Yorktown continue to trickle in. A Whisper from an alleged but unconfirmed insider says they're focusing on allegations of bribery. Sounds like the G-men are quietly asking a lot of questions of a lot of people around the Hill. The scandal has many people scratching their heads, as the rumors are all over the map and seem to point in multiple different directions at once.

Whisper 5 - Ticonderoga, the situation allegedly involving a female Member's relationship with her male Chief of Staff, continues to intrigue readers on the Hill. No new developments on this one specifically, but it has definitely jogged the memories of many regarding other Members' similar situations. Since yesterday, I've heard three separate rumors of Member-staff sexual misconduct. All three are old rumors that I believe may no longer be active relationships, but I'm going to keep my ear to the desk on this one.

Whisper 6 - Some developments on the "actual legislating" front: as you know, government funding runs out September 30, and to date zero work has been done to craft an agreement. Whisperers in the know tell me this may be about to change. Appropriators have actually begun having private discussions to put together a spending package that would balance the various demands of the major factions. Don't hold your breath, though - nothing will happen until after the Speaker election.

UNTIL TOMORROW, I have the honor to be,

Your obedient servant,

~QUINCY

Sign up at www.QuincysWhispers.com to get
every edition delivered to your inbox!
Watch for breaking Whispers on Twitter @quincyswhispers.

Hear something good?
Whisper it to me at tips@quincyswhispers.com.
All Whispers are reviewed and kept
strictly anonymous and confidential.

~

ANNA WAS ONLY HALF-AWAKE, but it perked her up to read about Montgomery in the Whispers yet again. She was beginning to understand Oscar Wilde's old quip: the only thing worse than being talked about is not being talked about. She started to question what else might be churning in the rumor mill.

What are people REALLY saying about us behind our backs? What will they say about us next? These rumors are a little out over their skis, but it doesn't really hurt to have people think Montgomery's more of a mastermind than he really is. And it's not terribly surprising that everyone's changing focus from factions to the Speaker's race and voting coalitions. It really feels like the speed of the Hill has quadrupled since The Collapse, and it's usually breakneck anyway... Yesterday's news might as well have happened a year ago.

Anna quickly leapt into the shower and continued getting ready for the day. By fast-forwarding her routine, she was able to get out the door only 10 minutes later than normal.

35

Anna made up for lost time by reading through more morning news recaps during her walk to the office. Coverage and analysis of yesterday's Speaker announcements filled every newsletter.

As Montgomery had expected, Christine Franklin had formally thrown her hat in the ring. Steven Reed of the Gadsden Guard and Nadia Lewis of the Warriors also were not surprises.

There still was no word of Ted Alber joining the race. Columnists speculated in every newspaper about his plans. His charisma and star power had spectators watching his every move. Everyone had a different opinion about his reasoning, but there was near consensus that he would instantly be a top-tier candidate if and when he decided to jump in.

Anna arrived and got to work. She had so many things still to do, it felt like she was drowning in uncompleted tasks. Even though she knew it was bad for her concentration, she kept one eye on the television while she tried to work through her backlog.

~

THE FEELINGS of tightness and anxiety inside Anna's chest continued to worsen throughout the morning. At 9:00, she decided to skip her usual coffee break and instead see if Peter Garibaldi might want to go for a quick walk to talk about the craziness of the past few days.

Anna exited the office as if making her usual coffee run. Once entering the hallway, she took the elevator down only one floor. Congressman Wilson, Peter's boss, had occupied an office on the first floor of Rayburn for the last two terms. This made it easy for Anna to occasionally drop in for a visit.

Anna had just read in the morning news that Wilson had been drafted Monday to be the Fiscal Front's standard-bearer in the Speaker's race. To a degree, she knew this meant she probably shouldn't be confiding in Peter. On the other hand, she really needed to talk to *someone,* and Peter was just about the only person she felt like she could reach out to who would understand what she was going through.

Besides, Wilson had next to no chance of winning the Speakership. Anna had actually felt embarrassed for Peter when she heard Wilson was running. She knew his heart wasn't in it, and he really had no business even trying. Tuesday afternoon, the Fiscal Front had gotten together to discuss strategy for the Speaker's race. The collection of bean counters had almost zero charisma among them, and no one who really wanted to run for the office. However, they decided that to have a voice at all in the race, they had better put someone forward.

As Anna had heard the story, the Members each put their name on a folded piece of paper and literally drew one out of a hat. Wilson somehow was the unlucky one who was chosen to carry the message of fiscal discipline for the next week and a half. Fate could hardly have picked a less enthusiastic candidate.

Fortunately, this morning Peter was in the office when Anna came by. He quickly agreed to take a walk.

Anna and Peter took the elevator to the Rayburn building's subterranean parking garage. Neither said a word as they made their way toward the open garage doors on the building's west side, unsure of who might be listening behind a pillar or crouching between cars. They walked through the northernmost garage door, which placed them 30 feet from Bartholdi Park.

Anna led Peter to her usual bench, out of sight from most prying eyes, and gestured for him to take a seat. She sat next to him and sighed deeply. Peter looked around in all directions before speaking.

"Are you okay, Anna?" he said in a hushed voice. "I don't think I've ever seen you look this worried."

"This week has been… well, it's been difficult," Anna said. It was hard for her to admit to struggles, even with someone she'd known as long as Peter.

"It sure has," Peter replied dryly. "Is there anything in particular that's bothering you?" He could usually recognize when Anna needed to vent.

"Well, it's just been hard," Anna began. "There's so much that's unknown right now. Literally everything is up in the air. I don't even know who to call for basic stuff anymore. There's no staff in charge of Floor debate. The Majority Leader's office is cleaned out and locked. The media is constantly hounding us. Constituents keep calling nonstop. Lobbyists are wanting to talk to me and Montgomery all the time. I'm working like 18-hour days, seven days a week. I think I'm even starting to feel paranoid. Really, I'm just worn out."

Peter took a few seconds to digest Anna's laundry list before responding.

"I'm exhausted from all of this too. Missing sleep, constantly overworked, not eating right. I feel like I'm catching the flu."

"Yeah, exactly," said Anna. "I just feel tired and run down and nauseous all the time."

Anna had been trying not to think about it, but she knew she'd lived this story several times before. In both high school and college, Anna had been so driven and overcommitted that she had almost run herself into the ground.

Peter had been very similar in college. Many Hill staffers had. The driven personality types that are drawn to Congressional work were usually no strangers to overcommitment and stress. He knew how tough situations usually affected people.

"Are you having any problems with anxiety?" Peter asked. "With Willis running for Speaker on top of all of this, I'm sure you're overwhelmed."

Anna let out another long sigh. She knew from experience that Peter wasn't asking so that he could gain some advantage – he actually cared about her wellbeing.

"Yeah, my chest seems like it feels tighter every day," she said. "When I'm working, I feel like I'm getting tunnel vision - I lose track of everything going on around me except the thing I'm working on at that instant."

Peter nodded and gazed across the street as he considered what Anna had said.

"Anna, you and I both know how hard it is to do this job when you feel thrown off your game. I've been feeling it too. I know it's easy to say and hard to do, but you have got to get some more sleep and find a way to relax."

Peter's reassuring tone calmed Anna. It was nice to at least hear that other people were in the same boat.

"I know you're right," Anna replied. "I feel horrible every morning, and I can't seem to keep my schedule like usual. It's the uncertainty that's killing me. As soon as this election is over, no matter what the result is, at least we'll have some kind of normal again. Until then, everything's just so crazy up here… I don't see how I can work any less or take time to relax for the next nine days."

"I know, Anna," Peter said. "It's hard to slow down, especially when you are afraid that you might lose a race by one vote. You'd always look back and wonder what more you could have done if you'd just slept 30 minutes less."

"That's exactly it," said Anna. "I would never forgive myself if I gave anything less than my full effort and we lost."

"Hey, I can't make you sleep or relax, Anna. I know that. But please do at least try. You'll be of much more use to Willis if you're rested than if you're overwhelmed."

"Yeah, I know you're right," Anna acknowledged. She decided to change the subject.

"Think you're going to make it to lunch today?"

Peter smiled as he answered. He loved Live Oak nearly as much as Anna, and was always glad to receive an invitation to her weekly lunch.

"Absolutely!" he said. "But I'd better go get some work done if I'm going to be able to get there."

He rose and faced Anna. He locked eyes with her and spoke sternly, hoping to get through Anna's tough emotional shell.

"You take it easy, Anna. I don't want to see you breaking down over all of this. The Speaker's race is important, but either way, life will go on next week. You need to be around for it."

Peter waved goodbye as Anna nodded silently. Peter walked back across the small park toward Rayburn. Anna closed her eyes and tried to relax to the sound of the water crashing down from Bartholdi Fountain. After a short three-minute rest, she stood and made her way back to the office.

~

At 10:30 a.m., Anna noticed the CNN "Breaking News" alert graphics popping up on her TV. She turned up the volume to see what was new. A reporter on a live feed from the Capitol was announcing a "major development" in the House of Representatives. The reporter stated that Karen Johnson, Alejandra Hernandez, and Marquez Williams would be holding a joint press conference from the House Triangle at 11:00 a.m.

The House Triangle was an outdoor spot just to the southeast of the Capitol that Members often used for announcements. The majestic backdrop of the Capitol dome was a striking visual that seemed to lend instant credibility to whatever message was being delivered.

Anna grabbed her phone and texted Montgomery.

> **AR**: Have you heard Johnson, Hernandez, and Williams are having a press conference at 11?
>
> **WM**: No. Talked to them yesterday. Sounded like they might start their own faction
>
> **AR**: That's what CNN's reporting now. Is it minority Members?
>
> **WM**: Yep
>
> **AR**: How many would it be?
>
> **WM**: Close to what we talked about yesterday. About 40
>
> **AR**: You called it.

Anna flipped around between cable news channels to get their different takes. All of them seemed to confirm the initial reports - a new faction would be forming under the banner of the "Minority Majority," with Jonathan Garcia their preferred candidate for Speaker.

36

The morning had flown by and Anna was shocked to hear Lily tell her it was already time to prep for her weekly lunch at Live Oak. They had skipped last week amidst all the post-Collapse commotion, but this week would be crucial.

At Montgomery's request, Lily had extended invitations to the Chiefs of Staff for all of his announced opponents. Unsurprisingly to Lily, most of them declined. Not only were they up to their eyeballs in work; most of them were incredibly skeptical of the motives behind such a request.

Nonetheless, three Chiefs of Speaker candidates did RSVP: Simon Belmont with Steven Reed, the leader of the Gadsden Guard from Wyoming; Linda Abrahamson with Henry Neville, a New Yorker from the Green Party; and Peter Garibaldi. The only common thread tying this group together was that they didn't stand a chance of actually winning the race. The rest of the lunch group was composed of a smattering of Chiefs coming from other factions.

Kyle was overwhelmed with media requests, so Josh stepped in to help drive guests to and from lunch. Des came along as well. This was going to be possibly the most important lunch Anna had hosted, and Des wanted to be certain they didn't miss anything.

Anna expected to discover at least one or two leads for either new converts to the Blues or potential votes for Speaker. But the lofty hopes the team had for the lunch did not materialize. Instead what she discovered was just how deep and strong the divisions ran among her colleagues.

Sometimes these lunches turned into a kind of focus group - or even a not-so-friendly argument - with a single question or comment setting off a broader discussion around the table. Today, with everyone exhausted and the House still unstable, it felt like the table sat atop a powder keg.

As everyone was finishing up their entrees, Simon Belmont decided to address the group. He had been silent to that point, but obviously wanted to get something off of his chest. Simon looked around the table as he spoke.

"The last week and a half have obviously been historic on the Hill. Steve and I have been talking with a lot of people since everything fell apart. Everyone is finally starting to realize that what we've been saying for years is true - the problem with Congress is not that people have been too ideological. The mainstream media has been trying to shove that lie down our throats for decades now.

"In reality, Congress has been getting further and further detached from our true American beliefs since the middle of the 20th century. We're now seeing the end result of abandoning our original principles. We have no foundation left to stand upon.

"The only way this body is going to pull together and correct our mistakes is if we turn our focus away from our own selfish desires. We've got to return to the values of our Founders - the way this country used to be run. For the first 150 years, America was magnificent. The "progressive" cancer has slowly eaten this nation from within ever since. The size and scope of our government is unsustainable. To help the people who need it most, we have to once again help our neighbors and return personal responsibility to its rightful place in society."

Anna could see tempers beginning to boil as Simon spoke. She mentally went around the table and tried to imagine the brewing reactions of her other eight guests.

There's one other Gadsden Guardsman, so Simon will at least have one person on his side. Maybe the Fiscal Fronter and Christian Conservative. But beyond that... two Green Party, two Minority Majority, and one Social Justice Warrior... ehhhh... not looking too good. The last thing we need today is a screaming match in the middle of Live Oak.

Oblivious to the brewing storm, Simon went on. "We want to work with any of you who share this vision. My entire life we've made minor tweaks to address symptoms here and there, hoping it would fix the massive underlying problems. It didn't work. Delaying the inevitable only made things much, much worse.

"If there was ever a time in our nation's history that called for radical change, now is that time. We are moving forward to re-envision our Congress, and therefore our entire government. Just let me know if you and your boss want to work with us on these goals. We will accept you and your friends with open arms. If you choose not to join us now, you might come to regret it."

Throughout this soliloquy, Anna had been slowly sinking deeper into her seat, wishing she could disappear.

The people don't want revolution! They want stability. *It almost sounds like he's threatening them. This group isn't going to take this well...*

Anna could see the rage building as Simon finished his speech. Although this kind of talk was normal among the constituency of the Gadsden Guard, Christian Conservatives, or Fiscal Front, it was poisonous to followers of the Green Party, Minority Majority, and Americans for Social Justice. Anna knew they would probably interpret Simon's rantings about returning to the good old days of the Founding Fathers as thinly veiled racism, and while many of them considered themselves political radicals, they were not the same brand of radical as Simon Belmont.

As soon as Simon finished, Anna tried to jump in to steer the conversation in a less argumentative direction. But before she could say anything, Linda Abrahamson exploded.

"Are you *seriously* trying to tell me that you think the lesson to take away from The Collapse is that America is calling for the Gadsden Guard to take over Congress? That's the nuttiest thing I've ever heard you say, and that's quite an achievement."

Simon was immediately combative in return. "What, do you think they want us to turn into a bunch of communists like you and your boss?"

The table erupted into yelling from all corners. Anna had completely lost control of the room. She looked desperately over at Des, who looked like a deer in headlights. Finally, Peter was able to calm his colleagues enough to speak. He had always been a good peacemaker.

"Alright, everyone just sit back and take a few breaths," Peter said. "Obviously tempers are still pretty hot all around town, and I completely understand why you are both so upset. Simon, I think it is not productive to call each other names. Linda, I am sure Simon would appreciate if we would hear him out, whether or not we agree with his conclusions."

Linda and Simon grumbled their acceptance of Peter's proposed olive branch. However, Simon wasn't ready to give up completely.

"Linda, I'm sorry if it hurt your feelings when I said that you and your boss are communists," he said. "But I *do* believe that the only way for Congress to be restored to its rightful place is to return to the principles our founders started with, and to turn our eyes back to God."

Simon's non-apology apology sent Linda back over the edge.

"Oh, you're sorry it hurt my feelings, huh? And I guess you think bringing back slavery is the cure to what ails us, huh Simon?" she said.

The room again erupted in anger. The group's waitress opened the door to the closed-off space to check on them. Patrons in the front of Live Oak could hear the shouting match, and several had complained to her manager.

Anna knew she had to defuse the situation, or else everyone at the table might blame Montgomery for the fight and never choose to join him. She stood, holding her hands up in front of her to quiet the room down. "Everyone, I know we are all feeling very passionate right now. This is an extremely tough time for all of us and we're all under a lot of pressure. I don't expect everyone to agree with each other at all. The only thing I ask at these lunches is for all guests to treat one another with respect."

The room was silent. All nine of her guests looked ready to be out of there.

"Alright," Anna said. "Thank you all for coming. If anyone needs to go ahead and get back to the Hill, feel free to head out. I'll take care of the check."

All nine guests' chairs scooted back in unison as the group made its exit. No one spoke to one another as they left the restaurant.

Anna sank back into her chair, overwhelmed. She and Des did not say a word to one another as each tried to process what had just happened. Anna felt a sense of helplessness and dread.

What the hell was that? Why can't people just be civil to each other? Arguments like that just make me feel sick. I mean, what was Simon hoping to accomplish by telling everyone they'd better get on his team or else? Does he really *believe things are that black and white; that the American people are on his side and everyone else is wrong? Can't he see that his boss's district - well, state - is wildly different than those of people like Linda's boss? We have to start looking past our own noses if we ever want to fix this place.*

~

ON THE WAY back to Rayburn in Josh's car, the silence was deafening. Josh instantly sensed that things had not gone well. He focused on making the 10-minute drive as short as possible, while Des stared out the window in a daze. Anna felt bad for not talking to them, but she felt so emotionally drained after the scene at lunch that she could not bring herself to relive it. She started mentally planning out what she needed to do for the afternoon.

Montgomery had decided to focus on Garcia, Franklin, and Alber as the only serious threats to his own Speaker campaign. Both Anna and Montgomery deeply believed in the value of relationships; the altruist would say it was the right thing to do, the cynic would say it was a strategy of "keep your friends close and your enemies closer." Either way, reaching out to opponents was standard procedure in their office. She decided to make contact with each of their Chiefs of Staff to create open lines of communication.

But Kit! Why does he have to be Alber's Chief of Staff? He's insufferable. Maybe he can wait for another day. Alber hasn't actually declared for the race yet, so talking to Kit really isn't necessary until he does. Garcia and Franklin - their Chiefs are definitely worth reaching out to for a conversation.

37

After returning to the office, Anna quickly turned her attention to her afternoon targets and tried to forget about the disastrous lunch.

Christine Franklin's Chief of Staff, Eugenia Dunn, had been on the Hill for two and a half decades. In a workplace typified by high turnover, she was a rare character. Her first day working in the House of Representatives was when Anna was still in kindergarten.

With Congressional jobs requiring only 20 years of service before retirement eligibility, a 25-year employee was almost unheard-of. The only people Anna had ever encountered who stayed on past 20 years were one of two things: policy wonks or power-hungry jerks. From what Anna had heard, Eugenia was both.

According to most Chiefs, Eugenia Dunn combined the worst of all worlds - the job passion of a multi-decade bureaucrat, the friendliness of a rock, and the intellect of a fox. Anna dreaded every interaction with Eugenia. She had only attended one of Anna's Wednesday lunches, and she had scarcely said a word, though her sharp eyes seemed to observe everything.

Anna consulted Alfred for details about Eugenia. Given her longevity, Alfred was sure to have *something* of use. Unfortunately, Eugenia's bland yet combative personality had not leant itself to sharing many personal details.

Anna read through the entire record twice. The only personal information she found was two entries from 15 years earlier - gifts from the past placed there by one of Anna's predecessors.

Apparently, Montgomery's former Chief had been sitting directly behind Eugenia for a party caucus meeting in HC-5, a large basement room in the Capitol. Before starting the meeting, the then-Speaker liked to play energetic songs to get the Members pumped up. As they waited for the meeting to begin, the Chief noticed Eugenia quietly singing along to a Bon Jovi song, "Livin' on a Prayer." Even then, this display of personality had seemed far enough out of the ordinary for him to take a note and feed it to Alfred.

The other item came from just two months later. Eugenia and Montgomery's Chief had both been in a meeting in the Cannon House Office Building. During the meeting, Eugenia made a passing comment about her sister's one-year-old daughter.

Anna made a mental note of both of these minuscule tidbits. They would have to do.

She checked the House Directory and saw that Franklin's office was in 2084 Rayburn, two floors below her own office. She took her phone and a notebook and quickly descended the two flights of stairs to see Eugenia.

After introducing herself to the Staff Assistant and handing over a business card, she asked if Eugenia was available for a quick second. The Staff Assistant disappeared into Eugenia's personal office and shut the door. A long moment later, she re-emerged and asked Anna to step inside.

Anna turned on her brightest charm and smiled as she shook hands with Eugenia. A middle-aged woman of 52, Eugenia looked like she had not smiled since before Anna was born. Anna was determined to break through and find a spark of humanity inside of this grumpy shell.

"Great to see you, Eugenia! Things have really been crazy around here lately… I'd bet you're not even fazed by it, given your experience."

"These are not normal times," Eugenia said glumly. "I don't recognize these events any more than you do."

"Is this what it was like during the Trump impeachment proceedings?" Anna asked, hoping to draw some conversation out.

"That was tame compared to this," said Eugenia. "At least we still had parties then. Can I help you with something?" She tried to get right to the point, already tired of small talk.

Anna's mind raced for some way to connect to Eugenia's humanity. Assuming from her gruff demeanor that Eugenia was a bit curmudgeonly, Anna ignored her question and tried to find a way to engage.

"I just thought that you might have some words of wisdom for me. I'm tired of listening to the younger staffers complain about all of the phone calls," Anna said. "It's like they can't even hear one harsh word without breaking down in tears."

At this, Eugenia shifted forward in her chair and allowed the slightest break in her frown.

"Let me tell you, things have sure changed around here," said Eugenia. "Back when I was a Staff Assistant, we took phone calls by the dozen. People would yell and scream at me, call me names, cuss me out… I just took down their name and number and thanked them for calling. Now these kids start to cry as soon as a caller raises their voice!"

Anna was breaking through.

"People just aren't as tough anymore," Anna said. "I just put on my headphones and listen to a classic rock playlist. Reminds me of better times."

Eugenia's eyes eased slightly from their usual basset-hound-like droop. "You know what?" she asked rhetorically, "I do the same thing."

She turned to her computer and showed Anna the music streaming app running in her web browser. The current playlist was titled "1980s Rock Classics."

"Hey, that's good stuff!" Anna said. "Love the '80s. What's your favorite '80s band?"

Anna thought she detected a momentary hint of a smile at the corner of Eugenia's mouth, but it disappeared before she could be sure.

"Oh, it's hard to narrow it down to just one," said Eugenia. "I guess I'd say Van Halen and Bon Jovi are up there, though."

"You're kidding me," Anna said. "Every time I take a run, the first song on my playlist is 'Livin' on a Prayer.'"

She unlocked her cell phone and opened her music player. She tapped on "Recently Played" and showed it to Eugenia. It was the first song on the list.

"Just played it this morning getting ready for work," Anna said.

Eugenia allowed the faintest grin to escape and linger on her face in response.

I think she's softening up a little - time to engage.

"Listen, I don't want to keep you long, I just wanted to touch base since our bosses are both running for Speaker."

"It's going to be a tough week and a half," Eugenia said. "I've been here a long time, but I've never been through something like this."

"It makes me feel better to hear you say that," Anna said. "I have hardly been here at all compared to you, but I definitely haven't dealt with anything this hard. Well, my only purpose in reaching out was to say that we are looking forward to a tough but honest race. We're planning to run on our record and proposals, and we will not go negative on your boss."

"That's magnanimous of you," said Eugenia. "I wish you luck in the race."

Anna had been hoping for a reciprocal agreement from Eugenia. It didn't sound like she was going to get it.

"I appreciate that," said Anna. "No matter the outcome, please know that we'll respect the results. If we lose, we intend to fully support the winner. If we win, Willis wants to work together with all of his former opponents to make the chamber better."

"Those are noble ideals," Eugenia said. "I do appreciate you coming by. Please let me know if there's anything we can do for you."

Anna thanked her and exited Franklin's office.

All things considered, not bad. At least the ice is broken.

38

Anna went straight from Christine Franklin's ground-floor office to the fourth-floor office of Jonathan Garcia. Gus Berger, Garcia's Chief of Staff, was someone Anna had not had much success connecting with over the past couple of years.

Like many Chiefs, Gus had come into his job by virtue of serving as the successful campaign manager for Garcia's eighteenth campaign five years earlier. Now in his 41st year in Congress, Garcia was a living legend. Serving as his Chief was a prestigious post. Gus had run countless political candidate and issue campaigns back in New Mexico and was a political animal through and through.

Coming to Washington, many of the skills and traits that had made him such a successful political operative were put to good use as Garcia's Chief of Staff. But they also caused some serious shortcomings.

Gus was what Anna referred to as a "Political Chief," a title she applied to about a third of her counterparts on the House side. He had zero concern for the actual job of running the taxpayer-funded Congressional office - a role for which he was paid a hefty taxpayer-funded salary. Instead, he spent upwards of 95 percent of his time trying to get money from donors or squeeze one more vote out of the next election.

Anna had seen this far too many times. Purely political Chiefs were often toxic to the other 15 or so people who worked in the official office. They disregarded any concerns regarding constituent services, unless the particular constituents were big donors. They often completely ignored anyone who was not part of their political base. And most certainly, they tended to ignore their staff and treat them like dirt. Gus prided himself on doing all of the above. It disgusted Anna. While she certainly wanted to do her best to help her boss be successful, unlike Gus, she actually felt an obligation to serve the taxpayers who paid her salary.

After saying hello to Garcia's front office staff, she asked to see Gus. The Staff Assistant ushered her in to Gus's office where he was busily going over spreadsheets. As soon as Anna entered the room, Gus turned off his monitor. She was pretty sure he was working on whip counts for the Speaker's race.

"Hi Gus," Anna said. "Thanks for taking a second to talk - I know you're busy."

"For a gorgeous lady like you, I'm always available," Gus leered. In addition to his lack of care for his employees, he also did not spend much time treating women with respect.

Anna tried not to let the disgusting line affect her.

I have to stay focused here. If he decides he likes me, it could make a big difference in how they treat Montgomery over the next week.

"Aren't you kind?" she said, then quickly turned to business. "I know your boss has a very respectable following and is going to make a strong run for the Speakership. I just wanted to come by and make sure we spoke face-to-face before getting too deep into everything."

"It's my pleasure. We're feeling pretty strong right now. I know Montgomery and a few of the others aren't going down without a fight, though."

"I expect it to be a spirited week," Anna agreed. "I also wanted to let you know that if he wins, Montgomery is serious when he says he wants to bring in his rivals on day one to see how they can work together. We are extremely concerned about this race causing more damage to the country than we already have."

"Well that would be pretty hard to do, wouldn't it?" Gus replied. "How about this? Why don't you and I grab a drink tomorrow night and talk about our plans. I bet we could have a very good place for you and your boss in the Garcia Speakership as well."

Anna's mind raced through her options.

If I say yes, it could buy us a few more days of Garcia staying quiet on Montgomery. But it would also mean feeling like I'm selling myself for favors... Actually... no. I'd never really go through with anything with Gus. I could just have drinks with him, and if he misinterprets that as me being interested that's his problem. Then, things would get back to reality as soon as the election happens.

She looked him in the eye and said, "That sounds great to me. I am tied up tomorrow night, but how about we get together Friday after work?"

Anna could see the excitement in Gus's face as she spoke. He straightened up and leaned forward toward her.

"I'll text you Friday," he said.

Anna stood and walked toward his door. Looking over her left shoulder, she said quietly, "I can't wait." She exited, leaving him to interpret her words however he wanted.

She shut the door to his personal office and walked to the main exit.

She stopped at the Staff Assistant's desk to get a squirt of hand sanitizer before leaving Garcia's office.

~

ANNA STRUGGLED to get to sleep Wednesday night. Every time she turned over in bed, she felt like she had finally gotten to a point where her comfort and exhaustion would override her racing mind and let her drift to sleep. Then the thoughts would come rushing back in, louder each time.

Delta could tell that Anna was unhappy. She moved from her usual spot on the far side of the bed and snuggled in close to Anna's head. The caring purrs helped calm Anna's mind, but they were not enough to get her to fall asleep.

At 1:15 a.m., Anna got out of bed to rifle through her bathroom drawer. After a few moments she found an old bottle of melatonin. She quickly downed two tablets, hoping this would bring the sleep she needed.

Within minutes, she could feel the sleep hormone taking effect. Unfortunately, it did not have enough power to quiet the cacophony of thoughts in her head.

What is going to happen with this race? Garcia seems confident... and Gus! Did I really tell him I would have drinks with him Friday? Maybe I can just sneak home and get to bed early... but then he'd be pissed and would probably retaliate against Montgomery... I can't do that. Have to go through with it. Gus is such a creep... I bet Garcia is the same way. Well, according to plenty of female staffers, he sure is. What about Christine Franklin? She seems like such a nice person - maybe too nice to win a Speaker's race... and before I really thought Eugenia was awful, but she actually seems like she's just old and grumpy. Now Alber... that guy is going to be a real challenge. He's got such a squeaky-clean image, there must be something seriously wrong under the surface. With a guy like Kit as his Chief, I would bet my life on it. Ughhhhh... Kit. That snobby spoiled brat.

Eventually the thoughts trailed off and Anna drifted to sleep around 2:00. It was a very short three hours until her alarm blared at 5:00 a.m.

39

THURSDAY, JULY 27

Anna's head felt like it had been squeezed in a vise. Three hours of restless sleep was not enough to keep someone at their full cognitive function. Her stomach was also tied in knots and aching like she hadn't felt in years.

She rolled out of bed and made her way to the bathroom in search of something to help ease the pain. After shuffling old boxes and bottles of medicine around, she settled on some antacid tablets. Maybe the stomach issues were just caused by something bad she'd eaten the night before. Surely this would calm it some.

Anna chewed three tablets and returned to her bed. She curled up under the covers and scanned through her phone to check on the overnight news.

~

From: Quincy <quincy@quincyswhispers.com>
Subject: Quincy's Whispers - Thursday, July 27
Date: July 27 at 4:39 AM
To: Anna Rothwell

Quincy's Whispers

261 days since the Midterm Election

467 days until the Presidential Election

8 days until the Speaker Election

What the House is whispering about...

but doesn't want you to hear.

Good Thursday morning! This Speaker's race is really rolling now. By my count, we have at least 19 announced candidates right now. I expect this to rapidly narrow as the next week progresses. The vote will occur in only eight days, so any candidate who doesn't get traction by the end of this weekend is probably toast.

I'm hearing about lots of maneuvering going on behind the scenes. Everyone is being friendly in public, but in the proverbial smoke-filled rooms, people are sharpening their knives. It's going to get ugly by early next week, if not before.

What I'm hearing today:

Whisper 1 - Is today the day we finally see Ted Alber (I-KY) join the race? Speculation has reached a fever pitch. My Whisperers seem to believe we will see an announcement this afternoon. I don't think anyone will be surprised to see Alber enter. The real question here is who he brings with him. Whisperers seem to agree we are likely to see Alber announce a large backing of Members; possibly even a new coalition of centrists. If it materializes, this could really shift the dynamics of the race.

Whisper 2 - Whisperers in the media (yes, even they like to Whisper every now and then) tell me the major television networks plan to form a polling coalition for the Speaker's election. With the entire race being only one week long, they've decided to pool resources and form a daily tracking poll of the public. Plans are to release data on five days next week, with each release consisting of a two-night rolling poll. Calls started last night; expect the first results tomorrow.

Whisper 3 - While attention has been focused on some of the bigger-name candidates like Christine Franklin (CC-ID), Willis Montgomery (BC-MO), and Jonathan Garcia (MM-NM), I believe the more interesting candidates to keep your eye on are some of the also-rans. Not because they're dark horses who might win (I think they're delusional if they believe that), but because their meager supporters will eventually have to go somewhere else. Cobble together enough of these votes and you could have yourself a real chance at victory.

Whisper 4 - Speaking of… trying to stay on top of an accurate whip count for this race seems a little like it must have felt to cover a frontline battle in World War II. The fog of war is thick. Information is scant, biased, and often fabricated to make someone look more heroic than they were in reality. I'm hearing nonstop Whispers about horse-trading and backroom deals… I know they're happening, but I have zero idea which ones are true.

Whisper 5 - As the Speaker race grinds on, several of the candidates have begun impugning one another's honor. Some of the most vicious attacks are coming from Steven Reed (GG-WY). At 7:00 last night, his office sent around a list of alleged "financial backers" of his opponents, seeking to engender guilt by association. The list is pretty out there, including most of the bogeymen whom the Gadsden Guard have accused over the years of funding everything from the Obamacare messaging fight to the Council on Foreign Relations and the Bilderbergs. Reed's specific allegations are unlikely to gain much traction (the GGs have cried wolf enough on this kind of thing), but expect much more of this from other candidates in the next few days.

Whisper 6 - Back to that sneaky whip count… The best Whisperers' info appears to have Willis Montgomery and Christine Franklin neck-and-neck for now. They generally expect Ted Alber to take the lead immediately upon jumping in. Once the first poll is released tomorrow, Members will probably start to blow with the political winds.

Until tomorrow, I have the honor to be,

Your obedient servant,

~Quincy

Sign up at www.QuincysWhispers.com to get
every edition delivered to your inbox!
Watch for breaking Whispers on Twitter @quincyswhispers.

Hear something good?
Whisper it to me at tips@quincyswhispers.com.
All Whispers are reviewed and kept
strictly anonymous and confidential.

Even though she'd been expecting that Alber would jump in the race, the news that it would be today made her heart pound.

I'm going to have to deal with Kit now. Why couldn't his boss just stay out of this? Probably just confirms that he's been following me around the past week or two, trying to keep an eye on me... what a weirdo. Seriously, what could he possibly think he's going to get out of me that will help him? Maybe I can just keep to myself and we won't have to interact directly. Bleh... I just want this to be over...

Delta seemed to notice a change in Anna's emotional state. She began to purr gently and rub against Anna's left cheek.

"Thanks, Delt. I'm fine. I just wish I didn't have to deal with some of these people at work."

Delta stopped rubbing against Anna's head and took a step back. She plopped down on her pillow and looked at Anna inquisitively.

"Who? Like this guy Kit. He is pretty much the epitome of everything that's wrong with Washington. Born with a silver spoon in his mouth, arrogant, entitled, handsome…"

A low rumble came from the pillow next to her.

"No, I can't stand him. And now I'll have to put up with his BS for at least the next week. I swear, if he tries to hook up with me… well, he'll never want to try it again."

Anna gathered all the motivation she could find and dragged herself out of bed.

Back to the grind.

40

The moment Montgomery stepped into the office, he began tossing tasks at Anna. He was a bundle of energy and clearly had plenty on his mind. Throughout all of the ups and downs of the past few days, he never stopped working. When he had told Anna that he had been preparing for this opportunity most of his political career and was not going to let it go to waste she had almost not believed him. But from the way he had acted since The Collapse, he meant it.

What Anna couldn't understand is how Montgomery maintained his energy and health through the countless hours he was putting in. It seemed like the harder she worked and more disheveled she looked, the stronger and more polished Montgomery became.

"I'm going to head over to Garcia's office in a few minutes to have a quick talk with him about the race," he said. "Could you check with Alfred and get me the most important details you can find? Garcia's a tough guy, so I had better come prepared."

"Yeah, tough guy is one way to put it," Anna said. "Seems more like an arrogant ass to me."

"Probably more accurate," Montgomery acknowledged. "Get me

anything useful - either positive or negative. I want to know every rumor that's been floating around about him, no matter where it comes from."

"Of course. I'll see what I can find."

A few minutes later, Anna delivered a one-pager to Montgomery highlighting the family details and some positive attributes of Garcia, as well as a long list of negative rumors. Finding positive attributes for a thrice-divorced serial philanderer who had spent over four decades in Congress was not exactly the easiest task she'd ever had, but he was a charismatic guy who had a big following. The rumor list was extensive and well-known. Garcia was a big personality and made waves wherever he went.

Montgomery thanked Anna for the information and started to head out the door. He stopped short and tossed one more item to Anna before leaving.

"I'm going to try and see Christine Franklin after I get back. Could you get me info on her too? Thanks!"

Montgomery was out the door before Anna could respond.

"Sure, no problem," she said quietly to herself after the door closed behind Montgomery. She returned to her desk and got to work.

After compiling a briefing on Franklin, Anna continued to trudge through her list of Chiefs and systematically follow up with them. Her goal was to check in every other day with each office that had committed to voting for Montgomery. Chiefs in offices that were still on the fence received a touch every single day. Anna was determined that no one would outwork her.

The downside was that all of this texting, calling, and emailing was monotonous and mind-numbing. By the end of each day she felt drained of all energy. Nonetheless, she continued to roll through the list like a machine. She kept telling herself there was only one more week until the election… and hopefully the mental burnout would be worth it when Montgomery became the most powerful man in Congress.

~

MONTGOMERY ENTERED Garcia's fourth-floor office and asked if he was available. The Staff Assistant quickly ushered him in to Garcia's personal office. The office was enormous - in a place where all real estate is determined by years of service, decades of seniority gets you a massive space.

When Montgomery entered, Jonathan Garcia was sitting at his large desk with the huge wall of windows behind him. He was deeply engrossed in writing something on a legal pad. Garcia did not even acknowledge that anyone had entered his office until Montgomery finally cleared his throat and spoke. "Good morning, Jonathan, thanks for taking the time to see me."

Garcia looked up from his notes and briefly acknowledged Montgomery. "Hi, Willis. What can I do for you today?" He returned to his work and kept writing, disregarding his guest.

Montgomery sat down in a chair directly in front of the desk. "I just came by to congratulate you on entering the Speaker race. It's going to be one for the ages, don't you think?"

Garcia didn't take his eyes off his notepad. He gruffly made a "harumph" noise in response.

This reaction was not atypical from Garcia. He had always been tough to hold a conversation with. Montgomery tried again to break through, this time with an item from Garcia's personal life.

"I bet Diana can't wait for this to settle down so you can spend some more time back home," Montgomery said. Garcia's fourth wife was a stunner, but he doubted Garcia was really anxious to get home to her.

"Mhm," Garcia replied. He was clearly not moved.

Montgomery decided to cut the small talk and get straight to it. "I wanted to let you know that I plan to run an above-board race. I'm not going to be taking any cheap shots at you or our other opponents. I say, 'may the best man win,' and it should be settled based on our actual qualifications, not mudslinging."

Garcia again did not respond. He continued to write.

Montgomery made one more effort. "Also, if I am fortunate enough to win the Speakership, I'd like to get together with all of the other candidates on day one to see how we can work together to move this chamber and our country forward. The skills and following you have are something that should be brought into the fold, and the same goes for many of the other very talented folks who are running as well."

At this, Garcia finally put down his pen and looked up at Montgomery.

"Willis, I do not intend to lose this race. In fact, I think the chances of you winning this race are incredibly low. *When* I become Speaker, don't expect me to come calling for your advice." Garcia returned to his pen and continued writing.

Montgomery was shocked at the frankness with which Garcia spoke. He did not know how to respond. Instead of continuing to sit in stunned silence, he decided to stand up and conclude the meeting.

"I appreciate your candor, Jonathan. I hope that you turn out to be incorrect. If you do, I will still be reaching out to you after my victory."

Garcia let loose an arrogant laugh without looking up from his notepad. He did not speak another word as Montgomery left his office. As he exited to the main hallway, Montgomery's face was calm and collected, not betraying a trace of what had just transpired inside.

MONTGOMERY PULLED out his phone and texted Anna.

> **WM**: Do you have the info on Franklin yet
>
> **AR**: Just finished it up!
>
> **WM**: Can you text it to me
>
> **AR**: Sure - just a second.

The PDF Anna sent contained all of the relevant information Alfred had accumulated about Christine Franklin over the years. She was generally known as such a nice, friendly Member, he knew it would be full of positives.

Montgomery scanned through the information and committed a few bits to memory, then looked up Franklin's name on the House Directory plastered to the wall near the elevator. He pressed the down button and rode to the ground floor.

He walked to Christine Franklin's office and asked the Scheduler if he could have a moment with her. Franklin came to the door herself and threw it open.

"I knew that was your voice I heard out there! Come on in and make yourself comfortable. Can I get you something to drink?"

The contrast from his previous meeting was striking.

"Thank you, Christine, but I am just fine. I don't need to take too much of your time. I just wanted to come by and congratulate you on getting into the race. I know it's not a decision you took lightly - I know I didn't myself."

"You have always been such a gentleman," Franklin said. "Come in and have a seat."

Montgomery lowered his large frame into a comfortable chair as Franklin found an opposing spot on her couch. He looked around the room and admired her decor. The photos and memorabilia on the walls were largely family-oriented, with many pictures of Franklin with her husband and children on vacation outdoors. It looked like they were very into visiting national parks as a family. Montgomery took mental note of these facts.

Franklin was cheerful as she spoke. "I truly am honored to have you just drop by to visit. You are a good man."

"And you are a wonderful woman," said Montgomery. "We all need to see a few friendlier faces these days. Speaking of which, how's Tom doing? I'm sure he's been missing having you home.

"Oh, you know Tom," replied Franklin. "He never wants to leave Idaho. All summer long he's out on the ranch fixing fence and who knows what else. We only get so much snow-free time to work on things up home!"

"I've always loved working outdoors," Montgomery said with a smile. "Frankly I'm pretty jealous of Tom right about now!"

Franklin laughed and agreed. "Just about anywhere seems better than the Hill these days."

Montgomery picked up this turn in the conversation. "That's for sure," he said. "How are you feeling about things with the Speaker race so far?"

Franklin looked to her left as she thought, then offered her thoughts. "I expect this race to be quite the challenge. So many good people are already in it - yourself included. I just hope that if I do not win, someone outstanding like you is our next Speaker. We may only have one more chance to turn this place around, and we had better get it right."

"You are far too kind," Montgomery replied. "I can honestly say the same in return. However, I do want you to know that if I am able to come out on top, I plan to bring together all of my former opponents on the first day of my Speakership. We will find ways to work together as a team. There is too much talent and potential for leadership in this group to let it go to waste. I don't hold grudges, and I hope you will not either."

"Oh, Willis, you know me well enough to have no doubt I will fully support you if you win. And I think your idea of bringing everyone together on the first day is brilliant. If I am fortunate enough to win this race myself, I will do the same and will be sure to make you a top lieutenant in my Speakership."

"I appreciate that. I think we have to all be in this together for the good of the country. Best of luck to you, and please let me know if you need anything from me."

Montgomery stood to leave the room. Franklin rose as well and walked him to the door.

"Thanks for coming by, Willis," she said. "And best of luck to you as well."

The door closed behind Montgomery as he exited the foyer and entered the main hallway. His face was sullen as he slowly walked to the elevator to return to his office.

41

While Montgomery was still meeting with Congresswoman Franklin, Anna left the office early for lunch. Typically, she exited her office at 11:45 on the dot to get a jump on the lunch crowd. Something just wasn't feeling right today, though. At 11:27 she picked up her wallet and phone and headed out. Lily gave her a confused look as she passed through the foyer but did not say anything. The staff was so used to Anna's clockwork schedule that any deviation made them curious, but they knew better than to ask her about anything personal.

Ever since Montgomery had told Anna about his plans to run for Speaker, she could feel a growing tightness in her chest. She hadn't paid much attention the first few days, assuming it was just a symptom of exhaustion. Today the sensation was multiplied. She struggled to come to grips with it as she walked towards the Rayburn exit.

What's the problem? Being in the middle of the action is exciting and what I've always dreamed of, but can my body handle it? Is it my mind? I feel like I can't focus on my work... So much I need to do, but I just can't bear down and do it.

Self-doubt was starting to eat away at Anna. Her old fear that every one of her counterparts was more experienced, smarter, and sharper than her had started to creep back into her thoughts. Everything was taking too long and her to-do list was growing by the day. The lack of sleep was killing her. She was not turning as many heads as usual when she walked down the hallways.

This is my chance! Why can't I get it in gear and just do the work?

The muscles in her face were now perpetually tight and aching; her shoulders were full of knots. She was struggling to stay a step ahead of what others were doing in this Speaker race and was starting to feel things slip. More than anything, she just wanted it all to slow down so she could have room to breathe and relax - to feel caught up.

Instead of her daily trip to the Rayburn salad bar, Anna decided she could use something more indulgent. She left through the Rayburn Horseshoe entrance and walked down Independence Avenue toward Pennsylvania Avenue. She veered southeast on Pennsylvania and walked two more blocks, then arrived at her favorite lunch spot.

~

THE LOCAL PIZZA SHOP WE, the Pizza had been around for several years before Anna arrived in D.C. She tried not to go too often, but when she was feeling down, the temptation was just too much. She joined the short line and read through the mid-day news updates as she waited to order.

"Hey Anna," said a male voice over her shoulder.

She closed her eyes and cursed under her breath. Kit again.

Seriously? Why does he have to keep showing up?

She turned around with dread, summoning up the most irritated facial expression she could muster.

"Hi," she said dismissively, then faced the register again.

"Are you ok? You look like something's off," said Kit.

"Have you been following me or something?" Anna asked with disgust.

Kit's ears turned red at the accusation and his smile turned into anger. "What the hell are you talking about?" he said, fury rising in his voice.

She turned to face him again. "We've never once crossed paths outside of work before, and now I've just mysteriously bumped into you what, like three or four times in a week? What a coincidence."

"Look, I don't know what's going on with you, but I just came to get some pizza. I'm not stalking you. Don't flatter yourself."

Kit seemed to have an instinct for pushing Anna's buttons. Her face turned red as she prepared to unleash a tirade in response. Other patrons in line for pizza turned to watch the escalating argument. Even the employees had stopped their work to watch.

"Excuse me? I'm not the one who just keeps randomly appearing behind you all over the place. And if you *are* somehow finding me on purpose, knock it off. If your boss wants to be Speaker, how about you win it by getting more votes, not tailing your opponents and their staff for whatever reason."

Kit gave Anna a disgusted look. "Whatever your problem is, you need to get back to reality," he said. "You're losing your mind."

Anna had heard enough. She gave him her most disdainful look and said, "Excuse me," as she passed by him and headed out the door.

She turned right and walked with rage for a block before slowing down. She glanced over her shoulder to double-check that Kit had not followed her. When she was sure he had not, she made another quick right into a small park. She found a secluded bench behind a row of bushes, sat down, and cried.

~

ANNA LET her tears flow for a good five minutes before she began to compose herself. She struggled to make sense of it all.

What is my problem? All the guy did was stand there to get pizza... what is so upsetting about that? Would he really be stalking me? Following me around? And if he is, why? What on Earth would he gain from that? I don't understand what's wrong with me... crying in public? In the middle of the work day? I've lost control. I can't do this.

The display was completely out of character for Anna. She had spent the past decade-and-a-half steeling herself against all emotions, becoming stoically unbreakable. Through her first four years on the Hill, she had never once cried - not a single tear, not a single time.

It couldn't just be the lack of sleep - could it? Since high school, mental toughness had been her proudest possession - why was it betraying her now, when she needed it most? No one else was going to feel sorry for her. If she couldn't toughen up and power through this, the other Chiefs would just run her over.

Eight days. Only eight more days of this and it will be over. A week from tomorrow - just push through and make it happen.

She sniffed and wiped away her lingering tears.

A little more sleep and better eating habits. That's all it will take. Eight days. It just feels like something's not right with Kit... in all these years he's barely said two words to me, and now all of a sudden, he keeps popping up wherever I go, trying to strike up conversations... what IS the story with him?

Anna rose from the bench and gathered herself. She put on her sunglasses to hide her red eyes, then crossed the street and dropped into the corner drugstore to grab some quick snacks to tide her over until dinnertime. She needed to get her mind off of her emotions.

Anna grabbed a bag of potato chips and a candy bar, then made her way to the checkout. She accidentally bumped into a middle-aged man wearing a baseball cap as she exited the candy aisle. The man seemed startled and quickly apologized, but Anna was so tired and lost in her own thoughts that she didn't even acknowledge him. He subconsciously covered his left cheek with his hand as he turned and headed for the candy. Anna bought her snacks and ate them as she walked back to the office, taking a back street to avoid bumping into any acquaintances.

42

Anna spent the next two hours continuing the grind of contacting Chiefs from across Congress. She checked in on them to see how they were doing personally, asked for insight into how their bosses were leaning in the Speaker race, and took notes about their potential support.

Around 3:00, while working through her contacts, she glanced up at the television. Anna habitually cycled through the cable news channels throughout the day, trying to get a feel for what all sides were saying. At the moment the TV was still on Fox News Channel.

As usual, the chyron at the bottom of the screen was blaring a "breaking news alert." Like the boy who cried wolf, these alerts had long ago lost their power. Still, Anna looked long enough to see what this latest story was.

The live feed showed an empty podium in front of a large set of white marble steps. Anna instantly recognized the background as the east front of the Capitol, just outside the House chamber. The live shot couldn't have been happening more than 1,000 feet from her desk. She turned up the volume to learn more about what was going on.

The afternoon anchor said that they were waiting on Congressman Ted Alber to speak any minute. He was expected to announce his candidacy for Speaker of the House.

Anna leapt from her chair and knocked on the passageway door to Montgomery's office.

"Come in," he called from his desk.

She opened the door a crack and poked her head inside.

"Sorry to bother you, but you might want to turn on the TV. Alber is about to announce."

Montgomery looked surprised. He looked through his desk drawer and found the remote, then brought his TV to life. Anna stepped inside his office and turned a chair to face the screen. Alber had stepped to the podium and was completing his preliminary niceties.

"This institution has stood for over 200 years as a beacon of light to the world. The petty disagreements and bickering that have characterized it over the past few years must stop now. It is time that we got the House in order.

"Since my first day in this historic chamber, I have stood firm for what is right and have never shied away from principled stands. I believe my colleagues know that, as do the American people. This is why I have decided to announce my candidacy for Speaker of the House."

While cameras clicked loudly, the press corps began yelling questions at Alber. Rather than answer them, he raised his hands to quiet the reporters.

"We're not done yet! I have more to announce."

The reporters quieted and returned pens to notepads.

"To this point I have remained independent of any faction. Many Members have approached me and asked me to consider their groups, and I greatly appreciate their interest in having me be part of their movements. However, I have not felt as though any of them truly stand for the thing our country needs most at this critical hour. Unity.

"Our country needs its elected officials to put factions and arguments aside. Our country needs us to do what is right, not what helps Congress. Our country needs us to unify behind our common interests, not special interests. Today I am announcing the formation of a group that will stand for these principles. A group that will work together and stop the petty infighting.

"This group will be known as the Unity Party. I am proud to be a founding Member. My staff will be providing you with a list of the other 44 founding Members of our Party, each of whom has graciously endorsed my candidacy for Speaker of the House.

"Together we can restore unity to the House and to our country. The Unity Party will lift the House back UP together!"

A small crowd of staffers and passers-by had stopped to witness the press conference. As Alber concluded his remarks, the crowd let out a cheer.

Anna was impressed with Alber's performance.

He really knows how to work a crowd. He's going to be a real challenge to beat.

~

AS THE REPORTERS again yelled questions toward Alber, Anna and Montgomery analyzed the situation.

"So, what do you think?" Montgomery asked.

"He is going to be the hardest to beat, that's what I think," Anna replied.

"The kid can talk, that's for sure."

"Yeah, and he seems so genuine and strait-laced."

"He's no Boy Scout," said Montgomery. "I can guarantee you he has something in his past that is not as good as it seems."

"This group looks like it's full of pretty well-respected Members," Anna said. She had just received a list from Alber's office via email. She showed it to Montgomery, who skimmed through the names.

"Sure is," he said. "These guys are going to need some special attention over the next week." Montgomery had an intense look on his face. He was dialed in.

"How have things been coming on your end?" Anna asked. It had been a couple of days since Montgomery had even updated her on his progress. She was starting to feel like there was something he didn't want to tell her.

"Well, I've been having less luck with the Gadsden Guard and Fiscal Front than I expected," Montgomery said. "The GGs are just stubborn as mules and don't want to even think about their guy not winning. Even though Steven Reed doesn't stand a snowball's chance in hell of being Speaker, they won't talk to me about second choices."

"What about the Fiscal Front guys?" Anna asked. "Aren't they a little more reasonable?"

"Yeah, in some ways," Montgomery replied. "But they're such risk-averse numbers geeks, they want to see you completely lay out your path to victory before they commit. Right now, they say mine is too speculative."

"Well that's frustrating," Anna said. "Maybe they'll start to come around once we close in on next Friday."

"I guess we'll see," said Montgomery. "For now, I think it's time we focus on learning more about our competition for Speaker," he said. "I'd like you to take the lead on oppo research. We have to learn everything about these guys we possibly can."

"Alright..." Anna said hesitantly. "What do you need?"

"I want to have the thickest file on each opponent that anyone's ever seen. We only have one shot at this and just a week to make it happen. I can trust you to be aggressive, right?"

"You know you can," Anna replied with more certainty than she felt.

I've never been a muckraker before... And besides, what are we doing digging up dirt anyway? I thought he had promised everyone that he would run a fair campaign.

"Good," said Montgomery. "You absolutely *must* work under the radar, too. No one can be able to trace your work back to me. You do know how to be discreet, don't you?"

"Of course," she said without thinking.

"Perfect," said Montgomery. "This is the most important job I can delegate for this race. I know I can trust you to do it well and keep it quiet. I want you to find out *everything* about these people. If they have ever had a girlfriend, a boyfriend, a business venture that went bad, extra money showing up unexpectedly - anything - I want to know about it. Find out who is most important to them, who in their family they're closest to, what they do with their free time. Anything you can imagine that tugs on their heartstrings, figure it out."

She tried to imagine how she could possibly handle this massive request. It would take a full team of people a month to do the job well. She probably had four days to get as much as possible and would be working alone. True to form, though, she automatically agreed to take on the work.

"Ok," said Anna. "I can do it."

"I know you can, Anna. You're the brightest Chief on the Hill. The stuff you find is what will launch us to victory a week from today."

Normally Anna would bask in this kind of praise, but her heart sank as the real meaning of Montgomery's directive finally clicked.

Oppo research will launch us to victory? But what about his promises to run on the merits? He's been pledging to everyone that he won't go negative... but what else would you do with oppo research?

She began to speak tentatively. "Um… okay. I just need to ask… didn't you say we're not going to do any negative campaigning?"

Montgomery laughed. "Of course we won't, Anna. I plan to win on my own merits. But for those who might be having trouble seeing why our merits are better than our opponents', some of our friends may want to be sure they are aware of the differences."

Anna was silent.

This just doesn't feel right. A clean campaign is exciting, but this is underhanded. Then again, there's some truth to what he's saying... people need to know what they're getting. Plus, it wouldn't be fair for our opponents to have carte blanche to smear us...

Montgomery sensed her hesitation and spoke to her gently. "Anna. None of this will be dishonest or untrue. Our friends wouldn't put anything out that is made up. They just want to know if there are any clear distinctions to draw between our record and theirs. I'm going to completely focus on my own accomplishments."

The distinction seemed very gray. Anna still didn't respond. Montgomery allowed her to sit in silence as she considered his explanation. Finally, Anna spoke.

"Do you think we can at least narrow it down to a few top candidates? That would make it a whole lot easier."

Montgomery was already there. "I still think the only ones we really need to worry about are Franklin, Garcia, and Alber. They each have serious national recognition and plenty of Members who will be on their teams."

"Okay," Anna said. "I think I can handle that."

"I know this will take a lot of work," Montgomery added. "I'd like Kyle to help out. You probably won't be able to finish it alone, and he is completely trustworthy."

This hit Anna like a punch in the gut.

He doesn't think I can handle it myself? Maybe he could tell I was crying at lunch... why can't I control my emotions? This will be really sensitive information... it'd be much better if I'm the only one working on it to make sure it doesn't get leaked.

"I don't think that's necessary," Anna said. "I can take care of it. We need complete secrecy on this project anyway."

"Anna, I appreciate your tenacity, but time is too short. You need help to do this right. Kyle has a Top-Secret clearance and was an Air Force intelligence officer for a decade before coming here. I'm pretty sure we can trust him."

This went against all of Anna's instincts. She loved working with Kyle, but she was skeptical of trusting *anyone,* especially with this particular job.

She decided to plainly lay out her feelings on the matter and leave the decision up to Montgomery.

"I know I can handle it myself. I could keep absolute secrecy and complete the job. But your name's on the door - if you tell me to work with Kyle, I'll do it."

"If we had more time, I would let it stay fully in your hands," he said. "It's not about believing in you or trusting you - I do both completely. I want you and Kyle to split this work up and get it done ASAP. Keep me up to date - let me know when you find out anything that might be useful."

Anna nodded in tacit agreement as Montgomery exited to his personal office.

43

She picked up her office phone and dialed Kyle's extension. "Hey, could you come here?" she asked.

"Be there in a sec."

Kyle entered Anna's office an instant later. She explained the situation to him. He didn't seem any more excited about it than she was.

"Do you *really* want to get in the middle of this kind of thing?" he asked.

Anna thought for a few moments. She was definitely struggling with Montgomery's orders.

This whole time he's been talking about bringing the House back to its former high-minded ideals... digging dirt is anything but high-minded.

"I really don't like it either," she admitted. "I just don't understand. He even said that if we found something, he wouldn't use it... but some of our 'friends' might."

"I don't like the sound of that," said Kyle. "Did he mention what 'friends' he was talking about?"

"No. Nothing more than that. I mean, he *did* say he'll still run his entire campaign on the merits. He won't attack his opponents."

"Anna. Come on. Does it actually make it *better* if we feed it to some shady 'friend' than if Montgomery says it himself?"

"I don't know. We wouldn't be making anything up. If we did find something truly bad, wouldn't it be best for everyone if it came out before the election so they knew who they were voting for?"

They both sat silently and thought it over. Kyle kept fidgeting and tapping his foot. Finally, he broke the silence.

"How on Earth are we supposed to keep our fingerprints off of this? You don't exactly blend into a crowd, and the only intel work I've done is behind a computer!"

"I don't know, Kyle. I'm going to be figuring this out right along with you."

"Alright, Anna. Look. The boss told us to do this so I'm going to do it. But to be honest, I don't feel good about it."

"I understand. If we start getting into dangerous territory, we need to promise each other we'll stop."

"I can live with that," Kyle said.

"Montgomery wants both of us on the case so we can get it turned around fast. We need to be able to trust you to never breathe a word of this to *anyone*," said Anna.

"That's a directive I'm very used to," Kyle said.

"Not a soul. Montgomery's name *cannot* be associated with anything we do."

"Got it."

Anna rose from her chair and walked across the office. She picked up a black dry erase marker and wrote on her large whiteboard.

Alber
Garcia
Franklin

"These are our three targets. Montgomery and I agree that Alber is the biggest threat. I'm going to focus fully on him. Garcia should be easy, so I need you to take on him and Franklin. Can you do that?"

"You're the boss," Kyle said with a smile.

Kyle's involvement was already starting to grow on Anna.

I like these ex-military guys. They'll do anything you tell them to, and they'll do it right.

"Great," she said. "Let's start off by figuring out who their opponents were in all of their past elections. Track them down and get their oppo file. Do whatever it takes. Once we have all of that, we'll see where it leads us."

"What about money? It's probably going to take some cash to make some of this happen."

Sounds like working in military intelligence also helped him learn how politics and government really *work.*

"If you need money, just let me know," she said. "I'll take care of it."

"That's all I need to hear… all I *want* to hear," Kyle said with a sly grin.

Even this joke made Anna feel a bit uneasy.

She was all business in her response. "Let's get moving. We don't have a lot of time."

"This all basically has to be done in a week, right?" Kyle asked. He was struggling to process the timeline. This was not going to be an easy assignment.

"Actually, more like half that time. The end of next week will be too late to make a difference. Can you do it, or do I need to find someone else?" Anna asked tersely.

Kyle snapped his attention to her and straightened up. "Yes ma'am, I can do it," he replied with an air of military discipline.

"Good. Don't let me down."

Kyle left Anna's office and closed the door. Anna reached inside her top desk drawer and unwrapped two antacid tablets.

44

Anna played some white noise through her computer to help her block out the office's buzz of activity. All of the phone calls, office conversations, and closing doors made it far too easy to get distracted.

Time to focus. We need this. I can't let our opponents go unchecked. If we lose because I didn't pull my weight, I'll never forgive myself.

What's the best place to start? No one's riding in on a white horse to hand over a video of a literal smoking gun. It's up to me. Focus.

She tried to think through the most-likely places she would find good dirt on Alber.

He's been so careful with his image up here, I doubt I'll find much unless I dive deeper into his past... probably needs to be stuff from before he got elected. If I do anything at all today, I have to track down the consultants and campaign managers for Alber's old political opponents. There's got to be something in their oppo files that's worthwhile. I'm sure there's at least one skeleton in his closet.

Alber had run successfully for Congress from his western Kentucky district three times. As with most Members, his first election was hotly contested, but his reelection bids were basically cakewalks. As was also fairly common, his opponent in both reelections was the same third-tier candidate - a nobody who just wanted to be able to tell his buddies he had run for Congress.

Anna ruminated on Alber's electoral history.

If there's going to be anything useful in opposition research files, it would probably come from his first campaign. Low-grade opponents like his re-elect usually don't even know enough to do oppo research, and they sure don't have the money to pay for quality work. I can probably just forget about them and home in on the first election. That'll save time.

She turned her focus to Alber's first race. After a few minutes of Googling, she came up with a batch of articles from early November, five years earlier.

Alber Defeats White by Five Points - *Paducah Sun*

White Comes Up Short in Battle for Former Davis Seat - *Kentucky New Era*

White No Match for Alber in Race for Congress - *Henderson Gleaner*

Alber Headed to Congress After Defeating White - *Bowling Green Daily News*

She pulled up the four articles and expanded them across her two computer monitors so she could review them all side-by-side. The article in the Gleaner was short and to-the-point. It laid out the facts of the election without much commentary:

"White No Match for Alber in Race for Congress"

Henderson Gleaner

By Mark Stillwell, staff writer

PADUCAH, Ky. — Last night, Paducah accountant and political newcomer Theodore (Ted) Alber defeated longtime Hopkinsville businessman Randall (Randy) White in the race to replace retiring Congressman Harlan Davis. With 99 percent of precincts reporting, Alber had received just over 158,000 votes to White's 142,000.

According to Alber's campaign manager, White called Alber around 10:30 p.m. to concede the race. The 52-47 percent victory places the tally outside the margin required for a recount. Alber addressed supporters at the historic 1857 Hotel in downtown Paducah just before 11:00 p.m. to thank them for their efforts and declare victory.

Pending formal certification of the results, Alber will be sworn into office on January 3 in Washington, D.C. The 39-year-old campaigned as a centrist who plans to work across the aisle once in office. His top legislative priorities are responsible budgeting, strengthening the social safety net, and providing federal assistance to impoverished regions.

About as milquetoast as it gets. Promising a balanced budget and federal investment to a rural, conservative, poor district is nothing remarkable. What about White's hometown paper... maybe they had something more interesting to say.

She enlarged the window containing the next article.

"White Comes Up Short in Battle for Former Davis Seat"

Kentucky New Era

By Susan Bennett, staff writer

HOPKINSVILLE, Ky. — Local businessman Randall White conceded defeat to Paducah accountant Ted Alber in last night's race to replace retiring Congressman Harlan Davis. At press time, Alber had collected approximately 52.5 percent of the vote to White's 47.1 percent.

White thanked about 400 of his supporters at The Bruce convention center at 10:30 last night. He informed them that he had just spoken to Alber and conceded the race.

After a bruising primary in which Alber defeated 10 other candidates and White emerged victorious from a pack of seven, the general election was relatively absent of fireworks. Although the formal messaging of both campaigns was above-board, several longtime local political activists we spoke with believe Alber's campaign was not as clean as it appeared.

"We had several incidents where Randy's campaign signs disappeared overnight," said Verda Johnson. "We never were able to capture it on video, but everybody knows it was Ted Alber's cronies who did it." Ms. Johnson was a volunteer on the White campaign.

Another White campaign volunteer, Bill Singletary, had similar experiences. "Yeah, I heard about the signs being stolen and vandalized," he said. "His people were also going around spreading rumors about Randy that I know personally were not true. As far as I'm concerned, Ted Alber would do anything to win - and he did just that."

Not everyone in Hopkinsville agreed, however. Longtime resident Gina Thomas said, "I met Mr. Alber twice this fall and talked with his campaign staff several times. They were all as nice as can be and never said a single bad word about Randy. I think he won it fair and square."

Local White supporters may not like the outcome, but it appears Ted Alber will be Hopkinsville's new Congressman come January 3.

Anna rolled her eyes.

Stolen yard signs is the best dirt they have? That's the kind of amateur BS college kids do, not actual Congressional candidates. Literally EVERY losing campaign has volunteers complaining about signs being torn down. And if Alber's campaign wasn't trying to start rumors about White, they weren't doing their job. This is useless. I do wonder about that primary, though... an 11-way race has to get dirty. Better find out more about that.

After reviewing Alber's primary opponents' Federal Election Commission reports, Anna was able to create a list of consultants and vendors who had been involved in the losing efforts. Just from looking at the FEC reports, Anna could tell that at least seven of the 10 opponents were not serious threats. The other three, however, knew what they were doing.

She compared her list of contenders to the primary election vote tallies and found that they matched up perfectly. The only candidates that drew serious votes were the ones with professional operations.

Anna dug and dug through seemingly endless reports with little to show for it. FEC reports are often filled out in a way that is deliberately vague, and this was no exception. It was hard to tell exactly who had done what.

Every few minutes Anna would realize her eyes had glazed over, forcing her to backtrack and pick up where her brain had left off. She felt like she was getting nowhere.

AFTER SIX HOURS of fruitless research, Anna was too frustrated to go on. She turned off her computer and put away the papers she had been going through, then packed up her bag and walked to Kyle's workstation.

"I think I'm ready to call it a night," Anna said.

Kyle stretched both hands as far over his head as they would go, then let out a big yawn. "Fine by me. This stuff is draining. You find anything worthwhile?"

"Eh, not really," Anna said, her disappointment showing. "Alber just doesn't seem to have much of a negative history. Well, at least not so far. I'm sure I'll find something. How about you? Any good news on your end?"

"I don't know. Franklin just seems like a sweet old grandmother," Kyle said. "I have a hard time seeing how she has anything serious in her closet. She's the harder of the two."

"Yeah, I feel like we're in the same boat on Alber and Franklin. How about Garcia?"

Kyle laughed. "The problem with Garcia will be trying to decide which scandals to focus on. Honestly, is there anyone who he *hasn't* tried to hook up with?"

Anna chuckled at this. "Yeah, true. That's a problem too, though. Everyone already knows he's a scumbag… what would we possibly uncover that would surprise anyone?"

This was an angle Kyle had not thought through. "That's a really good point. I guess I've kind of been thinking if I could just find actual proof of an affair or inappropriate relationship with a staffer, it would take him down."

"That's already baked into the cake," said Anna. "It would have to be a legit bombshell to really get anyone's attention."

Kyle nodded in agreement. "I'd better start doing some serious digging."

"Tomorrow," Anna said firmly. "You and I both need to get some sleep. And I could use a ride, if you don't mind."

"Sure thing," Kyle said. "I think my brain's fried anyway. We'll hit it hard here in a few hours."

KYLE DROPPED Anna in front of her building just before 10:00 p.m. She climbed the creaky stairs and slowly unlocked her apartment door. As always, Delta was there to greet her with a chorus of meows.

Anna entered and collapsed onto her bed. She stared at the ceiling as the emotional roller-coaster of a day replayed in her mind.

What in the hell was I doing at lunch? As if Kit didn't already think I was enough of a psycho... then I yell at him and burst into tears just because he happens to be in line behind me for pizza. And why? And then I start second-guessing my boss, the one person whose integrity I know I can trust in this sleazy town, just because he asked me to do something that everyone else is probably already doing anyways. What is making me this way? I can't even tell Delta. I can't take the judgment.

Delta snuggled up next to Anna as she drifted off to sleep. No matter what Anna had done, Delta was always there for her.

45

FRIDAY, JULY 28

The alarm went off at 5:00 a.m. Friday, as usual. Four years of this routine, and only the past few weeks had it started to feel like a pain. Anna used to love waking up early; getting a jump-start on the day, running on the National Mall, clearing her mind for work... but she hadn't exercised once since The Collapse. There was no such thing as getting a jump-start on the day anymore; the volume of work was so enormous, getting ahead of it was impossible. She couldn't even remember the last time her mind had felt clear.

Anna laid in bed next to Delta for another 10 minutes while she tried to summon her strength to rise. Dawn wouldn't come for another half hour, and the darkness made it feel like she had woken up in the middle of the night.

Rather than get out of bed, Anna started checking her phone for the overnight news updates. This was a category of effort she liked to think of as "productive procrastination."

~

From: Quincy <quincy@quincyswhispers.com>
Subject: Quincy's Whispers - Friday, July 28
Date: July 28 at 4:22 AM
To: Anna Rothwell

Quincy's Whispers
262 days since the Midterm Election
466 days until the Presidential Election
7 days until the Speaker Election
What the House is whispering about...
but doesn't want you to hear.

Good Friday morning! Everyone's biggest outstanding question has now been answered. With Ted Alber (UP-KY) joining the race - and bringing a new party along for the ride - all of the potential heavyweights are now accounted for. Alber has a wide following from his ubiquitous television appearances. His kind personality and charming good looks have made him a bit of a pseudo-celebrity across the land... or as close as a politician can be to such a thing.

What this means: the pedal will be to the metal over the weekend. I doubt you'll be able to turn on a television between now and Monday without seeing at least one candidate's face plastered across it. Come to think of it, I'll extend that to next Friday. It's a sprint to the finish!

What I'm hearing today:

Whisper 1 - Today's the day we finally get a taste of what the general public thinks of all of this. Results of the Consortium Poll (scooped right here yesterday morning) will be simultaneously released at 10:05 a.m. on ABC, NBC, CBS, Fox, and CNN. I won't even try to guess what the results will say. Keep in mind, this is a poll of the general public, not the Members of Congress who will cast the votes. If a wide disparity emerges between the two, we could be in for even more fireworks.

Whisper 2 - Ted Alber's announcement of the Unity Party is making waves through the political landscape beyond the Speaker's race. One Whisperer yesterday evening had this insightful observation: "No matter what happens with Alber in the Speaker's race, the Unity Party will be a powerhouse in coming legislative fights. This big a group of centrists could turn into the House's kingmakers, but only if they can stick together and keep it civil." Completely agree.

Whisper 3 - Yesterday I heard from several trusted Whisperers that Christine Franklin (CC-ID) was making significant inroads with Members of the Americans for Social Justice (ASJ) and the Watchdogs. Her following continues to grow. My armchair analysis is that Members are enticed by her pleasant demeanor and kind approach. They've had it with the fighting. Come to think of it, Ted Alber, who many see as the frontrunner in the race, has pretty much all the same characteristics. Perhaps the public really *is* looking for a uniter for once.

Whisper 4 - Alert readers will remember our previous reports on July 21 and 24 about Saratoga, involving a Speaker candidate's ugly sex scandal rumors. As much as I'd hate this to be true, it's starting to sound more and more plausible that there's fire beneath this rumor's smoke. Hold onto your seats, ladies and gentlemen. There's a good chance this isn't going away.

Whisper 5 - Financial markets are still roiling and probably will be at least until the Speaker vote is behind us. The VIX (a measure of stock market volatility) spiked above 93 in the immediate aftermath of The Collapse, a ridiculous level not even reached in the 2008 global financial crisis. It has since settled back into the mid-50s, which is still insanely high. Bottom line, there's a lot of fear out there, especially on Wall Street.

Whisper 6 - Brandywine has grown nuttier. A credible Whisperer tells me that the female staffer with whom a Member was allegedly involved is now telling her friends she plans to go public with the

> affair unless her "boyfriend" Member asks her to marry him soon. Get out the popcorn…

UNTIL MONDAY, I have the honor to be,

Your obedient servant,

~QUINCY

Sign up at www.QuincysWhispers.com to get
every edition delivered to your inbox!
Watch for breaking Whispers on Twitter @quincyswhispers.

Hear something good?
Whisper it to me at tips@quincyswhispers.com.
All Whispers are reviewed and kept
strictly anonymous and confidential.

THE REMINDER about the morning release of the first polling data was exciting for Anna. She knew it was going to happen, but with everything else going on it had slipped her mind.

Finally, something to look forward to... I wonder what it'll say about Montgomery. I bet being first to have all of those media hits about the Blues helped him get some national traction. It'll be fun to see, though. And what's up with this Saratoga deal? I have a bad feeling about that one. The other one with the love story sounds more like a soap opera, but this thing sounds like it might actually matter. Figures that a powerful Member would do something stupid and have a sex scandal... you can't trust any of these guys. Bunch of scumbags. But which one this time? Hmm... hold on... Quincy said this was a credible Speaker candidate... there's no way it would be Montgomery. He has his faults, but sexual misconduct just isn't one of them. Then again... accusations can come from anywhere... they don't have to be true.

The uncertainty ate away at Anna. Her stomach was so unsettled she thought she may actually vomit. She shot out of bed and into the bathroom. A slug of Pepto-Bismol calmed her queasiness, but the mental unease remained. Yesterday's opposition research failures must have been gnawing at her mind all night. Anna willed herself to get ready for work - today she had to get some answers.

46

Willis Montgomery was digging deep, using every connection he had ever built to try and gain an advantage in the race. The outcome of this election would ultimately define his political legacy. This was an inescapable fact of which he was well aware.

As election day drew closer, the GGs' and Fiscal Fronters' hesitancy to commit their backup votes to him was really throwing a wrench in his plans. It was time to consider Plan B.

On Friday morning, Montgomery swung by Christine Franklin's office to talk. It was about 9:45 a.m. - early for Washington, D.C. - and she had not yet arrived for the day. Her staff estimated Franklin would be in around 10:00. They promised to have her call him as soon as she got there.

Montgomery instead decided to kill a few minutes in the hallway outside of Franklin's office. He would catch her as she arrived.

Only three minutes later, Franklin appeared from around the corner and approached to her office. She smiled as she noticed Montgomery waiting outside her door.

"Well, what a pleasant surprise!" she said. "To what do I owe this great honor?"

"Christine... you are delightful. I just wanted to talk for a moment and your staff said you would be here any minute. I hope you aren't offended by my ambush!"

"I could never be upset with you, Willis," she said. "Come on in. Let me get situated."

The two entered Franklin's office and shut the door. Franklin put her briefcase and purse down, then took up a place on her couch. She offered a chair to Montgomery.

"How can I help you?" Franklin asked.

"I was thinking about our conversation yesterday, Christine. What you said about only having one more chance to turn the House around really resonated with me."

"Well, I truly believe that," said Franklin. "If we elect someone without real ethical backbone, we may not survive it."

"And unfortunately, I think you are probably right," Montgomery said sadly. "After you said that, I did some real soul-searching last night about the race. You know how I am - I don't want to name names... but I am very concerned that several of the people who are running for Speaker are not morally fit to hold such an esteemed position. And many are still looking at it as an opportunity to make a personal power grab. They're not in this race for something bigger than themselves."

Franklin seemed bothered. He was speaking her language.

"I have those exact same fears, Willis," she said. "I think if we don't turn our eyes away from personal glory and toward the good of the nation in this time of great need, we may lose our chance to ever do so again."

"Precisely," Montgomery said. "This is an existential turning point for our nation. If we mess this up now, hundreds of years from now our descendants may be studying how we lost the republic at this moment in time."

"You and I are doing the right thing, though," said Franklin. "Simply by being in this race, we are giving people a viable alternative to corruption and self-dealing. I trust you to do the right thing, Willis, and I hope you trust me as well."

"I have more respect for you than any of my other colleagues, Christine. You would make an outstanding Speaker. I would be honored to vote for you if I were not in the race myself."

"I feel exactly the same," she said. "I believe God has asked me to stand in this place and be a candidate for this position. If that were not the case, you would have my full support."

"You know, I think God really has been looking out for us both in this campaign, Christine. I prayed over this exact issue last night. I feel led to tell you that if I do not advance to the final ballot, I will support your candidacy. I will also use every ounce of my influence with my supporters to secure their votes for you as well."

"Bless you, Willis," said Franklin. "You are a selfless patriot. One of the last true statesmen. We need more people to put country before self here. I see no reason to not make the exact same promise. If I don't advance to the final ballot, I promise to support you and work to get my supporters to do the same. We need a man or woman of God - an ethical, moral leader - to be in this role if we want to restore our nation to glory."

"Christine, I don't know what to say. I was truly not coming here looking for a pledge from you. I am honored and humbled."

"Just promise me you will always hold true to the values that you have supported for so many years."

"I swear it," said Montgomery.

Franklin smiled. "Will you pray with me?" she asked.

They bowed their heads as Franklin offered thanks and requested God's blessing over them both. Montgomery then rose, said his good-byes, and exited her office.

47

Despite Anna's best efforts at focusing and searching, more than two and a half hours of additional research were unproductive. Anna finally accepted what she already knew to be true. If she wanted to get the real scoop on Alber, she would need to go straight to the source. She had to find and talk to the people who ran his opponents' campaigns.

As the clock approached 10:00 a.m., Anna became more and more anxious. The TV news channels had been teasing the initial Speaker poll all morning, and it was being publicly released at 10:05. She was so close to the situation, it felt impossible to get a true feel for where things stood. Everyone she talked to said positive things about Montgomery's chances, but she wasn't naive enough to expect anyone to tell her anything to the contrary. The uncertainty of everything was killing her.

Anna's office TV was on MSNBC when 10:00 came. The production value of the unveiling reminded her of the over-the-top theatrics of the annual NCAA basketball tournament bracket release shows. The graphics and dramatic music almost seemed like a parody, they were so over-done.

The anchor spoke in a serious tone.

"The numbers we are about to show you represent a scientific poll taken over the past two nights.

"Keep in mind, not all candidates had announced their runs yet when the first night of surveys was conducted. Subsequent polls will fully incorporate the impact of their announcements.

"The sample size of 842 adults from across the United States is sufficiently representative of the voting public to extrapolate the results to the entire population. However, the public at large will not be casting votes for this election - the only voters are the 435 Members of the United States House of Representatives. The numbers we are about to show you represent public opinion only."

Anna was getting antsy.

Get on with it already... we know how polls work.

The anchor continued. "Now, the moment we've all been eagerly anticipating: the initial polling for the Speaker of the House snap election."

Finally! Fingers crossed...

"In first place, with 25 percent support, is Congresswoman Christine Franklin, Christian Conservative from Idaho. Second is Congressman Willis Montgomery, Blue Collar Party from Missouri, at 20 percent. In third place, a candidate who only announced his run yesterday, Kentucky Congressman Theodore "Ted" Alber of the Unity Party, with 16 percent. Fourth is Congressman Jonathan Garcia of the Minority Majority, hailing from New Mexico, with 12 percent. Other candidates garnered 16 percent support, and 11 percent stand undecided.

"Polling will be updated every weekday morning at 10:00 a.m. through next Thursday."

Anna let out a quick yell of excitement at the mention of Montgomery.

Second place - great spot to start! Alber will probably make up a lot of ground once his announcement kicks in, though. The general public might not be casting actual votes, but it'd be impossible to win without broad public support.

She muted the television and stuck her head out of her office's main door. She looked back and forth between Lily and Josh. For once, Lily was not on the phone with an irate constituent.

"Hey Lily, could you tell everyone to hold any calls for me until I'm done in here?" Anna asked. "And don't let anyone come in unless it's extremely important, okay?"

Lily gave Anna a double thumbs-up. "Not a problem," she said cheerfully.

Anna closed and locked her door. She turned the white noise up louder and again buried herself in her work. She was more determined than ever to help her boss keep his momentum, even though it meant getting personal in researching Alber.

As Anna had learned from the newspaper articles, Alber's general election opponent in his first campaign five years earlier had been a businessman named Randall White. Deeper digging found that his most-competitive primary opponent had been a woman named Molly Grubbs. She looked for more information about who had run each of their campaigns.

The FEC reports filed by each opponent revealed the campaign consultants behind them. From what she could tell, White's campaign had been run by a local political operative from Paducah, Kentucky, named Loren Bolte. She had never heard of him or his firm, Bluegrass Advocacy, LLC. Sounded like a local shop through and through.

Grubbs, on the other hand, was backed by one of the best-known shops in D.C., Jefferson Square Strategies. Anna's spirits rose.

If I can figure out who her campaign manager was, maybe I can talk them into helping me... it's a long shot, but it might work. It'd better work... I'm really not finding much in the way of leads here. I really don't think I was cut out to be a private investigator.

~

AFTER THEY EACH grabbed a quick lunch in the cafeteria, Anna asked Kyle to come into her office and sit on the couch. Anna released a tired sigh as she sat in her desk chair. "So, I still haven't been able to find any good leads on Alber. I've checked his district's local newspapers, the FEC reports, his financial disclosures - everything. Every complaint about him from his district seems like either sour grapes or no big deal."

Kyle leaned his head back and let out a groan. "Well that sucks. All that work and still nothing? What are you going to do now?"

"Well, I've hit a dead end on every path I've explored on the paper trail. I think I'd better start meeting with people in person if I'm going to find anything worthwhile."

Kyle raised his eyebrows as he leaned back on the couch. "Who are you going to talk to?" he asked. "Do you have a source?"

"Eh... I wouldn't say that. I'm going to try to meet the campaign staffers who Alber beat in his first election - see what they know. Hopefully they'll at least be able to point me in the right direction."

"What're you going to say to them? You can't tell them who you are. If word got out that Montgomery's Chief of Staff was sniffing around for dirt, we'd be toast."

"I've been thinking about that. Maybe I'll just pretend to be a reporter. Tell them I'm looking for stories about all the leading candidates for Speaker."

"Alright, I guess that's about as good as any other dumb plan," Kyle said. "Not like we have a lot of great options here. Time's of the essence."

"Exactly. Fast is better than perfect." She turned back to Kyle. "How about you? Any progress?"

"Oh, I have a few leads. I'll let you know if I turn up anything real," Kyle replied vaguely as he unfolded himself from the couch and headed toward the door.

KYLE EXITED into the back room of the office and got back to work. Once Anna heard the click of her door latch engaging, she opened her research file on Alber and pulled out the FEC reports. She returned to her info on Alber's opponent Molly Grubbs.

After digging through some more paperwork, Anna determined that a consultant named Ashley Cookson had served as Grubbs' campaign manager. She searched the Jefferson Square website and quickly found her profile.

Jackpot. She's still there. Looks nice enough from the picture... I guess we'll see how good my acting skills really are.

Anna wrote Cookson's phone number down on a sticky note and left her office, making her way outside to Bartholdi Park.

48

Thursday night, Anna had used cash to pick up a prepaid phone card at a corner pharmacy. Even buying that little card made her squirm.

I haven't even touched one of these in probably 15 years. Who even uses them anymore except drug dealers and criminals? Just people who want to fly under the radar or cover their tracks... which is exactly what I'm doing...

While at the pharmacy, she had also picked up an extra roll of antacid tablets. She pulled out two and chewed them while walking toward the park.

There's nothing criminal about this. I'm not doing anything illegal... Alright, yeah, I'm using a name that isn't mine and a backstory that isn't exactly true... but I'm not trying to steal anything. We just need to get the truth, and we don't have time to wait for normal channels. I have to find intel on these guys. They'll almost definitely make up something about us, and if we don't have anything to throw back, they'll get away with it. Losing isn't an option... it's too important. Wait, too important for what? For America? For the House? For Montgomery? For me? Well... maybe it's a little of each.

Anna stepped into Bartholdi Park within five minutes of leaving the office. Checking her surroundings and finding the coast clear, she headed for the bench on the far side of the park. It was the same bench where Kit had bumped into her a couple weeks ago.

Let's hope that doesn't happen again.

She looked around one more time to ensure no one was within listening distance. The constantly-crashing water of Bartholdi Fountain would help to drown out her words to any would-be eavesdroppers anyway. She pulled the prepaid phone card out of her pocket and read the instructions, then dialed through to Ashley Cookson's direct line.

The phone rang three times. "Hello?" said a female voice.

Anna responded with a voice an octave lower than normal. "Hello, could I speak with Ashley Cookson?"

Oh my gosh, I sound like a cartoon character making a prank phone call. What an idiot...

Ashley didn't seem to notice. "Yes, this is she."

"Hi, Miss Cookson, this is Elizabeth Hughes. I'm a reporter for the *National Record* stationed here in D.C. How are you this afternoon?"

"Doing fine, thanks. How can I help you?"

"Well, I'm doing some research for a story on the main candidates for Speaker. I understand you have had some personal experience with Ted Alber."

"Yes, that's true. I ran a race against him a few years back."

"Right. I was wondering if you might be willing to talk with me on background to just point me in the right direction for my story."

Anna held her breath, hoping Ashley still held enough of a grudge to help. After a long pause, Ashley responded.

"Yeah, I wouldn't mind. Completely off the record, though."

"Absolutely. I never, ever reveal sources and will never tell a soul of our conversation. Well… except my editor."

That's what reporters do, right? They do have to reveal sources to editors... right?

"Ok, my first question," Anna started, but Ashley cut her off.

"Look, I prefer to do this in person. I don't want my bosses to hear me talking to the media. When and where can we meet?"

Panicking, Anna blurted out the first out-of-the way spot she could think of, a small park in downtown D.C.

"Ok, I'll be there in half an hour," Ashley said, and disconnected the call.

Anna stared at the phone in her shaking hands.

What have I done?

~

THIRTY MINUTES LATER, Anna sat on a park bench trying to quell the fear that was overtaking her. She took another two antacid tablets and chewed them while she waited. They didn't seem to be having much effect. Her anxiety was rising to a crescendo.

What in the hell do I think I'm doing? Sitting on a park bench wearing sunglasses, pretending to be a reporter... acting like I'm some kind of third-rate spy. This is insane. This woman is going to see straight through me. When she does it'll probably ruin me - she'll tell everyone what I've done... it'll make its way around the rumor mill and I'll be the laughingstock of this town. She might even know who I am! Lots of political consultants are crazy like that... they memorize every Chief they meet. No... no, I'm almost sure I've never seen her before. She won't know me. Maybe this is where it really does pay off to keep to yourself and stay away from the cocktail party circuit.

Despite staying below the radar of the D.C. social scene, it was nearly impossible for Anna to be unnoticed. Particularly during the summer months, when she couldn't use large coats, hats, and outerwear to obscure her features, her striking hair, stature, and attractive form prevented her from blending into any crowd. Even if Ashley didn't recognize her from any previous meetings, she certainly wouldn't be forgetting her in the future.

At 2:03 p.m., Anna saw a woman she recognized from the Jefferson Square Strategies website walking towards her. It was Ashley.

A tall brunette in her mid-30s, Ashley Cookson had long legs and a confident stride. She approached Anna directly. When she was three steps away, her right hand shot out as she introduced herself.

"Hi, Ashley Cookson. You must be Elizabeth?"

Anna rose and shook Ashley's hand.

"Yes, I am. Thank you so much for meeting me on such short notice."

Ashley began to walk through the park at a moderate pace.

"What can I do for you?" she asked.

Anna wasn't sure how to best approach the subject. She decided to just take a stab and see what happened.

"Well, as I mentioned on the phone, I report for the *National Record*. We're working on stories about all of the top-tier candidates for Speaker and I was assigned to Congressman Alber. I know you ran a race against him and wanted to see what you could tell me."

Ashley politely listened to Anna's thin story before responding.

"Are you new to the *Record*? I searched for your work and didn't find anything."

Anna's face turned beet red as her mind scrambled to do damage control.

Shoot. How did I not think of that? I totally should have picked the name of a real reporter... someone without a high profile... and without a headshot. Now what do I do? What's something believable...?

Finally, she came up with what seemed like a plausible explanation.

"Actually, to be honest, I haven't earned my own byline yet. Right now, they've just got me doing background research for the frontline reporters, trying to find leads."

"Alright," said Ashley. "Well good luck to you. I hope they move you up soon. You seem nice."

She bought it. Thank God.

Ashley continued. "Unfortunately, I really don't have much to tell you about Alber. During that primary, we turned over every rock in Paducah looking for info on him. I personally talked to probably six ex-girlfriends, went to his high school employers, asked his middle school teachers about him... the guy is a Boy Scout. Actually, an Eagle Scout. Literally. He's the kind of guy who would argue with the clerk if they gave him too much change. We tried to come up with stuff to hang on him, but nothing would stick. He was just too clean for anything to sound believable."

Well crap. That's about the last thing I wanted to hear. Seriously? Nothing at all?

Anna tried to hide her disappointment. "Are you sure there isn't anything you can remember? Anything interesting for me to take back to my boss?"

"Hmm... I'm trying to think... I mean, it has been five years. Really, the only thing I can think of is that he stole a couple of pumpkins from the front of a Wal-Mart in high school. Not exactly grand larceny."

"Yeah, I guess not," Anna agreed. "Well, if anything else comes to mind, would you let me know?"

"Absolutely," said Ashley. She turned and shook Anna's hand. "It was a pleasure to meet you… Elizabeth."

"Likewise," Anna said. She was bothered by Ashley's closing words.

I don't like the tone she used... she definitely knows I'm not "Elizabeth Hughes." I just hope she doesn't know who I REALLY am. Good Lord, I am terrible at this spy stuff. I'm never going to find anything.

49

Anna took the Metro back to her office and dove back into her work. She looked through her files to find something - anything - that might result in a lead.

Just after 4:00, her phone lit up with a text.

Shoot. It's Gus.

She had forgotten about promising to meet Jonathan Garcia's Chief of Staff, Gus Berger, for drinks. Unfortunately, he had not.

> **GB**: Can't wait to meet up tonight - Bullfeathers at 7?

Why, why couldn't he just forget? Or have some other girl to bother?

In addition to being disgusted by Gus, Anna had never been a big fan of Bullfeathers. A popular bar and restaurant just a block from the House Office Buildings, she had been forced to spend one too many evenings in fake conversation with lobbyists there. She debated what she could do to get out of the commitment.

I could just tell him I am stuck at the office... but he would come by here and drag me out. Do I really need to do this? His boss is such a jerk and plays so dirty, sweet-talking Gus might be the only chance we have of keeping him from kneecapping us... I think I'm just going to have to suck it up and do it.

Her stomach was queasy again. She popped another antacid tablet and texted Gus back.

AR: Sounds great to me! I'll see you there ;)

Anna threw her phone down on her desk and walked away from it, hands on her head.

This is the WORST. A winky face? Why am I doing this? Montgomery had better win, because all this nonsense had better be worth it. I've never lowered my standards as far as Gus Berger. Even his name is repulsive.

She paced back and forth across her office trying to calm down. She finally collected herself enough to sit back at her desk and get back to work. She had a couple more hours to research before she had to make her appearance at Bullfeathers.

AT 6:55, Anna was staring at the analog clock on her wall. For the past five minutes she had been debating if it was better to get to the bar right at 7 and get it over with or take some extra time and put off the pain. She finally decided there was no sense delaying the inevitable - the sooner she got there, the sooner she could get home.

Anna left the office and briskly walked through the underground tunnels from Rayburn to the Longworth House Office Building, then the Cannon House Office Building. She exited Cannon from the southeast door and arrived at Bullfeathers at 7:03.

She scanned the packed room in search of Gus. All the way in the back of the bar area, near the far end, she spotted Gus. He was halfway hanging off of an attractive young brunette who was clearly enjoying his company. It looked like he had gotten started at least a couple of hours ago.

This guy is absolutely disgusting. What's the point of this? Errrrrgh, I know I need to though. Just bite the bullet and go.

Anna approached the two and stuck her hand out towards the girl with confidence. "Anna Rothwell. Nice to meet you."

The young lady stared at Anna like a deer in headlights. She timidly grasped Anna's hand and shook it.

"I am… just going," she said. Within seconds she had disappeared to the other side of the bar.

Anna turned toward Gus, who didn't seem the least bit bothered to be caught. She pretended like she hadn't even noticed.

"Hey Gus," she said, summoning her most sultry voice. "Been waiting long?"

Is this how I'm supposed to do it? That's what it sounds like in the movies… I think.

Gus lit up ear to ear. Whatever movies Anna was recalling were clearly his type.

"Well well… the infamous Anna Rothwell. I had bets on whether or not you'd actually show."

Bleh… this guy.

"Why would I miss this chance?" she asked. "I don't feel like we've ever spent any real… quality time together."

Is he really buying this? I'm sure I've seen better acting at middle school plays. The alcohol is probably helping.

"A beautiful, intelligent woman like you and a strong, handsome man like me? Hard to believe we never had."

Oh, this guy is too much. What an ass.

Anna laughed and put her hand on his shoulder. "Oh Gus… you're something else."

Well at least *that* was true.

She continued. "So, tell me about things. How's Garcia doing with all of this campaign stuff?"

Gus let out a long whistle. "He's kicking ass. He's already locked up a ton of commitments, and it looks like more are coming tomorrow. He's going to win this thing bigtime."

Anna arched her eyebrows. "Is that so?"

Gus caught the hint. "Hey, I think your boss is a good Member. He's been around a LONG time. Nothing against him. I just think Garcia's going to win handily."

"Maybe you're right," Anna said. "Garcia is definitely a charismatic guy. I'm sure he has a good following. And what about you? You look like you're doing really well."

Gus smiled and put his arm around Anna's waist. It took everything in her to resist the urge to pull away. "I'm better now that you're here," he said.

Seriously, it's like he learned to flirt by reading a comic book! Does this kind of stuff actually work on girls?

Anna smiled and leaned into his shoulder. "It's good to get to know you more. Buy me a drink?"

Gus and Anna spent half an hour talking at the bar. Anna filled Gus with empty compliments; Gus coarsely praised Anna's physical features.

Thirty minutes was all Anna could handle. She decided to deploy her pre-made excuse.

"Well Gus, it's been great to catch up. Unfortunately, I told my boss I'd meet up with him at 7:45 to go over strategy, so I'd better head out."

"Let's get together again," he replied. "I'd like to see you somewhere... less crowded."

The hint was not subtle.

Anna hugged Gus, then leaned in and whispered in his ear, "You got it."

Anna turned and left, shooting a flirtatious look over her shoulder at Gus on the way out. As soon as her feet hit the sidewalk, the facade collapsed. Her smile disappeared and her confident strut turned into a power-walk. She just wanted to get home as quickly as possible and take a shower.

50

As Anna left Bullfeathers, she walked past a nondescript Chevy Tahoe parked along the street. Its driver watched her walk away down the sidewalk, relieved Anna had not seen him. Yesterday's accidental meeting in the drugstore candy aisle had been unnerving; he didn't need any more accidental encounters.

So far, everything had been going according to plan. As far as he could tell, none of the targets had noticed his men surveilling them. He had taken precautions in case any of them did get caught, though. None of his colleagues had any idea *why* they were following their marks, just that they were not supposed to let them out of their sight. Keeping information on a need-to-know basis had saved his bacon more than once in his career. He wasn't about to change that now.

The past 12 days had been brutal on his aging body. He couldn't handle the sleep deprivation and constant alertness like he used to. Fortunately, it now looked like an end was in sight. Only one more week until his mission would be complete.

On the other hand, his old friend had made clear that most of the action would happen in the next three or four days. The order to move could come at any moment, night or day, against any of the targets he had prepared for. Now was the time to focus and execute - the future of the country might depend upon it.

51

SATURDAY, JULY 29

Despite it being a weekend, Anna woke up at 5:00. She could not make her body break its early-rising rhythm. Delta was still dead asleep on the pillow next to her.

She took her phone off its charger and scrolled through the overnight news. The screen's light woke up Delta, making for a very grumpy cat. She tried to resettle herself out of reach of the phone's bluish-white glow.

Nothing interesting had happened since Anna returned home from Bullfeathers. She shuddered as she remembered the look on Gus's face as she left the bar. The guy had been practically drooling. Even the memory of his arrogant smile made her cringe.

Delta was back to her usual purring rhythm. Anna put down her phone and rolled over, putting one arm over Delta and bringing her under the covers.

As they cuddled together in the dark bed, Anna quietly began to tell Delta about her evening.

"I did something I'm not proud of last night, Delt," she half-whispered.

Delta continued to snore.

"This guy… he's everything I can't stand in men. Arrogant, self-absorbed, over-confident… he thinks every girl he meets should be honored to have him talk to her. He has zero charisma, no empathy… just out for himself."

She paused a few moments to think. Delta shuffled in place, probably dreaming about chasing a small rodent or bouncing through the park.

"But I spent half an hour, maybe 45 minutes flirting with him last night."

Delta woke up and let a small "meow" escape her tired mouth.

"I know. It was awful… I swear I didn't do anything physical with him."

This did not impress Delta, who rose from her spot and arched her back, stretching toward the ceiling. She sat down and looked directly at Anna's face lying on the pillow.

"I don't really want anything at all to do with him. Seriously. But he's Jonathan Garcia's Chief of Staff. Garcia is probably the most ruthless Member in the House, and he has a lot of power and followers. If we don't get on his good side this week, he'll almost certainly have some dirty trick to take Montgomery out. I can't just let that happen. It's too important."

Delta laid her portly figure back on the bed in the same spot from which she had just arisen.

"No… I don't trust him for a second. But I'm not trying to get anything out of him. I'm just trying to buy us some time. I have zero interest in dating him or anything like it. As soon as this Speaker's race is over, I'm never talking to him again if I can help it."

This final rant seemed to lull Delta back to sleep. She began to purr again loudly, snoring like only she could.

Anna whispered to herself. "It's worth it. We need to win."

She carefully rose from her bed and entered the bathroom. She prepared herself for the day and tried to stop worrying about Gus.

Delta retreated to the far corner of the apartment and curled up into a ball. Anna picked up her work bag, filled Delta's food bowl to the brim, and quietly slipped out the door into the hallway.

ANNA RESOLVED that as soon as she got to the office, she would start from scratch and go back over every shred of evidence she had gathered on Alber so far. She had already accumulated two file folders' worth of newspaper articles, FEC reports, voting records, and any other bit of information she could find. She hoped that if she looked closely enough at those hundreds of pages, some common thread would emerge.

When she unlocked the office door at 6:00 a.m., she was surprised to find the lights on in the foyer. To her right, Montgomery's personal office door was open.

Has he been here all night? Maybe it's just the janitors. They have weird hours on the weekends.

She loudly announced herself so as to not startle anyone. "Hello? Is someone here?"

"Hey Anna," Montgomery called from his room.

She peeked in the door and saw him sitting at his desk behind mounds of papers and an open laptop.

"Oh, hey," Anna said with relief. "I was thinking maybe someone was cleaning the office. What're you doing here so early on a Saturday?"

"There'll be time to sleep when I'm dead… or when I'm Speaker," Montgomery cracked. "Until then, it's a sprint to the finish."

"Alright, well you take care of yourself," she said. "We need you to stay healthy for the next six days."

"I'm fine, Anna. How's everything coming on your end?"

"I have it under control. Still a ton to do, though. I'm going to get to work. Let me know if you need anything."

"Will do," Montgomery said. "Thanks, Anna."

Anna entered her office, closed and locked her door, and started to attack her files. Four hours into the task, she felt like every single second had been wasted. She was absolutely no closer to an answer than she had been when she started. The frustration began to get to her.

How can I not even find a hint of a lead? People make campaign ads every day on less information than this. Even his voting record barely has anything to raise a real fuss over. Montgomery is going to kill me when he sees how little I've found... he might fire me before I ever have the chance *to be the Speaker's Chief of Staff...*

Anna decided that continuing to stare at the pile of paper wasn't going to help. She left the office and took a break in Bartholdi Park, listening to the soothing crash of the fountain.

52

Meanwhile, Montgomery had been working all morning on strategy. In the past week, Alfred had become his best friend - constantly offering him new information that could help him better connect with colleagues.

Just before 11, he composed a group text to the triumvirate of leaders that controlled the Minority Majority: Karen Johnson, Alejandra Hernandez, and Marquez Williams. After wargaming his plan and re-reading the text at least 10 times, he hit send at 11:02 a.m.

> **Willis Montgomery**: Hi Karen, Ali, and Marquez. Are you all around the Hill today? I'd love to talk with you three in private if you have a moment. -Willis

His phone buzzed with responses from all three almost immediately.

> **Karen Johnson**: I'm in the office today trying to knock out some work. Happy to any time.
>
> **Alejandra Hernandez**: same here- name the time/place

Marquez Williams: Shopping at ntl harbor, could meet around 2

WM: 2pm works for me. Where's best?

KJ: My office, 2438

WM: Thank you all, see you at 2

MONTGOMERY ARRIVED two minutes ahead of the appointed time. Karen Johnson's office was almost directly on top of Montgomery's, just two floors up. When he entered the foyer, the other three Members had already assembled and were deep in conversation.

"Hey there, how is everyone?" Montgomery said warmly.

The three Minority Majority leaders looked at each other, then back at Montgomery.

"We're sick of this!" Johnson said with a laugh.

"I sure am," said Ali Hernandez. "I can't wait for this thing to be over. The past two weeks I've had enough politicking for five years!"

The group made its way into Johnson's personal office and closed the door. No staff was in the office - Johnson had told them all to go home and not come in until Monday.

Everyone found a place to sit, then turned their attention to Willis. He began in a somber tone.

"I hope I can trust you all to keep this conversation confidential."

The other three looked at one another and agreed.

"I've been told by some friends that you might have some of the same concerns as I do about a... sensitive issue. I decided the best plan was to talk with you directly."

"Okay… what is it?" said Johnson. All three were looking at Montgomery with a mix of anticipation and confusion.

Montgomery looked from face to face. His expression was stern.

"I have some serious concerns about your colleague who is running for Speaker."

The other three looked at one another and back at Montgomery.

"Garcia?" asked Hernandez.

"Yes, Garcia," Montgomery said.

"Join the club," said Williams.

"Yeah, he's been a thorn in our side for years," said Johnson.

Montgomery looked confused.

"Then… why did your party choose him to run for Speaker?"

Johnson leaned forward. "It's pretty simple, really. Seniority."

"Seniority?" Montgomery said. "That's it?"

"Yes," Johnson replied. "When we founded the party, one of the main cornerstones of our charter was that senior Members get the right of first refusal to be the party's nominee for elected or appointed positions. We also agreed that whomever our party's nominee is will get our unanimous support. Respect for elders is very important to us, and our Members wanted our bylaws to reflect that. Garcia took a pass on serving as Party Chairman, which is how I ended up with the opportunity. But when we discussed the race for Speaker, he claimed the slot."

"Really," Montgomery said incredulously. "Huh. I had no idea. That explains an awful lot, actually."

"What are your concerns with Garcia?" Hernandez asked. "I've never been a big fan, but I don't have any specific examples of wrongdoing."

"Everything I have heard is secondhand," Montgomery admitted. "It just sounds like there are some significant skeletons in his closet. There is so much scrutiny coming down on all of the frontrunners, I will not be shocked if one or more of those skeletons comes out."

Johnson, Hernandez, and Williams exchanged glances but did not respond to the allegation.

"Why are you telling us this?" Williams asked. "Of course you already know that we have heard those rumors."

Montgomery could tell he was dealing with sophisticated and experienced political minds. They knew there was something he wanted. He decided he might as well be straight with them.

"My constituents and yours have an awful lot in common. Most of your voters are working-class folks. Your Members have a history of looking out for the little guy. I think we're very similar coalitions when it comes to the fundamentals.

"I'm not here to ask you to abandon Garcia. Of course not. He's your guy and you are people of integrity. I respect the loyalty you're showing to your most-senior Member."

The three Members nodded in response. Montgomery's message was resonating.

He continued. "The only thing I'm asking is this. If anything does happen to take Garcia out of the running, I would ask you to consider me as your second option. I think with the history we have, all the years we've worked together, you all know that we could be a very successful team. Most likely this will never even matter, but I want you to give it serious thought on the off chance it does."

The others again exchanged glances as they sat in silence thinking through Montgomery's proposal. Finally, Johnson spoke.

"Willis, I think what you say makes a lot of sense. Honestly, I would love to be able to work with you as Speaker. You've always been a straight shooter, and you know how much seniority and relationships mean to us. But my word is my bond, and Garcia will have our support unless something majorly changes."

The other two voiced their agreement.

Montgomery rose from his chair. "I completely understand that and respect you for it. Again, I do not expect that to change unless something major comes up with Garcia. But if it does, we'll talk again. Thank you all for your time on this Saturday afternoon. Please let me know how I can be of service."

The others rose from their chairs and accompanied Montgomery to the door to say their goodbyes.

Montgomery returned to his office with an extra bounce in his step.

53

After clearing her head in Bartholdi Park, Anna tried to get back to work and find a bit of normalcy. She still had plenty of Chief and Member contacts to follow up on and time was quickly ticking away. Des and Josh were in the office through the early afternoon helping pull together more intel on Members of the Watchdogs and Minority Majority. Anna had been focusing her touches with Chiefs on these two groups for the past few days with limited success.

The Blues' whip operation was strong and put extra attention on the Watchdogs and Minority Majority as well. The "go to bat for the country" schtick was a great messaging angle for the Blues, but Members were simply stuck in their positions. Anna hoped Montgomery was having more luck on the Member-to-Member level... they were going to need at least one of the groups to back him if they had a prayer of winning.

Anna remained focused and glued to her desk throughout the afternoon, taking only two breaks to get water and use the restroom. Being a Saturday, Rayburn was not open to the public, which allowed her to actually focus on her work. Des and Josh finished their work around 2:00 p.m. and Anna encouraged them to go home and get some rest. She spent the next hour and a half reviewing what they had given her, highlighting key portions and adding her own notes.

At 3:30 p.m., Anna heard a loud, persistent knock on the main office door. She went to the door and unlocked it. She gasped once she realized who was on the other side. Kit Lambert.

"Hey Anna, can I come in for a second?" Kit said. He seemed anxious and worried.

Anna gave him a skeptical look.

"Why?" she said coldly. All she could think about was their last encounter, two days ago at We, the Pizza.

"Come on Anna, I just need to talk to you. Please. I promise I'm being serious."

He does look really antsy. Probably not trying to pull a prank or something stupid. Okay.

"Alright," said Anna as she opened the door. "But any funny business and out you go."

"Thanks Anna," Kit said sincerely.

They went into Anna's office. Kit shut the door, then paced over to the window and looked out. He was on high alert.

"Are you the only one here?" he asked.

"Yeah, why?"

Kit was too preoccupied with his sweep of the office to answer.

"Could you turn on some white noise, please?"

Now Anna was more confused than annoyed.

"What exactly is going on, Kit?" she asked.

"Please, Anna, just do it. Just Google white noise and play the first video. Turn it up."

Anna followed his directions but made sure he knew how irritated she was.

"Thank you," Kit said. He scooted as close to Anna as he could, then began to whisper. "I'm sorry for coming to you like this. I know how strange it seems."

Anna was already sick of looking at him. She couldn't figure out what his angle was, but he was acting like a psycho.

"Go ahead," Anna said impatiently. "What is it." She did not even try to keep her emotionless voice down.

Kit was agitated by her indifference. "Anna, I'm serious. This is important."

Anna simply nodded in response.

Kit sighed and continued in hushed tones. "I know this sounds crazy, but... I think someone's been following me."

Anna broke out in laughter.

"Shhhh!" he said loudly. "Stop it, Anna! I'm serious!"

She tried to rein in her laughter and restore a sober countenance. "Kit... I don't mean this harshly, but you need to get over yourself. Why would anyone be following *you?*"

Kit's face scrunched up. This arrow had clearly struck a nerve. He tried to keep his cool.

"It's not just about *me,* Anna."

"Well it's obviously not about *me,* so why are you here?" she said with annoyance. "It's not like we're friends."

Kit was clearly frustrated. "Anna, listen to me. This could involve you too."

At this, Anna's defiant attitude vanished.

"What do you mean?" she asked. "Me? Why me?"

"Okay. So, for the past couple of weeks, every time I've been out of the office, I keep seeing the same two guys. They're normal looking; basically your average tourists. But seriously, they're *everywhere*."

"Alright… it could just be a coincidence. Why do you say it might involve me?"

"Gus Berger is a good friend of mine," Kit said.

Of course he is.

Kit continued. "I was talking to him at Cap Lounge last night. I said something about how I'd noticed these guys and thought they were following me around. Gus slammed his beer on the table and said he'd been having the exact same thing happen to him!"

Anna was skeptical. She recalled Montgomery's warning two weeks earlier that the Lambert family was prone to traffic in conspiracy theories. "I don't know that I'm going to worry too much about what a drunk Gus Berger says in a bar on a Friday night."

"Alright. Fair enough. But I started thinking about it. If we're not just seeing things, what do Gus and I have in common that could be making someone watch us? Then it hit me… both of our bosses are running for Speaker!"

Wow. Brilliant deduction.

"Okay… so?" Anna said. She was still far from convinced.

"So… this morning I went over to talk with Eugenia Dunn. I've known her a few years. Wonderful lady."

"Yeah, I like her too," said Anna.

"Anyway, I wanted to see if she's noticed anything weird. Gus and I walk to work, but Eugenia drives. She lives out in Fairlington - down I-395 in south Arlington. I explained to her what Gus and I had been noticing. No one had approached either of us or anything, but we'd had constant tails for a week or two.

"Eugenia said she thought she noticed something about a week ago. The same dark Tahoe had been about four or five car lengths behind her three days in a row. Something about the driver had made her notice him once when they got caught in different lanes and the guy went past her. He had a noticeable mole on the left side of his face and super-red hair. So red it made yours look brown.

"She said she could have sworn she saw the same guy yesterday while she was taking Franklin's dog for a walk. He was wearing a baseball cap and stayed a ways back. She said he did a pretty good job trying to look nonchalant. She made a few quick turns and doubled back so she could get a close look at him. As she passed him on the sidewalk, she saw the mole on the left side of his face. Red hair was poking out from the back of his hat."

Anna was done laughing at Kit - now she was taking him seriously. Most likely he was just losing his nerve under the stress of the past couple of weeks, but the description *did* sound vaguely familiar.

"Okay… I'll admit that's weird," she said. "But why would someone be stalking you guys? What's the point of that?"

"Well I have no idea," he said. "Obviously all of our bosses are top candidates for Speaker. Maybe someone's trying to get intel on us. Your boss is a top contender too, Anna. I think really the only other one who matters beyond Garcia and Franklin. Have you noticed anyone following you or anything weird like that?"

Anna racked her brain. She was usually so zoned out when walking to and from work, she was completely oblivious to her surroundings. She knew it was a fault she should work on.

"Honestly, I don't know," she said. "I wish I could say I pay better attention to that kind of thing, but I really don't."

"Well if I were you, I'd start paying more attention," Kit said. "I don't know what these guys are up to, but something definitely doesn't seem right."

Anna still wasn't completely convinced by Kit's tale.

If what he's saying is true, I'd definitely be a little worried. But he's such an elitist, he probably just saw a car more than 10 years old and decided the owner must either be a drug addict or a hit man. I don't know... I'm not going to hire a bodyguard just yet. I'll take a few looks over my shoulder tonight, though. I don't know about Kit, but if someone comes after me, I can take care of myself.

Kit was obviously shaken up. Even if Anna didn't believe the story, she was pretty sure he did. She decided it was best to be kind to him for once.

"Thanks for the heads-up, Kit," she said. "I appreciate you thinking of me. Let me know if you see anything else."

Kit stood up and made his way to the door.

"Same with you. You have my cell. Let me know."

The door shut behind him. Anna heard his footsteps fade away as he headed for the elevator. She locked the door and went back to her desk. She turned off the ridiculous white noise and got back to work.

PART IV

HOME STRETCH

54

SUNDAY, JULY 30

Sunday, Montgomery was booked on three of the major morning news shows: CNN's "State of the Union," Fox's "Fox News Sunday," and NBC's venerable "Meet the Press." His top opponents were also on several Sunday shows. Montgomery performed beautifully on each appearance - he was dialed in and knocking it out of the park.

On the way back to the office from NBC's studio, Montgomery took out his cell phone and began sending texts. He had long believed that being overly nice to political rivals was a much wiser strategy than treating them like poisonous enemies. That way, they might think twice before going scorched-earth on you… and they would also be less likely to see your own attacks coming.

Montgomery had just finished going toe-to-toe with Christine Franklin on Meet the Press. He respected her strength and resolve - she had more than held her own. He decided to text her a congratulatory note.

Willis Montgomery: Christine - great job back there. It's been a tough few weeks for all of us. Glad to see we have several quality people in the running for Speaker. -Willis

Christine Franklin: I appreciate that. This will be a challenging week. You are a good and honorable man.

WM: You are too kind. I hope all is well with you. Whichever of us pulls it out, let's get together and break bread in the Speaker's office as soon as it's over.

CF: We are all going to need each other. Let's do that.

WM: Have a great Sunday. God Bless

CF: Same to you!

Next, Montgomery sent a similar text to Jonathan Garcia.

Willis Montgomery: Jonathan hope you're having a good weekend. I thought you did well on your appearance on FNS. It's been a tough few weeks for all of us - will be good to elect new Leadership and move forward together. -Willis

Jonathan Garcia: Thx

WM: You still have my word I won't disparage you in this race. I think the best Member should win on his or her own merits.

JG: I plan to do just that

WM: Whichever of us pulls it out, let's get together and break bread in the Speaker's office as soon as it's over.

JG: K

"What an ass," Montgomery said to himself. "He can't even *pretend* to be nice." He moved his attention to his third target, Ted Alber.

Willis Montgomery: Ted - hope you're having a good weekend. You were solid today on SOTU. You're a good man and a great Member. I appreciate running against people as talented and honest as you. -Willis

Ted Alber: Thanks Willis. You'll be tough to beat. Great job at CNN too.

WM: Appreciate it. You still have my word I won't disparage you in this race. I think the best Member should win on his or her own merits.

TA: As it should be. I still feel the same too.

WM: Best of luck to you!

TA: Thanks, you too!

Montgomery put his phone back in his pocket and tried to relax the rest of the way to the office. He had a lot of work ahead of him.

55

Anna decided to work from home Sunday morning. Besides, her constant upset stomach made her afraid she might be coming down with something, and the idea of having Delta beside her for comfort made her feel at least a little bit better.

At 10:28 a.m., Anna's cell phone rang. It was Peter Garibaldi, Martin Wilson's Chief of Staff.

What could he want? He doesn't usually call without reason.

"Hello, this is Anna."

"Anna, have you heard?" Peter was out of breath and sounded upset.

"Heard about what?" Anna replied. His tone made her instantly tense with worry.

"I just got a call from Eugenia Dunn. Christine Franklin's husband was just killed in a car accident this morning."

Anna froze in place, mouth agape. She was absolutely stunned.

"Anna, are you there?"

"Yeah - uh, yeah, I'm here. I'm sorry. Did you say he's dead? Are you sure?"

Her voice was now shaking as much as Peter's.

What if... what about the crazy stuff Kit was talking about yesterday... No, there's no way.

Peter continued with more information. "Eugenia said she was with her boss a few minutes ago when Franklin got the call from the Idaho State Police. Eugenia and I have been close for years - I was one of the first people she called. I just figured your boss would want to know."

Anna was surprised to hear that Eugenia had any close friends. Then again, once Anna had gotten to know her a bit, she'd realized Eugenia wasn't as icy as she seemed on the surface.

"I'm... I'm shocked," Anna said. She grasped for words. "Do they know what happened?"

"Well, they don't know a lot yet. Right now, the State Police are treating it as a hit-and-run with possible foul play, though."

Anna felt another blow to her chest. Her voice cracked even more.

"What? Foul play? In a car wreck? How is that even possible?"

"I don't know, Anna. I guess there were no witnesses. His car got t-boned at an intersection near their house, which is in a pretty rural area. The other vehicle was big - maybe a truck or something - and was traveling at high speed, judging by the damage. Something about the scene made the cops think it might not have been an accident."

Anna tried to take it all in. She again felt the queasiness that had become so common in recent days.

Why would someone intentionally crash into Christine Franklin's husband? Did they think she was the one driving the car? Or just in the car with him? But she hasn't been home in weeks... if someone knew enough to plan out where their car would be in that much detail, wouldn't they be smart enough to know she wasn't even in Idaho?

The silence on the line hung thick. Anna realized she needed to say something.

"Is there anything they need? Can we do something?"

Peter sighed. "I don't think so. Eugenia was pretty broken up when I talked to her. I can't imagine her boss is going to be able to stay in the Speaker's race, though. This is too much to handle under even normal circumstances - she can't possibly run for the biggest job in Congress while she's dealing with this. Can you believe they'd been married 32 years?"

"Wow... 32 years," Anna said. "She must be devastated."

"Who wouldn't be?" Peter said sadly.

"Well... thanks for the call, Peter. I really do appreciate it."

"Sure. Just let your boss know. Hope you're well."

"Same to you. Bye."

Anna ended the call. She sat on her bed and stared at her phone.

Hit and run... That is NUTS. Intentional hit and run? That's even more nuts, but it's also murder...

This was the first time the m-word had crossed Anna's mind. It sent a chill down her spine. Every part of her felt like ice. Her thoughts dug deeper.

If that's true... IF... why would someone want to murder Christine Franklin's husband? Well... or maybe Christine Franklin herself?

The cold sensation only worsened.

Could someone really have tried to kill Christine Franklin over the Speaker's race? And if someone did this to Franklin's husband, could they try to come after Montgomery next? Surely not... there's no way. I bet this whole thing was just some idiot drunk driver who had been out all Saturday night, and Franklin's husband was in the wrong place at the wrong time. That's the most likely explanation. Occam's razor, right? When you have multiple explanations, the simplest one is most likely to be true. Planning someone's death by t-boning them with a truck is just too far-fetched. I'd bet money it was just a drunk moron.

Anna's conclusion made her feel marginally better, but not much. She still couldn't shake the feeling of dread that had taken up permanent residence in the pit of her stomach. After picking through the basket of half-empty medicine bottles in her bathroom, she found the ultra-strength Pepto-Bismol and downed a healthy slug.

~

AFTER TAKING a moment to collect herself, Anna dialed Montgomery's number. She had to tell him ASAP. The phone rang four times before Montgomery answered.

"Hello?" said Montgomery.

"Hey, sorry to call on Sunday morning, but I just heard some terrible news," Anna said in a shaky voice. "Just a little while ago, Christine Franklin's husband was killed in a hit-and-run accident near their home in Idaho."

Anna tried to steady her voice as she delivered the news. It was still hard to process. It didn't seem real.

"Dead? Not injured?" Montgomery asked.

"Apparently the Idaho State Police confirmed that he died on the scene."

"Well that's awful," Montgomery said. "Do they know who did it?"

Anna felt like Montgomery's voice seemed cold. She wasn't sure how to take his reaction.

Some people take news differently than others. I guess he turns robotic.

"No, they don't have any leads yet," Anna said. "But… but they *are* saying they suspect foul play."

"Foul play?" Montgomery asked with confusion. "Why?"

"I don't know for sure. I'm guessing because Franklin is a leading candidate for Speaker… maybe the driver thought she was the one in the car?"

"Hm. Well, who knows. Do you think she'll stay in the race?"

Anna was taken aback by this bluntly political question. She had just told him 30 seconds earlier that his opponent's husband was killed in a crash… and likely murdered. How could he already be thinking about how it might politically benefit him? This is the kind of stuff that made people hate politicians. She pulled herself together and answered.

"I seriously doubt it. They were very close. I presume she's an emotional wreck."

"Ok." Montgomery thought for a moment. "Make sure to send flowers to her office," he said. "I'll give her a call with my condolences. Thanks for the call. I'll talk to you later."

Anna looked at her phone quizzically and wondered what was going on with Montgomery.

I guess the stress is getting to him too. I can't wait until this is over.

AROUND 12:30 P.M., Montgomery dialed Christine Franklin's cell phone. It rang five times. He was certain she was not going to answer. At the very last moment, someone picked up the line. He could hear sobs on the other end.

"Hello?" said a female voice fighting through tears.

"Christine?" said Montgomery.

"Yes. Hello Willis." She said. He could barely make out her words.

"Christine, I just heard the news. I am devastated for you."

Franklin did not respond with words, only harder sobs.

"I cannot even imagine how you must feel in this moment," Montgomery said. "Just know that the Lord will be with you throughout. God does not give us more than we can handle. I am here for you, whatever you may need. And I guarantee the rest of our colleagues will be here for you as well. We take care of our own, and you are ours."

"Thank… thank you, Willis," she said between sobs. Franklin was completely overcome with emotion.

"Don't talk," said Montgomery. "I just wanted you to know we're here for you."

Franklin pulled herself together enough to begin to speak clearly.

"I have no idea how this could happen to Tom," Franklin said. "He is the most… was… the most careful driver I've ever known… He never even left our driveway without a seatbelt."

"There's not always a good explanation for why," Montgomery said. "Sometimes accidents just happen. We can't avoid them all."

"Oh Willis, I don't know how I can live without him!" Franklin again broke into hysterics.

"God will comfort you through this," said Montgomery.

Franklin again pulled herself together momentarily.

"Willis, I can't go on with the race. This is just too much to handle - I can't even think about politics. I want you to know I will honor my word and completely support you. I'll…"

Montgomery interrupted her mid-sentence. "Christine, I don't even want to hear it. There will be a time to discuss those things, but that time is not now. All I care about is getting you what you need. Please let me know how I can help you."

"Alright. Okay. I have no idea, really. I have so much to figure out."

"I'll let you go," said Montgomery. "I will be praying for you, and I will be there for you if you need anything."

"Bless you, Willis. Thank you so much for your call. It means the world to me."

56

MONDAY, JULY 31

Anna tossed and turned all Sunday night. She just couldn't get her mind off of Christine Franklin and her husband. Disjointed thoughts kept racing through her head.

Such an awful tragedy... their kids and grandkids have to be completely devastated. How can she even stay in Congress? If it happened to me, I'd be such a wreck I'd have to drop out. But she's probably tougher than me. No, I could stick it out. Whatever doesn't kill you makes you stronger, right? Does that apply to things that kill people close to you? Hmm... What about her staff? I bet they're scared to death they'll lose their jobs too. And what will it all mean for Montgomery?

Around 4:30 a.m., she finally decided sleep was not going to come, so she might as well get started with the day. As was her new usual routine, the first thing she did was check the overnight news stories.

From: Quincy <quincy@quincyswhispers.com>
Subject: Quincy's Whispers - Monday, July 31
Date: July 31 at 4:25 AM

To: Anna Rothwell

Quincy's Whispers
265 days since the Midterm Election
463 days until the Presidential Election
4 days until the Speaker Election
What the House is whispering about...
but doesn't want you to hear.

Good Monday morning! Unspeakable tragedy struck the Speaker race yesterday morning with the sudden death of Congresswoman Christine Franklin's (CC-ID) husband. The details are gruesome; Idaho State Police estimate the assaulting vehicle was traveling at over 80 miles per hour at impact. How in the world any vehicle was able to "run" after such a "hit" is a mystery. The State Police are treating it as an incident of foul play and have initiated a statewide search for the vehicle.

Back in DC... the House will gavel in at 10:00 a.m. today - buckle up for perhaps the Hill's wildest week in anyone's memory. No legislating will happen this week... again... but by Friday we ought to have a new Speaker.

What I'm hearing today:

Whisper 1 - Rumors are flying that Tom Franklin might have been intentionally targeted in the horrific crash that caused his death. This may all be premature, though. The Idaho State Police still have not identified the driver, so any speculation as to motive, or even whether or not Tom or Christine Franklin were intended targets, is just that. Speculation.

Whisper 2 - Sources tell me that, understandably, Christine Franklin is absolutely distraught over the death of her husband of 32 years. Yesterday afternoon and evening she was inconsolable. Her staff has arranged to get her back to Idaho late this morning. No one I've heard from expects her to stay in the Speaker race.

Whisper 3 - As most Whisperers expected, the initial Consortium Poll was dominated by Franklin, Willis Montgomery (BC-MO), Ted Alber (UP-KY), and Jonathan Garcia (MM-NM). Scariest for the others, though, is that Alber hadn't even announced his run until after the first half of polling had already finished. I expect Alber to rocket to the top of today's second poll. No telling what Franklin's numbers will be, but it's likely to be irrelevant. Most expect her to withdraw from the race today.

Whisper 4 - The whip rumors we'd been tracking over recent days are now effectively all moot. By all accounts, Christine Franklin had some of the strongest support, if not the strongest, of any candidate. What's more, many were fiercely loyal to her due to her deep moral convictions and kind personality. These Members will soon be free agents. The whole complexion of the race could shift depending on where they land.

Whisper 5 - This one saddens me and gives me anxiety. The Whispers around Saratoga keep growing in strength. I feel like it's close to reaching a breaking point. Frankly, the allegations sicken me. If they pan out, this will only further erode what tiny bit of respect the American people have for Members of Congress.

Whisper 6 - The news of Tom Franklin's death and the uncertainty it brings to the Speaker race appear to have freaked out Wall Street again. Overnight trading action has the market down 3.3 percent at this writing. The VIX volatility index is off the chart, shooting up to the mid-70s again this morning. Another bumpy week of trading is on deck.

UNTIL TOMORROW, I have the honor to be,

Your obedient servant,

~QUINCY

Sign up at www.QuincysWhispers.com to get
every edition delivered to your inbox!
Watch for breaking Whispers on Twitter @quincyswhispers.

Hear something good?
Whisper it to me at tips@quincyswhispers.com.
All Whispers are reviewed and kept
strictly anonymous and confidential.

~

THE WHISPERS DID nothing to improve Anna's mood. In fact, they only made her feel even worse. She couldn't get her mind off of Christine Franklin.

So senseless... if this does turn out to be a literal political hit job, and I sure hope it doesn't, it's going to destroy people's faith in government. The final nail in the coffin. Surely it's something else. Politics is dirty, but the odds are still best that this is all just a seriously awful coincidence.

Recovering from a night of zero sleep required extra coffee. Anna got out of bed to prepare a pot with her ancient coffeemaker. She downed a cup as soon as it brewed, this time adding double her normal artificial sweetener allotment. She took another cup into the bathroom to drink as she prepared for work.

57

As usual, Anna arrived at the office at 6:00 a.m. on the dot. She logged in to Alfred and began her normal routine.

About 6:15, she heard another loud, persistent knock at the door. This time she knew who it was. Kit's frantic pounding sounded exactly the same as it had Saturday. She unlocked the door and let him in.

Kit looked scared out of his mind. His breathing was short, and his voice was filled with fear.

"Anna… thank God you're here. Didn't you get my texts yesterday?"

In fact, Anna hadn't been responding to texts since Saturday afternoon. Frankly, she was just burned out on corresponding with people and decided to take a break. She knew she could catch up on Monday.

"Actually… I don't know," she replied. "I haven't really looked."

"Seriously? I thought something had happened to you! I even tried to call you three times."

Anna had seen the incoming calls, but the last thing she wanted to do in her free time was talk to Kit Lambert, so she had let them all go to voicemail. "Yeah, sorry. I was tied up doing other things."

Kit was exasperated. "Well I know you saw what happened to Tom Franklin. These guys are still following me around. What if I'm next?"

Anna rolled her eyes at this. "Kit. Again, I don't mean to be rude, but you're not that important. Tom's death was tragic, but I'm sure it'll turn out to just be an accident. And why are you here talking to me? Aren't you buddies with Gus and Eugenia? Go bother them for once."

Kit rolled his eyes. "I've already talked to Gus. He still thinks people are following him, but he just made fun of me when I brought up Tom. He's a dick. He's not going to listen to me."

"What about Eugenia?" Anna asked. "You said you've known her for years."

She still wasn't sure that this wasn't an elaborate setup by Kit.

"Eugenia's a good person, but she's more like my mom than a colleague," said Kit. "Besides, she's pretty grumpy and doesn't really seem like the type to take me seriously on this."

Anna pursed her lips. "So I'm the lucky one who gets to hear all of your conspiracy theories?"

Kit got more agitated. "These aren't conspiracy theories, Anna. This is for real."

Anna rolled her eyes dramatically. "Kit, no one is stalking you, and no one is going to kill you. And the only person I've seen following *me* is *you*. It's almost certainly nothing."

"Anna, you've *got* to start taking this seriously! Someone *died* yesterday. Tom Franklin is DEAD. Doesn't that seem suspicious to you?"

She tried to remain calm and logical. "A random car accident in middle-of-nowhere, Idaho, doesn't exactly seem like the stuff of spy novels, Kit. It was horrible, but I think it's almost certainly just a coincidence. Besides, are you saying Tom had spies following him too?"

Kit didn't appreciate her disdain. "I don't know, Anna! I can't exactly ask him. Maybe these people are just trying to get information from our patterns... they might be tapping our cell phones, looking through our trash! Who knows what they're finding out about us?"

Anna had heard enough. She wasn't going to buy into Kit's conspiracy theories and waste the most important week of her life worried about black helicopters and UFOs. Accidents happen; even oddly timed accidents. She had work to do.

"Thanks for coming by, Kit. I know you're very stressed right now. I hope you take good care of yourself and get some more rest. It's all going to be okay."

Kit was furious at Anna's dismissiveness. "God, you just don't listen!" he said. "Fine. I'm getting to the bottom of this myself. But don't say I didn't warn you when they come after you."

"Okay," Anna said. "I won't."

She escorted Kit back out the door and locked it behind him.

JUST BEFORE 10:00 A.M., Lily, Josh, and Des crowded into Anna's office to watch the release of the latest polling data. Kyle had a meeting out of the office but was sure to be checking for news on his phone. Today's data would include polling taken on Saturday and Sunday nights. This meant half of the responses were received after news broke of Tom Franklin's death.

Lily turned the television to Fox News Channel. At the top of the hour, the dramatic music and overproduced graphics kicked in. The anchor, a young lady with platinum blonde hair, had a stern expression as she explained the situation to the audience.

At precisely 10:05, text of the results dramatically floated onto the screen. The anchor reviewed the data and read it out loud.

"Over the weekend, Congressman Theodore "Ted" Alber, a member of the newly formed Unity Party from Kentucky, has surged into the lead with 28 percent support. Christine Franklin of Idaho, a Christian Conservative, maintained 20 percent backing despite the horrific personal tragedy she suffered yesterday morning. Keep in mind, half of the polling was conducted before her husband's death, and she is widely expected to withdraw from the race.

"In third place is Willis Montgomery of Missouri, founder of the Blue Collar Party. He held relatively steady at 18 percent. Jonathan Garcia, Minority Majority party member from New Mexico, increased two points to 14 percent. Other candidates totaled 12 percent. Eight percent were undecided."

The reaction from Team Montgomery was lukewarm. A few murmurs floated around the staff, but no one was particularly excited or disappointed. Anna continued to stare at the screen, trying to decide how the results made her feel.

Everyone's really pretty bunched up... If Franklin does drop out, I'm just not sure where her support would go. I could see her people feeling a lot of kinship with Alber's people... but some of them would probably like Montgomery too. I doubt many Christian Conservatives would head toward Garcia... he's not exactly their type. I guess we'll see in the next few days.

The team filed out of Anna's office without much conversation and got back to work. The phones were still ringing almost all day long, as they had been for weeks now. The staff looked like zombies, going through the same motions day after day. They were ready for a change.

58

At 10:28 a.m., Willis Montgomery was sitting at his desk working through papers when his cell phone rang. It was Christine Franklin. Montgomery quickly dropped his pen and answered the call.

"Hello, this is Willis."

"Willis, this is Christine Franklin."

"Hey Christine. It's so good to hear from you. How are you? What can I do for you?"

She spoke slowly. "Honestly… I'm not good. The past 24 hours have been the worst of my life. I can hardly even function. My kids are with me, but they're not doing much better."

"I am so sorry. I can't even fathom what you're going through."

Franklin sounded like she was in a daze. "I wanted to let you know that I'm going to drop out of the Speaker race this morning and endorse you. I'm going to instruct all of my supporters to vote for you in my place. God has selected you to be in this place at this time for a reason. I trust He has a plan for us all."

Montgomery struggled for an appropriate response. "Christine… I am so humbled by your gesture. I wish you were able to finish out the race. You are such an outstanding Member. I promise I will honor Tom's legacy and make you proud with how I run this race. If I am fortunate enough to win, I will dedicate my Speakership to him."

Franklin's voice was hollow. "Thank you, Willis. I look forward to that day. I will talk with you soon."

"Goodbye," said Montgomery.

He ended the call, dropped the phone, and stared blankly at his desk, deep in thought.

~

CHRISTINE FRANKLIN'S office announced an 11:00 a.m. press conference to discuss her future in the race. The studio space in the Capitol Visitors Center was packed with reporters who wanted to witness this emotional moment firsthand.

Eugenia Dunn entered the stage area and placed two pages of prepared remarks on the podium. Seconds later, Christine Franklin emerged from backstage and approached the microphone. Nearly a hundred camera shutters clicked at light speed. The noise was deafening.

Franklin looked like she hadn't slept in days - probably because she hadn't. She was likely already run down from the pace of the Speaker's race before her husband's tragic death. It was doubtful she'd slept since receiving that news. As she cleared her throat and adjusted the microphone, the room became silent.

"Thank you all for being here today," she said. Her voice was weak as she read off the paper. "My statement will be brief. The past day has been by far the most difficult of my life. Tom was my husband, my partner, my… my best friend for the past 32 years."

Franklin's composure cracked. She began to cry. Eugenia approached from the side and handed her two folded tissues. The camera shutters clicked nonstop, capturing every instant of emotion.

"Needless to say, I cannot continue in the race for Speaker of the House. I have far more important things to focus on right now.

"However, after praying intensely last night, I feel called to ask my former supporters to honor Tom's memory by turning their eyes and support to another righteous man of God. Our nation needs a statesman to lead this body through these tumultuous times. That's why I ask - I implore - my supporters to cast their votes this Friday for Congressman Willis Montgomery of Missouri. Thank you for your time."

The roomful of reporters began yelling questions at the top of their lungs, but Franklin simply turned and exited as if she heard nothing. Her withdrawal was completely expected, but no one thought she would be making an endorsement as well. The announcement promised to turn the entire race on its head.

AT 11:11 A.M., Anna knocked on the passageway door to see if Montgomery was available. She had just watched with astonishment as Christine Franklin endorsed him for the Speakership. Anna was stunned by the development.

Montgomery called for her to open the door. He was sitting at his desk furiously typing on his laptop as she entered. He looked up and gestured for Anna to sit down. She remained standing, arms crossed.

"How are things, Anna?" Montgomery asked.

"How are things?" she replied incredulously. "Did you know Christine Franklin was going to drop out and endorse you?"

Montgomery stopped typing and looked up from his screen. Peeking over his reading glasses, he looked mildly surprised.

"Yes, she called me earlier this morning. Did she actually do so on television?"

Anna wasn't sure how to take his statement.

If he knew it was even a possibility, why didn't he tell me? This is huge news for us! I need to know these things!

"Yes, she endorsed you and asked all of her supporters to vote for you on Friday," she said.

"Well that is extremely kind of her," Montgomery said. "She is a wonderful woman. What a horrible tragedy, what happened to Tom."

His response still seemed off, but at least his heart and mind were in the right place. "Yes, she is," said Anna, calming her initial frustration. "She's a lovely lady. And she has a lot of supporters - people who will now become your supporters if we give them some attention."

"I suppose that's true," Montgomery said calmly. "Would you please get me a list of all of her known supporters so I can personally reach out to them today? I'd like you to do the same for her Chiefs. Bump them up to a daily touch."

Montgomery had sometimes fallen into inscrutable moods in the past, but Anna was having an extra-hard time reading him today. He seemed so… unaffected by it all. So robotic. Maybe he was still in shock and denial about what happened to Franklin's husband. He and Franklin had known each other for over two decades, after all.

"Will do," said Anna.

"If we could get the Christian Conservatives' support, it would add 64 votes," Montgomery said. "Not counting Christine, of course. I assume she will not be voting."

"Right," Anna agreed. "If we could finally nail down the GGs and the

Fiscal Fronters, we'd almost have a lock on the Speakership. Any news on them?"

"I don't want to talk about them," Montgomery said dismissively.

Anna could tell Montgomery hadn't had any more luck. He quickly changed the topic to a different issue.

"How is the oppo research coming with Alber and Garcia?" Montgomery asked.

"Yeah… about that. Kyle's been focusing on Garcia. He has a list of affairs as long as your arm. A few of the unconfirmed ones were with his staffers. We're working to get proof… something that could really nail him."

"Anything out of the ordinary?" Montgomery asked. "Something particularly salacious, kinky, weird? If anything like that did come out, I'd sure believe it, and so would most other people. He's a sick dude."

Anna didn't like any part of this conversation. It still felt disingenuous to be devoting resources to dirt-digging while claiming to run a completely above-board campaign. But as long as Montgomery's name was on the door, he was the boss.

"Nothing yet," she said. "Kyle's good, though. I think he's onto some leads."

"Alright. What about Alber?"

"So… Ted Alber is about the cleanest politician I think I've ever come across. I've talked to old opponents, looked through local newspapers, turned over every rock I can find. Still zilch. I'm really not sure where else to look with him."

Montgomery looked frustrated. "The man's not a saint. No one in this business is. He's got to have *something* out there, and you're going to find it!"

Anna was taken aback by Montgomery's raised voice and harsh words. He had never spoken to her like this before.

"Yes sir," she said. "I'm going to redouble my efforts."

"Good," said Montgomery. "And find some new sources."

"Yes sir."

Montgomery must have noticed the look on Anna's face, because he softened his voice and said, "Thanks for your work on this. You're a great team member, Anna. I appreciate having you by my side in this."

Anna thanked Montgomery for his kind words and retreated to her office. He could be so hot and cold lately - one minute yelling, the next praising. Managing his roller coaster of emotions as well as her own was wearing her thin.

All day, Anna was in a somber mood. She had always really liked Christine Franklin, and cracking through the tough exterior of Eugenia Dunn had given her an even stronger appreciation for the two women. She couldn't shake the thought that Tom Franklin may have been deliberately targeted due to the Speaker's race.

Although she continued to dial Chiefs' numbers, she was struggling to focus on her calls. Each time a male voice answered, Anna thought of Tom Franklin on the other end of the line. They had never actually met, but every news report and personal anecdote over the past 24 hours made him sound like one of the kindest men who had ever lived. When a woman picked up the phone, Anna's mind went to Christine Franklin. She felt so sorry for Franklin. The feelings were overwhelming.

I absolutely can't imagine losing your husband of 32 years. It's obvious that the two of them loved each other so much. And to lose him during the most stressful week of your life! Unbelievable. Man, I've got to stop thinking about this... it's starting to affect my focus.

~

Monday night was another near-sleepless one for Anna. The effects of her insomnia were starting to compound; it was getting nearly impossible to focus on what others were saying in meetings. What's more, her usual lack of trust for others seemed to be getting worse. She feared it was turning into full-blown paranoia.

Delta was still there for her, though. Each morning she dutifully cuddled up to Anna and tried to ease a bit of the pain.

Anna wasn't looking forward to Tuesday. The mountain of work was only growing. She could feel others in the office were getting frustrated by her isolation. Every time she entered the door, several staffers would bombard her with questions and items for approval. Although she hated the idea of others thinking her weak, she simply couldn't keep up.

Four more days. I can do anything for four days. Once we get to the end, I am going to collapse in a heap. I don't know how people do this all the time. I guess it's a good thing I didn't go into the military...

59

TUESDAY, AUGUST 1

At 4:53 a.m., Anna picked up her phone off the nightstand and began to scroll through emails.

~

From: Quincy <quincy@quincyswhispers.com>
Subject: Quincy's Whispers - Tuesday, August 1
Date: August 1 at 4:27 AM
To: Anna Rothwell

Quincy's Whispers
266 days since the Midterm Election
462 days until the Presidential Election
3 days until the Speaker Election
What the House is whispering about...
but doesn't want you to hear.

Good Tuesday morning! WOW is this race getting crazy! I did not think things could get any weirder after Tom Franklin's untimely death Sunday morning, but today's Whispers drop yet another grenade into the middle of the pack.

But first, an important note: As anticipated, Christine Franklin (CC-ID) dropped out of the race for Speaker yesterday morning. Less expected was her simultaneous announcement that she would be endorsing Willis Montgomery (BC-MO) and encouraging all of her supporters to vote for him. The net political result of this tragic event will likely be a boon for Montgomery. He was already running well, and Franklin's supporters were numerous and loyal. Montgomery is looking very strong, although the circumstances are unfortunate.

That being said... get ready to throw it all in a blender again, because the (stuff) is about to hit the fan.

What I'm hearing today:

Whisper 1 - I've been dreading this day for weeks. The brewing scandal named Saratoga that I've been telling you about since July 21 is about to break the surface. Congressman Jonathan Garcia (MM-NM) has long been rumored to have had sexual indiscretions, although none have caused him significant trouble. Today will probably end that streak. A young man who interned for Garcia two summers ago is holding a press conference this morning to reveal lurid details of a sexual relationship he claims to have had with Garcia throughout his internship. Allegedly, he will outline at least three instances of outright rape and several more of coerced sexual behavior. He apparently has receipts and other evidence that he says corroborate his account.

Whisper 2 - As I have said in previous Whispers, this scandal sickens me, and it is probably immediately disqualifying for Garcia. His people have been frustrated at having to make excuses for his indiscretions in the past, but this will be a bridge too far. If he had a cleaner record, maybe he could fight these allegations. Realistically though, he's toast.

Whisper 3 - Whip counts still are about as useless as a week-old newspaper. Montgomery will almost certainly pick up a huge chunk of Franklin's support, if not all of it. This will likely put him within striking distance of Ted Alber (UP-KY). Whisperers tell me Alber had a fairly commanding lead before the latest craziness. Now... who knows.

Whisper 4 - As I predicted, Alber soared past his rivals to take command of the race in yesterday's second Consortium Poll. The biggest unknown: will Franklin's pledge to support Montgomery trickle down to the general public? The sympathy pouring forth for Franklin may give her endorsement more weight than the typical plug.

Whisper 5 - The Idaho State Police made a public statement yesterday evening about the crash that killed Tom Franklin Sunday morning. A witness claims to have seen what looked like a dump truck in the area with heavy damage to its front end around the time of the incident. Psychologists are working with the witness to attempt to draw out more detail from his memory. Governor Wyatt Mooney pledged to commit the full resources of the state of Idaho to solve this heinous crime.

Whisper 6 - A bit more on Ticonderoga. Not much to report on the substantive allegations, but I have received ironclad confirmation that the Member involved is NOT one of those running for Speaker. Thank goodness... I have enough craziness to keep track of with that. Still sounds like the situation is gaining steam, though. The news of the terminated pregnancy seems to have touched off several nerves on both sides of the former proverbial aisle.

UNTIL TOMORROW, I have the honor to be,

Your obedient servant,

~QUINCY

Sign up at www.QuincysWhispers.com to get

every edition delivered to your inbox!
Watch for breaking Whispers on Twitter @quincyswhispers.

Hear something good?
Whisper it to me at tips@quincyswhispers.com.
All Whispers are reviewed and kept
strictly anonymous and confidential.

~

THE NEWS of Garcia's rumored sexual abuse of a male intern struck Anna like a hammer to the forehead. For almost 10 minutes, she couldn't even read past the first Whisper. She struggled to make sense of it all.

He's always been such an asshole... and a scumbag. Even his Chief is the worst. Hold on - this means I never have to pretend to like Gus again! Oh, thank God. That guy was awful. I don't think I've ever hated myself as much as I did after that night at Bullfeathers... and what will this mean for Montgomery now? I don't think the Minority Majority has any other Members who are well-positioned to step in... and isn't it probably too late for a new entry anyway? Maybe some of them will come over to our side. This could actually happen... What if I was the Speaker's Chief of Staff on Friday?! No. Can't jinx it. So much more to do anyway. Man... this just keeps getting weirder and weirder.

She rose out of bed and prepared for the day. Delta was still sleeping on her pillow as Anna quietly closed the door and headed to the office.

60

After arriving at 6:00 a.m. and getting to work, Anna was unsurprised to hear a familiar pounding at the front of the office a few minutes later. She unlocked the door and opened it for Kit. She looked at him resignedly, ready to hear him out one more time.

"Yes, Kit?" Anna said. She didn't even move from the front door. His crazy talk didn't warrant a sit-down meeting.

"Did you read the news about Garcia?" he replied.

"Uh, yeah... who's surprised?"

"Don't you see what's happening? Someone's coming after each of the Speaker candidates! I don't know who it is, but these people aren't going to stop at Franklin and Garcia!"

Anna had heard just about enough.

"What the hell are you talking about, Kit? Did you not see the news? One of his former interns is holding an in-person press conference this morning to say what happened. It's not the Illuminati! Garcia is a bad man. Everyone knows that. And just because you're hearing footsteps doesn't mean there's anything to it. This is just a guy with a long history of abuse finally getting his due."

Kit put his hands on his head and paced the foyer. He couldn't find a way to get through to her.

"I swear to you, Anna. This is not my imagination. Something bad is going on here, and you need to help me figure it out!"

"If you're such good friends with Gus, didn't you see this coming?" she asked pointedly.

"Absolutely not!" Kit yelled. "Look, I know Gus isn't always a total gentleman and neither is his boss. But there's a big difference between that and these allegations. Garcia's just not that kind of guy."

"That'd be news to most people in D.C.," Anna replied. Garcia's bad reputation was strong and broad. Few people would give him the benefit of the doubt.

"Gus doesn't exactly keep sexual exploits to himself, if you hadn't noticed," Kit said. "If this kind of stuff was happening in his office, he would've been more likely to brag about it than cover it up. And do I need to remind you he had spooks tailing him too?"

Anna was sick of Kit's conspiracy theories. "Alright, Kit," she said condescendingly. "If these guys are following you, who are they working for? SPECTRE?"

"I don't know how else to tell you this, Anna. They already knocked out Franklin and Garcia. It's down to you and me now. We've got to work together and figure out who's behind this!"

She opened the front door and held it for Kit. "I'm sorry," she said. "I'm afraid you're talking to the wrong person. Best of luck."

Kit let out a frustrated yell as he passed by Anna and hurried down the hallway. Anna looked after him with pity.

He's losing his mind. I guess he can't handle stress. Must not have taught him practical skills at Harvard or Princeton or wherever he went to school. It's a shame. He really is a good-looking guy. If he wasn't such a psycho... and maybe if he wasn't so arrogant. Oh well... I'm already losing enough sleep as it is - definitely not going to lose any more over him.

THE TEAM GATHERED in Anna's office again just before 10:00 a.m. to watch the announcement of the latest polling numbers. The mood was noticeably more excited today. Everyone wanted to see what the impact of Franklin's endorsement would be on public opinion, and the news about Garcia was just starting to sink in. Des quieted down the team as the clock ticked to 10.

Today Anna had the television set to CNN. After the obligatory overdone music and graphics, the anchor got right to the results.

"Once again, Theodore "Ted" Alber of Kentucky leads the pack with 31 percent, up three percent from yesterday. Missourian Willis Montgomery made a strong move, gaining seven percent over yesterday's poll and placing second with 25 percent support."

The entire team let out a simultaneous cheer.

The anchor continued, "Congresswoman Christine Franklin of Idaho has lost significant support after dropping out of the race yesterday and is at 14 percent in today's poll. Congressman Jonathan Garcia of New Mexico received 14 percent support. However, extraordinarily troubling allegations about Mr. Garcia's personal life were just revealed this morning, leading many to question his viability as a candidate. Eight percent of respondents support other candidates and eight percent remain undecided. We will be back tomorrow at 10:00 a.m. to deliver the next-to-last poll in this important race to elect the next Speaker of the House."

The team again cheered and exited Anna's office. Somehow those ever-ringing phones did not seem as dreadful as they had just moments before.

Anna returned to her desk and kept plowing through her list of contacts. With both Franklin and Garcia now essentially out of the race, she had no time to waste. She had to get some intel on Alber, and fast.

But first things had to come first, and maintaining her systematic touches on Chiefs was even more important than muckraking. Especially with all of Garcia's supporters now potentially up for grabs. If she waited until Wednesday, they might all be committed. She moved the Chiefs of Garcia's supporters to the top of her list and began reaching out.

At 1:00 p.m., Anna received an email from Karen Johnson's Communications Director announcing a press conference for 2:00 p.m. in the Capitol Visitors Center. The listed speakers were Johnson, Alejandra Hernandez, and Marquez Williams. According to the email, the presser would be in response to the allegations against Jonathan Garcia.

CNN carried the press conference live at 2:00. Anna and the rest of the team again gathered in her office to see what new developments might come from it. At 2:07, Johnson, Hernandez, and Williams entered the press room and approached the podium. Johnson stepped forward to the microphone and began to read the group's joint statement.

"Thank you all for coming on such short notice," she said. "This morning, my colleagues and I learned of the disgusting and inexcusable allegations against Congressman Jonathan Garcia. Let me first say that all of us condemn these alleged acts in the strongest terms possible. While we do recognize that these allegations are just that - allegations - and not proven facts, we find them to be credible enough to be taken very seriously.

"Congressman Garcia has served this body for many years. He has never been a perfect man. We have stood behind him after previous allegations were made. However, today, we believe that this moment in history requires that we elect a Speaker of the House who does not have the looming specter of scandal.

"After consulting with our colleagues in the Minority Majority this morning, we have come to the unanimous decision to withdraw our support for Congressman Garcia's candidacy."

Camera shutters again roared like a freight train, capturing the somber looks on all three lawmakers' faces.

Johnson continued, "Furthermore, given the fact that the election for Speaker of the House will occur in only three days, the Members of the Minority Majority have concluded that there is insufficient time to put forward a replacement candidate from our party.

"After careful analysis of the remaining candidates in the race, our party has decided to give its unanimous support to Congressman Willis Montgomery. Congressman Montgomery is a statesman of the first order and has a proven track record of working with minority Members and supporting the interests of our constituents. We are proud to support him in this race and trust he will restore this body's reputation as one of honesty and integrity. Thank you."

Anna's office was dead silent as the reporters began to roar to life with questions. No one spoke - they didn't even look at one another. They simply continued staring at the television, mouths agape.

Eventually, Kyle reached for the remote and muted the television. He looked at Anna, who was still trying to make sense of what she'd just witnessed.

Anna lowered her gaze from the television to meet Kyle's eyes. Anna's astonished look morphed into a smile as she simply shrugged at Kyle. She was done trying to predict what was happening on the Hill. The two broke out into a mutual laugh as their good fortune began to sink in.

61

Anna knocked on the passageway door to Montgomery's office. He called for her to come in as he finished up some work on his laptop and closed its lid. Anna was bubbling with excitement as she entered.

"Did you see the Minority Majority press conference?" she asked, barely containing her joy. "They're endorsing you and throwing us their full support!"

"Well that's fantastic news!" Montgomery said. For once he seemed genuinely excited. "Where does that bring us?"

"Combined with the Blues and the Christian Conservatives, looks like about 196," Anna said after doing some quick mental math.

"That's still 22 short of a 218 majority," Montgomery responded dejectedly. "We *have* to get more. How's that oppo research coming on Alber?"

Anna ignored his question and asked her own.

"Won't the GGs or Fiscal Front come over to your side now that they see you're this close?" she asked. Anna felt like getting a handful of

Gadsden Guard or Fiscal Front commitments would surely be easier and more productive than continuing to dig for information on squeaky-clean Alber.

"Look, Anna," Montgomery answered. "The Fiscal Fronters have been clear that they will not commit to me unless it gives me a clear-cut victory. We need 22 votes. They have 17. The stubborn asses just won't do it."

"First of all, that's ridiculous," Anna said. "Even if it's true, though, why not go for the GGs? They have 29 votes. Couldn't you get three-fourths of them and get over the top?"

Montgomery was visibly frustrated. "I've been over and over it with them every day for the past week. They just refuse to wake up to reality and think pragmatically. In their eyes, if you're not for them, you're against them. Zero middle ground."

"Okay, well that does sound like them," Anna said. "It's just so frustrating."

"Tell me about it," said Montgomery. He rubbed his hands together, trying to think of another option.

"Let's keep working our people," Anna said reassuringly. "We've been touching our top targets daily and have a great finger on their pulses. In the next three days, I know we can get enough to come to our side to make the difference."

Montgomery stood from his desk and sighed deeply. "I hope you're right, Anna. One way or another, we have to win this race."

TUESDAY EVENING, Anna went home around 9:00. She was determined to get some rest before the final big push to the finish. After two more days of campaigning, it would be in the hands of the voters.

Delta was happy to have Anna back home. She was starting to be much more clingy when Anna was around - a sure sign she'd been gone too much lately. Anna opened a can of wet cat food and emptied it into Delta's dish. They were both feeling pretty good about things tonight.

Anna settled into her bed and began to watch a show on her laptop. She had a sleeve of Graham crackers and a jar of Nutella on the night-stand next to the bed. Every two minutes or so, she would break a cracker into fourths and dip each piece into the jar before eating it whole. Delta seemed disgusted by this sad routine, since it left crumbs all over her favorite pillow.

Just after 10:30, Anna's phone rang. She picked it up and looked at the screen. The caller ID said "Christopher Lambert."

What does he want at 10:00 on a Wednesday night? Surely not more conspiracy talk... Sigh... I guess I ought to answer though.

"Hello, this is Anna."

"Anna! It's Kit. I have to talk to you!" His voice was frantic.

Anna responded with annoyance. "Kit… what are you calling me for? It's past your bedtime."

Kit ignored her condescending tone. He had completely lost control of his emotions. His voice was near a shriek. "Anna, I just got mugged! At knifepoint!!! Oh my God… Why are they doing this to me!"

Anna sat up in bed, tossing Graham crackers across the comforter. Delta screeched and jumped to the floor.

"Mugged? What? Kit, where are you? Are you okay?"

"I'm fine! I'm fine. He took my wallet that had my keys attached to it and let me go. Oh God…" Kit was crying hysterically.

"Kit. Listen to me. Are you in a place where you are safe?"

"Safe?! Hahahaha… safe. Where is safe, Anna?"

Wow, I think this really pushed him over the edge. It's definitely weird though. Is it possible he's not just nuts?

"Alright, Kit. Just - why are you calling me? Have you called the police?"

"Anna, it was him!"

"What was who?"

"The guy! The one who was following Eugenia! The redhead with the mole on his face."

A chill ran the length of Anna's spine. She was silent for a moment.

"Are you sure?" she finally asked. "Couldn't it have been another redhead with a mole? There are a lot of gingers in Washington, D.C., with moles on their faces. Hey... are you prejudiced against my people?"

Anna said this last bit with a hint of sarcasm. She and other redheads she knew often joked that people tend to think they all look alike.

Her attempt at humor was lost on Kit. This was not the time. "No, Anna. I'm not prejudiced against redheads. Eugenia described him to me in detail when we talked this weekend. I have zero doubt in my mind it was him."

Anna kept looking for alternative explanations.

"It's almost 11:00, Kit. It's pitch black. Maybe your mind just tricked you into thinking he looked like that because you're already so obsessed with the idea."

"It was him. And right now, I really don't care who it was - either way, I just got mugged with a knife on my throat."

She thought about the facts Kit had told her. He was so upset, she thought it was worth trying to see it from his perspective and talk it through. If nothing else, it might calm him down.

"Alright. Tell me again what he took."

"It was a nylon wallet. Really just an ID holder with a keyring attached. They sell them in the House gift shop."

"And what was in it?"

"My Congressional ID, my driver's license, and my debit card."

"What about the keyring? Did you say you had keys attached?"

"Yeah… my office key and my apartment key. That's it."

"No cash? He didn't take your phone?"

"No. I had my full wallet in my back pocket and was just holding the ID case as I walked. He came up from behind me and put his knife to my throat. He said to shut up or I'd die. He grabbed the ID holder and thumbed through it with his free hand. I told him to take my phone if he wanted it. Oh my God!"

Kit broke down in tears again. Anna tried to get him to refocus.

"Okay, I'm still listening," she said. "What else happened?"

"He took the knife off my throat and spun me around. That's when I saw his face. He said, 'I've got all I need,' then punched me in the stomach and walked away."

What the hell... Kit's had some bizarre stories lately, but this really takes the cake. I guess his debit card could be worth quite a bit if you had the PIN, but the rest is pretty useless... and why not at least frisk him for a wallet or take the phone? And to think, a week ago I thought this guy's head was too big to fit through the door... now he's a whimpering pile of jelly.

Anna realized Kit was waiting on her to speak.

"Kit, are you still there?"

"Yeah, I'm here."

"We're going to find out who did this, okay? You call the police and get to a safe place."

"Alright. Thanks Anna."

"Of course. I'll check on you in the morning."

Anna ended the call and tossed her phone on her bed.

"Well that was weird," she said to Delta.

Anna swept the crumbs off the bed as best she could and carried them over to her trash can. She double-checked the lock and deadbolt on her door before laying back down. She didn't fall asleep until midnight.

62

WEDNESDAY, AUGUST 2

Once she finally drifted off, Anna slept much more soundly than the past few nights. Of course, it's hard to be worse than complete insomnia. Anna felt significantly better after five hours of sleep than she had after two days of none. Still, five hours is not enough for anyone to truly function well.

Delta appeared to be noticing. Instead of seeming irritated at Anna's 5:00 a.m. alarm each morning, she had come to take it as her cue to leave her own pillow and lie down against Anna's face. She would purr and purr while Anna stroked her back. These few minutes were enough to calm Anna's nerves and get her up for the day.

Once the sleep wore off, Anna's thoughts returned to the bizarre phone call she'd received from Kit the night before.

If he hadn't been acting so weird the past few days, I'd have thought that phone call was a dream. I ought to check in on him today just to make sure he's okay.

Anna dragged herself out of bed and got ready in the bathroom. While brushing her teeth, she skimmed the morning Whispers.

~

From: Quincy <quincy@quincyswhispers.com>
Subject: Quincy's Whispers - Wednesday, August 2
Date: August 2 at 4:33 AM
To: Anna Rothwell

Quincy's Whispers
267 days since the Midterm Election
461 days until the Presidential Election
2 days until the Speaker Election
What the House is whispering about...
but doesn't want you to hear.

Good Wednesday morning! Could things get any more nuts? The fallout from Jonathan Garcia's (MM-NM) implosion has roiled the waters in the Speaker's race even further. Once again, the luckiest guy in the room appears to be Congressman Willis Montgomery (BC-MO). This one speaks to the power of his relationships. If Montgomery hadn't been cultivating friends on both sides of the former aisle for the past two decades, he would never be in his current situation. Receiving the Minority Majority's full-throated endorsement - a group for which voting in lockstep is a literal prerequisite to membership - puts Montgomery neck-and-neck with Ted Alber (UP-KY). Your next Speaker is almost certain to be Montgomery or Alber.

What I'm hearing today:

Whisper 1 - This is now a two-man race. Knowledgeable Whisperers seem to think that even with the votes of former Franklin supporters and the Minority Majority, Montgomery may still be a few votes behind Alber. Hard to say, though. Not a lot of Members are publicly announcing their support, so there's lots of guessing involved in any whip count.

Whisper 2 - Today's polling should be interesting. Due to the two-day rolling sample, half of respondents will have taken the poll after news of Garcia's disgusting actions in Saratoga. He was polling at 14 percent yesterday… that's a significant chunk of support that will likely now make its way to either Alber or Montgomery.

Whisper 3 - Maybe the most interesting thing about the fallout from this is just how few people have come out to support Garcia. Despite his pledge to push on in his campaign for Speaker through what he calls a "witch hunt," I could only find evidence of two other Members making public statements backing him up. This is what you get for pushing the envelope for too many years - eventually you alienate everyone, and no one is there to support you when you really need it.

Whisper 4 - News on the Tom Franklin investigation is still elusive. An anonymous tip led investigators to an abandoned barn in an extremely rural portion of the Idaho panhandle yesterday, where they found a dump truck outfitted with a heavily reinforced front bumper. The truck had sustained serious damage to the front end. The reinforcements appeared to be very recent, lending more weight to the rumor that this was a pre-planned attack on a specific target.

Whisper 5 - I'm hearing an indictment may be imminent in Yorktown. For those who struggle to keep these things straight, Yorktown involves an FBI probe into alleged bribery and corruption of a Member. Still not getting a clear read on who is involved, but the allegations themselves sound like bombshells.

Whisper 6 - The markets seem to be comfortable with the two most-likely possible Speakers. Volatility was way down yesterday afternoon once traders had time to process the news about Saratoga. Montgomery is a known quantity and viewed as a calming statesman; Alber is well-liked and seen as a future President.

UNTIL TOMORROW, I have the honor to be,

Your obedient servant,

. . .

~Quincy

Sign up at www.QuincysWhispers.com to get
every edition delivered to your inbox!
Watch for breaking Whispers on Twitter @quincyswhispers.

Hear something good?
Whisper it to me at tips@quincyswhispers.com.
All Whispers are reviewed and kept
strictly anonymous and confidential.

~

Anna could hardly contain her anxiety over the state of play in the Speaker race. Things were starting to get real. Everyone now acknowledged that in two days, either she or Kit would be Chief of Staff to the Speaker of the House. The corollary to this, though, was that the loser would effectively become an outcast with no real political future. She couldn't take the suspense and uncertainty.

Her oppo research efforts had still not borne any fruit, and the deeper she dug, the more uncomfortable she became. She knew she was doing the right thing... getting this information might make the difference between winning and losing. But rather than making her feel more confident, she now was more of a mess than ever.

Staring back at Anna from the mirror was a haggard middle-aged woman. The gorgeous young redhead she was used to seeing had turned into a bedraggled adult with bags under her eyes and ever-deepening worry lines.

Two more days. That's it. It'll all be over. Two more days.

She finished up getting ready, said goodbye to Delta, and headed out the door to work.

63

Wednesday morning, Team Montgomery's excitement was impossible to contain. Now that the Speaker's race was effectively down to Montgomery and Alber, the adrenaline rush was pushing everyone to a state of near ecstasy.

In the midst of the morning chaos in the office, Anna forgot to check in with Kit. She had a massive amount of work to get done for the Speaker race. She was two days from achieving her wildest dreams, and her mind was focused on making them come true.

At 10:00, the team gathered in Anna's office for polling results. Des sent the phones to voicemail as everyone squeezed in the small room. This time Montgomery happened to be in the office. He entered Anna's office through his private passageway and watched alongside the team.

Kyle turned up the volume so they could hear the NBC anchor lay out the situation.

"For the third consecutive day, Congressman Ted Alber of Kentucky leads the Consortium Poll. His tally increased 12 percent from Tuesday, pulling in 43 percent support. Hot on his heels is Missouri

Congressman Willis Montgomery at 37 percent, also an increase of 12 points."

The team whooped and high-fived each other, happy to be keeping pace with the frontrunner. There was still plenty of distance to make up over the next two days, but they were within striking range. At the mention of Alber, Anna thought about Kit for a split second, but the idea was quickly swept away by the anchor's closing sentences.

"Embattled Congressman Jonathan Garcia of New Mexico has quickly faded, only carrying eight percent in today's poll. Six percent support other candidates and six percent are undecided. Stay tuned to NBC News for all of the latest updates on this developing situation."

Anna muted the television. Montgomery turned and addressed the team with a grin.

"Well guys, what do you think?"

The team cheered in unison.

"We are most definitely headed the right direction!" he said. "I can't tell you how much I appreciate all of your hard work - and we're doing this the *right* way. Two more days to victory!"

THE REST of the day seemed to fly by for Anna. She happily knocked out her list of calls and texts, double-checking with supporters to ensure they didn't have any last concerns before Friday's vote. She was in her own little world - and a happy one, at that.

At 3:15 p.m., her phone buzzed to alert her to an incoming text message. She quickly glanced at the screen and saw it was from Peter Garibaldi. She unlocked her phone and checked the text.

> **PG**: Hey Anna, have you heard anything from Kit today? He left me a really weird VM just after lunch. Tried to call him back but no answer.

Shoot. I was going to call Kit this morning and totally forgot. I'd better check on him.

AR: Nothing today. He called late last night and was pretty upset, but that's the last I've heard from him. I'll try to get a hold of him.

PR: K, let me know if you hear from him. Tell him to call me.

Anna had been too engrossed in helping Montgomery win the Speaker's race to worry about Kit's mental breakdown and conspiracy theories. Then again, he did seem legitimately upset last night. Anna decided to just text him. She really didn't want to deal with another long, emotional phone call.

AR: You doing ok today?

She set her phone aside and worked on a few other things on her computer. Several minutes later, Kit still had not texted her back.

Hm, weird. He usually responds immediately. I'm sure he's busy with Speaker race stuff though. Well, if he's not in the looney bin.

Another 10 minutes elapsed before her phone finally buzzed with Kit's response.

KL: Yeah. I'm fine. Police are looking for the mugger, but no news yet. Trying to focus on the race.

At least he's not dead. I hope he can just keep himself together for another two days. I really don't need any more late-night wake-up calls about bogeymen.

She wrote a quick line back.

AR: Good, glad you're ok. Let me know if you need anything.

Anna exited the text with Kit and shot a quick text to Peter to let him know Kit was alright. She dove back into her work, pushing Kit out of her mind.

Anna made sure to stay alert on her walk home that night, but she did not see any questionable redheads or suspicious vehicles following her. She laughed at herself as she opened the door to her apartment. She decided that she wasn't going to let Kit's overactive imagination infect her too.

She scooped Delta up into her arms and showered her furry friend with attention. Delta's warm, purring body helped calm her. As Anna drifted off to sleep later that night, she thought smugly that all the privileged, Ivy League training in the world was no match for her Midwestern self-taught mental toughness.

64

THURSDAY, AUGUST 3

"FBI, open the door!" A fit man in his early 30s rapped his knuckles against the thick oak door five times. "This is Special Agent Burgess with the Federal Bureau of Investigations," he said. "We have a warrant to search the premises."

Agent Burgess's voice echoed down the long, empty corridor against the marble floors and 15-foot ceilings of the Cannon House Office Building. Two hundred feet away, a solitary janitor blasted music through headphones and pushed a large trash can slowly away from them. She paid no attention to the team of five armed agents serving the warrant. A 1950s-era analog clock ticked above her head showing 2:27 a.m.

He knocked again. "Open the door or we will have no choice but to enter by force."

After several moments, sounds of movement came from the other side of the door just as Agent Burgess was preparing his final warning. "What do you want? It's 2:30 a.m." the irritated voice responded.

"Are you Congressman Theodore Alber?" asked Agent Burgess.

"Yes, who's asking?"

"Special Agent Burgess with the FBI. We have a warrant to search your office."

"A warrant? Why? What for?" Alber said from behind the closed door. He sounded confused.

"We have orders to search the premises for any evidence related to public corruption."

"Corruption?" Alber erupted. "What the hell is this? Is this some kind of joke? Did Dan put you up to this?"

"I'm sorry sir, but this is exactly what it appears to be. If you open the door and cooperate with our team, we will do our best to leave your office in the condition we found it."

Congressman Alber unlocked the heavy door and cracked it open. He squinted as the light hit his eyes. "This is crazy. I follow the law to the letter. There's no way I've done anything wrong. Is it even legal for you to search this office? What about separation of powers?" His brain was spitting out a stream of poorly formed thoughts as it did its best to wake up and process the scene.

Agent Burgess was sympathetic but stern. "This warrant pertains to evidence of public corruption. The FBI has jurisdiction over such cases."

Alber cursed to himself, then opened the door fully. He was barefoot and wore only boxer shorts and a wrinkled white undershirt. His office was filled by a large sofa bed that he had obviously been sleeping on moments earlier. These days many Members of Congress slept in their offices - especially young, male Members. It helped them save money by not renting an exorbitantly overpriced D.C. apartment, and it had the added benefit of making them seem more relatable to their constituents.

"I know this is a mistake, and I know I've done nothing wrong," he said. "You won't find anything here. But I am a law-abiding person and don't want to cause trouble. I'm going to let you come in. Please just be careful with things. Even a fruitless search of an innocent man's office can ruin his career if it's found out."

"Understood," said Agent Burgess. "We recognize the sensitivity of the situation and will do our best." He turned to the other four men in the hallway and motioned them inside.

Alber paced constantly, getting more upset as he thought about the consequences of this raid on his political situation. The election was only 30 hours away - was this a political hit job?

"Can I see that warrant?" he asked Agent Burgess. "I want to know which judge in which court issued this. I find the timing of this whole thing incredibly suspect. I am running for Speaker of the House, the election is tomorrow morning, and I have done *zero* wrong. This *has* to be political. And if it is, this will make Watergate look like a kids' picnic. You had better have an incredible team of lawyers, because I will *not* let this go."

Alber's face was beet red. He tried to contain the steam building inside of him while keeping his voice as low as possible. He was being railroaded - he knew it.

"I understand your frustration, Congressman," said Agent Burgess. "I can assure you the warrant application was approved by the absolute highest levels of the Justice Department and was reviewed in excruciating detail by the issuing judge. The law was followed to the letter."

The agents searched the small office top to bottom, carefully examining the contents of desks, file cabinets, and closets. Congressional offices were tiny, so the staff made good use of the space they were allotted. Every surface had something on top of, behind, or underneath it.

After thoroughly searching the legislative staff's space and coming up empty, the agents proceeded to Alber's personal office. They gently tipped over furniture and tapped each piece to listen for any potential voids or hidden compartments before returning them to their prior homes with care.

The tallest agent, who looked like he had been a linebacker not many years earlier, began to go through the contents of Alber's personal closet. The Congressman watched from the closet's doorway as the agent looked through each box, shirt, and suit; even the pile of laundry on the floor. The agent was getting a firsthand view of the true glamour of many Congressional lives. He eventually removed two suitcases from the back of the closet and knocked his fist along the wall above the baseboard. A faint smell of paint wafted from the closet.

As he passed from left to right, the solid thumps turned to hollow echoes, then back to solid thumps. The agent called for Burgess before going further. He then reversed his tapping motion and outlined a void in the wall. The agent took out a black permanent marker and drew a rough line on the wall that followed the hole's edges. Visually it appeared the same as the rest of the wall.

The agent was wearing blue latex gloves. He took one finger and ran it across the plaster. When he looked at his fingertip, it was covered with a white smear.

Alber stood at the closet's entrance appearing unimpressed. He knew what the agents were thinking, but he knew he'd never concealed anything in that wall or anywhere else. "They tell me this closet used to be a bathroom back when Cannon was built," he said. "It's more than a century old. I'm sure there are a thousand old holes patched up in these walls."

Agent Burgess told his tall colleague to open the void and inspect the wall. After two minutes with a carpenter's hammer, the agent had broken the false covering loose and revealed a two-foot-by-one-foot empty space. Burgess asked the other agent to step aside as he entered the closet himself.

Bending to his knees, Agent Burgess clicked on his flashlight and shined it inside the hole. Without saying a word, he reached inside and pulled out a huge stack of fresh hundred-dollar bills. Burgess turned and looked at Congressman Alber, whose mouth hung wide. His face was completely white. Burgess inspected a few of the bills and announced that they had been printed the previous year - the money was new. He removed several more stacks of money from the wall and neatly piled more than $250,000 in cash on the closet floor.

Agent Burgess wiped the dust off of his hands as he rose and stepped toward Alber, who stared at the money in shock. "Congressman," he said, "you are under arrest for the crime of bribery with intent to influence an act of a federal official."

CONGRESSMAN TED ALBER was having the worst day of his life. The 2:30 a.m. FBI wake-up call had been rough enough. Watching Agent Burgess pile stack after stack of crisp $100 bills next to his shoes and dirty socks had made him physically ill. He wanted to vomit as he watched the pile grow.

Alber was able to talk Agent Burgess into letting him put on some fresh clothes, brush his teeth, and comb his hair before leaving his office. He knew there was no avoiding embarrassment now - he would be arrested, booked, and jailed. His mug shot would be on every national news station within hours. Anxiety overwhelmed him as he imagined his promising future rapidly circling the toilet.

Agent Burgess and his team were professional and courteous as they took Alber to the holding facility to be processed. The fingerprinting and photographs only took a few seconds, but the paperwork dragged out at least an hour. Finally, the last blanks were filled in and Alber was taken to a cell. The large clock at the entrance to the cell block read 5:03 a.m. He silently stepped inside and sat on the floor against the wall. His eyes were vacant. He looked like a man who had just lost everything.

65

Anna woke up at 5:00 a.m. with a burst of energy.

Tomorrow's the day. Tomorrow's the DAY! All of this will be over, one way or another, in about... let's see... 30 more hours! There's still sooo much to do between now and then, but we can see the finish line. And it's a two-man race: Alber and Montgomery. We're going to give it all we've got.

Anna grabbed her phone and began to check the overnight rumors while brushing her teeth in the bathroom. Seconds after opening the Thursday Whispers, she froze in complete disbelief.

~

From: Quincy <quincy@quincyswhispers.com>
Subject: Quincy's Whispers - Thursday, August 3
Date: August 3 at 4:39 AM
To: Anna Rothwell

Quincy's Whispers
268 days since the Midterm Election
460 days until the Presidential Election

1 day until the Speaker Election
What the House is whispering about...
but doesn't want you to hear.

Good Thursday morning! Ok, I'm done making predictions about how crazy things can get. There are simply no words for what you're about to read. Let's just get to it.

What I'm hearing today:

Whisper 1 - We should see charges filed today linked to Yorktown. I can't begin to find words to express the shock I am experiencing. I have confirmed that the lone indicted Member will be none other than the frontrunner for Speaker of the House, Theodore James Alber (UP-KY).

Whisper 2 - Since originally reporting on it July 18, I have heard credible speculation that Yorktown possibly involved literally dozens of different Members. Never once did I hear the name Ted Alber. But, according to a Whisperer in the Department of Justice, it sounds like the feds have him dead to rights on bribery and public corruption charges. Whisperers tell me that last night, an FBI team raided Congressman Alber's office in Cannon. After a thorough search, they apparently discovered $250,000 in cold, hard cash stuffed inside the walls of his closet.

Whisper 3 - The Attorney General is expected to announce the charges at a press conference this morning at 9:00 in the J. Edgar Hoover Building.

Whisper 4 - Support for Jonathan Garcia (MM-NM) cratered in yesterday's poll. Despite his defiant pledge to carry on, the American public seems to have all but abandoned him. Today's poll will have his scandal fully baked into the results. Expect to see his support disappear.

Whisper 5 - But let's be real. That poll isn't going to matter. The timing on Yorktown couldn't be worse for Alber, and the consequences are clear. Turns out my code-naming of this situation was prescient: this looks to be the end of the war. Alber's bid for Speaker is over... and probably his days in Congress as well. The reality is obvious: Willis Montgomery is your next Speaker.

Whisper 6 - I expect the stock markets to jump once this news hits. Montgomery is beloved by Wall Street types, not so much for his specific financial policies, but for his statesmanlike persona and years of experience. He's seen as a steady hand at the tiller.

UNTIL TOMORROW, I have the honor to be,

Your obedient servant,

~QUINCY

Sign up at www.QuincysWhispers.com to get
every edition delivered to your inbox!
Watch for breaking Whispers on Twitter @quincyswhispers.

Hear something good?
Whisper it to me at tips@quincyswhispers.com.
All Whispers are reviewed and kept
strictly anonymous and confidential.

ANNA'S VEINS ran completely cold. The color drained from her face. Her clammy hands could hardly operate her phone's touchscreen. They were shaking so badly, she could barely even hold it.

She dropped her toothbrush into the sink and set her phone down on the counter. Her hands were moving wildly now, looking for something solid to hold onto. She talked to herself as she tried to find something stable.

"It can't be right. It can't! There's no way. I've been looking and looking and looking and I haven't found *anything* on Alber! He's clean as a whistle! Him? How is it even possible?"

Delta jumped off of the bed and made her way into the bathroom, pushing open the cracked door. She wasn't used to Anna talking to herself. Anna kept mumbling as she paced frantically.

Without warning, Anna dropped to her knees and violently vomited into the toilet. The stress had finally broken her. Again and again she retched, crying as she tried to get control of herself. Long after everything had been evacuated from her stomach, her body finally gave in. She collapsed backward against the bathroom wall. She continued to think through the possibilities.

Kit kept saying someone was after them... But they found cash in his personal office closet wall. No... no. That just can't be faked. What if Kit was just trying to lay the foundation to cover for his boss? He must have figured out that the G-men were on to them and tried to come up with a story. Yes! That explains the wacko call I got from him about the mugging - he wanted me to think some redheaded hitman stole his ID and keys to break in Alber's office and frame him! But the FBI has been on this case for weeks - it didn't just happen last night. His story just wouldn't add up. Wow is that insane.

Delta walked toward her, jumped into her lap, and curled into a ball. Anna didn't have the strength to speak.

Alber was taking bribes... the FBI found cash in his walls. There's no other way to explain it. Alber did it, and he's just one of the best con men I've ever seen. What was I thinking? I had almost convinced myself maybe he was honest. No one *in this business is honest. When am I going to learn that? The only person you can trust is yourself.*

Anna pulled herself together enough to reach for the Pepto-Bismol on her bathroom counter. She lay back against the side of the bathtub and took several long chugs. Then another thought struck her.

Alright, but what if it is a frame job? Another hit on a candidate? Franklin is a stretch, Garcia probably DID do it, and this seems impossible to fake... but what if someone really did? Montgomery... he could be next! I've got to warn him... if someone takes him out before the election tomorrow, we'll lose everything we've been working for! It just can't happen. We have to figure out who's behind this and stop them, plus keep Montgomery safe until the vote.

The fear gave Anna a jolt of adrenaline. She had to get to the bottom of this before something worse happened. As she hurriedly got dressed, she again began to doubt herself.

There's no way this is some big conspiracy... it's just our good luck. I don't want to sound like a nut job to Montgomery. I can't risk him not taking me with him to the Speaker's office...

She shot out the apartment door with barely a goodbye to Delta, still throwing on her clothes as she raced down the stairs.

66

The office was empty when Anna arrived at 5:55 a.m. Montgomery usually came in around 6:30 on Thursdays. He had a weekly pickup basketball game with some other Members that he absolutely never missed, and he always dropped by the office before heading to the gym. Anna tried to think through what to say to him once he arrived. There was just so much to consider. She chewed on three more antacid tablets as she thought.

What's Montgomery going to think about Alber? It's just so far-fetched. Ted Alber... Saint Theodore... taking $250,000 cash as a bribe?

She laid down on her couch and tried to relax. Her mind kept rehashing the arguments for and against Kit's theory.

There's no way all of that could have been pulled off. Kit has to be lying. The FBI doesn't make stuff up, and they wouldn't search his office without a warrant. A judge wouldn't issue a warrant without other evidence of wrong-doing... so there must *be something to it. Kit made up that BS story two nights ago to try and build an alibi... What a psycho! He's got to be some kind of sociopath to be that good of an actor...*

Anna closed her eyes as she rested on the couch. Some of the story still just didn't feel right.

Why today? Literally the day before the Speaker election? Didn't the FBI learn not to get in the middle of this kind of stuff back when Comey reopened the Clinton email inquiry right before the 2016 election? Then again, if they're moving forward, it probably means they have some airtight evidence this time... and they wanted to get it out there before the election so it wouldn't make Congress implode further if Alber won and then this came out. But what do I know?

The competing arguments were pulling Anna's mind apart in different directions. She desperately wanted to just sort it out and pick a side.

Okay, if Kit's telling the truth, about 100 things would have had to happen in exactly the order he said. Really the chances of it being some conspiracy like that are pretty minuscule. I bet Kit just wants to be Chief to the Speaker and can't stand that it's going to be me. He freaked out when he got word what was going to happen and tried to cover his rear.

But then again... what if he's right? I can't just sit on it and say nothing to Montgomery. I don't care if he thinks I'm nuts, I have to at least mention it. What if something happened to Montgomery and I hadn't warned him? I'd never forgive myself.

Through all of these thoughts, she still hadn't fully internalized the implications of Alber's arrest. As of this moment, no legitimate contenders remained in the race. Tomorrow, Montgomery would be Speaker.

ANNA WAS STILL in the middle of a debate with herself when Montgomery arrived just before 6:30. As soon as she heard his key insert into the lock, she rose from the couch and stepped out of her office to meet him.

Montgomery opened the door and saw Anna inside the office. His face immediately lit up in ecstasy as he jumped forward to embrace Anna. He let out a loud "woo-HOO!" as he squeezed her in excitement. Anna was stiff as a board. She was so confused by all of her emotions, she was having trouble making sense of how she felt, let alone Montgomery's reaction.

Montgomery recognized something was wrong. Anna was neither smiling nor returning his hug. He let go and stepped back.

"Are you ok, Anna?" he said. "Didn't you see the news about Alber? We're going to win this thing!"

Anna stared blankly at the door. Her eyes moved slowly toward Montgomery and she forced a fake smile.

"Yeah, I saw. Great news for us."

Montgomery's smile disappeared. Anna's response was very out of character. She may not show many emotions, but he knew enough to see that this was not normal.

"Come into my office," he said.

The two stepped inside Montgomery's office and shut the door. Anna sat on a chair and Montgomery stood leaning against his desk.

"Tell me what's wrong, Anna," he said.

"I… I don't really know," she stammered. "It's all just so… so much. It's so much to process. I don't know what to think."

Montgomery laughed. "Ha! What to think is you're about to be Chief of Staff to the Speaker of the House!"

Anna cracked a slight smile. Despite her uneasiness, hearing these words come out of Montgomery's mouth were satisfying. This had been her dream since first setting foot on the Hill, and now it was all but hers.

Her reply was emotionless. "Yes. Yes, I suppose so. And I'm excited for that, I really am. I can't wait to get started with it."

"Then what's the problem?" Montgomery asked. "Are you okay?"

"I'll be fine," Anna said. "It's just... Alber. I have looked and looked and looked for *anything* about him that might be helpful. I never even found him misplacing a nickel, much less taking a quarter-of-a-million-dollar bribe. I'm just not sure it's legitimate."

Montgomery laughed again. "Not legitimate? Anna, the FBI had probably been investigating him for months. They found the cash stuffed in the wall of his personal closet. Sometimes people are just good at deceiving others."

Anna felt a chill at Montgomery's final words. Trusting others had always been such a struggle... it still seemed like every time she started to believe in someone, they let her down. Alber really had her fooled - she had bought his choir-boy persona. She beat herself up internally as she struggled to put her emotions into words.

Never again. You can't trust ANYONE. Add Alber to the list. How many more will it take before I realize to never trust other people?

"Ok," she said. "I guess you're right. It's sad though. He seemed like a good person. One more thing that's bothering me. I don't know if it's anything, but I feel like I should mention it."

"Yeah, what's that?" Montgomery asked.

"Well, I've heard a few people speculating that this stuff with Franklin, Garcia, and Alber wasn't just coincidence. Some people think it was all orchestrated."

"Orchestrated?" Montgomery said incredulously. "Orchestrated by whom?"

"I have no idea," Anna admitted. "Maybe someone who just wants to sow chaos. Could be the Russians, the Chinese... hell, it could be someone domestic for all I know. Honestly, after Tom Franklin's death, I started thinking it might be Garcia trying to take out his opponents."

"Whew, that's a pretty big allegation," Montgomery said. He thought for a moment before continuing. "Let me ask you, have you encountered evidence that would support any of these theories, or is it all speculation?"

Anna thought about it for a minute or two.

Kit's frantic pleas, the rumors floating around... none of it was based on facts. It was all feelings and fears. It's a weird set of incidents in a short amount of time, but each one has a totally plausible honest explanation. The circumstantial evidence lends itself to curiosity, but the facts don't seem to support a conspiracy.

"I guess you're right," she said, finally. "It's all just rumor and innuendo. Probably nothing more than people trying to connect dots that don't actually go together. Some people were even telling me that you and I needed to watch our backs because we could be next."

Montgomery chuckled and said, "Well, I sure hope we're not next. But I don't think we need to worry. We just need to make plans for tomorrow - we're about to win this thing!"

Anna was finally coming around. "Yeah we do... we have a lot of organizing to take care of. I can't believe we're the last ones standing. If people didn't know better, they might think we were masterminding all these incidents," she said jokingly.

Montgomery's face went white and his smile disappeared.

"Why would anyone think that?" he asked tersely.

"Just, well, you know how crazy the rumor mill can get," Anna sputtered weakly, completely thrown off by Montgomery's sudden mood swing. "You know, people looking at who ended up benefiting from each person's withdrawal or scandal. *Cui bono*? - who benefits. Kind of like a 'follow the money' thing."

"Well if you hear anything like that from anyone, you let them know that I had absolutely nothing to do with it. I play above board and am going to win this race fair and square. You understand?"

Anna was again taken aback by Montgomery's emotional outburst.

"Yes sir," she said.

"Good. The last thing we need is people spreading fake rumors, trying to call me a murderer and such."

"Absolutely. I'll be on the lookout."

"Alright," said Montgomery. "Now let's get moving. We have a lot to do."

AT 10:00, Anna turned on her television but left it muted. She sat in her chair as she watched the final poll results drop onto the screen: Alber 47%, Montgomery 40%, Garcia 3%, Other 4%, Undecided 6%. She knew the numbers were meaningless. All that mattered now was the Members' vote. With the morning's revelations about Alber, she knew it was all but over.

Strangely, Anna didn't feel the level of excitement she expected. Despite Montgomery's reassurances earlier, she still felt uneasy.

If some kind of bad actors are behind this, they could still come for Montgomery before tomorrow. No, no, no, that's crazy talk. Franklin's crash was an accident, Garcia's rumor is probably true, and Alber is just another corrupt politician. We just happen to have the good fortune to benefit from it all. That's it. I just need to accept that we had good luck for once and take the win.

An absent stare returned to her face as she remained deep in thought. Her stomach began to churn again.

67

FRIDAY, AUGUST 4

Anna didn't even try to sleep Thursday night. She knew it would have been a complete waste of effort. Instead, she stayed in her office and worked late into the night. Her veins were flowing with more coffee than blood. She felt like hell, but at least she was still upright.

At 3:00 a.m., Anna decided it would be a good idea to at least lie down for a while. She had read once that lying down for a couple of hours can actually provide many of the same benefits of sleep. She had no idea if this was remotely true, but it sounded pretty good at that moment, so she did it.

The excitement of the morning's upcoming vote made it almost impossible to stay put, though. She would do anything to just be able to skip forward a few hours. In less than half a day, she would be Chief of Staff to the Speaker of the United States House of Representatives. It seemed impossible that this was really happening to her. Her ticket had actually come through - she was about to win her career equivalent of the lottery.

At 5:00, she finally allowed herself to go back to checking emails and reading the news.

From: Quincy <quincy@quincyswhispers.com>
Subject: Quincy's Whispers - Friday, August 4
Date: August 4 at 4:30 AM
To: Anna Rothwell

Quincy's Whispers
269 days since the Midterm Election
459 days until the Presidential Election
Day of the Speaker Election!
What the House is whispering about...
but doesn't want you to hear.

Good Friday morning! What started as a dogfight appears to be ending in a coronation for Congressman Willis Montgomery (BC-MO). Barring another insane development, the House will elect him Speaker late this morning. I don't know about you, but I'm ready for a nap.

The House will gavel in at 10:00 a.m. today. After preliminary formalities, the vote for Speaker of the House is expected to occur around 11:00. The new Speaker will likely be sworn in around noon.

What I'm hearing today:

Whisper 1 - If and when Willis Montgomery is sworn in as Speaker of the House, he will become only the second Speaker from the state of Missouri. As I'm sure you know, James Beauchamp "Champ" Clark was the only other person from the Show Me State to hold that honor, serving as Speaker from 1911-1919.

Whisper 2 - Yesterday's indictment and arrest of Ted Alber (UP-KY) continues to baffle everyone on the Hill. Judging by the chorus of

Whispers coming in yesterday, even Alber's biggest detractors did not think he was corrupt. Usually corrupt politicians are surrounded by substantial rumors - smoke is seen before the fire.

Whisper 3 - The lack of smoke surrounding this curiously timed fire have led to all kinds of speculation and conspiracy theories about Alber being framed. Combined with the foul-play death of Tom Franklin and the suspicious timing of the rape allegations against Jonathan Garcia (MM-NM), many Whisperers are looking to the last man standing and asking questions. Might Montgomery meet a similar fate? Is Montgomery just a fabulously lucky beneficiary of these three unbelievable events? Or could something more sinister be going on?

Whisper 4 - However, at this time there is absolutely no evidence tying Speaker Montgomery to any of these incidents. The most-likely explanation is that with stakes this high, the deepest dirt-diggers went into overdrive on Garcia and Alber. As for Tom Franklin, we may simply never know. He could easily have been an incredibly unfortunate victim in a case of wrong-place, wrong-time.

Whisper 5 - What we do know is that today the House will turn a corner. We will soon emerge from the darkest period of this august body's long history and begin a new era. After what we've all been through, this is cause for celebration.

Whisper 6 - Response from the stock markets appears jubilant. Overnight trading indicates a massive rally is likely today. Montgomery seems to be the captain of the ship traders have been begging for.

Let's hope next week we can start over with a clean slate and put this nightmare episode of our nation's history behind us.

UNTIL MONDAY, I have the honor to be,

Your obedient servant,

. . .

~QUINCY

Sign up at www.QuincysWhispers.com to get
every edition delivered to your inbox!
Watch for breaking Whispers on Twitter @quincyswhispers.

Hear something good?
Whisper it to me at tips@quincyswhispers.com.
All Whispers are reviewed and kept
strictly anonymous and confidential.

THE WHISPERS WERE pure joy for Anna. She read the email over and over, smiling and laughing each time. She was slightly annoyed that rumors impugning Montgomery had made their way in, but she figured it was just sour grapes from the other candidates who knew they didn't have a shot. She was not going to let that kind of pettiness bother her today. She was about to become the most powerful staffer on Capitol Hill. She decided she had better put on her best outfit and really pay attention to the mirror - today her image would be in news reports from every country in the world.

68

Des and Lily took charge of arrangements for Montgomery's post-election celebration. They reserved a large room in the Capitol and ordered mountains of hors d'oeuvres and drinks for the occasion. They special-ordered a congratulatory cake and had it delivered. Anna worked with Josh and Kyle to ensure all of Montgomery's biggest supporters and donors received personal invitations. Everyone was floating on air. The sleepless nights, the endless phone calls, the incessant work - all of it had been worth it.

Montgomery arrived in the office around 8:30 a.m. He was positively beaming. Any stress he'd been feeling in recent weeks had evaporated. The staff had never seen him this happy. Everyone on the team received hugs and thank-you for all of their work on the race. Montgomery knew it was a team effort, and he wanted them all to know he appreciated them.

Kyle was frantically fielding telephone calls and emails from members of the press. Everyone wanted a chance to talk to the next Speaker of the House. He couldn't wait until Montgomery got elected - the Speaker's budget for communications staff was probably 10 times that of a personal office. They were going to need it.

Made in the USA
Middletown, DE
26 January 2020